FATAL INNOCENCE

David Berardelli

FATAL INNOCENCE

FICTION4ALL

PART I

The Hunt

CHAPTER 1

Monday, the First Week

The girl lounging out by the hotel pool was definitely trouble.

The black strips of material barely covered her smooth, tanned flesh. To make the volatile situation even worse, she was fifteen years old.

Watching from a tinted window in the dark, air-conditioned hotel bar, Adam Brooks sipped his Manhattan. He knew this wouldn't take long. Yesterday, it took the girl less than half an hour to attract a victim. The day before, thirty-seven minutes. She was just a kid, but she was also a knockout, and obviously knew how to reel in a man.

Kids grew up much too quickly nowadays. Renee, his younger sister, started developing at about the same age and was a knockout at sixteen. But that was nearly two decades ago. Each generation made the transition a year or two quicker. Soon these kids would be walking into bars at twelve and being served without question.

Adam's job wasn't to criticize or judge. He was a private eye – he wasn't qualified to provide professional criticism or analysis. He found people and brought them home as requested. He also caught people in compromising positions.

Sometimes he was paid to take incriminating pictures. Sometimes he was paid just to warn someone from doing something stupid. He left criticizing, evaluating, and all that other mumbo-jumbo to the guys in tailored suits making hundreds of bucks an hour.

The tall, slender waitress made her second trip to his table to see if he wanted a refill. Once again, he smiled and shook his head. She smiled back, but he could tell she was a little peeved. Bars didn't make their money on customers who sat at their tables and bought just one drink. But it didn't matter. He couldn't get soused on the job. He needed to stay sharp and alert. Once he got back to his apartment, he could do as he pleased. But right now, he was earning his two-fifty a day.

Five minutes later, he realized the action was about to start. He glanced at his watch. Twenty-four minutes this time. The girl was getting better. By this time next week, she wouldn't even have to bother looking for a lounge chair. She could just wander out to the pool, push her hand through her hair, and lead the way back to her hotel room.

The girl's new companion looked like money – designer shirt and slacks, imported shoes that probably went for a couple of bills, top-of-the-line visor, and red-tinted sunglasses. The Rolex on one wrist and gold bracelet on the other conveyed the true image of the rich businessman on the prowl. He was around forty and fairly slender, but with a slight expansion around the midsection – probably from too many martinis and porterhouse steaks. His lack of tan told Adam that the man was probably here to attend a convention or a series of business meetings.

He stood beside the girl's lounge chair, smiling down at her, but his leering was obvious even behind the shades. The girl sat up, stretched, and reached up to arrange her dark brown hair more provocatively over her shoulders. Then she grabbed her towel and spent some time blotting the perspiration from her cheeks, shoulders, and arms before draping it over one shoulder. Her companion watched every move. Adam felt sorry for the poor guy. *He's toast. If he only knew... He will. Shortly...*

They crossed the pool area, making their way across the lush garden leading to the wing of hotel rooms. Adam left some bills on the table, got up, and hurried out of the cool, dark room.

Although he didn't particularly like this sort of work, it paid the bills. As a private eye, he did other people's dirty laundry – no more, no less. He talked to people his clients didn't want to talk to, dealt with people he wouldn't be caught dead associating with otherwise, listened to lies, both from his clients and the people he was being paid to deal with, and collected money when the job was finished. Sometimes he actually got paid. Other times he didn't. If the check cleared, he celebrated with a little booze, paid a bill or two, and got back in the saddle. If it bounced, he chalked it up to experience and promised himself he'd be more careful the next time, even though he knew that sort of thinking was useless. Being careful only helped in a perfect world.

The two walked quickly toward one of the rooms on the other side of the pool. The man already had his arm around her tiny waist. He'd only met her five minutes ago but had already gotten physical. The bottoms of her feet probably wouldn't see much of the carpet once they went inside.

They stopped in front of Room 12. The girl reached into the bottom piece of her bikini for her key. The man had already begun groping her. She had to push him away so she could open the door. He bent, burying his face in her hair at the base of her neck. She pushed him away again, then reached for the door. As soon as it opened, he shoved her inside.

Adam decided not to wait very long. It wouldn't take the man any time at all to rip off her bikini scraps and send them flying. This had to be done as quickly and as cleanly as possible.

He knocked on the door. Nothing. He knocked again, this time harder.

"No one here!" the man announced gruffly.

Adam pounded this time.

The door clicked open. The man's red, angry face appeared in the six-inch gap. "What the hell do you—"

"Sir, I don't know who you are." Adam kept his voice calm. "Quite frankly, I don't want to know, but—"

"Whatever you're selling, I'm not—"

"I'm not selling anything. I'm giving it away."

"What the fuck are you talking about?"

8

"I'm offering you your freedom. You want it or not?"

The door opened a few more inches. The man gripped the doorknob with his right hand. With his left, he held his shirt in front of him to hide his nakedness. "Listen to me, whoever you are." His voice was a harsh whisper. "I'm about to get laid, and I don't like interruptions. I'll give you just ten seconds to tell me why the fuck you're–"

"Sir, I don't know if you're aware of this, but you're about to have sex with an underage girl."

The man's face paled.

"The girl is fifteen. She won't be sixteen for nearly a year, and her father has instructed me to have the police here in fifteen minutes if you don't comply with his wishes and just walk away while you still can."

The door slammed shut.

Adam stepped aside and waited.

Seconds later, the door was yanked open. Shirt wide open, the man charged out of the room, fastening his belt as he ran.

***

Perched on a barstool, Richard Warden sipped his double vodka martini while the late-afternoon Orlando sun pierced the cloudless sky beyond the big, tinted windows.

Gino's was nearly packed. Local businessmen and vendors rubbed elbows with sloppy-dressed tourists taking a break from their street-prowling. The bar maintained a cool 72 degrees – a welcomed respite from the approaching summer brightness already filling the late March sky.

9

Richard Warden was tired. Following a long afternoon of back-to-back board meetings, he could feel the vodka gently nudging the tension away. The tension was a by-product of frustration. And anger. Years of listening to nonsense, of supervising a room filled with well-dressed idiots, was taking its toll. Once again he considered firing them all and starting from scratch.

Richard had known long ago that his company, WarCo SoftSystems, Inc., would have to make harsh decisions if they wanted to stay ahead of the pack. People would have to be laid off. Departments would need to be absorbed. Products would have to be cut or improved. It was the American way. Profit was always the bottom line. WarCo would have to grit its teeth and take no prisoners.

But he couldn't just sit back on his haunches and let Lou Berchfeld run things his way, could he? Even though the two men went back more years than either of them cared to remember, this was serious business. If Berchfeld couldn't take the initiative and start kicking some high-powered corporate ass, Richard would have to jump in and start slamming butts himself. Even if it meant opening the door and tossing the bunch into the street.

Jack Koslo was a prime example. The jerk was a computer wiz, and had graduated from MIT before he was twenty. With an IQ of 160, Koslo came to WarCo with glowing reports, a brilliant portfolio, and contacts up the ass. Berchfeld did some serious scrambling to get Koslo behind the helm of the WarCo subsidiary, RKW ChipTics. And as a result, Koslo had done nothing but bring RKW stock steadily down.

Koslo's specialty was outsourcing. The man thought nothing of eliminating a department of high-salaried, well-trained technicians and transferring the work to a larger group of low-salaried incompetents, to manufacture products of considerably lower quality.

In one instance, Koslo's outsourcing scheme had resulted in so much lost work and cancelled contracts, Berchfeld was forced to step in and recall those who'd been dropped, making them consultants at a much higher rate of pay. A very expensive fiasco, indeed.

Koslo and Berchfeld were related – making the situation sensitive as well as tense. Regardless, Richard wanted Koslo to stop his reckless shenanigans. It came to a boiling head just an hour ago in Richard's office, following the meeting in which RKW's questionable future was discussed.

"Bottom line, Jack. And don't give me any of those stupid stats that don't matter."

Despite Richard's firm request, Koslo consulted his figures. To Koslo, they meant everything. He'd resort to them even though his plan had just gone down the shitter. "The chip factory is a seven-twenty-four operation. Electricity alone is costing us–"

"I don't give a rat's ass about electricity," Richard snapped. "All I care about is the bottom line. Your figures don't mean a thing. You've got five good people – brilliant techs, every one of them – producing excellent products, and they're making

11

upwards of seventy-five K, plus another fifteen K in health benefits. Their products are bringing in ten million in revenues per year – which comes out to two million a head.

"You pop into Walmart for groceries, or McDonald's for a cheeseburger and fries, and you see these kids working their butts off for pennies. And you think – for whatever stupid reason – that you should run RKW in the same fashion. You fire all your accomplished techs and hire ten worthless incompetents who wouldn't know a good product if it bit them in the ass. But this is just fine, because these people are only making twenty K – which is all you care about. It doesn't matter that their products aren't selling or that the ten million the other crew was bringing in has dwindled down to less than three. So now we've got to fire the incompetents, squeak by the usual lawsuit bullshit, then hire back the original guys short-term for nearly twice what we were paying them before."

Richard loosened his collar and unbuttoned the single button of his fifteen-hundred-dollar Luciano Carreli pinstripe. *Wiz kids. The bane of humanity*.

"Refill? "Frieda had come over. Her sweet perfume brushed against his skin.

Frieda was a good-looking chick, even though she was on the wrong side of forty and had brought three kids into the world. Her frosted hair was still thick and shiny.

"Sounds good."

Less than a minute later, she placed a new glass on a clean napkin in front of him and took the empty away.

12

He lifted his glass and got ready to drain it when he suddenly stopped. *Careful, now. Take it easy.*

Not too long ago, he could pull down half a dozen martinis in an hour. But since he'd turned fifty, many things had changed, forcing him to realize moderation might actually be the intelligent way to go. It had been more than three years since the incident. Though he'd managed to overcome it, his attorney Bob Dalgren had ordered him to cut way down on his drinking. "The less you're seen in bars," Dalgren had said, "the better."

Easy for him to say.

Richard was paying Dalgren a shitload of cash for his personalized legal services. The least the little nerd could do was cut him some slack. Three years had passed, for Christ's sake. Richard had grown, had matured. He'd learned a few things along the way. Moderation turned out to be more reasonable than he'd initially thought. Binges at age fifty were ten times worse than when he was a kid. His body could no longer tolerate the abuse.

Anyway, Richard's drinking was no longer out of control. And he no longer reached the point where he couldn't quit when he wanted to. There hadn't been a time in his life when he didn't have the self-control to stop whatever he was doing whenever he damned well pleased. Except, of course, for sex.

And why shouldn't he enjoy himself? He was still young, strong, and vital. A sexual powerhouse at fifty. He'd spawned two kids and enjoyed hundreds of sexual encounters over the last twenty years – no small feat for a man who had, according to his smug, overpaid doctor, passed his prime. And what would the doc know about anyone else's prime? What would any of them know about anything?

He picked up his glass, drained it, and motioned to Frieda for another refill. Two down. He'd stop at three. *A man with no self-control couldn't stop at three, could he?*

He turned on his stool. Across the room, a gorgeous redhead sat by herself at a table in front of the window. She was smiling at him.

***

"May I join you?"

She smiled. "Please." The blinking of those thick lashes sent his pulse pounding. Her heavy red hair cascaded in shiny swirls down to her shoulders. Her large glittering green eyes held him fast, taking in his suit as well as his tie, his smile, and his hair. Her high cheekbones tapered down to a firm jaw line. Her swollen, pouty lips made his heart sputter.

"I'm Richard. Richard Warden."

"I know."

"You ... *know* me?"

"You were pointed out to me."

He straightened in his seat. Being talked about always pumped up the old ego. This happened frequently to him, as owner of a software empire. Sometimes it was damned hard not to appear too smug – especially when such a lovely babe was involved.

"I take it you've seen me before, then?"

She shrugged. "Right here. You spend a lot of time in this place."

So much for the old ego boost...

Her blank expression didn't give him any additional information. Had she said it to criticize? The rehab program had ended two years ago, leaving him sensitive and self-conscious. And for good reason. A man of his caliber? Reduced to swapping sob stories with tramps, drunks, and street scum? The experience was humiliating. But at least it was over.

He found no reason to take offense. He didn't know her, so he couldn't be certain about her disapproval. She may have merely stated a fact. Besides, it was easy to overlook her comment. No man in his right mind could criticize this perfect package in her blue suit and white silk shirt with the top three buttons undone, exposing a deliciously tanned cleavage. Not to mention the shapely legs or the strong fragrance of lilacs in her hair. Although she was obviously close to thirty, which was a few years older than what he ideally preferred, he knew that with a little luck, he'd eventually be able to snare her without too much difficulty.

"You have me at a disadvantage. You know my name–"

"Brittany. Brittany Weber."

At least the awkward formalities were over. So far, everything was progressing nicely. The next step, logically, would be to clear the air. It wasn't necessary, of course, but he decided to let her know why he spent so much time here. "Gino's is my favorite, uh, watering hole. My offices are on the

15

twentieth floor. And since this place is so convenient, I just pop down here for lunch, or when I need to get away from those irritating board meetings." He gave her a relaxed smile. He wanted another drink but decided to hold off.

Instead of replying, she sipped her drink and studied his tie.

Was it his imagination, or were her eyes lowering? *Don't jump the gun, sport. You're fifty, not fifteen...*

"And where do you work, Brittany? Orlando?"

"I've got my own home business. I sometimes do seminars."

"What do you sell?"

"Software programs. I'm a wholesaler."

"Good and solid right now. I ought to know. I'm CEO of–"

"WarCo SoftSystems. Yes, I know. I've seen your stuff on the Net."

He puffed up again.

She finished her drink. He signaled for Frieda.

"No, thanks. Gotta go." She glanced at her watch. "It's almost six, and I've got to get back to my place and finish up some work."

"Why not have another drink with me?" He wanted to get to know her. It had been a while since he'd met such an attractive, interesting woman.

She smiled. "Thanks, but I've really got to go." She reached for her handbag and opened it. He waved her down, quickly producing two crisp twenties and dropping them on the table.

A wrinkled frown appeared on her face. "Mr. Warden, I'd much rather–"

16

"Richard."

"It's really not necessary to–"

"My pleasure."

"But–"

"I'll let *you* pay next time."

Her smile drifted back. "Perhaps. Maybe."

He not only liked this woman for her looks, he admired her independence. She obviously liked paying her own way. She did exactly as she pleased. *His* kind of woman.

She snapped her handbag shut, looped the thick leather strap over her left shoulder, and stood.

He joined her, hoping she'd suggest getting together again. But she didn't. He decided to take the initiative. "Perhaps we could repeat this another time? Tomorrow? After lunch?"

She held out her hand. "It was nice meeting you, Richard." He took her hand in his, wincing at its coldness – probably from her drink.

"It was nice meeting you, too. I hope we can–"

"Maybe we'll see each other another time."

He opened his mouth to reply, but she'd already turned to leave the bar.

He crossed the room, moving to the tinted windows viewing the front lot. He wanted to see those gorgeous legs moving on the pavement ... the white heels bringing out the muscularity of her shapely calves ... the late afternoon sun playing on her bouncing red locks.

But there was no sign of her.

He hurried out through the lobby. The sun was hiding behind a swollen gray cloud. Heavy rush-hour traffic roared past. People marched up and down the aisles in the main lot, talking on cell phones.

He ran down the walk, turned the corner, and scanned another section of parking lot. Brittany Weber had disappeared.

***

"How much is my old man paying you?"

Adam Brooks pulled out onto the main drag. Beth Ricci sat beside him in the seat, her hair a mess, her face streaked with mascara and tears. The tears were mostly from anger. Once again, Adam had ruined her fun afternoon. For the third day in a row, he'd interrupted her private sex party to send her partner packing. The first two times, she'd tried flirting her way out of it, flashing her breasts to get him to forget what he was supposed to be doing. But it didn't work. This time, she'd silently put her clothes back on while he waited patiently at the door.

"It's not the money," Adam told her. He felt sorry for her father. An attorney, Domenic Ricci represented a big developer in the Central Florida area. In Adam's world, being an attorney and a developer were two out of three strikes. But as much as he detested both professions, he respected Ricci for at least making an effort to get his daughter back. Ricci was divorced and raising his kid on his own. He was away most of the time and rarely saw her. When he was home, he usually spent most of his time in his study, arranging deals on his phone. He loved his daughter, but like so many fathers, he had no idea how to show his love.

18

"What is it, then?" she asked. "You don't like to see people having fun?"

"You're a kid. You're too young to be–"

"Oh, fuck you. You're no better than him."

"Despite what you think, he loves you."

"My fucking ass."

"Why else would he pay someone like me to follow you around and make sure no one hurts you?"

"News flash, asshole. He doesn't want me having any fun."

"I've got a news flash for *you*. He doesn't want you ending up dead. Or beaten half to death."

"The guys who pick me up are okay. They've got money and everything. Why d'ya think I always go to places like Holiday Inn?"

"You don't even know them. How could you? You pick them up and you're having sex with them five minutes later."

"How can I have sex with them when you're following us around, pulling them off me all the time?"

"I can either do that or bring in the cops. Then your party becomes a memory anyway. Your new boyfriend's brought up on statutory rape charges, and you're sent back to your dad."

She crossed her arms. "I *really* luck out, don't I?"

"You don't even know how good you have it."

"Yeah. I have it real fucking good. Half the time I can't stand it."

"You have a father who cares about you."

"He so doesn't care about me."

19

"How can you say that?"

"I never even see him half the time."

"He's a busy–"

"Yeah, yeah, yeah. He's successful. Works his fucking ass off. Yeah, I got that. Believe me."

So did Adam. Her attitude said a lot. It also said that if she couldn't spend time with her father, she'd have no trouble spending it with other men. It didn't matter how she spent it. It only mattered that she felt wanted. Desired.

"I guess you wouldn't wanna just leave me off somewhere and tell him I slipped away, would ya?"

"No can do."

"What would it take?"

He didn't want to get into this. She'd already flashed her breasts and even tried putting her hand on his crotch.

"How 'bout a blowjob?"

He just sighed.

"I'm good at it. I can do it right now, while you're driving. How 'bout it? Just don't kill us, okay? I'll get you off, then you let me off. Just tell him I slipped away while you were pumping gas or something."

"I can't do that."

She huffed. "Now I get it. You're gay."

"Actually, it's worse than that."

"What is it?"

"I suffer from a strange condition you don't see much anymore."

She moved closer to the door. "You mean, like, a disease?"

"I accept responsibility when it comes my way. And when someone pays me to do something, I do it."

"What are you? Some jerk who thinks he's a superhero?"

"Just an ordinary jerk doing his job."

"What if I pay you to let me go? I've got money." She opened her purse. "I've got–"

"Like I said, it's not the money."

"Then I'll just get you off and that'll be that."

"You're underage."

"For a blowjob? That's not even sex. Everyone knows that."

"I hate to burst your bubble, but if it involves the sex organs, it's sex, and just because one of our former presidents was too stupid to figure that one out doesn't make it right."

She sat back and watched the road in silence. After about a minute she said, "I guess you never fucked around when you were a kid."

"Sure I did. I got into trouble a lot, too."

"Then why won'tcha give me a break?"

He felt uncomfortable about all this. He didn't have kids, so he couldn't easily relate. And he couldn't take her side when her father was paying him. Even if he did, she was clearly in the wrong. She was fifteen – much too young to entice strange men into motel rooms. She had issues. But then, so did everyone else. Still, he couldn't help feeling sympathetic toward her.

Was it because of his sister? Their father had left home when Adam was fifteen and Renee fourteen. Their mother had done her best, but like most parents, she just couldn't handle both roles. Adam hated his father for years. The hatred eventually subsided, becoming a heavy dullness surrounding an ache he felt each time he permitted the man to enter his thoughts. It brought Adam closer to Renee and their mother, making the three of them a very tight-knit group. But even so, a day seldom passed when he didn't think of his dad, hoping he'd see him again. He'd looked for him during high school basketball and football games, hoping he'd see his dad sitting in the bleachers. High school graduation was not a pleasant memory because of their father's absence. He dreamed of the time his dad would return and they could go fishing together. Or hunting. Or maybe even attend a Magic game.

But Adam never saw his dad again. Neither did Renee.

"They're assholes, aren't they?" Beth stared straight ahead at the SUV in front of them. "Fathers. I don't even know why they bother. My old man doesn't even–"

"At least you still see him," he said flatly.

Her eyes blazed. "And I'm supposed to think that's a good thing?"

"It is good," he said softly.

"How the hell can it possibly be good?"

"You wouldn't understand."

***

Richard Warden sat picking at his food at the dinner table.

Renata, their housekeeper, had prepared one of his favorite dishes – a wonderful pot roast. Renata

22

was a terrific cook. She could make a feast out of just about anything. But this evening, Renata's culinary skills were the least of his concerns. As was his wife's detailed account of how the renovation work on the guest house was coming along.

He hadn't been able to think of anything else but Brittany Weber since he left Gino's. The woman's unique essence filled his mind just as much now as it had at the bar.

"Well, are you?" Adrienne's smoldering black eyes focused on him.

"Am I what?" He was surprised at the testiness in his own voice. He put it down to resentment for having his thoughts interrupted – as well as the fact that his wife was sitting across the table instead of Brittany.

"You're not paying one bit of attention to me, are you?"

He picked up his wine glass. "Guess I'm preoccupied."

"Don't tell me you and Louis are butting heads again."

His wife's distorted reflection came into view as he tilted his glass. Adrienne was still a good-looking woman, but despite the grays popping up, the crow's feet slicing into the corners of her dark-brown eyes, the wattle pulling loose the once-firm chin, and the thickening of her hips, it was clear that what had survived their relationship was anything but physical. The years, the kids, and the problems that had come and gone, had turned them into two very different people sharing the same house. What had once been a solid relationship had transformed into a corporate merging, with each division head pursuing his – or her – own separate interests.

Richard knew Adrienne was painfully aware that he often strayed. But in spite of her suspicions, she lacked the evidence required to drain him of his fortune. In choosing his partners, he'd always been fortunate to find women who could keep their mouths shut. Usually, money proved to be the only requirement to ensure their necessary silence. A couple had posed a potential problem, requiring a considerably larger payoff, but they too had vanished quietly, once their financial desires had been sated.

Adrienne continued watching him. So did his daughter Katie, who sat on his right.

"It must be something really serious," his wife said.

He stiffened. "What was that?"

"Whatever you and Lou are fighting about."

He sighed. *I need to be more careful.* "It's worrying me a little." To satisfy her curiosity, he gave her a capsulized version of the Koslo problem.

"You think you'll have union problems?" she asked.

"Their union isn't very strong. Florida's right-to-work situation helps us. But since RKW is seventy-five percent management, their union representation doesn't matter much. Koslo has a history of using inexperienced workers to save money, and it always backfires."

"I remember now. Jack Koslo, outsource king extraordinaire."

"His experiences with IBM and AT&T should have taught him something, but he's so dead-set against paying benefits, he's liable to have them cranking out enough bad chips to cause the stockholders to panic and start pulling out."

"What does Lou say about all this?" Adrienne looked worried. And she had every right to be. Much of her own money was tied up in RKW.

He shrugged. "Koslo's kin. This means a lot to Lou."

"I understand that. But I can't see that man letting relatives screw up a company that does more than ten million in exports–"

"This has to be addressed, and quick. I let them both have it this afternoon, but it's up to them to fix it. I can't go behind Lou and pull something. He's the president, after all."

Renata scuttled by with another bottle of red wine. She picked up the empty and was gone in a flash.

"I'm gonna need more money for books," Katie interrupted, obviously waiting for a lull in the dinner conversation to spring her request on him. "Next semester, my psychiatric nursing books alone will cost a fortune."

His daughter never failed to bring a smile to his face. She had a special glow that brightened any room. "If it's for school, it's justified," he said. "Just let me know what you'll need."

Katie smiled. "You wouldn't consider getting me a new car, would you? I'll only use it for school. The one I'm driving is kind of funky and–"

"Nice try."

Katie shrugged. "Can't blame me, can ya?"

"That clunker you've been driving is two years old now, and your friends probably all have something fresh from the showroom – right?"

She reddened. "I guess that *was* kind of obvious."

Katie was a pretty girl. Not beautiful, but the kind who'd produce good-looking offspring. She'd always been serious about her education, but it wouldn't be too long before she'd be getting married. She'd brought over this Kevin character several times during the past few weeks. The boy seemed nice enough, but like all the others, there was something about him Richard just didn't like.

He knew it would only be a matter of time before he was forced to give his daughter away to some wild-eyed jerk that needed hosed down. But whatever happened, she'd always be his little girl and would have a special place forever etched in his heart.

"At least you're not as bad as your brother. Nick was turning my hair gray by the time he'd graduated high school. But now that he's running sales at Directron, the kid has finally settled down and taken on his share of responsibilities."

"Daddy, you know Nicky's just like you. Don't you remember those times you and Mom argued about why Nicky got into so much trouble?"

It was strange, her remembering that. She was only four or five when Nick was becoming a pain in the ass in high school.

Adrienne started on the guest house again. Getting the cable company out there to add an extra line was high up on her list of priorities. And the main bathroom was bugging her to death. The Roman tub was entirely too large for the room. She saw no reason why it should be so large when the shower already took up so much space.

He tuned her out. Brittany had drifted back into his consciousness.

Renata appeared five minutes later, wheeling in the dessert tray. When she reached across Richard to set down the engraved silver ice cream dish in front of him, he realized he'd developed an erection.

"Something wrong, Daddy?"

"What?" He shifted in his seat and repositioned the monogrammed towel in his lap.

"You've got this really worried look on your face."

He smiled sheepishly. "I'm okay. Just a little tired."

*****

Half an hour later, as Richard Warden sat in his den in front of the computer screen, he cursed himself for being so obsessed. Yet he found that he didn't really care. He wanted to see Brittany again – it was that simple.

Finding her online quickly proved to be a fruitless venture. As far as he could ascertain, the only thing he knew about this beautiful woman was her name. She'd mentioned working at home, selling wholesale software programs. But her information had been vague at best. It made him wonder if she actually owned the software company or merely worked for one.

From his experience, he knew there could be five thousand such companies in Central Florida alone. Looking up the name Weber hadn't led to anything promising.

Had she told him the truth? Or was her company called something else?

A search in the online phone book directory quickly produced several full columns of Weber's in the metropolitan Orlando area. He dropped to B and carefully scanned the list. Two Bs, a B. A., a B. L., several Bobs, three Bills, a Bradford, and a Bradley.

He tried the first B. Not in service.

The second B was answered by an elderly man who said his name was Barclay and that he did not appreciate being interrupted during his dinner.

Richard apologized, then sat back and stared at the French doors leading out to the lit gardens in the back yard. This was going nowhere. If he really wanted to find her, it would probably be much better and less frustrating to let someone do it for him.

Ellen, his personal secretary, could save him time and aggravation. But that wouldn't work. Ellen was a damned fine secretary, but much too interested in other people's business. Besides, Ellen and Adrienne had been on friendly terms for more than a year.

A professional would be safer and much more discreet. Last year he'd used ABC Investigations on East Robinson, when he was considering taking over Genesis, Inc., and needed some dirt to give him leverage. Thomas Cravell was a good man. He not only knew how to keep his mouth shut, but also had a healthy respect for big money. He'd been running ABC for ten years – a long time in an unpredictable place like Orlando.

He dialed the number from the card he'd kept in his wallet. When Thomas Cravell answered, Richard gave his name."

"Mr. Warden?" There was a slight pause, then Cravell said, "Genesis, right?"

"Good memory."

"How can I help you?"

"I'm trying to locate someone. A woman."

"All right..."

"But it won't be easy. The only thing I know about her is her name."

"And the hard part is...?"

"Not knowing anything else."

"That's why I'm in business, Mr. Warden."

"Then I take it you want the job?"

"Of course."

***

Though Domenic Ricci was probably on the wrong side of fifty, he looked good and kept himself in shape with tennis and golf. The golf was probably what kept him away from the house so much, particularly when he was in the middle of closing a deal. Otherwise, he would've spent much more time with his daughter.

Adam Brooks knew better than voice his opinion about something that shouldn't concern him. In his view, the hardest part of the job was keeping his mouth shut, especially when supposedly intelligent people repeatedly made stupid mistakes that could be easily corrected.

Ricci was sitting behind his desk in his book-lined home study, writing a check when Adam entered. Adam welcomed the sight. He assumed the check was being made out to him. At least, he hoped so. If he was right, he promised himself to be especially pleasant during this particular visit. He didn't want to say anything to sour the deal.

"How'd you do with the latest boyfriend? " Ricci asked.

"He wasn't exactly what I'd call a boyfriend."

Ricci's pen stopped moving – which irritated Adam. "What *would* you call him?"

Adam sat uneasily in the armchair facing the desk. He knew he shouldn't have said anything. Now he had to squirm out of this gracefully. He shrugged. "Just some guy who happened to see your daughter sunning herself out by the pool."

"Older guy?"

"Thirties, I guess."

"He wasn't a sleazebag, was he?"

"Sleazebag?"

Ricci shrugged. "Tattoos? Nose rings? Leather?"

Adam couldn't see what that had to do with anything. "Actually, he appeared pretty prosperous."

"At least that's *something*." Ricci went back to writing the check, then ripped it out of the book. Adam knew better than to mention the pony-tailed biker he'd seen Ricci's daughter the other day.

30

Ricci stared at the check, then at Adam. "I work for some powerful people."

"Developers." Despite Adam's willpower, he'd let that response come out flat.

"Anything wrong with developers?"

"You really want my opinion?"

He handed Adam the check. "I asked, didn't I?"

Adam took it, glanced at it, then folded it carefully and pocketed it. "I'll sum it up in three words. I love trees."

Ricci grunted. "Progress, Brooks. People hear the word and get all bent out of shape and causey. They bitch about raping the environment, killing trees, and destroying the ozone. Then they turn around and complain that they have to drive ten miles to the closest Wal-Mart or Dollar Store when someone should clear the vacant field two miles down the road. People." Ricci shook his head.

"They're assholes. I agree."

"Everyone knows how messed up people are. But I've gotten off the subject."

"What is the subject?" Adam didn't want to ask, but could tell the man had a lot on his mind and obviously wanted to talk about it.

Ricci sat back and rubbed his eyes. He suddenly looked tired. And defeated. "I'm just stalling, I guess. The real subject is kind of painful."

"You want to know what's happening with your daughter."

"That more or less covers it."

Adam got up from the chair. "I can't tell you what to do here, Mr. Ricci. I don't get involved in other people's business."

"I asked your opinion, dammit. You've got something to say? Say it."

"Your daughter's in her room now, crying her eyes out. She wants her father."

"I'm right here."

"Yeah." Adam crossed the room and stopped a foot short of the door. "You're right here. And she's right there. Do I honestly have to say more?"

Ricci appeared genuinely confused. Adam felt sorry for him again. "Come right out with it, Brooks."

"I just did, but you didn't get it." Then he left before he had a chance to say something that would *really* hurt.

CHAPTER 2

Tuesday, the First Week

At nine o'clock, Richard Warden left Conference Room A with the single-mindedness of a man leaping from a sinking ship.

The workday had started with another ChipTics crisis, this one concerning their New York plant. Koslo had apparently ruffled the union's feathers – which wasn't a wise thing to do. New Yorkers frequently turned radical and violent when someone threatened their bargained-for benefits. But Jack Koslo seemed unconcerned about the union or its seventy-five members. His rants about 'obscene wages' and 'ridiculous benefit demands,' followed by threats to close the New York plant and open a new one in Jacksonville, proved more than Richard could endure before lunch. Giving Berchfeld a simple, "Handle it now!" before bowing out of the picture was the best thing he could do.

Thomas Cravell, looking sharp in his dark suit, sat in the receptionist area, reading a copy of Fortune Magazine. He stood up and smiled. "Mr. Warden. Hope this is a good time."

Ellen was busy working on the monthly report. Richard gestured for Cravell to follow him into his office. "No calls, Ellen."

The plump, middle-aged woman didn't skip a beat with her keyboard. Her nod was slight.

"And when Stephanie is finished with the minutes, I want them copied, distributed, and faxed as quickly as possible to our West Coast offices."

In his office, he gestured for Cravell to sit. He closed the door behind him and circled the massive desk. Behind him, the bright Orlando skyline reflected the brilliant metallic skyscrapers in the huge, tinted window.

Richard opened a drawer and produced a small cigar. It was a single green leaf made expressly for him by an independent Cuban grower, individually wrapped and packaged at ten dollars apiece. The five a day Richard allowed himself had helped keep the little Cuban in business the last ten years.

Richard got the leaf going and tossed the gold monogrammed lighter in the drawer. "What have you got?"

Cravell lit a cigarette and pocketed the hotel matchbook. "I'm afraid we're gonna need to work this from a different angle." Cravell sat forward and flicked a tiny gray ash into the glass ashtray on the small table beside the chair. "All we have to go on is a name. I've already tried the phone directory but came up empty."

"I did the same thing last night. Unlisted, maybe?"

"Tried that angle, too. Got a contact in the phone company's databanks. Either this woman doesn't have a phone or gave you a fictitious name. And how many people these days operate without a phone?"

Richard sat back and considered the hopelessness of the situation.

Cravell blew a slim trail of cigarette smoke toward the ceiling fan. "How serious are you about finding this woman?"

"You don't need to know. I'm paying you to find her."

"All right. So let's talk about my 'different-angle' theory."

"I'm listening."

"We have no phone number, no car, and no address. Nothing from DMV. All we have is a name – no doubt fictitious – and a description. Am I right?"

Richard nodded.

"Where did you meet this woman?"

"Downstairs, in Gino's."

"She a regular?"

"Don't think so. At least, I never saw her there before."

"Doesn't mean anything. Tourist, maybe?"

Richard shrugged.

"She tanned?"

He recalled the delicious cleavage. "A little. But this is only March. Beach weather doesn't start for another month or so."

"Anything strange about her clothes?"

"They fit her extremely well."

"Notice anything else? Labels? Logos? Brand names?"

"Nope."

Cravell finished his smoke and stubbed it out. Then he leaned back and rubbed his palms. "Here's my proposition."

"I'm listening."

"I follow you."

"Why?"

"Hear me out first ... please?"

Richard sat back and sighed. "All right."

"I follow you for the next few days. A simple tail, but you won't see me. I'll be in Gino's whenever you're there. If this woman comes in, let me know by some subtle gesture. Scratch the back of your head."

"No good. I do that a lot."

"What don't you do a lot?"

Richard made an impressive smoke ring and watched it float lazily across the room. "I saw Bogart tug his earlobe in a movie once."

"Think you can remember to do it?"

"I'm sure I can."

"I'll lay low, then tail her when she splits. If circumstances cooperate, I should be able to find her car, where she lives – everything you need to know. How's that?"

"Good, except for one thing."

"What's that?"

"What if she leaves with me?"

A curious expression touched Cravell's fine features. "You just told me why you want this woman followed."

***

At six o'clock that evening, Richard Warden sat at a center table in Gino's, sipping a martini, his eyes glued to the entrance doors. He expected Brittany to appear at any moment.

Less than twenty minutes ago, a small group of stockholders tried to shanghai him into a conference room to grill him about something they'd heard on CNN about the War-Met contract with Singapore. Richard referred them to Ken Olson, President of War-Met Labs. Olson had all the answers. Besides, Olson loved getting together with stockholders. Bullshit was oftentimes the only way out of a sticky situation.

As he sat in the dark, air-conditioned room, Richard wondered where Cravell was. Gino's wasn't crowded, but there were several strangers amongst the regulars. Any one of them could've been Cravell in disguise.

The details didn't matter. Since meeting Brittany here the previous day, Richard couldn't keep his mind on much of anything else. She was the most beautiful creature he'd ever seen, and he wanted – *needed* – to see her again.

Frieda came by to check on him. He ordered a refill. For the first time since he'd first met Frieda, her tight outfit didn't even register. He was only concerned about what Brittany would be wearing when she came in – if she came in.

The possibility of not seeing her shrouded his thoughts in a heavy blackness. Trudging back to his car and driving home after having three drinks alone would be too much to bear. Sitting at the dinner table, forcing himself to pay attention to Adrienne, would be torture. Listening to Katie and her latest adventures would undoubtedly cause his eyes to glaze over.

Brittany appeared at just a few minutes before seven. She wore an emerald-green suit, the skirt just an inch shy of the knee, the silk top low-cut, revealing her smooth cleavage and three simple gold necklaces. She sauntered over to his table and stopped, looking down at him, her smile warming him even more effectively than his drink. "Didn't know if I'd see you here tonight," she said.

He practically smashed his kneecap against the table leg, scrambling to his feet. His fascination at watching her come in had done much to switch his mind off. He found himself staring at her hair, her arm. She flicked some hair from her shoulder, and he bathed himself in her sweet perfume. Still watching her, he fell into his own chair and nearly missed the seat. When reality finally returned, he realized his mouth was open. "I-I've been w-waiting ... t-to see you since ... all d-day..." For the first time since grade school, he was stuttering. He had to take a few deep breaths to calm down. *CEO, remember? Corporate tycoon? A little class might work wonders...* "It's really good, seeing you again," he managed, his voice firm and in control again.

She smiled. "For a while, I didn't think I could get away."

"From where?" It escaped his lips before he even realized it.

"I had some errands in town, and barely made it to the bank before they closed."

It was vital to find out where she worked, lived. What car she drove. What colors she liked. Movies. Music. Favorite flowers, sex positions–

Then it dawned on him. Cravell. The signal... As subtly as he could, Richard tugged his right earlobe.

Brittany suddenly smiled.

He swallowed. "Something ... funny?"

"Humphrey Bogart did that."

"What?"

"That earlobe-pulling thing."

He flushed, sitting up sharply. Now he felt like a child who'd been caught scratching something dirty into his desktop. "W-What made you think of *that*?"

"Saw one of his old movies the other day and remembered."

Richard sat back and waited for his heart rate to return to normal. *Damn, that was close...*

Brittany tilted her head. Some heavy red tresses brushed down her arm. "Aren't you gonna buy me a drink?"

"Shit. I mean – I'm awfully sorry..." He practically smacked his knee again, straightening. One of the waitresses came right over.

"Tom Collins," she said.

He ordered a refill for himself, then sat back and resumed staring.

"Something wrong? "She pushed some heavy red locks away from her face. "It's a little windy out there. Looks like it wants to rain."

He grinned. "Everything's ... just perfect."

Brittany blinked. "You don't mince words, do you?"

He'd intended to let Cravell earn his money. But right now, he wanted her to know just how he felt. "I ... want you to know something, Brittany."

"What's that?"

39

"You're one of the most beautiful women I've ever seen." He hadn't wanted to sound so dramatic, but it came out automatically. He quickly found that he wasn't even embarrassed for saying it.

She laughed. "I'll bet you say that to all the girls."

"No. I don't. I really don't. In fact, I don't think I ever said that to anyone before."

Her large green eyes focused on him. "That wouldn't be a line, would it? To get me in the sack?"

He felt his cheeks reddening. This woman didn't hedge around, either. "To answer your questions, no to the first and yes to the second." Then he cursed himself for being so brazen.

When the drinks came, she picked up her slim frosted glass and sipped sparingly. Richard downed half of his and sighed.

She shrugged. "You don't beat about the bush."

"Life's too short."

"Yes. It is. *Very* short."

"Brittany, are you married?"

"Divorced."

"How long – if you don't mind my asking?"

A shadow touched her face. "Not long enough."

Her tense expression made him realize he'd said the wrong thing.

"Eric's very ... obsessive."

"How so?"

She drank more of her drink and set it back down. "He likes to ... follow me."

"He's stalking you?"

A nod.

40

"How long?"

"The last six months."

"But the courts... Can't you get them to–"

"I've already filed an injunction. It hasn't worked. He's come to my place three times since."

"But can't you–"

"I'd rather not talk about it, if you don't mind." She drank more Tom Collins. "It really upsets me."

"I understand."

"You've been stalked?"

"No, but–"

"Then you can't possibly know what I'm going through."

"Obviously not." He pulled at his martini, furious at himself for upsetting her. "I'm sorry, Brittany. If I'd known–"

"Let's not ruin our drink, okay?"

"What about dinner? Have you eaten?"

"I have to get home."

"But we've got to have at least one more drink together." The prospects of this gorgeous creature leaving so soon made his heart ache.

"Wish I could." She shrugged. "But some things have to be done."

"Let me take you home. Please."

"Oh, no. That wouldn't work."

"Why not?"

"I couldn't possibly bring someone else into this. Surely you can understand."

"I want to make sure you get home safely. I could follow you, make sure–"

"I appreciate it. Really. I can take care of myself. I could never forgive myself if I involved you or anyone else with my problems."

"Please..."

"Thanks anyway." She patted his hand." We'll talk about it later, okay?" She gathered her shoulder bag and stood. "Right now, I have to make a stop."

"Of course." He watched her as she marched to the ladies' room near the double glass doors. Then he sank back in his chair and smiled at the delicious thoughts of the beautiful redhead in the john, sliding her panties down those smooth, shapely thighs...

***

At eight-thirty, Brittany still hadn't come out of the ladies' room.

The room had turned into a solid, disorganized crowd. Women flocked in front of the restroom, some disappearing inside, others coming out and returning to their tables, or leaving entirely. The waitress working with Frieda moved quickly, squeezing between tables, her cluttered tray delicately balanced on her raised palm.

Richard waited until she'd finished delivering a big order to the table next to him. He caught her by the crook of the arm. "A good-looking redhead was sitting here with me a while ago."

She frowned. "Tom Collins?"

"That's right. Do me a favor." He handed her a ten. "Take a trip to the ladies' room and make sure she's okay? She's been in there quite a while."

She folded the bill and pushed it carefully into a pocket of her laced apron. "Back in a minute." Then she hurried away.

42

Richard sat back and finished his drink.

One minute later, the waitress returned. "She's gone, mister. No one's in there."

CHAPTER 3

Wednesday, the First Week

Following a night of little sleep, Richard Warden arrived at his office early the next morning.

Despite his punctuality, he wasn't in the mood to talk to anyone about company business. He wanted blood. And the blood he wanted belonged to Thomas Cravell.

He called Cravell's office promptly at nine. The detective answered on the second ring. *Lucky for him.*

"How the hell could you let that woman slip right through your fingers?" Richard glared at the phone; it was set on speaker. He wanted to reach into it, yank Cravell out by his shirt collar, and wring his scrawny neck. "What the hell were you *doing*, for God's sake? Taking a nap?"

"This is extremely embarrassing," Cravell said softly. "Nothing like this has ever happened to me before. I was in Gino's, sitting at one of the little round tables against the wall. You knew I was there – you even looked at me."

"Were you disguised?"

"Slightly. I had my eye on her when she walked by on her way to the john. Mr. Warden, I never took my eyes off that hall entrance. That woman never came back out!"

Richard sat back and took some deep breaths. He needed calm. That's what he'd learned many years ago, as a young college grad just starting out in the corporate world. *Calm and collected*. When you could think clearly, you could achieve anything.

Maybe Cravell wasn't totally at fault. There could have been any number of things that had happened. "She wasn't in there when I paid the waitress to check on her," he said.

"I just don't understand it. She *couldn't* have slipped out without my spotting her."

"There a back way out?"

"No."

"You sure?"

"First thing I checked when I went there. Before I went in the bar yesterday evening, I knew that place like the back of my hand."

"What about the ladies' room?"

"I could only do a quick check before lunch, as soon as the place opened. But I did see what I needed to see."

"Any windows?"

"The only other exit from the bar is on the opposite wall. It feeds into the restaurant on the other end of the lobby."

"I've seen it."

"I'm really sorry, Mr. Warden..."

"It's okay." Letting the little guy off the hook was the only sensible thing to do right now. At least Cravell had done his homework. He couldn't help it if the woman had outsmarted him. Women being stalked learn to be resourceful as well as– *Yes. That had to be it*. "Listen, Cravell. Something just occurred to me. This can't be your fault. Brittany told me she's being stalked."

"Husband? Boyfriend?"

"Ex-husband. From what she said, the man's mental. We can't blame her for being able to slip in and out of the picture without anyone noticing. She's damned sharp. Noticed my earlobe tug right off."

"This ex of hers got a name?"

"Eric."

"Same last name?"

"No idea."

"I know a couple of strong-arms, live in Orlando. Retired OPD. They like to pick up a couple of bills once in a while. Cigarette money, booze, you know. If I had a name—"

"Just Eric, as far as I know."

"Am I still on the case?"

"Until I say otherwise. Check and see if there's an Eric Weber lurking around somewhere. I want to know everything about her – and him. Understand?"

"Completely."

***

Richard had little to say at dinner.

He was much too busy thinking about Brittany and the events of the previous evening.

Adrienne started talking about someone she'd run into at the Mall, but when she realized he wasn't paying attention, she put both elbows on the edge of the table and glared. "You're insulting Renata's cooking. The woman prepares this magnificent scampi, and you're sitting there, playing with it. I hope this isn't about that business with Jack Koslo."

Only then did he realize what he'd been doing. Since sitting down at the table he'd been moving the

46

shrimp around in the dish instead of picking up one and eating it. He loved scampi. Renata knew exactly how to prepare it. But this evening, he just didn't care about food.

"You know I'm right, don't you? " Adrienne asked.

"Of course you are," he replied. His wife had said something about Jack Koslo. But he hadn't heard anything else and didn't want to antagonize her by asking her to repeat it. Agreeing with her seemed simpler.

Katie started talking about her boyfriend, Kevin.

He quickly tuned out again, focusing instead on what had happened at Gino's. How could such a strikingly gorgeous woman slip through the hands of a professional detective? The idea was incomprehensible. Men were fascinated by such exquisite beauty, and women were intimidated by it. There is no way a woman looking like Brittany could go anywhere without being closely watched. Aside from the highly unlikely possibility of her becoming invisible, it wasn't possible for such a beauty to just disappear. But the fact remained ... she'd vanished again.

Despite his initial misgivings, Richard found himself considering Cravell's offer. The idea, at first, was revolting. Richard had never condoned violence. It was too risky and threatened reputations and careers. And the danger of legal prosecution always lurked much too close for comfort. But in this case, he'd somehow grown comfortable with the idea. Brittany had said the man was violent. He was ruining her life.

Richard Warden suddenly realized that the idea of possessing such a beauty might require him to readjust his attitude toward violence.

CHAPTER 4

Thursday, the First Week

The next morning quickly became hectic – phone call after phone call, an emergency meeting with concerned stockholders, and a frantic call from Adrienne asking him to get with the contractors working on the guest house. Apparently they wanted to talk only to the man financing the project.

"I'll get to it," he promised, irritated for the disturbance. "Maybe after lunch."

"You know I don't call you at work, Richard. But sometimes it's so aggravating, dealing with men. You know what I mean. Last week, when they finished tuning up the Cadillac and brought it back to the house, I asked them a simple question, and you'd think–"

"I understand, Ade. I'll call them." He didn't want to waste time arguing with her. Suppertime would come soon enough.

He hung up. Thirty-nine new email messages showed on his monitor, most of them concerning RKW or War-Met. He decided to scan the list and pick out the ones he really wanted to read.

The phone rang again. The bleeping red light told him it was his private line. *Probably Adrienne again. What is it now?*

He picked it up and heard the soft, sultry voice whisper, "Richard?"

Brittany. He swallowed a warm lump and searched for his voice. He had to clear his throat to bring it out. "I-I didn't think I'd ever ... hear from you again."

"I told you we'd talk again, didn't I?"

"Yes, but ... the way you just *disappeared* the other night–"

"Sorry." She sighed. "I told you, I have to be careful these days."

"Your ex-husband, I take it."

"If I even suspect I'm being followed, I pull out all the stops. I could sense someone watching me as I left for the restroom."

Cravell. She'd spotted the detective and pulled a quick vanishing act. Or maybe Eric was in the bar. Either way, someone had spooked her.

This was incredible. He'd just met the woman of his dreams, and someone was hell-bent on turning this into a nightmare.

"Brittany ... I'd like to help you."

"You can't do anything. Besides, it's my problem. I can handle things myself."

That independent streak again. "I understand, believe me. And I respect you for it. But listen. I'm a successful man. I've got all kinds of contacts. I can help you."

"I don't know..."

He stared at the reflection of the golden sun shining in the window and wondered what his next move should be. Whether he should take Cravell up on his offer of strong-arming. Too extreme, no matter how he felt. He was considering maiming or even murdering someone for a woman he barely knew. This alone made him wonder what was happening to him. How long had he actually known this woman? A few days? And how much time had he spent with her? An hour? And here he was, stepping right in, making plans, promises...

In exchange for what? A relationship? A quick toss in the hay?

He'd cheated on Adrienne countless dozens of times. Women had literally thrown themselves his way for favors, money, referrals – anything they could get their hands on. It was difficult, if not impossible, to fend them all off. And only a man in his position could know this.

Unlike all the others, this woman was not throwing herself at him. For the first time in his life, Richard Warden wanted someone so badly, he knew he could quite possibly kill for the pleasure of her company.

"I ... want to see you again," he said, his voice constricted.

"I want to see you, too. Name the place and time."

"How about dinner? Tonight?"

"Sounds good. Where?"

"That French place in Altamonte. *Le Cuisine*. The food's great, and it's very private."

"What time?"

"Seven o'clock?"

"I'll meet you there."

***

Adam Brooks sat in his tiny office, gazing at the tinted window that looked out onto the main parking lot of the shopping mall.

51

His neighbors did manicures and tattoos, sold tee shirts, peddled swimming pool accessories, and served takeout Chinese food. Across the eight-lane highway, a rental car agency provided frontage for a major Toyota dealer. Farther up, a huge furniture wholesaler advertised seventy-five percent off all items marked with a red tag.

His glass door was marked *Brooks Investigations* in black stenciled letters he'd applied himself nearly ten years ago, when starting his business. He was no artist, so the letters weren't evenly spaced. But none of his clients noticed or considered the subject important enough to bring up. His office sat next to the tee shirt shop, enabling him to watch many of its patrons coming and going. Since most of them were young girls in shorts and tank tops, the view made the act of sitting in an empty office, waiting for the phone to ring, a pleasant experience.

Straight ahead, a skinny blonde in a short black skirt and white sleeveless blouse got out of her black Vette. Her four-inch spikes made her shapely calves look sensational. Whoever had invented heels definitely knew what they were doing.

The blonde pulled a large brown handbag out of the Vette, slung it over her shoulder, and slammed the door shut. It looked heavy, sliding down her arm and nearly pulling her off-balance. Like most women, she probably carried her makeup supplies, an extra pair of shoes, her lunch, and maybe even her boyfriend, in it. She managed to pull it back up, then pranced off toward the mall across the grassy courtyard.

She looked like she was in her mid-twenties but drove a Vette and wore expensive clothes. An attorney, maybe? Or the part-owner of the beauty salon? You really couldn't tell nowadays. Twenty years ago, sensational-looking babes were usually doctors' wives, models, or bank tellers. Now they ran companies, acted as attorneys for high-profiled clients, and headed successful medical practices.

You're bored. Make some coffee.

His last client was Domenic Ricci. He hadn't had a phone call in two days. This wasn't unusual for the business he was in, just aggravating, especially when he had to sit here and wait for something to happen. He wanted to go back to the apartment, strip, and jump in the complex pool. But that wouldn't be practical. Someone might call. They could leave a message, but if they were in a hurry, they might just look for someone else. He didn't want to miss a job – especially if it turned out big.

He knew he should start putting his cell number on his cards, but he didn't want too many people to know how to contact him and discover where he lived. In this business, there were plenty of crackpots to deal with, and he'd made a healthy list of enemies. The same rang true for just about every business, but in this one, the enemies frequently turned out to be dangerous.

His cell buzzed. The name displayed was a familiar one – Bob Dalgren. He'd known Dalgren for several years. He was the attorney for Richard Warden, CEO of WarCo, and had asked him to do several important jobs for him. Adam knew he

53

didn't have to wear his 'professional' hat with Dalgren. He picked it up and immediately went into a spiel he'd wanted to do for quite a while. "Adam Brooks Investigations, I'm not in the office right now, but if you'll leave your name–"

"Very funny," Dalgren said.

"Sometimes I like to amuse myself in strange ways."

"Let's not go into that right now. You have time to talk?"

"You sound serious. For an attorney, that is. Not that you don't have a humorous side – as far as attorneys go."

"I just need to know if you're busy, Adam."

Something was going on. Bob usually joked around a bit more than this, before getting down to business. But right now, that could be a good thing. Dalgren paid top dollar and paid on time. Dalgren was, in fact, probably the only client who actually paid on time – and without balking about the charges.

"Of course I'm busy. Matter of fact, the phone hasn't stopped ringing all day."

"Too busy to make some extra money?"

Money was the key word. Adam figured it was past time to cut the silly act. "What can I do for you, Bob?"

"I've got something you might be interested in. It pays well, and you don't have to risk your life. Or even put yourself in an embarrassing situation."

"There's something new."

"It involves Richard Warden."

"Ah. What's the big guy been up to?"

"I'll tell you when you come over here to my office."

"This is beginning to sound really serious."

Dalgren sighed. "I'm a little worried about Richard and would like to find out what he's been up to."

"I thought you saw him every day."

"Not every day..."

"What's the problem?"

"That's just it. I don't know. That's why I'm hiring you."

***

Le Cuisine rested quietly in a grove of pines on five or six acres of wooded, hilly property in Altamonte Springs.

Not visible from the main highway, the chalet-type building sat at the end of a long, winding path more than two miles from the closest major intersection.

A French-run business, the restaurant employed the best chefs and waiters brought over from Paris. The food was excellent, the wines top of the line. Its clientele consisted mostly of wealthy businessmen who didn't mind spending several hundred dollars for a relaxed candlelight dinner.

Richard Warden arrived promptly at six-thirty and slipped the host twenty dollars for the corner booth overlooking the brightly lit gardens and fountain in the courtyard behind the building. A vodka martini was placed in front of him soon after he sat down.

The place wasn't yet crowded. The atmosphere was warm and mellow. Mellow was what he needed tonight. The martini would help, of course, but it wouldn't solve their present dilemma. Brittany had to accept his help before he could bring in Cravell. Once her stalker was removed, Richard would be free to pursue this exceptional beauty at his leisure.

Le Cuisine was perfect for such a rendezvous – candlelight, soft piped-in violins, extravagant prints of Parisian courtyards and gardens covering the walls, and the strong hint of romance in the air.

He was finishing his second martini when Brittany entered the candlelit room. She wore a low-cut silk dress that clung tightly to her perfect figure. The dress accentuated her exquisite cleavage and her shapely legs.

The host escorted her to Richard's table. Richard could not speak as she slid into the booth next to him.

"Am I late?"

"It ... doesn't matter," he said, noting how bizarre his own voice sounded. Time seemed to have stopped for the moment.

She patted his arm. An electric shock danced up and down his limbs. "I'm thirsty. What're we drinking?"

"Whatever you want."

She thought for a moment. "I think I'd like champagne."

Richard signaled for the wine steward.

Later, as they sipped the excellent imported champagne, Richard discovered that he couldn't stop gawking. She appeared to have stepped from the pages of *Glamour*, or *Cosmopolitan*.

"You're staring."

"Can't help it."

She had more champagne. Her smile had disappeared.

He sensed the sudden mood swing. "What's wrong?"

"Just thinking."

"Of what we were talking about earlier?"

She nodded.

"Tell me about him."

Her eyes lowered. "It's just like any other sob story you've ever heard. Girl meets boy, falls in love, marries boy. Boy changes overnight and turns into a psycho. Wifey becomes Golden Boy's punching bag, putting up with this abuse for a whole year before throwing in the towel. But Golden Boy doesn't accept the split; he also doesn't agree with the court's decision to keep them apart."

Richard fought the anger down. The thoughts of anyone hurting or abusing this beautiful woman made him want to spit blood. That jerk had to answer for this. He struggled to keep the rage out of his voice. "Is his last name Weber too?"

She studied her half-empty glass. "He's been following me around for more than a year. Once he flattened my tires. Another time he poured sugar in my gas tank. I rent cars now so he can't keep up. But he still manages to find out where I am."

"Where's this character live?"

"Once, not too long ago, I went to see my folks at the cemetery. I went there one Sunday afternoon with fresh flowers. As I was walking back to my car, Eric was standing there, holding a crowbar." She sipped her drink and replaced the glass roughly on the table, nearly upsetting it. "He smashed out every window while I watched. The windshield, too. There was a smile on his face. After each blow, he turned to me and grinned. It was like ... like he was hitting me instead of my car."

"And the court injunction. Did you pursue it?"

She shrugged. "Complained till I was blue in the face. The judge didn't seem interested."

"What's the judge's name?"

"Doesn't matter."

"Yes it does. I can help, believe me."

Her eyes flickered in the candlelight. "I keep forgetting. You're very wealthy. You own companies. Have hundreds of people you order around."

He didn't know how to respond. Was there cynicism in that last remark? Some hidden meaning? Or was she just upset over the rehashing of these unpleasant events?

"Yes." He ignored his petty suspicions. "I have contacts, friends in high places. Let me use my resources to help you."

"What's in it for you?" she asked flatly.

He finished his drink, poured another, and added a splash to her glass. The vibes she was giving off had turned into something he hadn't anticipated. He raised his glass and averted his eyes from hers, but it was difficult. He couldn't ignore the heavy red tresses resting on her shoulders, her gorgeous eyes – every delicious inch of her. He wanted her more than ever. And he was certain she knew how he felt. "I'd like ... to get to know you better." Then she scowled, realizing how silly his statement sounded.

"Haven't heard *that* one in a while."

"Sounded pretty lame, huh?"

"Very."

"I just didn't ... I didn't want to come right out and say–"

"If you want to have sex with me, say it."

His pulse sputtered as he gawked at her.

"You want to, don't you?"

He reddened. But he knew he was in way too deep to back out now. Besides, he didn't want to back out. "Brittany, I know you must've been told this a hundred times before but let me say it. You're one of the most beautiful women I've ever seen."

"Was I right?"

"About what?"

"Do you really want to have sex with me?"

"Yes. I really do."

"And this is why you want to spend your money to help me get rid of Eric?"

"That and many other things."

"Like what?"

"Brittany ... if you'll just let me help you, I can–"

"I'm hungry." She put her empty glass down. "Let's talk about it after we eat, okay?"

***

Bob Dalgren presently maintained two law offices.

He ran his Orlando office during regular working hours from the third floor of the Orlando Center Building off Magnolia Avenue. His

Altamonte office rested in a small strip mall directly off Altamonte Boulevard, between a liquor store and tee-shirt shop. It was less than two miles from his Spanish villa, built in an exclusive section of Altamonte Springs. Dalgren worked out of his Altamonte office in the evenings when he didn't want to contend with the heavy Orlando traffic.

Coffee was brewing when Adam came in. Dalgren sat talking on the phone, but motioned Adam to help himself to some coffee. Adam grabbed a Styrofoam cup, added a sugar cube, and poured. By the time he took a sip and sat, Dalgren had put the phone down. "It's been a while," he said.

Adam put the cup down carefully on a corner of the metal desk. Outside, bumper-to-bumper downtown traffic inched by, exhaust smoke forming a filmy haze in the air. "Miss me?"

Dalgren grinned and sipped coffee from his mug. "So, your schedule's pretty clear for the time being?"

"You could say that. What's happening?"

"Like I said before, I wish I knew. Richard Warden has been acting strange lately, and I can't pin it down."

"Define strange. He is a multi-millionaire, you know. None of them have shown any evidence of using their brain cells like normal people – at least in my humble opinion."

"Point taken. But I'd need to make a list of what's bothering me in this case.   He seems to be sleepwalking – not paying attention at meetings. Not saying much or contributing. Acting secretive."

60

"I thought he always acted that way."

"Up to a point. There's something else going on. When Richard Warden presides at a stockholder's meeting and acts like he doesn't even want to be there, you know something's wrong."

"Kidnapping?"

"You mean Adrienne? Or his daughter? Highly unlikely. I would've been told about it."

"Extortion? Blackmail?"

"Don't know."

"So you want me to find out, one way or the other?"

"Exactly."

"Discreetly, I take it."

"I'd like you to shadow him for a few days. See where he goes. If he's meeting someone. Who this someone is."

"What if it's just a babe he's boffing on the side? Babes have the ability to turn a man's brain into mush without even working up a sweat."

"In this case, I hope it is. I sincerely hope he's not being blackmailed or conned. Too many crucial things are going on now that could be stymied if he's involved in anything illegal."

"So a babe squeezing his nuts is okay, but anything else is not?"

"If, of course, the babe is just a sex thing. If she's working for someone else, we'll need to know. If you find him meeting someone other than another woman, find out all you can, but for God's sake be careful."

"In that case, I'll take pictures."

"That would be fine. The more we can find out without actually blowing anything wide open, the better."

"I think I've got the idea."

Dalgren opened his checkbook and began writing. "The market's too volatile at the moment to let anything affect it. If Richard's involved in some secret merger, acquisition, or anything of that nature, I should've already been told about it by now. Otherwise, he's committing corporate suicide." He finished writing and ripped the check free. "The man's a corporate genius, but he's done many things in the past that border on sheer idiocy, and he's put me in the position of making sure he doesn't go overboard." He handed Adam the check. "Here's two grand. Let me know when you need more."

CHAPTER 5

Friday, the First Week

The next morning, Richard Warden stared out his office window and tried desperately to determine what had gone wrong the previous evening at Le Cuisine.

The dinner itself had gone well. However, nothing had been resolved. Brittany had managed to talk about everything but her ex-husband. She'd used distraction to skirt the issue, accomplishing it with a simple smile. Or accolades about the cracked crab, the Beluga caviar, or the champagne.

Steering the conversation in his direction also didn't seem to hurt. WarCo, War-Met, RKW – they all seemed so big. So successful. Where were all the branches, the subsidiaries? Did he leave the country very much? How many employees were on his payroll?

It didn't matter what she'd asked. She'd played him like a fine violin – puffing him up, getting him to talk about his business. No problem. Want to lead Richard Warden around by his nose? Just ask about his empire.

It was the oldest trick in the book. Richard was proud of his position, his corporation. He'd started up WarCo all by himself. Why shouldn't he use every given opportunity to flex?

But Brittany needed help. Certain issues had to be discussed. He should've shoved everything else aside and focused on her.

He'd known what was going on at the time. He'd also known what he needed to do. But jumping into her problems and offering his assistance had to be done gently. The first step, of course, was to steer the conversation away from him and nudge it back to her. It could be done tactfully and without her realizing what he was doing. And since he did it successfully every single day in his business dealings, he shouldn't have had any problems, should he?

Of course not. He needed a couple of minutes to collect his thoughts. Then he could work at his leisure. After coffee and brandy, Brittany excused herself and went to the ladies' room. This provided the perfect opportunity for him to organize his strategy. For the next fifteen minutes, he emptied his mind of all else and focused on presenting Cravell's proposition as gently and as tactfully as possible under the circumstances. However, he soon discovered his efforts had been in vain. Brittany had already left the restaurant.

***

At ten o'clock, two reps from War-Met Labs conned their way into Warren's office to discuss an urgent matter.

War-Met, a small WarCo subsidiary, employed less than fifty people, most of them PhD's with vast experience dealing with state-of-the-art processors and multi-faceted laser technology. War-Met's primary function was high-tech robotic research and utilization of highly sensitive software information. Since the old-fashioned data center had become obsolete, War-Met's resolution had moved toward mini-silos half the size of the average chest-type freezer, and processors as compact as toasters.

There had been a growing concern about War-Met's Singapore-based robotic arm-making plant. Singapore, sensing political mayhem with the U.S. Government, had intervened, slowing things down to a painful – and very costly – deadlock.

"The arms we received last week were unacceptable." The first rep, a short, skinny man in his late fifties, coughed noisily into the silk handkerchief he kept wadded up in his right hand. "We assembled an arm and installed it in silo number three at the plant. There was an immediate malfunction when we put the silo online and designated it to test mode."

"What kind of malfunction?"

The second rep, a younger man of Chinese origin, wore thick glasses and an expressionless face. His ID said his name was Wu. "The arm would not perform the simplest functions."

"Workmanship?" Richard wanted to get to the root of this problem and move on.

The reps nodded in unison.

Richard suspected this last strike was going to do some damage. He'd warned Olson about Singapore workers being impulsive, but Olson hadn't seemed too worried. He'd assured Richard any dispute would be quickly resolved. "Could it be the result of the strike?" he asked.

The first rep, whose name was Tompkins, shrugged, coughed, and covered his mouth.

"I consider this sabotage, sir," Wu suggested. "The arms we'd received before the official strike notice were perfectly designed and ready for assembly. This defective batch was made afterward."

"When was the strike announced?"

"Approximately mid-February."

"I've been informed these arms take nearly three months to complete."

"There was some delay." Wu shrugged. "The plant was in the process of renovation. The area finishing the arms was moved to another section of the building. This took place in early January."

"Olson informed me about that but never disclosed the details. Why move anything? Especially in the middle of a contract?"

"There was a scare that shook up everyone."

"What kind of scare?"

"Hazardous waste contaminating the ground near that section of the building."

"Toxic?"

"Yes."

"American?"

"Most definitely."

"Son of a bitch." Richard opened his drawer, reached for the bottle of Tums, and munched on four.

Wu adjusted his glasses. "The delay offered the workers time to postpone the present shipment. We think they rushed off a bad batch to fulfill the contract."

"Anyone looking at the contract?"

Both men nodded.

"I hope you discussed all this with Olson."

Wu nodded. "Mr. Olson is on his way to Singapore as we speak."

"So I assume you want me to get with Olson to speed this up."

"It would be appreciated greatly."

After they left, Richard sent off a priority email to Olson, then went into the War-Met site to familiarize himself with the robotics arms contract. It was a standard international contract. However, since this business dealt with a toxic issue, he knew what extent the damage would be. It was eggshell-walking time. The Singapore government had quite possibly the most stringent laws in the world. They would not, under any conditions, tolerate American business coming in and doing any illegal dumping.

Richard sat quietly, thinking about what the dumping would cost WarCo in terms of diplomatic relations, and what a lengthy strike would cost War-Met in terms of lost work, contractual delays, and possible sabotage. *I don't need this. I have other things on my mind.*

***

Thomas Cravell called just before one that afternoon.

"Where the hell were you?" Richard couldn't keep the agitation out of his voice. "I thought we'd agreed on frequent reports in this case."

"Sorry, Mr. Warden, but I only just got back to the office."

"You have a cell phone, don't you?"

"Uh, yes, sir..."

"Why didn't you use it?"

"I guess I was too busy with the woman, sir."

Richard perked up. "You managed to stay with her? After our dinner date last night?"

"For a while."

"What the hell do you mean, 'for a while?'"

A pause. "I mean just that, sir. She pulled the same swift move as the other night. She just up and vanished."

***

Later that afternoon, Richard sat with Cravell in a corner booth at Cokie's, a small bar near Church Street Station in downtown Orlando.

The afternoon sun burned bright against the window facing the street. The skinny, brown-haired waitress squeezed between them to pull the blinds shut.

"I'm getting a bad feeling about this woman, Mr. Warden." Cravell sipped his bourbon and water. He kept glancing at the No Smoking sign posted near the entrance. "I mean, avoiding an abusive stalker is one thing. Shaking a seasoned professional like me is totally different."

"What are you getting at?"

"She got away from me too damn easily."

Richard sipped cognac and looked Cravell right in the eye. "And you don't think this is because of anything you did or didn't do? Is this what you're saying?"

Cravell studied his glass before answering. "Mr. Warden, if you're hinting at a fuckup on my part, I'm not denying anything. I'm human – I admit it. There could be several things I might not have considered that could've made this much simpler for both of us. For all I know, I could be going at this all wrong. What I'm trying to say is this. The woman has definitely been followed before. She knows how to dump a tail."

Richard shrugged. "Of course. Her damned ex-husband–"

"It's more than that."

"How so?"

"Too many other things just don't add up."

"Go on..."

"For instance, the car she was driving."

"What about it?"

"It was a rental."

Richard shrugged. "She told me that herself. Doesn't want her ex to be able to tail her."

"There's more to this than what she's been telling you."

Richard sighed tiredly. He didn't like all this hedging around. "I'm waiting patiently for you to come out with whatever you're implying, Cravell, and I don't have all day."

"I tried doing a check on the rental."

"And what did you find?"

Cravell finished his drink and put down his glass. "Plate was stolen."

CHAPTER 6

Saturday, the First Week

After a quick breakfast of toast and coffee, Richard Warden slipped into his home office and called Ken Olson in Singapore.

In Olson's view, the issue of the robotics contract was simple. "The locals are scared, Dick." Olson's normally calm voice sounded edgy. "They know about that business years ago in Mexico with kids born without brains, thanks to that big Chicago firm that bought land down there and then dumped chemicals into the town's drinking water. But you really can't blame us for this fiasco. These ecology people stampeding to Washington to get all these restrictive regulations passed are the culprits."

"How the hell did Singapore find out about the dump?"

"They won't say."

"I take it the dump is ours rather than Singapore's?"

"Our lab techs have been dumping non-hazardous materials in that open field for the last two years."

"I was told the materials were toxic."

"War-Met uses only environmentally safe chemicals and materials. The dump is miles from the closest water source. There isn't an aquifer anywhere near that area."

"You're one hundred percent certain?"

"I've brought over a team of independent testers with me. I figured Singapore wouldn't want anyone from War-Met involved in the study."

"Where'd you find them?"

"I let the EPA pick their own."

"Smart."

"Singapore is assembling their own ground-sniffers as we speak."

"Everything above board?"

"As long as I have a hand in it."

Richard sat back and sighed. "This whole thing is bullshit. I thought we had people in Washington keeping a lid on that kind of stuff."

"This one took off like a scalded cat. What's scaring them is that the area's a potential drain-field, with the plant on the ass-end of the dump. They brought in their own local landscapers and did all kinds of studies and proposals. The Singapore government wants the damned thing capped."

"Who can we give this to?" This had to be handled quickly. "I had a friend with Washington connections, but he died last year of a heart attack. I just don't have the time right now to fool with this myself."

"I've got a contact who deals with the environmental people all the time. Knows what questions to ask, which lawyers to grease, who to get with to launder the right amount of money–"

"Find him and get him on this. We need to get it capped and checked, then stick those assholes back on the assembly line. Contract's costing us millions every day production's down."

***

Richard spent the rest of the morning at his desk, gazing out the French doors. Beyond them, the gardens glittered with fresh morning sun. A hundred yards down the cobblestone walk, the two-story guest house sat half-hidden in a grove of scrubs and pines. The workers would be arriving shortly to replace the Roman tub. After that, there would be some minor trim work to finish, and the place would be ready for guests.

Guests. Brittany, perhaps?

He smiled at the thought. Setting her up in the guest house would be impossible. Wonderful, but impossible. The biggest kink in the works would be Adrienne. If only he could get her to drive to Tampa to visit her parents for a few weeks... Then all he'd have to do was make sure Katie didn't go near the guest house. That would be another kink, but not nearly as tricky as keeping Adrienne away. Katie was busy with that Cassidy kid and school. The last thing Katie cared about was the guest house. And with Katie and Adrienne occupied, there would be no more hassles.

But what about Cravell's latest findings? The stolen plate. If that wasn't a hassle, he didn't know what was.

His thoughts went back to their evening at Le Cuisine. Had Brittany mentioned anything to suggest she'd been forced to break the law? Richard couldn't come up with one logical reason why the woman would put a stolen plate on a rental car. He tried rationalizing this from her point of view. *I'm escaping an abusive relationship. The psycho I was married to follows me everywhere, and the only relief I get is dodging him, getting away, and slipping by him. I'm scared – so scared, in fact, that I do strange, impulsive things, like switching plates on a rental car so Mr. Badass Ex can't keep close tabs...*

Maybe the plate wasn't actually stolen, but taken from another rental and–

That wouldn't wash. The fact that Cravell had already looked it up and found it on the hot sheet disproved that idea. The plate was reported stolen several weeks ago.

But somehow the idea of that babe getting down on her knees and switching plates just didn't wash, either. Maybe someone else? Perhaps the person who'd rented the vehicle *before* Brittany?

Just how meticulous were the people running the rental agencies? Orlando was one of the biggest suppliers of rentals in the country. They couldn't possibly keep a tight handle on every car coming and going from their lots.

Other tidbits raked at him even more than the stolen plate. Cravell had said she'd bolted when she spotted him. Not only did she bolt – she'd disappeared in a matter of seconds. The woman was obviously so terrified of her ex, she dropped out of sight at the slightest suspicion. Using instinct as her guide, she'd probably rationalized that being overly cautious was far better than the alternative.

But what Cravell had discovered going through the court's records unnerved Richard worst of all. In the last six months, there had been dozens of stalking injunctions reported in Orange County, in the city of Orlando. Not one of these cases even remotely resembled Brittany Weber's situation. Richard had told Cravell that Brittany's injunction might have been issued a year ago – maybe even two years ago. Brittany had said something about this jerk stalking her for about a year. Hence, the injunction could have been issued between twelve and twenty-four months ago. But nothing existed in the court records.

The 'Eric Weber' theory also led to a dead end. According to Cravell, the only Eric Weber in the Orlando area was seventy-four years old, a paraplegic, and lived in a retirement community off South Orange Blossom Trail, near the Florida Turnpike.

Richard's phone rang. It was Linda Voss, Executive Director of Marketing & Research, RefurbNet, Ltd. RefurbNet, another WarCo subsidiary, supplied routers, hubs, terminal servers, switches, adapters, and other hardware locally. The strongest of WarCo's union shops, RefurbNet experienced recurring problems with labor stepping on management's toes.

Richard sat there for the next twenty minutes, listening to Voss's status report about the present temporary union slowdown. But another part of him worried that Cravell might actually be right in his assessment. There was something very wrong – and suspicious – about Brittany Weber.

***

Nick Warden switched off his computer.

He never liked working on a Saturday. However, his old man had asked him to make it a common practice. As Sales Manager of Directron

Digitals, Nick had to admit the old man was right as usual. It set a good example and inspired admiration among his subordinates. Where there was admiration, there was also loyalty. As the old man had said, loyalty was one of the few things that couldn't be bought.

This request had been made six years ago, when Nick was coming out of grad school. He hadn't really got along with his old man since junior high, but the big guy knew his stuff about running things, and Nick was determined to go as far as he could with Directron – even though the software business bored him to tears.

It bored him almost as much as being married.

Wendy was a great wife. She knew how to cook, kept the apartment clean, and cooked up a storm in the bedroom, as well. She was a little messed up, but he hadn't known a prime piece of ass that wasn't. But as great as Wendy was, Nick remained his old man's son. One woman would never be enough. Even if he managed to catch one of the hottest Hollywood babes on the planet, he'd still prowl around at night. As long as he kept a close eye on the drinking.

Nick was very proud of his self-control. It was no problem at all to have wine with his meal and a couple of beers later on, when he went clubbing. Wine with your meal made the food taste better. Drinking beer when you were trying to hook up with a horny babe eased some of the tension.

The old man was another story. Despite his claims to the contrary, the great Richard Warden lacked the willpower to stop. Even though he'd gone through hell and nearly lost everything, the man couldn't resist the old 'one more for the road,' even when lying flat on his face.

Nick approached the matter much more rationally. When he was drinking, he was as horny as a bull. And since Wendy wasn't exactly the sharing type, she'd drain him as dry as a baked clam shell if she ever caught him giving it to someone else. This sort of reasoning kept him out of trouble. But it was Saturday, and the strippers would be out in droves. Nick had promised himself a night on the town once a week. Managing Directron kept him busy nearly seventy hours a week. After so much mind-blowing stress, he deserved a little fun.

He picked up his cell phone and dialed his apartment. Wendy answered on the second ring. "Hi, honey. What's up?"

"Bad news."

He heard her sigh. "Somethin' at the office?"

"Gonna be late."

"Darn. I was hoping we could go out for supper tonight. Haven't been out in a while."

"We were just out."

"When?"

"The Outback."

"That was two weeks after New Year's. Remember? We were invited to your folks' place that same week."

Dammit. It amazed him that females as stupid and as naïve as Wendy could get the jump on a guy so damned easily. "That long, eh?"

"I had my heart set on going out."

"How about tomorrow night? We could maybe drive on over to Disney Village, see what's happening."

"That sounds good. Promise?"

He didn't like it when she put him on the spot like that. But things could be a lot worse. At least she wasn't throwing a tantrum. "Unless something else comes up."

"But something always does." He could tell by her voice that she was pouting, doing that thing with her lower lip. "Sometimes I think you like that office more than me."

"Not true. Our bed isn't here. Neither is that hot little body of yours."

She giggled. It didn't take much.

"All kidding aside. I'm gonna be here a while. I might go out later and grab a bite."

"Think you'll be that long?"

"You know how things get around here."

"I won't wait up, then."

"I'll be home as quick as I can."

"Love ya."

"You know it, baby."

***

The pink Spanish-style stucco building dominated the intersection.

Rows of floods highlighted the entrance and most of the parking lot. A bright blue and yellow neon sign advertising *Babes Bountiful* flashed over the large double doors. The dark interior fluttered wildly with more neon. The loud thumping juke in the far corner made the walls vibrate. Half-naked dancers slid up and down their shiny metal poles and thrashed seductively in rubber cages.

A hot blonde sat by herself at a table on the other side of the room, near the window. Perched on a bar stool, Nick Warden let his eyes linger on the girl's shapely legs. He ordered a rum and coke and tried not to stare, but it was impossible. The chick was gorgeous.

He drank some of his drink. The dancers were sensational and sizzling hot. Except for sequins and sheer panties, they were naked. Yet, he kept turning back to the attractively dressed blonde. She was smiling at him.

Lordy ... I've died and gone to heaven...

He picked up his drink, jumped nimbly off the stool, and moved briskly to her table. "Mind if I sit down?"

Her smile widened. "I was hoping you'd join me. You wouldn't believe how many weirdoes have already tried picking me up."

"Oh, yes, I would." He put down his drink and sat.

Close up, she was one dazzling babe. Her curly blond hair covered her shoulders in heavy tresses. Her blue eyes were large and piercing, her cheekbones large and swelled, like a model's. Her low-cut electric-blue dress exposed a delicious cleavage and medium-sized breasts. Their nipples pushed brazenly against the thin material of the dress.

"I'm Nick Warden." He held out his hand.

"Jackie Marks." She took his, squeezed, then released it.

"Come here often? This place isn't exactly right for unescorted women."

She smiled. "I kind of had the feeling I'd be meeting someone nice. I'm glad I was right."

Lordy, Lordy... He struggled to ignore the erection straining against his dress slacks.

Since he considered himself too sophisticated to proposition a woman after only two minutes of pleasantries, he decided to try for some meaningful conversation. Besides, she was too classy for such trashy treatment. A far cry from the usual pickup. "I come here a lot," he said, "but I don't remember seeing you here before."

"My first time. People have been telling me about this place, so I had to come see for myself. The dancers are good, aren't they?"

The hottest-looking numbers in this place never gave me the boner you've just given me, baby... "If you wanna know the truth, they don't hold a candle to you."

"That's sweet. Your parents must've brought you up right."

He frowned. *Why the hell did she have to say that?* This was not exactly the right place, time, or circumstance to think about your parents. He decided to ignore the remark. "You didn't say where you were from."

"I didn't, did I?" she teased, still smiling.

Was she playing with him? It was hard to tell. That would be ironic. Playing mind-games with women was one of Nick's favorite activities. He'd been doing it since he was a kid and did it well. And despite his old man's subtle claim of having

79

invented the art, Nick prided himself in doing it better than anyone. But her shifting the game plan had unnerved him.

"Let me guess." Maybe he could bait her, shift things back into his own ballpark. "Las Vegas?"

"Why Vegas?"

"You could be a showgirl."

"Nope."

"New York?"

She shook her head and turned to watch one of the dancers going at it on top of the bar.

Nick grinned. She was definitely playing with him. Before the night's end, he knew he'd end up in bed with this woman. "You a tourist?"

Again, she shook her head. "How about you? You obviously live around here."

"I've got an apartment just a few miles up the road. I usually–"

"You're married, right?"

He forced himself to maintain his smile, but it was difficult. *Now why the hell would she say something like that?* "Do I *look* married?"

She nodded.

He scowled. That was an insult if ever he heard one. Nerds with bad haircuts and ill-fitting clothes sitting on wallets crammed with baby pictures and driving station wagons. Those morons looked married. Not Nick – no siree. For one thing, he was always careful about his looks. He watched what he ate, made sure he went to the best salons to have his hair professionally styled, and spent a fortune on his clothes. *Married-looking, hell!* He was just as dapper and buffed as those male models fresh from

80

the runway. What could this hot but obviously ill-informed chick be thinking? "Tell me why you think I look married."

She shrugged. "You're covering your wedding ring hand."

He looked down. That baby had been dumped just a few months after the wedding. He'd intentionally caught the appropriate finger in the closet door and relied on Wendy's soft heart to get him to take it off permanently once the bleeding had stopped. "But I'm not wearing a ring."

"Doesn't matter. The fact that you're unconsciously covering it tells me you're feeling guilty."

"You a shrink?"

"Just picked up a few things along the way."

He drank some rum. *Bitch. Playing with me, eh? I'll show you...* "How about you?" he asked.

"Divorced."

"How long?"

"A couple of years. Does your wife know you're here tonight?"

He sat back and forced himself to ride out the hot wave. *Easy, now. Don't fuck this up.* This was the hottest chick he'd seen in many a moon. He wasn't gonna lose it just because she happened to be squeezing his balls in her hot little hands. He had to get back his cool and show her what he was made of.

"She doesn't know," he said evenly.

She shrugged. "Don't feel guilty. Lots of guys cheat. Girls, too. How long have you been married?"

81

Shit. Why did the hottest-looking chicks always have to be bitches?

He thumped his elbows down on the table and moved closer, so he didn't have to shout over the roaring juke. "How about if we don't talk about my wife, okay? If I wanted to talk about her, I wouldn't be here at all. I'd be with my in-laws, having supper and watching *Desperate Housewives,* or something on the *Lifetime* Channel."

"I getcha."

Now he wanted this chick even more. Taking her to a motel would serve two purposes. It would get him off and shut her up as well. "Anyway, I'd much rather talk about you."

"Not much to talk about." She played with the ring of water her glass had made on the table. "Like I said, I'm divorced. I was married twice. My last husband died. He was rich. Owned a software business."

Nick perked up. "My old man's pretty high up in software."

"Really?"

"WarCo SoftSystems. Heard of it?"

Her slim brows bumped together. "I don't think so."

"The largest software supplier in Florida and you've never *heard* of it? You're obviously not from around here, are you?"

"WarCo ... WarCo..." She was mouthing the word softly, making her lips pucker.

This chick knew exactly what she was doing.

"Is WarCo corporate?"

"Damned straight. Five other companies have merged with it, most of them with international offices. We've got plants in Singapore, China, Australia–"

"Sounds pretty big. And your father *owns* WarCo?"

"Sure does." He grinned in spite of himself. The old man was a dickhead, but he sure packed clout. "Last name's Warden, remember? Where do you think the 'WarCo' comes from?"

"Didn't think of that. Do you work for your father?"

"I'm Executive Manager in charge of Sales for Directron Digitals, one of WarCo's subsidiaries. Matter of fact, Directron's almost as big as WarCo, since we've just taken over three multiplex operations. Directron furnishes multiplex components all over the world. Sydney, Australia, has recently become our largest buyer."

"Have you been to Australia? I hear it's beautiful."

"Not yet. But I'm hoping I can squeeze in a weekend or two down there one of these days."

The waitress brought them fresh drinks. He took a sip and put down the glass. He was beginning to relax. This chick was not only a knockout, but she was also easy to talk to. A broad like her would have to be dynamite in bed. "So you're a widow."

"Yes."

"And you said your husband was wealthy?"

"Moderately."

"How long's he been dead?"

"A year."

"Have any trouble with con artists?"

"Not really." A dark look crossed her face.

"What's wrong? Did I say something I shouldn't have?"

"It's not what you said. It just reminded me of something I don't want to think about."

"Tell me about it."

She shrugged. "I don't think–"

"C'mon. You can tell me. I'm a good listener."

She stared at him. Her dark look stayed.

"C'mon, Jackie. Maybe I can help."

"How?"

"Don't know yet. You haven't told me anything."

She had more of her drink and put down the glass. The darkness in her eyes had turned into fear. "Someone's following me."

***

Later they sat in Nick's silver Continental in front of Babes Bountiful while the heavy Saturday-night traffic roared down Semoran Boulevard straight ahead.

Jackie kept glancing out her window. The parking lot was now half-filled, but it didn't seem to make a difference. She was very tense.

Nick was growing impatient. *Just my luck. I find a dynamite babe, and she's even more messed up than Wendy.* "We can go somewhere else," he said. "Somewhere ... less crowded."

"It won't matter," she whispered, looking down at her lap.

"Whaddya mean? We can–"

"I was married twice. First time lasted just a few months. We were both young and foolish. I didn't know he had a ... terrible drug problem."

"Heavy stuff?"

"Heroin."

"But ... why would he be following you?"

"For my money – why else?"

"But he can't possibly have any claim, can he?"

"He doesn't need a claim."

"Why don't you get the cops involved?"

"Bill may be a junkie, but he's very smart. He's got this sixth sense for staying out of trouble. No one has seen him following me."

"Why not hire someone?"

"Already have."

"What happened?"

"The jerk took five hundred dollars from me and called me a week later, saying I was making it all up. No one was following me, and I should get psychiatric help."

"What an asshole."

She turned to him. Her eyes were bright in the darkness of the car. "You believe me?"

"Why would you make it up?"

"I could be a certified fruitcake, for all you know."

"Maybe ... but I don't think so."

"We only met an hour ago. You don't even know me."

"I'm capable of judging a person's character."

She smiled.

"What's funny?"

"The trouble you men go through – humiliating yourselves, learning and memorizing all sorts of lines, listening to a girl's troubles, doing anything she wants. Just to get laid."

He laughed.

"Well, isn't it true?"

This chick was as sharp as a tack. "You're supposed to think I'm genuinely interested in your story."

"And, of course, you're not."

"Don't get me wrong, Jackie. I really want to get you between those sheets. But I'd also like to help you get rid of that jerk."

"Come over here."

He moved toward her, and they kissed. When his left hand covered her right breast, she suddenly tensed up, grabbed his wrist, and pushed him away.

Dammit. He *hated* when they did that. "What the hell's wrong?"

"Listen." Her hand was cold. "Did you hear that?"

"Hear what?"

"I think Bill's out there, prowling around."

"You sure?"

"Positive."

Nick snapped open the glove box and removed a small automatic pistol.

Jackie stiffened, twisting away. "What's *that*?"

"Don't be alarmed. I carry this because I handle money for the company. I'm gonna go out there right now, and if he's hanging around–"

"Don't *kill* him, Nick." Her trembling hand touched his arm. "Please?"

86

He smiled. He had no intention of killing the pervert, but it was nice, seeing her all tense and scared. When they were like that, it was easier getting them in the sack. The sex was always much better, too. "Don't worry, I'm just gonna scare the asshole."

He opened the door carefully and slipped out into the cool night.

***

Five minutes later, Nick returned and pulled open the driver's door. Jackie gasped at the sound.

"Relax." Nick slipped behind the wheel and pulled the door shut. "Nobody's out there." He tucked the gun safely away, back in the glove box, and rested his hand on her left thigh. "You probably just heard someone getting in their car."

"No." Still shaking, she made no attempt to push his hand away. "It was Bill. I'm sure of it."

"Okay." He decided to let her have her way. If it made her feel better, so be it. Anything that would get her in the mood was fine. Right now, all he wanted was to reach down beneath her dress and hike off those panties. "But I think we scared him off."

She rested her hand over his. "Thanks, Nick."

"Let's go somewhere."

She moved closer, reached up, and cradled his neck in her hands. After pulling his face to hers she kissed him again. "Wherever you want," she whispered when the kiss ended.

***

Jackie slipped into the bathroom, turned on the light above the sink, and came back out.

She left the door half-open, providing a triangular beam of light spreading out onto the carpet. The darkness was a precaution. Didn't want anyone to know she was in here. No problem. Nick could be cautious if it meant nailing this hot, sassy babe. "Now what?" he asked.

"Sit down."

"Why?"

"You want to see a show, don't you?"

Without another word, he sat tensely in the chair beside the door. *A show, huh, baby? Sure. No problem. Start performing. I'm ready.* He loosened his shirt collar to ease the pressure in his neck. It wouldn't be long before he'd have to unbuckle his pants as well.

Only five feet away, Jackie stood beside the bed in the haze of the bathroom light, her gaze on him as she undressed, one garment dropping silently to the floor at a time. The dress slipped quietly down her perfect form and lay in a discarded heap on the carpet at her feet. She reached behind her and unhooked the lacy bra, then let it fall silently as well. Her boobs were sensational – round and perky, their nipples erect.

The panties were next. She hooked her long-nailed thumbs beneath the sheer fabric and pushed them down, an inch at a time, until they cleared her knees.

"Faster." His voice was a frail croak, his sex hot and throbbing. He couldn't hold it much longer. "Get those babies off!"

88

She let them drop to her ankles, then raised a foot and stepped away.   Turning slightly, she gave him an excellent view of her perfect round ass.

His blood thrashed violently through him.

She placed her hands on her hips, turned toward him, and suddenly stopped cold.

"Now what?" His temples throbbed loudly.

"Someone's outside!" She covered her breasts with her forearms and began backing away.

Shit. Here we go again... "Dammit, Jackie!"

"No. It's him! I'm sure of it. Bill's outside. He followed us here."

Despite the hot, pulsating tightness in his pants, Nick got up from the chair and approached her. She twisted away and groped for her clothes. "Gotta get away. Gotta get the hell *out* of here."

"Jackie, listen!"

"Can't let him *find* me here!"

"If you'll just calm down and let me handle this..."

The slamming of the bathroom door silenced the rest of his statement.

***

Two minutes later, fully clothed, Jackie slipped out of the bathroom. "Please, Nick. Check outside."

Even in the dim motel room lighting, he could tell that her face was as white as a sheet. *This bitch is scared shitless.* "Jackie, let me take you–"

"No. *Please*." Her eyes glistened in the darkness. "Check outside. I'll phone for a cab."

"I'll take you wherever you–"

"I don't want you to get involved."

89

He approached her. "I'll take you back to the club. Your car's there."

"No. He was back there. He's seen the car. He'll wait around until he spots me..."

"Jackie..."

"No. Please. Let me do this my way. I'll get a cab while you check things outside. It's the only way."

His blood boiled. He wanted to forget about her stupid suspicions and just pin her down on the bed. He also wanted to run outside and strangle whoever was out there. He knew better. There was no psycho ex lurking about. This chick was so scared, she'd probably heard someone near the ice machine and went apeshit.

He had to play this game her way. He'd known a few nut jobs back in college. Hell, even though Wendy had gone through her own craziness a few years back, she still had her moments. But a guy had to make concessions to get a chick to spread her legs.

"I'll go check. But you have to promise me we'll see one another again."

"Sure. Anything."

"What should I do if – when I see him?"

"He'll probably just make tracks if he thinks he's been spotted. That's what he usually does."

He moved toward the door and snuck a peek through the front drapes. Darkness. A light outside the motel room door. He turned around. She stood trembling in the darkness, her hands covering her mouth. "How can we get together again?"

"I'll call you."

"When?"

She shrugged. "Tomorrow night?"

"Six o'clock?"

"Just give me your number. But *please* ... go out there and check?"

He opened his wallet, removed a card, and handed it to her. Then he shuffled outside. The parking lot, as he'd suspected, revealed nothing suspicious. No one in the shadows, hiding beneath the steps, or wandering around in the parking lot. Just some tourists lugging bags through lighted doorways.

Jackie wasn't in the motel room when he got back. Tired and frustrated, he got back in his car. Farther up, a cab pulled away from the front entrance. It was too dark to tell if anyone was sitting in the back seat.

He promised himself he'd nail that beautiful but crazy bitch if it was the last thing he ever did.

CHAPTER 7

Sunday, the First Week

The next morning, Nick sat at the desk in his home study, glaring at his laptop, trying not to visualize the gorgeous but totally fucked-up Jackie Marks on the screen, wriggling out of her clothes, then forcing him away.

Damn that messed-up bitch with her drop-dead gorgeous–

A knock on his door stopped his imagination cold. He took a deep breath. *Calm down. Remember where you are. It's probably Wendy. Remember? Your wife? And she shouldn't see you like this because she'll ask what's wrong.*

"C'mon in."

"Breakfast's ready, baby." Wendy opened the door and approached him, then bent and wrapped her arms around him. Her hot breath brought him around. *Still worked up about last night, no doubt.*

He'd returned home around one o'clock. Still frustrated over what had happened at the motel, he'd marched into the bedroom, stripped, climbed into bed, yanked the sheet away from his sleeping wife, woke her with a passionate kiss, and ravaged her. In the darkness it was easy to imagine Jackie lying naked beneath his thrusts. However, his concentration deteriorated when Wendy suddenly called out his name. He covered her mouth with his hand – a tactic she'd always liked – and Wendy once again became Jackie. It was the best sex he'd had in weeks.

Her arms still around his neck, she kissed his right ear. He closed his eyes and once again pretended Jackie was caressing him. She kissed the back of his neck. "Want your breakfast now? Or later?"

Wendy knew how to turn him on in seconds. Or maybe it was his residual frustrations about the previous evening. Whatever it was, he'd quickly become tense and throbbing. "Kind of early ... for breakfast."

"You worked up an appetite in me, lover boy."

Her hot breath, so close, singed his flesh, making him rock-hard instantly. "Sorry about that. Was I too rough?"

A giggle. "I guess I forgot. Maybe we can go at it again, so you can help me remember."

He forced himself to focus on other things. He did have some work to tend to. It was the stuff he'd put off doing the day before, when he'd gone to Babes Bountiful. "Not this morning, Wen. I've got some stats to look over."

"Stats, stats. It's all you talk about anymore." She straightened. "I was surprised you decided to look me over last night. You must've been really horny."

"Yeah, I guess you could say that. But why such an early breakfast? It's not even eight o'clock."

"I want us to be hungry when we go out for supper tonight."

"Supper?" He sat up. *Damn. Jackie was supposed to call at six.*

Wendy's smile vanished. "Did you forget *already*?"

"Listen, Wen. Something's–"

"Don't tell me you're not taking me out tonight." Her little-girl voice suddenly sounded threatening. As usual, when she was about to throw a tantrum.

His mind immediately went into overdrive. "Something has come up. There's a buyer coming to town today, and I wanna make sure everything goes as planned. Listen. How about we go to the Magic Castle for lunch?"

"The *Castle*?" She was already grinning. It was one of her favorite spots. Eating there made her feel like a princess. "For *lunch*?"

"Okay with you?"

Her smile grew. "Wowee. It'll give me a chance to wear that flashy new red skirt I just bought." Without another word, she spun around and rushed back out, pulling the door shut behind her.

CHAPTER 8

Monday, the Second Week

Though Nick didn't want to be at the office at all, he hoped it would help get his mind off Jackie Marks.

Thankfully, the coffee was ready. He wouldn't have to waste too much time exchanging small talk with his secretary, Ann. Besides, she was too busy handling calls to ask how his weekend was.

He poured a cup of strong black coffee, closed his office door, fell into his chair, and immediately found himself getting angry again. Not a word. Nada. Six o'clock came and went without Jackie's call.

It had been ten years since a chick had pounded his brain into mush. But back then, he deserved it. He was just an immature punk with an attitude and a hard-on to match. Now he was rich, bright, and resourceful. He boasted dozens of prestigious business contacts, money in the bank, a stock portfolio, a father who would always be there to bail him out, a wife who loved him, and real estate investments certain to earn him tons of healthy respect. He had the world by the *cojones*.

Why, then, would he let a chick squeeze them?

Easy. She was a knockout. The kind of babe every guy dreamed of nailing.

Wendy was a hot-looking number. Skinny, with small round tits, a nice ass, and a terrific pair of lips. But Jackie made Wendy look like a drowned cat.

Nick figured he should be the one calling the shots here. He was sitting pretty. At twenty-eight, he was more of a success than ninety percent of guys twice his age would ever be. Why should he let anyone lead him around by his dick?

At eleven o'clock, Ann buzzed him. "Mr. Warden? Some woman wants to talk to you, won't say who she is. Shall I put her through?"

He sighed. "I'll take it." He flicked it on speaker. "Nick Warden."

"Nick? It's Jackie."

He stiffened, then grabbed the receiver. "J-Jackie?"

"I'm terribly sorry about last night. I really feel awful about everything. Bill came to see me at my place. It ... wasn't pleasant."

"Are you okay?" Suddenly all barriers dropped with a resounding bang. His anger had dissipated like a wisp of smoke. Now it was important to see her, find out what happened. He could tell by her voice that she'd also had a rough night. "Did he hurt you?"

"I'm fine. I sort of ... I stayed away for a while, until he got tired and left. Can we ... can I see you, Nick? This evening, maybe?"

His pulse hastened. "When? Where?"

"I was wondering if we could meet in some out-of-the way place. Miles from here. Kissimmee, maybe. I'd feel a lot safer, and I could concentrate better on ... on us."

He smiled. His pulse continued fluttering. "How about *La Bohème*, on 192?"

***

"Why the hell haven't you called me, Cravell? It's been *two days!*"

Richard Warden had to force himself to keep from yelling into his office phone. He hadn't heard from Brittany all weekend. Cravell had better tell him what was going on and what he was doing to earn his money. "Where the hell is Brittany?"

"I didn't call because there was nothing to report," Cravell replied in his usual soft voice. "To put it bluntly, I have no idea where that woman is."

Not the sort of thing Richard wanted to hear. "I'm paying you a grand a day, and all you can come up with is that?" Richard's resolve to remain calm seeped away like air from a punctured balloon. He knew he was going to have to pace himself if he wanted to keep the blood pressure in check.

High-class. It was a catchphrase he'd always used in tight situations. He'd programmed it into his brain years ago. The simple idiom never failed to pull him out of whatever rut or hole he found himself in. It reminded him that he stood head-and-shoulders above the average Joe, and that he could never behave like others of lower class.

"Mr. Warden, I'm doing the best I can."

Somewhat calmer, he fished for one of his cigars. "I'm interested in results, not promises."

"Like I've already said, this woman is good. I don't know why she's good. But she's obviously better than I am. This tells me several things. The most important, of course, is that she's expert at losing a tail. But this also raises an important question. Why should she know how to do something like that?"

Richard didn't reply. He wasn't interested in going that route.

"And I'm still suspicious about that stolen plate," Cravell said. "I'm convinced she was the one who switched it."

"Now how the hell would you know *that*?"

"These rental agencies scan their vehicles. They come out with their scanners and meters and check the car from bumper to bumper, inside and out. You don't think they'd spot something as conspicuous as a stolen plate?"

"When you've got a company paying its workers minimum wage with little or no benefits, you'd better get used to more than one of them skimping on company procedures."

"Are you saying someone at the rental agency ignored standard protocol?"

"I'm saying anything is possible. Believe me, I know. I own a plant in Singapore that's chafing my ass because the little jerks have just figured out how much shit they can splatter by whining about a toxic dump that won't even affect them. I've outsourced a great deal of work to foreign countries because American labor was bleeding me dry. On the other side of the scale, one of my presidents is outsource-happy because he's got this thing about medical benefits and doesn't want all that money going to–"

"What's this have to do with a stolen plate?"

"When you cut costs, you sacrifice quality. Mistakes will be made. Minor blunders squeak by that can transform into a giant fuckup. Like a shipment of defective robotic arms. Or shopping for meat at the grocery and finding packages that should've been thrown out a week earlier. Or discovering a stolen plate on a rental vehicle."

"So are you saying you want me to forget about the stolen plate?"

"I'm saying I want you to find Brittany Weber."

Richard hung up and fixed a drink from the credenza behind his desk. It was still morning, but he didn't care. He needed a stiff belt.

***

La Bohème, a gray stone building half-hidden by ivy, trimmed hedges, and palm trees, sat almost unnoticed amidst multi-lane intersections, strip malls and the endless trail of fast-food kiosks littering the busy highways.

Dressed casually, Nick chose a booth in a dark, secluded corner of the restaurant. He'd hurried home after work just long enough to shower and change. On his way out the door, he gave Wendy a detailed lie about entertaining an international client visiting Orlando.

Jackie appeared in a black crop-top, white shorts, and red tennis shoes. Her heavy golden mane was pulled back and tied with a red rope. As usual, she looked fabulous.

Spotting him, she hurried right over. The smile of relief on her face made him feel like the most important guy in the world – especially when all male heads turned their way.

"I know I'm late." She slid in the booth and dropped her tan bag on the padded seat beside her. "There's a lot of traffic."

"You're fine." He found himself gawking helplessly. Her sweet smell perked him right up. "Well worth waiting for."

"Always the charmer." She glanced at his glass. "What's that you're drinking?"

"Rum and coke. What would you like?"

"I could go for something slightly stronger after fighting that traffic. Something that'll calm me. Vodka and orange juice sounds heavenly."

He signaled for the waitress, who asked if they wanted to eat. "Later," Nick said, and ordered the drinks.

After the waitress shuffled off, Nick decided to focus on their earlier conversation. For one thing, he was curious. For another, he wanted to know a little about the man responsible for ruining their evening. "Tell me what happened with your ex."

"Sure you want to know?"

"That's why I asked."

Jackie waited until the waitress came with their drinks. She immediately sampled hers. "It wasn't very exciting. I mean, it wouldn't make a good suspense story for TV. But when it first happened, I did have the feeling I wasn't gonna come out of it very well."

"He didn't attack you, did he?"

"I'd just taken a shower and was getting ready to call you when the doorbell buzzed. I went to the door, saw him in the peephole, and made sure the chain was on the door. He heard me and started banging and yelling. I was afraid he was gonna get me kicked out of the place. I had no other option, so I opened the door, but left the chain on. I only did it to keep him from making more racket."

"What did he want?"

She shrugged. "What he always wants. Forty or fifty bucks – more if I could manage. So I let him in, gave him what I had, and told him to leave. But he sat down in the chair and started his routine to get me feeling guilty."

"What sort of routine?"

"He always whines about the lousy breaks he'd had when we were married and makes sure I remember that he never had any luck because of his addiction. Then he reminds me that he would've been successful if he hadn't got started on coke."

He found it amazing that anyone would fall for a spiel like that. "And this works for you?"

She sighed. "I guess I understand where he's coming from. He probably could've really made something of himself if he hadn't been hooked. He went to college and studied architecture. He was really good at it, too."

"But why should *you* feel guilty?"

"He knows about my second husband's wealth and wants us to get together again. He always knew how to get under my skin. I guess that's why I married him. That, plus the fact that he was always so great in bed."

Nick frowned. Guys just didn't like hearing stuff like this.

Jackie sighed. "It's true. When we were going at it, that man could literally make my eyes roll back into my head."

"You oughta give me a chance," he said. "I just might surprise you."

She picked up her drink. "You'll get your chance. Sooner than you think."

***

After supper, they left the restaurant and crossed the front, where the motel awaited them next door.

Jackie stopped suddenly, then turned back toward the restaurant. She was staring at his Lincoln, which was parked in the space next to *La Bohème's* huge neon sign. "Nick. Your car."

"*Damn...*" His blood instantly turned cold. All four tires were flat. Someone had obviously let the air out. There was no way all four steel radials had gone flat at once.

"My *God.*" With her hands covering her cheeks, Jackie backed up. "Bill ... he was *here*. He ... he *found* us."

"This is ridiculous." Nick pulled out his cell phone. "That asshole can't get away with this."

She gawked at him. "Who are you calling?"

"The cops. Who else?"

She grabbed his wrist. Her hand was ice-cold. "But ... you c-*can't.*"

"Why the hell not?"

"What'll you tell them?"

"Some asshole snuck over here, let the air out of my tires, and–"

"Will you give them your name?"

102

He hadn't thought of that. This could be bad.

"You know how they are. They'll ask for your ID. Then they'll ask for mine. They'll check with the motel registration. Before you know it, everyone will know what's happened. You know you can't afford that. Neither can I."

She was right. The cops would turn this into a real show – especially if they started asking questions. Who knew what would happen? And if Wendy got wind of it, he'd be fucked.

"I don't want your wife to find out about this. I sure don't want you to suffer for something I did."

"But we can't let that moron get away with this."

"It would be worse for us than for him. I'll bet no one even saw him come out here. That's how he operates. He's as smart as a fox."

"This really chafes my ass."

"Mine, too."

"And it ruined our evening."

"I was looking forward to it, too." She brushed his cheek lightly with her palm. He immediately felt the effect in his groin. "But we need to keep a lid on this for both our sakes. Why don't you just call for road service and let them take care of it?"

"Why can't we just finish what we'd planned?"

"Oh, no, Nick. I couldn't *possibly* relax after this."

His heart sank. "*Please*, Jackie..."

"I'm sorry. Another time."

As the truck arrived at the motel, Nick watched Jackie walk back to the restaurant and disappear behind the building, where she'd parked. He wanted to see the vehicle she was driving, but someone behind him yelled, "Hey!"

Flinching, Nick turned.

The tow truck operator opened his door. "You the guy, called about the flats?"

Nick wanted to deck the man for interrupting his concentration. He sighed. *Cool it. Things are bad enough.* "I'm him."

His shirttails flopping in the breeze, the big guy climbed down from the truck. He eyed the flattened tires and gave a low whistle. "Somebody's got it in for you, buddy."

"Yeah." Nick fought down the heat crawling heavily up his spine. "And whoever it is doesn't know who he's messing with."

CHAPTER 9

Tuesday, the Second Week

With a deep sigh, Richard Warden dropped Olson's fax on the blotter in front of him.

Just as he figured. It was all the ammunition Singapore needed to turn this into a first-class boil. Every damned chemical listed could be directly traced to War-Met.

Five years earlier, War-Met Labs owned a small site a mile up the road from the RKW ChipTics plant that was used specifically for chemical testing. As soon as the test lab opened, the EPA had sent a package containing strict guidelines about illegal dumping. Apparently the information hadn't been taken seriously. Now everyone was going to take the heat for this.

Ellen buzzed him. "A woman named Brittany Weber wants to talk to you, Mr. Warden. Would you like to take this? Or should I tell her you're busy?"

"I'll take the call." His heart raced, waiting for the click.

"Richard?"

"Where have you been, Brittany? And why haven't you called?" He'd wanted to keep the urgency out of his voice, but just couldn't manage it. Despite the chaos during the last few days, he hadn't passed a single waking moment without Brittany dominating his thoughts.

"I'm terribly sorry, Richard. But I've been in a great deal of trouble and haven't been able to get a free moment until now."

That Eric bastard. It had to be. Her desperation had weakened her voice. "Are you all right?" he asked.

"My ex found me again. The other night."

"What happened?"

A deep sigh. "He showed up Friday at the 7-Eleven, while I was pumping gas. I managed to slip away, but he obviously saw me because he was outside my apartment complex Saturday morning, when I went out to put trash in the dumpster."

"What was he doing?"

"Just standing in front of my place, leaning against my car."

A chill flickered through him. "The crowbar routine again?"

"Didn't have it with him this time. I guess he just wanted me to know he could find me any time he wanted. So...I moved."

"You *what*?"

"Just packed up what little I had and got out. Found a cheap station wagon, tossed everything in the back, and moved in the middle of the night. I spent the night at a motel, then found this cute little efficiency."

"Brittany, you *can't* keep doing that!"

"Don't want him knowing where I live, do I?"

"But what about your security deposits? Damages? Those other expenses you forfeit when you up and move?"

"I'd rather lose a little money than my life."

106

He leaned back in his chair. This was incredible. A beautiful woman like Brittany having to live scared all the time, looking over her shoulder, moving around like a gypsy. And all because of a crazed bully. "Brittany, please let me help you."

"Why?"

"Because–"

"I know. That sex thing."

His cheeks flushed. "When you put it like that, it sounds so–"

"It's true, isn't it?"

It took him a few moments to reply. "It's much more than that. I enjoy talking with you, being in your company."

"You're married."

A strange coldness developed on the back of his neck. Adrienne, dark, and ominous, flashed in front of his eyes. "Yes..."

"I remember reading about you in *Orlando* Magazine. Last summer, I think it was. They showed your offices, your mansion, your family. Full color shots. Your wife is very attractive."

"Please ... don't–"

"You know she is."

He sighed. "Adrienne was always a striking woman."

"But you screw around anyway."

The sharpness in her voice could be felt as well as heard. It probably came out because she didn't want him to be married. It made him almost ashamed to have had a life before meeting her.

107

"How long have you been married? Your son – isn't he pushing thirty? And your daughter's around twenty, right?"

This was accomplishing nothing. He just sighed and hoped she'd get her frustrations out of her system.

"It must be nice to have children," she said in a whisper. "To see them grow up, become adults..."

The sudden eerie quality in her voice alarmed him. He had to snap her out of this. "Brittany, I want to help you. I've got the juice – and the horsepower – to do it. And I'd like to discuss this with you, if I can. Can we see each other? How about lunch?"

"I don't know..."

"You name the place."

Silence.

"If you don't trust me–"

"It's Eric I don't trust."

"I understand. But like I said, I've got leverage here. Let me make a couple of quick phone calls, get us some protection."

"What do you mean?"

"I could get a private detective to watch–"

"No!"

"But–"

"I've got enough to worry about, Richard. Do you honestly think I could be calm and relaxed if I knew there were two men out there, watching me? I'll call back when I think of something, okay? But like I said, I don't want any private investigator hanging around. Understood?"

"But if you'll just–"

108

The click echoed sharply in his ear. With a heavy sigh, he quickly dialed Cravell's number. "This is Richard Warden. Get over here."

"But I'm on the other side of—"

"Get your ass over here now. I've got a brand-new job for you."

***

Half an hour later, Cravell nervously took his seat across from Richard's desk. "You sounded really upset when you called."

Richard forced himself to keep the anxiety down to a tolerable level. "I want you to tail me again. Day and night. And God help both of us if that woman spots you this time."

"What exactly do you have in mind?"

"I want to see Brittany, but I can't. There's a psycho out there making her life a living hell. Because he's following her, she's gun-shy, and doesn't want anyone else hanging around. Understand?"

Cravell lit a cigarette and sat back.

"Something on your mind?" Richard asked.

"I knew this chick once. A knockout. Big jugs, dynamite face – the works. Couldn't go down the street without someone propositioning her. I went out with her once. That was the end of that." Cravell pushed out a cloud of cigarette smoke. "She was just too much trouble. Had exes all over the damned place. Husbands, boyfriends – the whole nine yards. I took her to a bar, and there were three guys at our table when I came out of the fucking john. We went to a nice, quiet restaurant later on, and this guy comes out of nowhere, asks her how she's been

109

doing, why she hasn't called, why this, why that. And her cell must've gone off a dozen times during our date. She didn't answer any of the calls, fortunately, but it was still damned irritating." Cravell stubbed out his smoke. "Last time I stood in line was in the damned Army. I don't take a number to get laid."

"I don't see where this is going..."

"Women like her are all the same. You know it, and so do I. So does every damned guy who's been around the block. It's nothing but a game for these women. They love it when guys fight over them. I guess it's got something to do with a feeling of security."

"Brittany isn't that way. She's just having a rough time."

"Her ex, right?"

"Yes..."

"They're all alike. More trouble than they're worth."

This sounded like the ravings of a jilted man, but Richard could well understand. Cravell was average height, slender, and nothing to write home about in the looks department. Anything he picked up would have to be second-rate. The woman he was talking about was probably the best thing he'd ever snared in his life. He'd no doubt stumbled upon her purely by accident and couldn't accept the fact that she was out of his league. Cravell's personal resentment toward Richard or women like Brittany might prove an obstacle here. If this job had jinxed him, now was the time to find out. "Are you saying you want out?"

"Not at all. I'm just warning you about women like her. I'm sure you know a lot more about them than I do, but I think you're being too damned subjective in this case. In my opinion, you're throwing your money away."

"Let me be the judge of that."

"All right, then. We both know where we stand."

Richard leaned forward. "I'm waiting for her to call me back. When she does, we'll set up a rendezvous. I'll get with you and give you the details. You follow me at a safe distance, and when I meet up with her, you stay as close as you can without letting her see you. Can you do that?"

"Been doing it for ten years."

"Don't forget how good she is."

"No need to worry. I can't be fooled more than twice."

"All right. And when this asshole ex of hers shows—"

"You still don't have a description, do you?"

"No. But from the way she talks, he'll be easy to spot. Man's unstable, nervous, bad-tempered. A psycho. Do what's necessary to get him away from us."

"Strong-arm stuff okay?"

"As long as she doesn't know about it."

Cravell gave Richard a puzzled look.

Richard shrugged. "That's the job."

"The strong-arm stuff will cost you extra. I'll need a pro for this. Maybe an ex-boxer. Someone who can take down this character and put him in the hospital. But they cost money. A coupla hundred extra, maybe a C-note if you want the job done really well."

"Give him a grand and put it on my tab."

***

Nick Warden spent his lunch hour quietly by himself in a small cafe at Church Street Station, staring at his untouched shrimp salad and the half-finished whiskey sour at his elbow.

His mind wasn't on food or his drink, but on Jackie Marks. He knew full well he was acting like a moron. He couldn't just sit here, feeling sorry for himself. He was Nick Warden, a corporate chief in the making. In five years, he'd be running Directron. And when Big Daddy retired or bit the dust, Nick would undoubtedly be chosen to man the helm.

It didn't matter if Jackie was gorgeous. Or that he developed a hard-on every time he saw her or talked with her. Even if she turned out to be the world's wildest lay, she was serious trouble.

With his head back where it was supposed to be, he went out into the bright sunlight and crossed the street. For the rest of the afternoon, he'd concentrate on business. Nothing else. And he'd forget all about Jackie Marks and her messed-up life.

Ann switched the call over as soon as he'd returned to his office. It was Jackie Marks. "Nick, I want to see you tonight."

Dammit.

Sighing tiredly, Nick sat back and stared at the white plaster ceiling. He wanted to hang up and forget about her. *Just do it. She can't do you if she*

112

can't talk to you, can she? All you've gotten from her are empty promises and more than your fair share of aggravation and bullshit. Now she's calling as if nothing's wrong. Hang up.

He pulled the phone away from his ear, then stopped.

Now what the hell? What's going on?

As always, he surrendered to the familiar tightness in his lap. Jackie was breathing into the phone and, despite everything she'd done, everything she'd put him through, all he could think about was the delicious smell of her.

Stupid, pussy-whipped moron.

"Nick? You still there?"

"Listen, Jackie..."

"Tell me what's on your mind, Nick."

"I really don't want to discuss it on this line."

"Why don't we get together and–"

"Before we start making any plans, I have a question to ask."

"What's that?"

"Why the vanishing act last night? As soon as the road-service guy fixed my tires, I was just fine and dandy. But you'd long gone. You made me feel like a shithead."

"I'm *so* sorry about that. Really and truly. I promise I'll tell you everything when we see each other again, okay?"

He sat forward. Should he or shouldn't he?

She's a problem. A big one. Last night, it was four flat tires. And don't forget that fiasco in the motel room, right after she'd stripped naked and

113

showed you all the great stuff you wouldn't be getting. Now she wants to do it again.

Could this be just another ploy? Maybe to play for some time to map out a good excuse? Didn't matter, did it? The image of those gorgeous breasts wouldn't go away. Nor would the memory of those beautiful legs. He wanted her again. He could hardly stand it.

"Name the time and place," he told her.

"We could meet somewhere for drinks, then have dinner. And later on, we could, you know..."

His suspicions, his anger – everything – had collapsed around him, as if someone had just detonated a bomb. The power this woman had over him was frightening. He didn't like it one bit. He had no idea how else to deal with it, but he knew to remain wary. Despite how much he wanted her, she could not be trusted. "Got a place in mind?"

"The Kingston, on International Drive. They've got a really nice bar, and their rooms are way in back. Very private. If we don't want to eat there, there are hundreds of restaurants up and down that stretch."

"What time?"

"Eight o'clock?"

Once again, his inner voice told him to hang up. The billowing heat emanating within him forced him to ignore the voice. "Eight o'clock's perfect."

***

Richard Warden scowled at the digital clock on his desk.

Almost four o'clock and Brittany still hadn't called – still miffed about his detective idea, no

114

doubt. She was doing it again. Playing him as if he were a child wanting an expensive toy. Why was she torturing him? Couldn't she see what she was doing?

No. It wasn't that at all. It was her damned ex fouling up the works. If it was the last thing he ever did, Richard would make sure the asshole suffered for this.

He got up from his desk, deciding to take the elevator down to Gino's. The day was already a bust. No point in hanging around any longer. A few martinis, a change of scenery, and he'd forget all about this.

His line buzzed. It was Brittany. "I had to get over being angry with you," she said.

"Was it my detective idea?"

"Yes."

"I understand, but all I want to do is–"

"Let's just forget about it."

He wanted her to know he couldn't get through one minute without thinking about her. She was affecting his work, his life ... but he didn't want to say anything that would cause her to end this conversation.

"Wanna meet somewhere tonight?" she asked suddenly.

His head instantly grew warm. Everything he wanted to say evaporated. "Yes. Of course. Where?"

"The Stonehenge, on International."

"Great place." He'd enjoyed many other liaisons there. The hotel had terrific food, great atmosphere, and the staffers went to extra lengths to make sure their guests were given every convenience. "What time?"

"Nine o'clock?"

"I'll be there." He waited for her click, then dialed Cravell's number.

CHAPTER 10

Tuesday Evening, the Second Week

Nick's heart thumped as he entered the Jamaican Lounge in the Kingston Hotel a few minutes before eight.

Jackie sat in a corner booth, watching him. She wore a dark skirt and a sleeveless white blouse with the top two buttons unbuttoned. A yellow scarf hung loosely around her neck. Since it was the same shade as her hair, he didn't see it right off. He wondered why she wanted to hide her beautiful swanlike neck. But it didn't matter. He'd given up trying to figure women out long ago. Besides, he wasn't really concerned about the scarf. His biggest challenge was to keep down the drooling as he slid into the booth beside her.

"Aren't you a little early?"

She smiled. "I was running ahead of schedule, so I decided to get here and reserve the room while traffic wasn't so bad."

He licked his dry lips. "You already ... got the room?"

"It was all right, wasn't it? Did you have something else in mind?"

"No, that's fine." *Thank God for independent females.* "In fact, you saved us a lot of time and aggravation."

"Shall we order our drinks first?"

He blinked. "First?"

Her hand rested warmly on his thigh. "Before we go find our room."

Nick forced himself to ignore the sudden urgent throbbing and waved for the waitress. He wanted to forget the intermediary bullshit and haul this gorgeous chick off to the room. But that wouldn't be proper. Heating up the inevitable with drinks, flirting, and intimate conversation would make the sex much more memorable.

***

Sophie's, the dark, air-conditioned bar down the hall from the three Stonehenge restaurants, smelled of the small seafood buffet placed in the corner of the room. Tourists and locals alike helped themselves to the fine cuisine.

At eight-thirty, Richard Warden sat at a table, sipping his first strong drink. He didn't care about the seafood, but about Brittany and her problem with her ex-husband. He didn't want this woman slipping through his fingers and would do whatever it took to eliminate anything that threatened their future relationship.

But he knew to tread carefully. Adrienne had her claws into much of his assets and would pull out all the stops if she suspected he was about to threaten their thirty-year marriage.

Once he and Cravell had gotten Brittany's ex out of the picture, Richard could put her up in one of the Disney Village condos he'd secretly bought a few years ago. If Brittany decided to go along, he certainly wouldn't mind suffering through the considerable time, details, and expense such arrangements demanded.

118

Some arrangements were worth the trouble.

***

From the dirty white van parked five spaces down from Richard Warden's Cadillac, Thomas Cravell had a really good view.

The light spring drizzle had stopped just as abruptly as it had started, making the evening slightly cooler. Mr. Bigbucks sat in the bar – probably getting himself slightly soused before Red showed.

Tom wore his usual disguise – brown suit, plain black shoes, white shirt, gray tie. Dressed in this outfit, he could get in someone's face and duck out of the picture without anyone remembering what he looked like. The two-day growth of beard and unkempt hairdo helped, too. He looked like a street person sobering up for a meal.

The greatest contributing factor to his anonymity, however, was what Mother Nature herself had bestowed upon him. Tom was five-seven, average-looking, and weighed one-thirty, soaking-wet. People didn't care for diminutive, ordinary men. It made them think of mediocrity and failure. Though this had bothered Tom as a kid, he overcame his shortcomings through therapy. And once he decided to accept himself for what he was, he realized he could make his anonymity work *for* him, rather than against.

He experimented by walking into stores, taking things from shelves, then leaving without paying for them. He did it once, then twice, then three times at the same store. No problem. And certainly no challenge. Spurred on by these revelations, he decided to make the situation more complicated. He entered a different store, picked up a few items, approached the cashier, security guard, or floor manager, and engaged in light conversation before smiling and walking out with the stolen items. Again, he encountered no problems. In the short span of two weeks, Tom lifted sixty toothbrushes, more than a hundred DVDs, six DVD players, two radios, a digital camera, countless articles of clothing, and two twenty-four-inch color televisions, before the idea presented itself.

Anonymity. Using it for profit. Maybe even as a career. Private investigation seemed the perfect choice. He could snoop around and sneak in and out of places – for money. He could also learn about people, get dirt on them, and, as a result, score a terrific chunk of cash.

This job was getting better by the day. For a thousand bucks a day, all he had to do so far was follow Red. She was definitely bad, but Mr. Bigbucks didn't care. However, Tom *did* care, but for a much different reason. When the mark was bad, the pot turned infinitely sweeter. The more Tom snooped, the more he found. He hadn't found much about her yet, but he planned on making up for it tonight.

He had a feeling he'd be cleaning up very shortly, and that his 'rainy day' account would soon be fat and happy. His nest egg had been growing steadily over the years. Its purpose was plain and simple – to buy a mansion in Rio, where he could live like a king for the rest of his life. Tom already had piles of clear photos tucked away in a safe deposit box in his bank in downtown Orlando. Dynamite color glossies of nearly a dozen Orlando big shots taken in compromising positions. Photos valuable enough to generate one million dollars in extortion money per victim when he decided to retire in style.

Richard Warden was the perfect patsy to polish off Tom's gold-plated nest egg. If Warden and Red would cooperate and show their stuff for some treasured Kodak moments, Tom would have no trouble at all. He couldn't blame Warden for going after a chick as sweet as Red. He had met Warden's wife before. The woman was frightening – a nut cracker in every sense of the word. He could easily imagine her offing her husband if she suspected he was giving it to another woman.

This job had turned seriously tricky. From what Warden had said – not to mention what Tom had already learned – Red wouldn't tolerate a tail. Spotting him would be all she wrote, and he could kiss this job good-bye. But he still needed to move around freely. Thanks to the zoom lens on his camera, he wouldn't get careless.

Tonight, things had to go down in order. Hopefully, Red would serve as bait for her stupid ex. Once he showed, he'd been taken quietly out of the picture. When Warden and Red felt they could lower their guard, Tom would move in with his camera.

Fernandez was anxious to do some strong-arm stuff. Getting the big spic ex-boxer out here was no problem. If Fernandez could intervene when he was supposed to, there would be no need to sweat out

121

the rough stuff. Fernandez would have the ex bundled up and carted away in the pickup.

Tom knew to stay on his guard. He wasn't one hundred percent sure about Red's story. Going by Warden's position and by the man's supreme arrogance, Tom figured this could be something totally different. It might be a simple matter of someone – an old enemy, obviously – trying to get Warden. Tom wouldn't be surprised if this 'ex' was actually someone Warden had fucked in the past. Some angry jerk using Red as bait.

But Tom was prepared. Fernandez had his orders. He was a human fist – he didn't care who the punching bag was. Neither did Tom. No one else was allowed to rip off Warden while Tom was planning the deed himself.

Red was certainly a choice piece of bait. Warden was rich and successful, but he was still a man. And no man in his right mind would pass up such a prime piece of ass.

Tom lit another cigarette and took a big slug of hot coffee from the thermos on the seat beside him. This reeked, all right. But by tonight's end, he'd definitely have everything figured out.

***

"What's this ex of yours look like?" Nick asked. "Is he a big guy?"

Jackie just sighed and stared at her glass.

Nick had to find out about this psycho. He knew that as long as that moron was out there, things wouldn't improve. "I need to know what I'm going after, the next time you ask me to go outside to look for him."

122

She picked up her drink with a shaky hand. A dark look drifted across her beautiful face. "He's only an inch or two taller than I am. And fairly skinny, from all the heroin. He's always had a problem with his self-image."

"What's he look like?"

"Nice-looking. Well, he used to be. But he hardly shaves anymore and wears cheap clothes he gets from the Goodwill box, since he never has any money." Her blue eyes blazed. "Is that enough for you?"

He hated himself for upsetting her. "Jackie, I'm sorry. I didn't–"

"It's all right. You just want to help."

"I promise I'll never bring him up again."

"My makeup's smudged."

"Listen..."

"Be right back." She got up and slung the strap of her oversized bag onto her shoulder.

"That bag looks like it weighs a ton."

She just smiled.

"Who have you got in there?"

"A new face."

"The one I'm looking at is just *perfect*."

She touched his shoulder.

"Don't take too long."

"Don't worry. I'll be back long before you start missing me."

"In that case, you're already running late."

She mussed his hair, then hurried away, making her way for the restrooms out in the lobby. Nick's gaze never strayed from her as she left the room.

Don't be long, baby. I'm about to burst.

***

It was just a few minutes after nine when Brittany came into Sophie's.

His heart thumping, Richard Warden jumped to his feet. It had been much too long since he'd seen this woman. The sight of her now in the dark, candlelit room, was a genuine orgasm for the eyes. She was wearing a simple black skirt just above the knee. The light-blue silk blouse was opened at the neck. A yellow scarf was tied loosely around her tiny waist. Her lilac scent made him warm all over.

"Brittany..." He grasped her outstretched hand. It was warm and firm. His heart skipped a beat. "It's been ... too long."

"I know, and I'm sorry about ... well, you know–"

"Don't apologize." He watched her as she sat. She was even more beautiful than he remembered. Everything about this woman was perfect. His dream girl in the flesh. He couldn't bear being separated from her again. "We have to talk, Brittany. There are things we have to discuss. I really want to see you on a regular basis, and I'd consider it an honor if you'd let me–"

"We can talk about that later, okay? I'd like a drink first."

He gestured for the waitress and ordered a Tom Collins for Brittany and a third refill for himself. He reached for her hand. "I hope there'll be time for a lot of things later."

Her nod was slight.

***

124

For a private eye to do his job well, he has to be able to tolerate sitting around for hours and observing human nature at its most mundane.

As strange as it sounds, human nature is amazingly interesting, a source of constant entertainment.

Adam Brooks sat by himself at a corner table, drinking his coffee while studying the clientele. Sophie's, an expensive, high-class place, still couldn't stop the idiots from coming in. A group of young men sat at a table, engaged in a frantic napkin-tearing contest. Two tables down, two tanned, well-dressed females in their late twenties chatted away endlessly about their latest cosmetic surgery experiences. The room also had its share of nosepickers and crotch-scratchers, as well as the obligatory screaming toddler at the other end of the room, that everyone tried very hard to ignore.

Richard Warden sat by himself at a table near the bay window, glancing at his Rolex every ten seconds. He seemed nervous and anxious, occasionally touching the Windsor knot of his tie – probably to make sure it felt right.

A leggy, well-dressed redhead walked in. Warden immediately jumped up and stood at attention. His eyes swelled as he watched her approach. He circled the table and stood behind her, carefully pushing in her chair before awkwardly returning to his own seat.

Judging by the tension in Warden's face and attitude, this looked like a simple candlelight rendezvous. Adam was too far away to hear their conversation, but decided it wasn't necessary.

Interpreting body language was an important skill for a private eye to learn. In many instances, correct interpretation could mean the difference between life and death. Oftentimes, a quick evaluation of a situation could either open or close an investigation.

Both Warden and the redhead were obviously flirting. Hell, a blind man could pick up on the signals the redhead was sending out. She sat forward, her back arched, elbows on the table, tits clearly presented. Her legs were crossed beneath the table, her foot just inches from Warden's. It wouldn't take much effort on her part to slide her foot up the side of his calf, heating up the coals already burning within him.

Nothing new here. Warden was a known womanizer. The woman was a knockout, sure, but as far as Adam could see, there was nothing out of the ordinary going on. This was standard behavior for a forbidden rendezvous. Unless Bob Dalgren wanted pictures or snippets of conversation, this was a simple case of Warden stepping out on his wife again.

However, if the redhead was working for someone else – a competitor trying to get the drop on Warden – she could be luring him into corporate sabotage. Warden was worth serious money. He was also Bob Dalgren's biggest client. If something illegal or wrong was going on, Dalgren would definitely want to know. She could be some sort of well-chosen paid decoy or distraction. But then again, she could just be a well-stacked broad trying to get ahead through Richard Warden. Until he knew for sure, Adam felt she should let Dalgren know what was going on. Adam pulled out his cell and dialed Dalgren's number.

"Find out anything?" Dalgren asked.

"You want the short version or the long one?"

"Short."

"Your boss is having a drink with a gorgeous redhead, and the way it looks, they'll probably be getting a room within the hour."

"I figured as much. Anything else?"

"Not that I can tell."

"You're sure it's not a business meeting?"

"My gut's telling me this is sexual."

"Adam, we're talking millions here. Describe the woman."

"Nice..."

Dalgren sighed. "Can't you do a little better than that?"

"How about if I say none of the best Victoria's Secret models have a thing on her?"

"Now we're getting somewhere. That sounds like Warden's speed. But it still could be something other than a pick-up."

"I'll put it this way. You'd probably have to soak him with gasoline and light him up to get him out of that chair."

"That's usually what happens when he's in his stud mode. He sees and hears nothing else. Where are you right now?"

"International Drive. Sophie's at the Stonehenge."

"That tells me a lot. Warden uses that place frequently. It's discreet, and the staff never asks questions. You could be right about all this. If you

127

are, there's really no point in sticking around to find out who the girl is."

"What if I'm wrong?"

"If she's already getting him lathered up, we can't do a thing right now. We'll have to wait and see what happens. Can you get a picture of her?"

"I could use my phone camera, but it's dark in here. I'd have to follow them out to see where they go, find a good place to hide, then get them when they come back out. I can do it, but it'll probably take a few hours. And if they don't come out until morning–"

"I don't see the point. But at least we know now what's been bothering him."

"Tell me, Bob – what were you really worried about?"

"His drinking – what else?"

"Well, he's certainly drinking."

"He's not supposed to be. Not in public, anyway."

"You want me to tell him to stop? I personally don't think he'll listen to me."

"I want you to pull out. You've done your job. We'll consider this finished for now. Send me the rest of your bill."

"You've sent me more than enough. Want a refund?"

"Not necessary. I have a feeling I might need your services later on."

***

Tom Cravell's binoculars were trained on the bar window when Red sat down with Warden.

The dash clock said 9:09. Red was pretty much on time. Too bad he hadn't been able to spot her driving in. Entirely too much traffic on International. Besides, he knew better than try and keep tabs on someone who could switch tags on a rental and disappear at will. Good thing her hair and her knockout figure made her stand out.

So far, nothing out of the ordinary, but it was still early. If someone was slithering around in the shadows, Fernandez would show up. It had been a while since Fernandez had won one. The big spic could stand a good, clean KO for a change.

Tom opened the console between the seats and made sure his camera was where it should be and loaded with fresh batteries. He picked up his binoculars just as Red and Warden unexpectedly jumped up from their table.

***

"Eric's been making himself very visible the past few days," Brittany said, playing with her straw.

"How visible?"

"I just saw him a couple of hours ago."

Richard stiffened. "He found you again? Since you moved?"

She nodded.

This was insane. "But ... how the hell could he find you?"

Brittany shrugged. "I told you he was good, didn't I?"

He stared at the flickering candles lighting their table. Despite their hazy golden softness, he saw red. *This isn't the time to lose it. Candlelight.*

129

Romance. Brittany was sitting right across from him. Her lilac scent so close, so delicious. Why ruin the moment? *No, this wasn't the time for seeing red. It was time to handle things rationally. It was high-class time.*

His secret code word worked, and he calmed down almost immediately. "What happened?" he asked softly.

"The day after I'd settled in my new place, I spotted him in the supermarket."

"And then...?"

"Nothing, really. He was just letting me know he was close again." She picked up her glass with a shaky hand, drank a little, and set it down crooked. It fell over, liquid and cubes sliding across the surface, splashing her blouse, scarf, and lap. "Damn!" She jumped up, snatched a napkin, and began blotting herself. "This is a new blouse, too. Damn that man."

"Here." He handed her his silk monogrammed handkerchief. She took it gratefully. The drops on her cleavage glittered in the candlelight.

"I've got to take care of this." She picked up her oversized bag.

"I'll be here when you get back."

"Won't be long." Then she was gone.

***

Tom Cravell kept the binoculars steady until the slender figure disappeared through the entrance door.

It had been too dark to see exactly what happened, but both Red and Warden had definitely jumped up from their table at the same time.

130

A spill, maybe? No biggie. Hell, Tom spilled things all the time – drinks, cigarettes, pens, pencils. He'd burned holes in the carpet so many damn times, it made him wonder why he hadn't been thrown out of more places. People fell, stumbled, dropped things. Nothing odd at all about spilling a drink, was there?

***

Sighing impatiently, Nick Warden gave his watch another glance – 9:20, and Jackie was still gone.

That made it nearly forty minutes. *What the hell's she doing in there?*

He drained his drink. He'd give her five more minutes. If she wasn't back, he'd have someone check on her. He was about to order another drink when his cell phone buzzed. He pulled it out of his jacket pocket and flicked it on.

"Nick? Jackie."

"Where are you?"

"Nick ... you've got to come, help me..." She sounded out of breath.

"What's wrong?"

"I'm across the street, at the Stonehenge. Bill – he was waiting for me in the lobby. Near the exit door in back. He tried ... he almost ... I barely got away."

"I'll be right there. Are you in the hotel right now?"

"In the lobby. I had to run across the street to get away from him. I almost got hit. The traffic, it's so awful... I see him coming in through the back door. There's a bunch of people in the parking lot.

131

Maybe if I can get near them, he won't be able to do anything..."

"Listen. Stay put. Try to get a manager or—"

She'd already hung up.

Nick dropped two twenties on the table and ran outside. Luckily, he'd parked the Lincoln close to the glass doors. He could get his gun out while he drove over there. He'd never shot anyone before, but he was angry enough to do it now. Anyway, who could blame him? Nobody in their right mind would mourn the death of a stalker.

***

Warden studied his wristwatch, then stared at the other end of the room.

Then his watch again. Then he had more of his drink – showing all the signs of a horny, frustrated man.

Don't worry, Tom Cravell wanted to say, *Red'll be back in just a few minutes*.

Then—

The figure emerging from the side door caused Tom to jerk bolt upright. It was Red. She hauled ass through the parking lot, making her way for the wing of rooms behind the main building.

What the fuck?

He dropped the binoculars on the seat beside him and picked up the cell phone. Fernandez didn't answer. Tom tried again. "Goddammit. You fucking lush!"

He knew damned well he shouldn't have paid the asshole that hundred up front. The dickwad had no doubt snuggled up to a bottle of Wild Turkey in the back of the pickup.

Groaning, Tom groped for the compact Sig Sauer in his shoulder holster. He didn't like guns, but sometimes there was a need for them. And in this dangerous business, it was best being armed. He checked the magazine, jacked one into the chamber, took it off safety, and replaced it in the holster. Then he pushed open the door, climbed out, and took off.

***

The front lot of the Stonehenge swarmed with tourists and short trains of vehicles easing past, searching for a parking space.

The big picture window displayed an excellent view of the brightly lit lobby. More tourists wandered around. The desk clerk tended to a young couple renting a room. Behind them, another family waited to check in.

But no sign of Jackie.

Dammit. Why the hell didn't she stay put?

Because she's scared. You don't think rationally when you're scared.

Nick found an empty spot on the side, toward the back, and parked the Continental. The side lot was filled. Except for tourists and customers coming and going, he didn't see anything out of the ordinary.

He began walking briskly down the long row of cars. The buildings extended in several different directions. He was certain he could spot Jackie's golden hair. He just had to stay alert and keep looking.

The walkway leading to the pool provided a clear view. It was a cool, damp night, but a couple of young jerks, probably from Canada or Alaska, were doing laps. The pool itself was well-lit. If Jackie was trying to hide or get away, she wouldn't come this way to–

A flash to his left caught his attention. He spotted Jackie sprinting toward the rear parking lot of the motel adjacent to the pool and the main building. Something yellow covered her head and flapped in the night breeze – her yellow scarf. No doubt she was using it as a flimsy disguise.

Nick took off after her.

**

Tom Cravell crossed a different section of the parking lot and saw Red again, moving quickly past the trail of palmettos lining the walk.

At least he thought it was her. Something about her was different. The hair. The getup. And she'd taken the yellow scarf from around her waist and wrapped it over her head. She was obviously using a disguise again. This is probably what had happened at Gino's, when she'd given him the slip the first time. No wonder she'd been able to walk right out of the ladies' room without him even noticing.

You won't lose me tonight, you clever bitch...

Tom moved quickly in her direction. Twenty yards later, as he veered around the corner of the pool area, someone else appeared in the shadows. Tall, slender, well-dressed. *That Eric bastard, maybe? Or whoever was in on this with her? But if the two of them were in on this together, what was all the running about?*

134

The possibility stabbed at him. Suppose Red was on the up-and-up. Suppose she was actually being stalked by her ex, just as she'd told Warden all along.

This whole nasty business had suddenly turned bad. It had to end. Right now. *All right, asshole. Your days of fucking with my nest egg are all over.*

Without breaking stride, Tom closed his hand around the butt of the Sig in its holster.

***

After running down the walk spanning the length of the pool, Nick squeezed through a short row of hedges separating the path.

About fifty yards straight ahead, the grassy hill ran down the slope, leading to the annex of motel rooms.

The scream penetrated the night air.

He sprinted the last few yards, stopping short of the end room. The lights were on inside. Someone was probably peering out through the blinds. The guest inside probably heard the scream. Hopefully, the cops had already been called.

Keeping close to the building, Nick slipped past the door and eased around the corner. Beyond the brick wall, a row of thick shrubbery extended down the property line to a five-foot-high chain-link fence. A dozen or so small, carefully tended spruce trees lined the back. A scrap of bright clothing – Jackie's scarf? – dangled from a low branch of one tree.

His hand gripping the gun, Nick edged carefully down the row of shrubs. The back lot wasn't well-lit. A streetlight tossed some sleepy orange haze farther down, to his right. But as he drew closer, the cool night breeze dislodged the scarf from the branch.

Nick bent and picked it up. It was heavily-scented with the aroma of lilacs – the same fragrance Jackie had been wearing this evening.

He turned and searched for some sign of her among the trees. He saw nothing. He was about to slip between their branches when a man's harsh voice directly behind him yelled, "All right, motherfucker. Don't move." Jumping with a start, Nick turned.

***

Flinching at the sound of Tom's voice, Red's stalker turned slowly.

Nearly out of breath, Tom swallowed the lump in his throat. "I said, don't move. And drop that gun before I blow your head off."

When he'd peered around the corner, Tom had seen Red's stalker half-kneeling in the grass near the trees in front of the chain-link fence. He had his back turned to Tom as he gripped Red's scarf in his left hand. A small black gun grew out of his right fist.

Tom couldn't remember hearing a gunshot, but with the commotion of the passing traffic, how could anyone tell? The scream was enough.

The man's arms were slightly out from his sides. The hand holding the gun was almost totally hidden behind the man's back.

"I said, *drop the gun!*"

"Listen here." The man's face was totally in shadow. The gun remained out of sight. "Maybe we can work something out. Just tell me what you'd—"

"Drop the gun. Or I swear I'll blow your fucking head off!"

The other man turned a few more inches. His face was still in the darkness, the hand holding the gun still hidden.

Tom forced himself to stay calm. *Damn that Fernandez. I'm no killer—I don't even like guns. This jerk was supposed to get beat up, not killed. Maybe I can try reasoning with him.* "Listen here, sport—"

"Why don't you just leave Jackie the hell alone? If you just go away, we'll both forget all about this. I won't even care about what you did with my tires—"

"What?" *Jackie*? Who the hell is *Jackie*? And what tires? "What the fuck are you *talking* about?"

"I'm telling you to stay away from Jackie—"

"Just who the hell is this Jackie you keep talking about?"

"Don't play stupid, pal." The man turned another few inches. His posture was very rigid. Tom still couldn't see the gun. "You've been fucking with her, and I want it to stop. Now. This second. You're getting in my way, understand?"

Tom stepped out of the bushes. His gun had not strayed from the other man. The yellow scarf suddenly fell out of the man's hand, dropping gently to the ground. Tom's eyes automatically followed its lazy descent for one fatal instant.

***

137

Distraction was the only way out of this.

Nick planned to set things right. Jackie would be his, goddammit, and if all it took was nailing this psycho, that was how it had to be.

He could claim self-defense. It would hold up in any court. Both he and the other guy had guns. It was a no-brainer that any hardware a stalker had would be illegal. Nick had a carry permit. The law would be on his side. No way would the scales of justice lean in the direction of a convicted stalker.

Nick let the breeze play on the scrap of golden silk in his hand. He subtly separated his thumb and forefinger and released it, keeping his eyes on the other man as the scarf drifted softly to the damp grass at his feet.

The haze from the streetlight shone in the other man's face. Nick could see the man's eyes as they watched in silent fascination. In the next instant, his expression changed to total confusion. The gun suddenly jumped in his hand.

Nick brought up his arm, gritted his teeth, and fired.

***

A huge sizzling fist smashed violently through Tom.

It felt as if someone had kicked him in the gut with a huge foot of hot iron. He was knocked backwards, landing against a shrub, then dropped to his knees. He was able to hold the Sig steady for the single agonizing second it took to squeeze off a round. The automatic roared, jumping in his hand. The jerk was knocked off his feet, slamming to the ground and landing flat on his back.

Tom lowered his arm. The searing pain in his gut had turned everything into a blinding white light. The cold, wet grass pressing against his knees made him shiver. No wonder – it had rained an hour ago. An hour ago he'd been warm and comfortable in his van, drinking coffee, watching Warden and Red...

An hour ago. An eternity ago, more likely. Red and Warden. Having drinks. Red getting up, leaving the bar, running outside, then wrapping a scarf over her head...

Weird. Something strange ... and not making sense...

The cold slowly moved up his thighs.

The jerk was getting back up. First on his side, then pushing himself up with an elbow. When he was halfway supported by one knee, he began looking for something in the grass.

The gun.

Fascinated, Tom watched. The blinding light began to dim. The cold had reached his hips. *Cold. Rainy. Rain in sunny Florida. Ain't that a real kick? Plays hell on the hair, though. Makes women do all sorts of strange things, like wrapping scarves around their heads, even when it ain't raining...*

Favoring his side, the punk picked up his gun and moved awkwardly on all fours, until he faced Tom. A strange moaning sound escaped his throat. The man's face was no longer in shadow. Funny, how he suddenly favored Richard Warden. *Hey, Mr. Bigbucks, what the fuck are you doing out here in the wet grass? You're supposed to be back in the bar, getting soused. Well, I got news for you. Red*

139

ain't coming back. You ain't gonna see her again. She's out here, lying in the grass behind those trees, and it's because of you and your fucking big bucks that I ain't ever gonna see Rio or those black-haired beauties ... and if you think I'm going down quiet, you're even dumber than I thought...

Using the last of his draining strength, Tom raised the Sig. The cold had reached his arms, turning them into two heavy blocks of ice. Cradling the gun in both shaking hands, he took aim and shot Richard Warden in the face.

***

Standing in front of the bathroom mirror, the slender young woman ran a brush through her short brown tresses.

Then she picked up her bags, left the motel room, locked the door behind her, and hurried down the walk. The crowd had grown considerably where the walkway joined the pool area. Since she'd parked on the other side of the complex, she faced no major delays.

She put her bags in the trunk of the rental, slid behind the wheel, and pulled out. A medical unit inched by the gawkers. She eased around the corner, to the lobby. Then she parked, hurried inside the building, and dropped off her key.

The parking lot hummed in utter turmoil. Cops patrolled the lot and carefully directed the heavy night traffic buzzing up and down International Drive. Luckily it wasn't the weekend. Otherwise, a hundred cops would be needed to contain the havoc.

The cop at the motel entrance waved her on. She pulled out, disappearing in the swarm of traffic.

***

Across the street, Richard Warden sat at the bar, downing another vodka martini.

Brittany hadn't returned. By the looks of things, he didn't think she was going to. Didn't matter. He was past his mad, past worrying – past just about everything, actually. If the fucking bitch wanted to continue squeezing his balls, let her have her fun.

At the other end of the counter, a hooker easily reeled in the stupid tourist asking her directions. That didn't matter either. Let her have her damned tourist. They deserved each other.

The bartender asked him if he wanted another drink. Richard told him it didn't matter, then pointed to his empty glass.

Two guys came in and chose stools farther down. They were talking loudly about two stupid assholes who'd just wasted themselves across the street, behind the Kingston. Probably drugs, they'd said, since both were carrying automatics. And everyone knew those drug guys used automatics. One of them mentioned an Uzi, and his friend started on the Muslims.

The bartender said, "Let all those damn ragheads kill themselves off, and God'll sort it all out."

Richard gulped half his strong beverage and used both hands to put the glass back down without spilling the contents. *Let 'em all kill themselves. All those fucking crazy assholes. Those fucking crazy bitches, too. Especially the ones that like squeezing your balls. Let God sort it out...*

CHAPTER 11

Wednesday, the Second Week

The lead story on the morning news showed an aerial evening shot of International Drive. Then came a large close-up of Richard Warden, with an inset photo of his son Nick, filling the screen.

Adam left the kitchen and picked up the remote from the couch. He turned up the volume and stood there, dumbfounded as Sky Cam focused on the heavy evening International Drive traffic, quickly zooming in on the huge neon sign in front of the Stonehenge Hotel. The scene shifted to the three cop cars parked out front, their lights flashing. A brief close-up of the crowd gathering outside the hotel followed, then another scan, this one showing the medical units parked off to the side. A moment later, the camera settled in on four men in white paramedic uniforms, wheeling two gurneys up the walk near the hotel pool. Each gurney carried a body enclosed in a black plastic body bag.

The solemn-looking brunette standing in front of the white News Nine van spoke quickly into her mike. "Orlando police haven't yet determined just what transpired in this double homicide. Neither of the two men involved was associated with organized crime or narcotics. One of the victims, Nicholas Warden, age twenty-eight, served as the Sales Director of Directron Digitals, a WarCo subsidiary owned by his father, Richard Warden..."

Adam dropped the remote onto the couch. He couldn't take his eyes from the screen as the words of the newscaster echoed in his head. '...Nick Warden, son of Richard Warden, a victim of a double homicide outside the Stonehenge last night.' This double homicide happened last night.

He ran his fingers through his hair. *I was in the hotel bar last night, spying on his father, who was having a drink with a gorgeous redhead. What the hell is going on?*

He pulled himself away from the TV screen, grabbed his cell from the kitchen counter, and dialed Bob Dalgren's number. Busy. He tried again. Still busy.

He put the phone down and tried to think. His thoughts kept looping over Richard Warden meeting a gorgeous redhead, and Nick Warden behind the hotel pool, involved in a gunfight. Something was very, very strange.

***

His head still pounding, Richard drove back to the estate shortly before noon.

He'd spent the night at the Stonehenge, in one of the luxury suites in the main section of the hotel. He'd tossed his cell in the trashcan as soon as it went off. He'd wanted no disturbances, no matter what they were.

He surrendered to unconsciousness as soon as he hit the bed, awakening hours later with a heavy throbbing in his head and a sour taste in his mouth. He suspected the sourness wasn't the aftertaste of the whiskey, but the result of what his life had become.

He wanted to strangle Brittany for what she'd done. She'd easily reeled him in and turned him into a horny, brainless fool – a rich, successful CEO brought down to the level of a nervous junkie aching for his next fix. But since she refused to give him the fix, he'd drowned his frustrations in drink. And he did that well, which was no surprise, since he'd done it so many times before.

And he'd endured this same madness once before. Despite the Detox, the rehab, and the legal horrors resulting from his carelessness, the craving remained. He suspected it always would. But at least he'd possessed the sense last night to realize that, in his drunken state, the ten-mile, heavily congested trip would lead to disaster. His subconscious would not subject him to the same horror he'd endured three years earlier.

After a good night's rest, he was awake and alert, and ready once again to deal with life's challenges. Brittany Weber headed the list. That last episode with her finished the deal. She was out of his life forever.

As he drove home, he tried putting himself in a better frame of mind. He'd bought a bottle of aspirin at the hotel drugstore before having a quick breakfast at the restaurant. After forcing down some dry toast and black coffee, he could feel the aspirin slicing away at the thumping in his head. Now, it was a dull, distant throb. In another hour, it would be barely noticeable. And once he reached the estate, he could slip in through the side entrance, retreat to his study, and relax on the couch for an hour or so. After a nap and more aspirin, he'd be able to face whatever hell Adrienne had in store for him.

As he approached the estate, he saw half a dozen vehicles parked in front. He recognized a couple of them. Bob Dalgren's red Ferrari. Katie's compact. But the others – plain, dark in color, with official-looking plates – were foreign to him.

He parked and got out of his car. Bob Dalgren met him at the front door. Bob's clean-shaven, usually serene face was twisted into a tight swell of creases. "Richard, we've been trying to reach you all night."

"Lost my cell." It seemed the easiest explanation. But he couldn't ignore the feeling of profound sadness enveloping him as soon as he stepped into the dark foyer.

Dalgren took a breath. "There's been ... a terrible accident."

Sobbing wafted from the living room down the hall. It sounded like Adrienne, but he couldn't be sure. His mind fought to clear the cloud of confusion. The shroud of sadness enveloping him grew heavier as he heard more sobbing, and whispers accompanying the sobs. The throbbing in his temples increased. He felt as if he were trapped in a strange dream. "What's ... going on?"

Dalgren grasped his elbow and steered him down the hall. He opened the study door and gently coaxed him inside. "It's Nick," he said softly, then closed the door behind him.

Richard moved stiffly, his body heavy and sluggish, his mind swimming. *Sobbing. Whispering.*

Strange cars. A terrible accident. Nick. What's happening here?

He hoped his friend's gentle touch would bring him to. Maybe he'd wake up in the motel room bed. He was probably still having that stupid dream where he'd killed Brittany. That was it. In his dream, he'd strangled her. Now it was time to wake up. It wasn't Bob Dalgren guiding him, it was someone else. The maid, calling from the door, "Mr. Warden? Wake up. Checkout time." And he'd left.

He blinked, hoping his vision would clear. But it didn't. Bob Dalgren stayed Bob Dalgren.

He'd left the motel. Had breakfast. Driven home. Now he and Bob were in his study, and Bob was acting very strange. A terrible accident, he'd said. Something dreadful had happened. Dalgren motioned for him to sit. He did so, but Dalgren said nothing. His face resembled bleached bone. "Bob," Richard urged. "Talk to me."

Dalgren sighed. "Nick's...dead."

A strange coldness drifted slowly up Richard's spine. It was almost as if someone was lowering him into a vat of ice water. He studied the attorney's somber face. Was this some sort of joke? Some tasteless, practical joke? "Bob," he managed weakly, "what did you say?"

"Your son. He's dead."

Richard pushed himself forward. The light-headedness grew. He remembered some old movie he'd seen a while back, where the main character had been told the same thing. That was fiction – it didn't really happen. Nick was alive. Right now, the boy was probably sitting at his desk, sipping coffee, going over sales packages, proposals...

Dalgren's words chipped away inside his head. *Dead. Your son. He's dead.*

Richard took a deep breath and found his voice. "What the hell do you mean ... *dead*?"

Dalgren moved closer. "Richard, I'm so sorry. He was shot last night, outside the Stonehenge, off International Drive."

International Drive. The Stonehenge. It all came back in a hot, disordered cluster – a series of meaningless events thrashing around in his head, like debris in a twister. *International Drive. Brittany. The Stonehenge. Brittany spilling her drink, getting up and leaving. Not coming back.*

My son. Nick. Dead. Shot to death.

This time his voice, loud and strong, boomed off the paneled walls. "What the hell do you *mean*, Bob? How could my son be dead? Who the hell *shot* him?"

Dalgren placed a manicured hand gently on Richard's shoulder. "Thomas Cravell shot Nick. Nick also shot Cravell. Both men are dead."

Cravell. Dead. Nick. Dead.

One last image of Brittany frantically mopping up the spill drifted past his vision. The angry look on her beautiful face. The glittering drops on her smooth skin. The wet marks on her skirt and blouse. Her last words, "Got to take care of this."

What happened? Why the hell did Cravell shoot my son? What happened? What the fuck happened? A dark fuzziness filled his head. Dalgren had grown lighter, hazier. *What's happening now? Am I willing*

Bob to evaporate? What would be the sense in that? Do I think I can undo any of this? It's possible, isn't it? Bob had brought bad news. It makes good sense to make him evaporate. With Bob gone, things would revert back to how they were before. It wouldn't take much – maybe just twelve hours or so. Twelve hours ago, Nick was alive. If I can close my eyes and will Bob to evaporate, Nick will be alive again.

Richard rubbed his eyes. When he opened them, the room had grown lighter. He didn't know why. He hadn't seen Dalgren adjust the blinds. It also had gotten warmer. Bob Dalgren leaned toward him and began whispering things in his ear. Richard closed his eyes once more. When he opened them again, the room had grown darker.

Then everything went black.

***

After a long shower, two strong belts of Wild Turkey, and nearly half an hour of pacing the apartment, Adam tried Bob Dalgren's number once again. This time, Dalgren answered on the first ring.

"I just saw the news," Adam said. "Any idea what the hell happened?"

"We messed up, my friend. From what I was just told, Richard's son Nick and a private detective named Thomas Cravell shot one another behind the Stonehenge last night."

"I got that, too. Photos, close-ups, even pics of the bodies. But what was this all about?"

"No one seems to know at the moment."

"I was at the Stonehenge."

"Yes, I remember."

148

"And this happened last night."

"It seems so."

Adam's blood grew cold. His next question was probably the most important, yet he was afraid of the answer. Still, he had to ask. "This obviously happened after I left. At least, I hope it did. The news report didn't say exactly when the fireworks took place, but since I didn't see any cop cars on my way out, I'm assuming all this happened after I left. Tell me it didn't happen while I was there. Please tell me..."

"From what I understand, it happened after, but not too long after."

Adam's pulse had calmed down somewhat. But he was far from out of the woods. This was much too serious to dismiss as a coincidence. "So ... if I'd stayed–"

"Adam, this has nothing to do with you. You were watching the old man, not his son."

"I know." Oddly, that didn't make him feel any better.

"Even if I suspected something like this was going to happen, I couldn't very well ask you to watch both men, since you can't possibly be in two places at once."

That simple bit of logic didn't make him want to celebrate, either. "I know that, dammit."

"Then why do you sound so angry?"

"This reflects on me. I'm a private detective. This business is full of close calls – I'll admit that. But the pendulum swings both ways, and even when you steer clear of one disaster, you end up nearly getting slammed by another, and it gets to you.

149

Even when you're in the business as long as I've been, it gets to you."

"You weren't responsible for this."

"I feel as if I was."

"Are you telling me you knew what was going on somewhere else?"

"This wasn't somewhere else, Bob. This was right behind the hotel. On the same night. And probably within the hour."

"You're beating yourself up unnecessarily. You weren't with Nick Warden, and you weren't with Cravell. You didn't—"

"What's Cravell's first name?"

"Thomas. Know him?"

"I don't believe so. There are a couple of hundred private eyes in this area. I doubt if I know a dozen of them. What was he doing out there in the first place?"

"I don't know yet."

"Who was he working for?"

"He's worked for Richard before, but since no one seems to know exactly what went on out there, I can't tell you anything about that, either."

"Have you talked to Warden?"

"He's lying down. He was given a strong sedative."

"How long before you can talk to him?"

"Who knows? I'll call you."

"Please do."

"And Adam?"

"Yes?"

"Try to remember, you were watching Richard Warden. I was paying you to do that. I wasn't paying you to watch the whole family."

"I know."

"But you're still going to blame yourself, aren't you?"

He wanted to, he just didn't know why. He felt responsible and didn't know why, either. Maybe it was because he felt stupid. He was sitting in a bar, watching a rich, successful man cheat on his wife while his son was wandering around behind the hotel with a handgun, ready to partake in a deadly gun battle. It shouldn't have happened. Even though it wasn't Adam's fault, the fact remained – it shouldn't have happened.

"I don't know," he told Dalgren. "I'll have to get back to you on that."

***

A hazy white form drifted in Richard Warden's direction, growing bigger, broader.

Along with it came the smell of talcum powder, medicine. The wall of white obscured his vision, and the haze grew more distinct as the nurse moved closer. A smile touched her plain, gaunt features. She held something shiny in her hand – a hypodermic. He let her pull his arm gently, then move it to his side. A dab of something cool. A tiny pinch.

The nurse mumbled something he could not distinguish. What the hell was this? Had someone stuffed cotton in his ears? He wanted to tell her to speak up, to bring Nick in here to clear up this awful mistake.

151

Bob Dalgren drifted into his consciousness. Bob Dalgren and his ashen face, his sad expression, leading him down the hall, to his study. Behind them, sobbing and whispering floated softly from the other rooms.

Cravell. That bastard killed Nick. Killed my kid. Sorry son of a bitch cocksucker.

The room abruptly began spinning around, growing hazy ... then dimmed.   Richard closed his eyes.

Nick. My dear sweet son...

The darkness drifted back, turning everything mellow.

***

Richard awoke sometime during the night.

After several clumsy attempts to sit up, he grunted out of bed and held onto the bedpost until his equilibrium sluggishly returned. With it came the nausea. He closed his eyes and waited until it passed, then let go of the bedpost and stumbled down the dimly lit hall.

Bob Dalgren sat alone at the kitchen table, an empty glass on the counter, inches from his grasp. He saw Richard and jumped up. "Richard ... are you all right? What're you doing up?"

"I need a drink."

"Do you think that's wise? The medication–"

"I'm thirsty." He opened a cabinet door. A wave of warm dizziness filled his head. He took a deep breath and leaned against the counter. Fight it. Go away. Then he found a glass.

"Where's Ade? Katie? "The urge to regain control had quickly returned. Things made better sense when he was in control. "How about Wendy? Has her family been told?"

"Everyone knows. Adrienne's family is coming over from Tampa."

Richard poured half a glass of cognac and sat down heavily. He was still shaky and wondered what the nurse had given him. It didn't matter. His curiosity took precedence over everything else. When he found out a few things he'd feel much better. "The funeral arrangements. What have you–"

"Everything's been taken care of. I've made the necessary calls. The services will be Friday. I've arranged for the service to be simple and private. I've taken the liberty to refuse an open casket viewing." Dalgren paused. "It's all right, isn't it? I haven't been able to discuss this with Adrienne, of course, but that's to be expected."

Richard forced himself not to dwell on that. Nick was at peace. There was no need to dwell on the macabre specifics of the situation. "Everything else all right? The cemetery? Limousines?"

"You don't have to worry about anything."

He tipped the glass and swallowed half its contents. The warm elixir quickly rushed to his center, relaxing him. "You're a true friend."

Dalgren shrugged. "You and Adrienne – and Katie, of course – you all need to heal. There's no reason why I shouldn't–"

"That bastard Cravell." Richard stared at his drink. Funny how pretty cognac became in a certain light. But when he thought of Cravell, he saw another color instead, and the hairs on the back of

153

his neck bristled. "I want that son of a bitch brought here and—"

"He's dead, Richard."

The word turned his blood ice-cold. He stared dumbly at his friend.

"Nick shot him. I already told you, but it's understandable that you don't remember."

"I remember." Richard closed his eyes and let the cognac continue working its magic. "Good thing. Otherwise..."

Bob Dalgren nodded but said nothing.

"What happened, Bob? All the facts in yet?"

"The police are on it." Dalgren patted Richard gently on the shoulder. "You need to rest. We'll give you the particulars in a few days when you've had time to recover."

Terrific. Everything will be just dandy in a few days.

Richard drained his drink. He got up heavily. The room began spinning again. Nausea filled his gut. That damned medication... He could've managed much easier with booze. "I think I need to ... go back to bed. Will you be here in the morning?"

"If you want me to be."

"You're a good friend, Bob." Had he said that before? He couldn't remember. *Maybe it'll all come back later on, when this damned medication wears off...*

CHAPTER 12

Thursday, the Second Week

The next day, after the drugs had finally worked their way out of his system, Richard Warden sat in his den, trying to think clearly. He and Bob Dalgren were alone in the house.

Ade and Katie were staying at Wendy's parents' four-bedroom condo in Casselberry. Wendy had literally come apart and had to be given a strong sedative by Ade's doctor. Although Ade was taking Nick's death hard, she'd always been a strong woman. Doing something meaningful enabled her to maintain stability. Helping Wendy was all she needed to preserve her own equilibrium.

In Richard's case, maintaining order in his universe required deep analysis. And that meant going back several years to make sense of all this.

Richard and Nick had been close when Nick was a kid. But like most father/son relationships, theirs had dissolved as Nick grew older. In the past few years, they'd become little more than strangers. Richard first noticed signs of estrangement when Nick was in high school, trying out for football. Those were tense days. Too many factors prevented a smooth father/son relationship. Peer pressure. Girls. The fine art of becoming a man. The discovery of the many things in life you were never taught or warned about. The struggle to break away from the suffocating confines of being your father's little boy.

Richard expected his own son to be perfect, but reluctantly realized this sort of thinking was silly. People were masses of imperfections. They displayed their flaws automatically at every given opportunity. Nick was definitely a product of his old man. Like most fathers, Richard could not accept seeing his own flaws revealed so strongly in his son. And like most sons, Nick refused to believe he was gradually turning into a clone of his dad.

Nick was his one and only son. He'd been born a lifetime ago, when Richard and Adrienne loved one another. His birth was the result of an act of love. Now the boy was dead, and the family faced the excruciating task of committing their only son to the ground.

"I don't understand any of this," Richard said, gazing out at the lush back yard through the double French doors.

"All the facts aren't in yet." Bob Dalgren appeared to have just run a marathon. He'd been playing phone tag with the Orlando Police the last two hours, and that had obviously taken its toll.

"What do they know?"

"The way the cops figure it, Cravell snuck up on Nick behind the Stonehenge, and the two shot it out."

"What the hell was Nick doing out there in the first place? And why was he carrying that gun?" Richard gripped his bloody Mary tightly in both hands.

Dalgren rubbed his eyes. "If you'll remember, I was the one who helped the boy acquire the carry permit in the first place. You can't imagine how this makes me feel."

"He would've gotten the permit with or without your help. Nick wanted one when he started making weekly payroll runs on his way home. But that was all he used it for. I don't believe he ever fired the damned thing. It was strictly for protection." He slugged down his drink. "I want to know what he was doing out there, and why."

"The police questioned the hotel personnel working that night. First the Stonehenge, then the Kingston. No one at the Stonehenge remembers seeing Nick at the bar or in any of the rooms. But the bartender and two of the waitresses at the Kingston remembered seeing him in the hotel bar with a woman. Apparently she was very attractive. A blonde."

"Hooker?"

Dalgren shook his head. "No one saw her there before that night." The attorney raised a brow at Richard. "Know anything about this, Richard?"

"Why the hell should I? Kid moved out of the house ten years ago. He was a grown man with a mind of his own. I had no idea what the hell he was doing there."

"Let me put this another way." Bob Dalgren stared awkwardly at Richard. "Did you know Nick was sowing wild oats?"

"Like I just said–"

"All right, all right." Dalgren waved it aside. "Just trying to cover all the bases."

"Is that what this is about?"

"Richard." The attorney's face turned sour. "Your boy was murdered two nights ago. Shot to death in a gunfight behind a hotel, across the street from where he was seen with a strange woman. The other man in the gunfight was a private detective who, I recall, you've used before. The police are having a rough time piecing this together. I'm surprised they haven't been here yet, questioning both you and Adrienne. I'm trying to get to the bottom of this before something comes up that implicates you in this."

"How the hell can *I* be implicated? He was my *son*, for Christ's sake."

"Cops get cranky when someone gets killed – especially when there aren't any clues to help them solve it. They start digging, and when they dig, they pull up any dirt they can find. If they check Cravell's records and see your name anywhere, they're gonna be knocking on your door."

"It's up to you to stop them. That's what I pay you to do."

"Yes. That's what I do. And it's a service I'm paid handsomely for. But I need something, and I need it before they show up on your doorstep. So tell me."

"Tell you what?"

"Tell me what Cravell was doing out there."

Richard finished his drink, got up, and shuffled over to the wet bar.

"How many *is* that, Richard?"

"Don't worry about it. My son's dead, remember?"

158

"Even so, you shouldn't be–"

"I'm a grown man." He mixed another drink and had a healthy sip. His eyes burned at the attorney as he lowered the glass. "Let me mourn in my own way."

"You're not mourning. You're doing exactly what you were doing three years ago, when–"

"Don't remind me."

"You need reminded."

"You'd make a good mother."

"Ease up and tell me what Cravell was doing out there."

"I don't know what he was doing there."

"Don't lie to me."

A sour taste drifted up Richard's throat. He knew how radical Dalgren could get. It was better just to let him have it and be done with it. "I had him watching someone."

Dalgren gave him an accusing look, but Richard said nothing. "Talk to me, Richard."

During the last fifteen years, Bob Dalgren had lied for him, covered up for him, provided alibis, made excuses. Richard had always convinced himself that Dalgren did it for the seven hundred and fifty thousand dollars Richard tossed him each year. But that wasn't the whole story. Bob was his friend. He deserved the truth. "I ... met this woman in Gino's last Monday, after work. It was like ... like she was just *there*. Like I was meant to meet her. It's hard to explain, but that's what happened."

"You've been married thirty years." Dalgren's words were cold, emotionless.

159

"I wasn't exactly going out of my way, looking for a quick roll in the hay."

"*There's* a switch."

Richard stiffened. "Don't go religious on me, now."

"Richard, you obviously don't remember those dozens of other 'quick rolls in the hay' I've seen you involved in the past two decades."

"I also seem to recall the two or three affairs you got yourself tangled up in over the years. So don't preach."

The attorney's face reddened. "I know I'm not in the position to be self-righteous. But I never had the same problems you had. I never had to make a quick payoff because I couldn't keep my dick in my drawers."

Richard drained his drink. He went to make another. "Don't forget how rich I happen to be. Men in my position–"

"Fall prey to the notorious gold digger. Yes, I know. How many times have you told me that?"

"Obviously not enough. Otherwise, you wouldn't be preaching."

"Richard, you were at the Stonehenge when Nick and Cravell were killing each other, weren't you?"

Richard turned pale. "How the hell did you–"

"You were there, weren't you?"

A deep sigh. "Yes."

"With that woman. The redhead."

"How did you–"

"Just answer the question."

160

"All right. I was with her. I didn't know anything about her, and I wanted to find out a little something. So? I hired Cravell–"

"My *God*, Richard."

"If you think I had anything to do with my own son's murder..."

"I'm only looking at these facts objectively. The same way the police are going to see them. I just want to get a clear picture of what happened. And since you were only a few yards away from your son, who was engaged in a fatal gunfight, you could say this looks kind of suspicious – don't you think?"

"I see your point. I just don't know why one thing should have to be related to the other."

"As I told you, I need to know the whole picture, so I can put together some facts for the police."

"And like I said, I was with a very special lady I'd just met last week."

"Her name?"

"You don't ... need to know her name."

"Her *name*."

Richard sighed. "Brittany Weber."

"What else do you know about her?"

"Nothing. Which is why I employed Cravell."

"And what did he find out?"

"Not much."

"What actually prompted you to hire him?"

"This woman kept disappearing during our dates. She always seemed to be on edge, watching her back. The only thing she ever talked about was her ex-husband, who was stalking her. That's why I employed Cravell. I wanted him to tail her and find the ex. I wanted Cravell to scare the ex away."

"Why?"

His temples throbbed. Dalgren was turning this into something agonizing. "Goddammit, Bob, I wanted to fuck the woman!"

Bob Dalgren nodded. "Now we're finally *getting* somewhere."

***

Later that day, Bob Dalgren drove back to his Orlando office to catch up on some paperwork and make a few important phone calls.

About two hours later, he returned to Richard's den to continue their talk. "When you found out the plate on this Weber woman's rental car was stolen, what did you think?" he asked.

Richard was tired of this constant questioning, but realized it was necessary. But he'd rather talk to his friend about this than the cops, and knew that if he played his cards right, Dalgren would keep the cops away. "Bob, the poor woman had been dodging her asshole ex for so long, could anyone really blame her for taking additional precautions?"

"Like stealing a license plate from someone's car?"

Richard shrugged. "Hell, the damned injunction she'd filed against the bastard wasn't working. What else could she do?"

"That's another thing that puzzles me about all this. I got in touch with the courthouse about an hour ago."

"You didn't find an injunction, did you?"

"No."

"I think there could be a legitimate reason for that."

"Which is?"

"I don't think Brittany Weber's her real name."

Dalgren shrugged. "So ... where do we go from here?"

"I think we ought to start by going back to why Cravell and Nick had that shootout."

"Here's the scenario. You're at the Stonehenge with a woman whose name, supposedly, is Brittany Weber. While you're with her, your son Nick is at the Kingston across the street with a blonde. Am I right so far?"

"I guess so."

"You're at the Stonehenge at around eight o'clock. Nick is at the Kingston at the same time. Then, for some inexplicable reason, Nick leaves the bar, drives across the street, and shoots it out with a private eye hired by you to stay close to the woman you're having your drink with. How's that?"

"Sounds about right."

The attorney ran a palm across his thinning dome.

Richard got up to fix another drink. "Tell me if there's anything you can do to keep the damned paparazzi away from my short curlies. At least for a little while."

"Are you talking about the funeral? Or the murder investigation?"

"Both."

"I'll try very hard to swing it. Family grief, for starters. Even the most selfish, arrogant reporter can identify with that. I can always throw them a bone,

163

promise to get them chewing on something juicy later on. The cops are the ones we need to be careful with."

"I want them to go through you."

"I'll use the same procedure I've used before."

"Whatever you think will work." Richard didn't want to think about the past. He was depressed enough.

"All right. But they'll probably want to talk with you directly, later on. After the funeral, of course."

"Any way I can squeak by that?"

"I don't think so. They can slap us with all kinds of things, and we'll end up with even more publicity. We'll probably be subpoenaed. Then there will be hearings to attend. But I'll be present. You know the drill."

After some thought, Richard said, "I'm a little worried about Directron."

"You should be. This kind of publicity will definitely bring the stock down. Remember what happened to AT&T years back, when their CEO gave himself a multi-million-dollar bonus and later announced a layoff of forty thousand workers?"

"This isn't the same thing."

"Stockholders are a damned sight smarter and more informed than ever before. They've got CNN, the Net, *Fortune* magazine, *Wall Street Journal*, web sites – all kinds of instant information sources. If something upsets the cart, they'll pull their resources in a New York second." A shadow drifted across the attorney's face. "If you don't think I'm right, go back three years and you'll clearly remember what hap–"

"I wish you'd quit bringing that up." Richard put down his drink and rubbed his temples.

"Only to ensure that you don't make the same mistake."

"No need to worry about that."

"There is, as long as you keep lifting that elbow."

"I've already told you. It's controllable."

"Prove it, then. Finish that one and call it a day."

"No problem." Richard drained his drink, got up, and washed out the glass. He closed the cabinet door, sat, and lit a cigar.

Bob Dalgren nodded. "I'm relieved. And impressed."

"Told you I could do it." Richard puffed on his cigar, enjoying the attorney's obvious discomfort.

CHAPTER 13

Friday, the Second Week

Nick's funeral quickly turned into chaos.

Since the family had decided against any sort of viewing, the press stayed away from the church for the service but waited eagerly at the cemetery long before the lead vehicle arrived. A news van showed up, in addition to reporters from the Sentinel and more than fifty curiosity-seekers, many armed with digital cameras.

Richard wanted to get this over with as quickly and as quietly as possible. He stayed in the background during the services, mourning privately in his limousine. Since both he and Adrienne were raised Roman Catholic, the service was performed by the Catholic Church. However, Richard hadn't been to church in years and, despite Adrienne's repeated protests, refused to participate.

Two reporters rushed over to the limo. One of them, an attractive brunette, was followed by a skinny young guy balancing a camera on his right shoulder. The woman held a microphone with one hand and repositioned the cord running down the collar of her stylish brown suit.

The second reporter, a slender blonde about twenty-five years old, motioned impatiently for her cameraman to get a good close-up shot of the gravesite.

A third reporter, a tall guy in his early forties, stood beside the hearse, shouting angrily at the two men setting up their equipment on the cemetery lawn.

A middle-aged man in Bermuda shorts and black knee socks emerged from a utility vehicle. His camera was aimed at the small crowd wandering over to the gravesite. The man adjusted the lens before aiming it.

Richard and Bob Dalgren sat in the second limo, watching. Richard wasn't in the mood for this. He scowled at Dalgren. "I thought you were going to see to it that this shit didn't happen."

Dalgren produced his cell from his breast pocket. "OPD was supposed to be here already."

Dalgren made several quick calls. Within minutes, OPD appeared, cordoning off the area, pushing people out of the way, and barking orders at the newsmen.

Richard sat back in the leather seat and closed his eyes. His mind instantly went into overload, recalling treasured moments he hadn't thought about in years. Nick's birth. His christening. The first day of school. A third-grade school play in which the boy portrayed an oak tree. His first black eye. The first high school touchdown. The day he started college. His college graduation. First day at the company. Bringing Wendy home to meet them a very short time ago.

Why is my son dead?

His thoughts immediately shifted to Brittany Weber. It angered him to think of her on this solemn occasion, but he forced himself to realize that she

167

might somehow be connected. He just didn't know how. The fact that she was in the same area when Nick was killed proved too coincidental. It also posed a giant puzzle, as well as a disturbing question, one that had been surfacing more and more frequently the last few days. Had Brittany somehow triggered all this? And if so, why?

Just a hundred feet away, the crowd of approximately forty people dressed in black stood in the bright Florida sun, heads bowed, hands clasped in front of them.

Sobbing hysterically, Wendy slouched over the polished casket, her father and mother behind her. The black veil concealed her grief-stricken, tear-streaked face.

"Shame about Wendy," Dalgren said.

Richard didn't want to comment. The girl was a fruitcake. When she and his son first began dating, Nick told his parents Wendy had a serious cocaine problem and had already been to rehab by her twentieth birthday. But Nick wasn't too concerned about it. When they began getting serious, she did a great job turning her life around.

Richard couldn't help thinking the little bitch had tricked his boy into marrying her. A false pregnancy during their first year triggered the whole thing. Nick had confided in Adrienne several months later, saying Wendy hadn't been exactly sure about the pregnancy. He also told Adrienne he would've married Wendy anyway. But Richard was convinced his son was just being diplomatic to appease everyone.

168

The casket was lowered. The crowd began to disperse. Richard scanned the crowd, taking in everyone he knew. The familiar figure caught his immediate attention. No. It just couldn't be. His eyes were deceiving him.

There she was. The thick red hair partially covered by the sheer black scarf. Her shapely figure dressed in black, Brittany crossed the paved drive, moving toward the line of parked cars.

"Something wrong, Richard?"

The scattering crowd quickly obscured his view. Cars and limousines and mourners were everywhere. He wanted to jump out of the limo and run after her. No. That would not only be stupid, but also disrespectful.

He waited tensely for his view to clear. By then, the redheaded figure had vanished.

***

That afternoon, as Richard Warden stared at the paneled walls in his study, a bloody Mary in his hand, he wondered what was happening to his world.

Why nothing made sense anymore. Why everything had suddenly begun to slip away. Why life and its complications had become so strange...

Why was Brittany at the cemetery? Even with her red hair partly concealed beneath the black scarf and her slender figure hidden by the black suit, he knew it was her. But why would she come? Had Brittany attended Nick's funeral out of her respect for him – or for some other, more sinister reason?

It involved Tuesday night. There was something oddly suspicious about that fateful

169

evening at the Stonehenge. Something had been lurking in the back of his mind all this time, not wanting to reveal itself ... until now. But why now?

His suspicions settled on what happened at Sophie's, when he and Brittany were having a drink – until she spilled her glass, got up, and left the bar. Spilled her glass. Purposely? Why would she leave so abruptly and not come back?

She was upset – which was to be expected. She'd been talking about her ex. The subject had enraged her, made her edgy ... nervous ... clumsy. Had he been the one to bring up the subject, or had Brittany brought it up herself? He had. He'd always been the one initiating the conversation about Eric.

He finished his drink, mixed another, and started back at square one.

The two of us meet at the Stonehenge for a drink and dinner. After just five minutes, I ask her about her ex. Brittany becomes upset, spills her drink, gets up, and leaves to clean up. At the same time, Nick is across the street at Kingston's, having a drink with a blonde. While this is going on, Thomas Cravell is outside the Stonehenge, watching us. But just minutes later, Nick and Cravell are behind the hotel, engaging in an old-fashioned gunfight.

What the hell happened, for Christ's sake? Why would Nick leave the Kingston, meet Cravell behind the Stonehenge, and shoot it out with him? Who was the blonde Nick was with, and where did she go? And why would Brittany show up at Nick's funeral?

170

He sat tensely, going over these events, again and again. Three more drinks and one hour later, he fell asleep in his chair.

CHAPTER 14

Saturday, the Second Week

At nine o'clock the next morning, Lou Berchfeld, President of WarCo, called to tell Richard he wanted to meet with him at his Orlando office.

This was highly irregular. Berchfeld never made a habit of going into the office on a Saturday. He preferred his golf.

"We need to replace Nick as soon as possible," Berchfeld said as soon as Richard came in.

The hair on the back of Richard's bristled. He was in no mood for this. "And you skipped your Saturday golf game to come in and tell me this?"

His bushy black brows bumping together, Berchfeld shifted uncomfortably in his seat. He obviously realized he'd stepped into a highly sensitive area. "I ... considered it necessary that we talk about this as soon as possible."

Richard wanted to grab Berchfeld by the neck and strangle him. He circled his desk and forced himself to ride out the hot wave. "Why'd you wait?"

"Pardon?"

"You could've come to the funeral and asked me."

Berchfeld reddened. "I don't deserve that."

Richard realized right then that he needed to regain control. This was a multi-million-dollar business, after all. Berchfeld was only thinking of the overall picture. "I'm sorry. My nerves..."

"I understand."

Richard opened the blinds to let in some fresh morning sun. It seemed to dissipate some of the tension in the room. "I was coming in anyway. I wanted to pull up some files and see where we stand." He opened a drawer and found a hand-rolled cigar. He didn't offer one to Berchfeld, who despised smoking.

"We need to cover this as quickly as possible," Berchfeld said. "Get everyone's mind back on business. There are several top sales boys we've got in line. I think Jack can use his influence to have Phil Maguire come over from RKW."

Richard puffed on his cigar. A dynamite salesman, Maguire had the kind of sharp, go-getting personality needed to head that department. Maguire had been around much longer than Nick. No reason why he shouldn't be offered the position. But somehow, the idea of replacing his own son made his gut throb.

The phone buzzed.

Richard wondered who in the hell would be calling on a Saturday morning. He picked it up and answered gruffly. His mood changed instantly when he heard the soft, feminine voice respond, "Richard? It's me, Brittany."

He glanced at Berchfeld, who was examining a non-existent smudge on the sleeve of his jacket. He placed his hand over the receiver. "This is, uh, personal, Lou. Give me ten minutes, okay?"

"Huh? Oh." The other man grunted into a standing position. "Let me see if the coffee machine's working in the snack room. Can I get you some?"

"I'm good, thanks." He waited until Berchfeld had closed the door, then spun his chair around and lowered his voice. "Brittany ... where have you been? What happened the other night?"

"I'm terribly sorry about your son. I ... heard – saw it – on the news."

"Where did you go? That night. You never ... came back." It was the most important question of all for Richard. For some strange, despicable reason, Nick's death had taken a back seat. Despite his intentions, he cared only about what had happened at the hotel. "Why did you leave me?" He didn't know any other way of asking.

"I was followed. My ex ... he found me there."

"You mean he followed you – us – to the Stonehenge?"

"He was waiting for me when I came out of the bar. He saw me heading for the ladies' room and followed me in."

"He followed you into the ladies' room?"

"Luckily for him, no one else was in there. Luck always seems to be on his side. Anyway, he forced me into one of the booths. He had a knife. He ... put it to my throat."

The heat settled on Richard's shoulders, scalding his flesh. "Brittany, you need to get the police in on this!"

A deep sigh. "If only you knew how many times I've called them. How many times I've tried

174

to get them to listen to me. The injunction. The times I've had to face him in court. Richard, I don't think the police really care."

"Then it's about time we did something to make them care."

"That sounds good, but–"

"You have the right to be safe – just like anyone else. Why should you suffer for the laziness of the police department?"

"Like I said, it sounds good, even though it may not be very practical."

"Brittany, they need to know."

No reply.

"Let me help you."

A chuckle. "All this for ... sex?"

He hated when she said that. "It's more than that."

"What is it?"

"I'd ... like to do something unselfish for once in my life."

"Down on yourself?"

"With good reason."

"What happened ... with your son? Was he really in some sort of gunfight with a private detective? I saw it on the news broadcasts. Is this true?"

"Yes."

"Tell me what happened."

"I'd like to. In person."

"I ... don't know."

"Why not?"

"Eric. I don't want him bothering us."

"I'm not afraid of Eric."

175

"He's crazy, Richard."

"I can be crazy, too."

"I'm sure you can."

"Where can we meet?"

"How about that steakhouse on Semoran and East Colonial?"

"What time?"

"Six o'clock?"

"See you there."

***

Katie Warden sat on her bed, drying her hair.

The afternoon sun spilled in through the blinds. Her TV showed some tattooed, half-naked diva doing one of her famous music videos. The sound was off. Katie wanted peace and quiet. The birds squawking in the back yard were almost more than she could tolerate.

Her cell phone buzzed. When she answered, Kevin asked, "Feeling any better?"

She sighed, rolling over on her back to stare at her ceiling. "Not really. I mean ... Nicky and I hadn't been close the last couple of years, but he was always there when I was growing up."

"He was kind of older than you?"

"He was nine when I was born. My big brother ... always protecting me." She sighed again, her chest feeling heavy. "I still can't believe he's gone."

"I just wish there was something I could do to cheer you up."

"It's gonna take a while. But just knowing that you care is a big help." Katie managed a small smile, but even that took some effort. Don ... always so sensitive. More than she could say about most

176

other guys. And she appreciated that quality, especially now, when she really needed it. She'd only known Kevin six months, but going by the way things were heating up, this might turn serious.

"What say we go out for a burger and fries?"

"I don't know..."

"C'mon, Kate. Lemme get you out of there for a little while. That place is a damn mausoleum."

"But Mom–"

"She'll be okay. Aren't her folks staying there with you guys?"

"They're staying in the guest house."

He laughed. "You mean that mansion in the back yard that's bigger than my entire apartment complex?"

Katie hated it when people ridiculed her family's wealth. It was only their jealousy coming out. But she knew Kevin was just trying to lighten the moment. "It's not that big and you know it."

"And why are they staying there? You've got more than enough room in the main house."

"Daddy's weird in some ways. I think he sort of feels threatened with other people around. Some kind of strange control thing, I guess. Who knows?"

"He doesn't exactly make me feel welcome, either."

"I ... I'm not sure that he actually likes you, Kevin."

"Maybe he thinks I'm after the family fortune."

"Could be." She smiled. "Aren't you?"

"Haven't you figured out by now why I'm always buying you junk food? I want you to get fat and sloppy, so no one else looks at you anymore."

177

Katie laughed despite her depression.

"I haven't heard you laugh in too long. How about that burger and fries? Maybe I'll let *you* pay this time."

Another laugh. "Oh, all right." What harm could it do? She did need to get out for a little while, didn't she? If not for some fresh air... "Pick me up at two, okay?"

***

Kevin brought over the tray and set it down on the table. He slid into the booth and pushed the giant Coke in Katie's direction.

The parking lot was nearly deserted. Only a shiny black BMW, a white 350 SL, an emerald-green Volvo, and Kevin's tan VW Bug sat in front of the big, tinted window. The other five customers – Rollins students, by the looks of them – wolfed down burgers and fries across the room.

"Since we both love ketchup, we can share the fries, okay?" Kevin dumped the two large orders on a napkin in the center of the tray. He placed the four small paper cups of ketchup beside the pile.

Katie pouted. "I really shouldn't pig-out on the fries or the ketchup. Gotta watch the old figure, you know."

"You women are all alike. You're perfect, Kate."

She stuck a fry in her mouth. "You'd be the first to say something if I porked up."

"Not *this* guy." He opened his burger, centered the lettuce directly over the meat, the pickle in the center of the lettuce, then closed it carefully. "I'm

178

smart enough to know better than mention a lady's weight."

"A very wise decision."

He had a big slug of Coke. "If I've learned anything growing up in a house full of females, certain criteria ensure a healthy, happy, and safe relationship. A man should never notice – or mention – physical deformities, maladies, or any sort of imperfection. And a woman's weight definitely heads the list."

"Tactfully said. I'm impressed."

"By the way, how's the family doing?"

She sighed. "As well as expected. Daddy's not able to grieve – not properly, anyway. He's too busy running the corporation. And now he's got to find a replacement for Nicky."

"Your brother was in charge of the sales department, right?"

"He was their director."

"How long had he been doing that?"

"Three or four years, I think."

"Did he like it?"

Silence.

"Did I say the wrong thing?"

A dark look shadowed her face. "It's just that ... I didn't want to talk about this. Not this soon."

"I'm sorry. We need to be talking about other things. The weather, maybe? Politics? Adopting a dog? How about those Gators? How about this ... do you think men should wear underwear beneath their kilts?"

She forced a smile. Kevin was trying so hard... "I really wish I could be better company."

"Hey, he was your only brother."

"Kevin, would you be really mad if I asked you to take me home?"

"Are you sure?"

She nodded.

"All right, then. On one condition."

"What's that?"

"That we do this again very soon. Not the leaving-before-the-food-gets-cold part, the leaving-after-we-stuff-ourselves part."

She laughed in spite of herself. Kevin never failed to cheer her up. And she needed it. "Maybe in a few days."

***

Brittany was the first person Richard saw when he entered the dark, air-conditioned Steakhouse bar.

She sat at the end of the bar, sipping her drink. Her eyes were focused on him. Despite the anger and confusion consuming him during the last few days, he experienced the same excitement he always felt in this woman's presence. Only hours ago, he'd told himself she was out of his life. Seeing her again would only lead to more misery and torment. But now he realized just how futile that line of thinking really was.

He climbed onto the stool next to her and ordered a double vodka martini.

Brittany continued staring at him. "It's terrific seeing you again," she said softly.

"I was thinking the very same thing."

The barwoman brought his drink. Richard picked it up and downed half in one swallow. Its potent warmth settled in his gut, spreading out quickly and relaxing him. He sighed, hoping that maybe now he'd have the courage to find out a few vital things. "Tell me what happened that night." He was surprised his voice still worked.

"It's like I told you on the phone. Eric showed up at the motel that night ... the night your son was killed. He followed me into the ladies' room and started up with his usual threats."

The same despicable thoughts suddenly took over, driving everything else out. Pushing away decency and honor, pride and self-respect. Nick's death was once again tossed into a dark corner of his thoughts, like a box of old magazines. The gunfight with Cravell no longer mattered. Nor did the fact that Nick lay dead in the wet grass, his face blown half off, while his old man sat in a bar across the street, getting drunk.

But this wasn't about Nick or Cravell ... or even why Brittany hadn't come back from the ladies' room. It was about something much more important. Something he needed to know more than anything else. "Brittany ... were you at Nick's funeral?"

She blinked, her eyes searching his. "Now why would you ask me *that*, Richard?"

"I ... could've sworn I saw you there."

"That would've been awkward, don't you think? You didn't *expect* me to be there, did you?"

Idiot. He should've known better. He cursed himself for bringing it up.

"Are you sure you saw me there?"

He shrugged. "Maybe my eyes were playing tricks. I guess I was just thinking of you at the time, so..."

She placed her hand on his. "That was touching. Thinking of me while you were burying your dead son."

He flinched. *Why the hell did she have to put it that way?* It made him sound even more cruel and heartless.

He put down his glass. Strange. He hadn't given this any thought before. But now, the possibility was becoming obvious. Brittany's ex was constantly following her, staying close. The idea of a certified psycho being around when Nick was killed suddenly didn't seem as coincidental as before. "I think your ex-husband may have had something to do with Nick's murder." It came out even before he realized it.

"That's insane."

"The more I think about it, the more suspicious it seems, his being out there while you and I were at the Stonehenge–"

"But why would Eric want to hurt your son?"

"I don't know."

"Did they know one another?"

"I don't know."

"Then why would you think he had anything to do with that?"

"I don't *know*, Brittany." His pulse raced. "There are a lot of things I don't know. But the more I don't know, the more I don't like it. Why was Nick out there in the first place? I know he sowed his wild oats. He had no choice. He was my son, wasn't he?"

That last statement made him feel genuine disgust for himself, for what he was. But it was true. And it cleared up at least a small part of this messy, unpleasant puzzle. *My son. A chip off the old block. The apple never falls very far from the tree.*

Funny how those ancient aphorisms always sounded innocent. Until now. How Nick's drinking and womanizing never really posed much of a problem. Until now.

"Richard, the news reports said the man who killed your son was a private detective. Is this true?"

"Yes..."

"Do you have any idea what that detective was doing out there?"

He couldn't reply. There was no way he could admit hiring Cravell to follow her. She'd been trying to evade a wild, abusive man who was ruining her life. How could Richard justify hiring someone to follow her on top of all this?

"You know, don't you? "Her eyes probed his.

His pulse raced as his brain feverishly worked on something that would sound acceptable.

"You knew that detective, didn't you?"

"Brittany..."

She sat bolt upright, her eyes searching his. "Tell me ... about him." Her voice had become a tense whisper.

"I ... knew the man."

"What was he doing out there?"

Silence.

"Tell me."

183

"He was ... working for me."

"Why?"

"I'd hired him to ... to watch out for you."

"To *what*? "Her eyes blazed.

"Brittany, I ... I couldn't help it."

"Are you telling me you were paying that detective to follow me?"

He picked up his drink and emptied it just as the barwoman brought him a new one. He was going to need many more of these tonight.

Brittany slid down off her stool and stood tensely, her neck muscles quivering. The hatred, the betrayal, the hurt – everything showed in her face.

How could he tell her how much she meant to him? That he'd become obsessed? So much so that he had to find out every single thing about her and get rid of any obstacle that might threaten his quest to possess her?

No words could justify what he'd done, what he'd tried to do. His quick corporate mind had switched off, refusing to work under such adverse conditions. No calls, no suggestions. Not even the hint of a fix strategy. Mr. CEO's super brain had suddenly gone out to lunch.

Before he could even think of a suitable explanation, Brittany stormed out of the bar, bumping into a waitress and nearly knocking over a tray of frosted beer mugs.

He rushed out of the room. "Brittany!" He caught her outside, in the front parking lot facing East Colonial. He tried to grab her elbow, but she pulled away with a vengeance. Their faces were inches away. He flinched at the hot fury filling her.

184

"How *dare* you hire someone to follow me!"

"Brittany..." He searched for the right words. They were far off, in some locked vault. Desperation had set in, closing up shop. A thick cloud had settled over him, obscuring anything vaguely intelligible. He struggled to make it work. There was no way he could let this beautiful creature storm out of his life. Not like this. "I wanted ... I wanted to get someone ... after your ex. To get him away from you. To–"

"I told you no, Richard. I told you I didn't want you to do that. Don't you remember?"

He couldn't reply. The thick cloud preventing clear thought hovered steadily above him. He'd reverted to the role of a small boy being scolded by his mother.

"Always the manipulator. Pulling strings. Pushing people out of the way."

He felt himself growing smaller. As if all his air steadily trickled out of him. His brain remained useless.

"I ... don't ... ever ... want ... to ... see ... you ... again ... Richard." She said it calmly, carefully, making each word separate and distinct. The effect was just as excruciating as if she'd stabbed him with each separate word.

"*Please*, Brittany..."

"And I don't want you hiring anyone else to follow me. Get it?"

Smaller, smaller...

"We're through. Understand? You've pulled your last string with me. Go pull them with your associates and your employees and all the other

185

little people who fear and worship you. But let me be. I mean it. Do you understand?"

"But all I wanted—"

"Do you *understand*?"

He couldn't look at her anymore. Too much hatred and fire oozed from her. He could understand her anger. But he couldn't comprehend the scorching fury behind it.

He nodded numbly, knowing he'd never be able to get through this. This woman had aroused him more than anyone else ever had. It was this fact that made him realize that despite her seething anger, her hatred, he would indeed see her again.

"Richard," she said in a much calmer voice, "I want you to go back inside."

Most of the heat had gone, but her expression remained tense.

He didn't reply. He stood there silently, shaking, his face numb.

"I don't want you to see me leave. Can't have you finding out what car I'm driving."

He continued searching for the right words that might fix this.

"Do you see what you've done here? You've totally destroyed my respect for you, my trust; and you've killed a possible relationship – all in one savage stroke."

"Brittany, I told you why I–"

"I want you to go back inside and do what you do best. Drink, order people around, and feel sorry for yourself. Understand?" She made a gesture similar to flicking away a pesky insect. "Now go."

The heat rushed up his limbs, settling in his spine. He could feel his hands curling into fists, his stomach tightening. How *dare* this woman talk to him this way! How *dare* she make him feel like a child!

"Inside, Richard. Drink up."

Obediently he turned on his heel, trudging heavily toward the double wooden doors on feet that weighed a ton, cursing himself for letting this woman treat him like this. For getting to his very core. He stood at the entrance, contemplating his dark reflection in the opaque glass window. His right hand inched slowly toward the brass door handle. Then reality hit him full in the face. No one talked to him like this. *No one!*

He shook himself out of his daze, spun around, and took two steps in her direction.

She'd already gone.

CHAPTER 15

Sunday, the Second Week

Kevin Cassidy glided the Gillette disposable gently over his delicate twenty-one-year-old cheek and rinsed off the blade.

He splashed cold water over his face, blotted dry with a towel, and slapped a little Aqua Velva over the works, wincing at the burst of tingling pain. He spent the next few moments in the closet doorway, searching for a clean shirt and tie to wear to Mass.

Kevin Cassidy was far from religious. The whole mindless routine – Communion, Confession, Catechism class, Heaven, Hell, Limbo, Purgatory – bored him to tears. It wasn't why he went to church nowadays. Kevin's present commitments dealt with something infinitely more satisfying.

He'd felt this way the last five years, since his first sexual encounter, which happened during a high school party. The girl's name was Elaine. She was tall, blonde, slender, and two years older than Kevin. Fully developed, Elaine sported a pair of mouth-watering tits and could already do things that Kevin, up to that point, had seen only in porn mags and downloads.

After his liaison with Elaine, Kevin was never the same. He would never again be able to look at a girl in the same light and would never go more than a few seconds without thinking of sex. He'd find himself embarrassingly erect in biology class, when one of his female classmates squirmed in her seat, stretched, or picked up a pencil from the floor. He could no longer watch a girl bent over the water fountain without developing a burning hard-on. Nor could he glimpse the girls' volleyball team or cheerleading practice, without making a sudden trip to the rest room.

Church was great for girl-watching. The Catholics really cranked out good-looking babes. He'd met Katie Warden in church. She wasn't religious but enjoyed the relaxed atmosphere. It gave her the opportunity to meditate. Katie liked Eastern philosophies. She wanted to experience a meshing of the mind with the spirit and hoped her presence in church would help.

They hadn't yet slept together, but Kevin knew it was only a matter of time. He strongly believed the gentleman approach would succeed in this case. And it would be well worth the trouble. The lucky guy who married into the Warden family would have it made for life.

Katie was sweet but kind of plain, and her tits were disappointing. They were firm enough, but there just wasn't much to them. He didn't think Katie would do a lot of things the other girls did, especially those with less successful backgrounds. The real kickers were the chicks from the other side of the tracks. They were often the less attractive girls who had to prove themselves better than the babes with that nose-in-the-air attitude that said *I'm beautiful, I can be a real bitch, and if you don't like it, you can go screw yourself.*

189

He'd seen babes like that all over the damned place – especially whenever he walked into a drugstore. There always seemed to be a gorgeous number standing behind the counter, filing her nails. At first he'd tried talking to them, but the result was always the same. Talking to a wet sponge would be much more entertaining.

The lookers were too stuck on themselves and thought they were too special to open up on the mattress. And the well-off babes were much too busy soaking Daddy's golden plastic to waste their time.

Katie wasn't selfish or materialistic. She might not have been the greatest-looking chick around, but she had more than enough on the ball to heat him up whenever she wanted to. Kevin was convinced she'd go all the way for her man.

Kevin wanted that type of woman. He was determined not to waste his life like his parents, who'd been working their tails off in someone else's drugstore the last twenty years. Kevin needed success. And if he played his cards right, Katie would come through for him.

The kink in the works was Katie's father. The old man could scare off a grizzly bear with a look. Kevin could tell Katie's old man knew where his true motivations were coming from. Kevin was almost certain the old fart could read his mind. But Kevin Cassidy was no quitter. He followed his instincts. In this case, he'd have to tread carefully if he wanted to become a member of Katie's family.

After inspecting himself once more in the full-length mirror and approving his 'good-boy' image,

Kevin left his tiny Winter Park efficiency and hopped down the concrete steps to his car, which was parked in the small gravel lot behind the brick building.

Across the street, a beautiful raven-haired chick in a short red skirt and sleeveless tan blouse was bent over, inspecting the flat tire on the shiny red CL600.

"Bummer, you've got a flat." Kevin knew that sounded stupid, but sometimes a stupid, innocent line was the best way to start talking to a chick.

She straightened and shook her head. He couldn't see her eyes behind her wraparounds, but figured they were probably large and long lashed. Possibly brown or chestnut. "Yeah. Of all the damned luck. And I'm late for an appointment." She reached up and pushed some thick black hair away from her gorgeous face.

The scent of lilacs drifted his way. This woman was probably about thirty, but somehow it didn't matter. Not to him. A guy didn't think about age when checking out a woman like her. She was seriously hot. He would've been turned on no matter how old she was.

"I can change it for you." The offer jumped out of his mouth before he realized it.

She shrugged. "You're all dressed up. I'll bet you're going to church, right?"

He didn't reply. Not at first. He didn't want to admit it. She might consider him a momma's boy, or fanatic. *Funny how a hot babe could change your attitude so quickly.* "I don't usually go to church, but I had some free time this morning and decided to give it a shot – just for the hell of it."

"I still couldn't ask you to–"

"No. Please." He was already loosening his tie. The prospects of sitting in an uncomfortable wooden pew just for a glimpse of a few well-dressed Catholic girls suddenly seemed stupid. This chick was gorgeous, with a smoking bod, and she was talking to him. He'd definitely enjoy some good memories of this later on. "Just take a couple of minutes. Then you'll be on your way."

She was smiling. He really wanted to see her eyes. Were they brown? Gray? Maybe even blue? He hoped she'd remove those damned wraparounds.

"I can't thank you enough." She placed a hand on her hip and rested her fine ass against the side of the car. "You're a life-saver."

So put me in your mouth, baby. He forced himself to hold back the silly grin. "It's nothing."

She took his jacket, folded it neatly, and held it close against her – which turned him on even more. Later he'd sniff it and relive all this. He rolled up his shirt sleeves and followed her to the back of the car, where she bent to open the trunk.

Her sweet scent was even stronger up close. She tilted her head. The raven-black hair spilled over her bare shoulder as she reached for the jack. She was careful to keep his jacket away from the tools in the small area.

"I can get it." This babe had a dandy set of knockers. They weren't big but looked perfect. Perky. Proud. "You'll ... get your blouse dirty." His voice sounded funny.

192

She backed away and reached up to push the hair behind her. Her scent was intoxicating. "Let me at least pay you for your time..."

"No, it's cool." He focused on the jack, the changing of the tire. Later, maybe, this babe would be grateful. So grateful that–

No. That was one fantasy he didn't want distracting him right now. It was important to get this done without developing a hard-on.

"You're really a nice guy." She held his jacket against her, hiding those beautiful tits. "You a student?"

Her legs were terrific. She obviously took care of herself. He rolled out the tire and leaned it a foot or so from the flat. "Third year."

He knelt. Forgetting himself, he turned to look at her. It was a mistake. If it weren't for his jacket hanging down in front of her, he might've caught a glimpse of her crotch. *Shit...* She stood, those yummy legs nearly two feet apart. It didn't help. He wondered if she was doing this on purpose. He pulled his eyes away from her and picked up the X-wrench.

"You seem so ... mature."

"Twenty-one," he said proudly. "Drinking age."

"I would've guessed twenty-four or -five."

He beamed in spite of himself. *Fix the flat. Concentrate. Then you can puff up.*

Ten minutes later, he bent over the trunk of her car and slid in the flat. "Better have this fixed quick. You get another flat, you'll have to be towed next time."

"I really appreciate this. I'd like to repay you somehow."

You can repay me by sitting on my face.

She was standing close. As he pulled on his jacket, he couldn't help noticing how her lilac scent lingered on it. It was gonna be impossible paying attention to those Catholic gals, with this babe's fragrance all over him. "It's okay. Now you won't be late for your appointment." He wondered what kind of appointment it was, seeing how she was dressed.

"It's in half an hour." She consulted the expensive gold watch on her wrist. "Shouldn't take more than an hour. Can we meet again? Say, at two o'clock? For an early dinner, maybe? A drink?"

He suddenly felt light-headed. "You sure? I mean–"

"Of course." She pulled back her hair and raised her breasts, which did a number on him just as effectively as an intense hand-job. "My treat. There's a little Italian restaurant just a couple of miles down the road, on Park Avenue."

"I know it." His pulse hastened. "I'll meet you there at two."

"Don't be late."

***

Richard Warden awoke on the couch.

He surveyed his surroundings. His den. Somehow he'd managed to make it home last night without breaking his neck. Had he driven? He must have. But he couldn't remember, and this was what scared him.

194

Should he check the Cadillac? Go on out there right now and make sure there were no dents or other signs that he'd hit something? A horrible thought.

Everything's fine. Nothing happened last night. Nothing at all. You're just upset. And you should be.

It came back like a fist to the jaw.

I meet the hottest, most beautiful chick I've ever seen. From that day on, she steers me on one wild ride after another. During all this madness, my son is murdered. And when this woman finds out about the investigator I've hired to follow her, she stomps out of my life.

He tried sitting up. An enormous wave of warm nausea slammed into him. His temples throbbed mercilessly. A heavy ball of fire filled his gut. It had been three years since he'd drunk that much, and he hated himself for doing it.

Despite his fierce determination to keep the nightmare tucked safely away in the black recesses of his mind, it flashed across his vision. The unspeakable horrors of what he'd gone through. The single incident that would forever change his life.

The fuzzy drive back to the hotel following four hours at the bar, where he'd tried relaxing after three long, hectic days at Tampa's Annual Software Convention. Then, finding out what he'd done. What they'd said he'd done.

The frantic call to the authorities. The horror-stricken call to Bob Dalgren, telling him what had happened. The gut-wrenching call to Adrienne. The arrest, the breath test, the fingerprinting. The total humiliation of being locked up with worthless scum.

The trial. Dredging up every painful fact. The judge reprimanding him, talking to him as though he were some disgusting thing that should be put away forever. The deal his friend Bob Dalgren had cut for him, greasing everything, as usual, with giant wads of money.

Over the last couple of years, he was careful to drink in dark, secluded places and to keep his consumption minimal. The follow-ups helped. But what kept him honest was his personal realization that although what he'd done was despicable, it wasn't something he was ever likely to repeat. It kept everything in check. Until yesterday.

Go back inside. Drink. Do what you do best. Order people around. Feel sorry for yourself.

Strange, how Brittany knew so much about him. He had the eerie feeling she could actually see into his soul.

***

La Scala, a small, white stucco building with a red Spanish-tile roof, was surrounded by lush gardens and a small courtyard out in front.

The restaurant was owned by Italian immigrants who cooked their own food using age-old family recipes. The food was good, but extremely expensive.

The red CL600 sat in the side lot. Kevin entered the cool, dark foyer and slipped through the archway that led into the main dining room. The gorgeous brunette sat in a booth in the rear, smiling at him.

196

He couldn't believe his good luck. He'd been afraid all this was just a figment of his imagination. How often did a guy like him meet such a hot-looking woman? And on a Sunday morning, no less...

He was surprised at himself for coming here so easily. Shouldn't he feel some guilt for getting together with another woman? After all, he'd been dating Katie for months. And even though they weren't exactly going steady, it was mutually understood that they wouldn't see other people.

He'd done this woman a favor. She wanted to repay him for his kindness. He couldn't deny her rewarding him, could he?

She'd changed into a different outfit – a red tank top, white shorts, and white open-toed high heels. Her hair was pulled back and tied with a red rope. Several gold necklaces hung around her neck. She also wore gold earrings on each ear, a gold bracelet, and gold rings on each hand.

"You look fabulous," he said, sitting down.

She smiled and finished her drink.

The waitress came to the table. He ordered a gin and tonic and asked if she wanted a refill.

"Sure." She put down her glass and rested her arms on the table. The valley between her tits deepened.

It was impossible to ignore those babies. He guessed they were compliments of Dow-Corning, going by their perfect shape and how they pushed against the material of her top. The way her nipples mashed against her top told him she wore no bra.

"I don't even know your name," she said after the waitress brought their drinks.

"I'm Kevin. Kevin Cassidy."

She held out her hand. "I'm Monique Lasko."

Her touch was electric. He cleared his throat and reached for his drink.

"Something wrong?"

"Uh, no. Nothing. I'm okay." The drink was exactly what he needed. Hopefully it would relax him.

She watched him, her large hazel eyes taking him in. It was the very first time such a beautiful babe had looked at him like that. Was he making too much of this? He'd done the woman a favor by changing her tire. A simple kindness. And she intended to repay him with dinner and a drink. Nothing more, nothing less.

Kevin had learned long ago to accept his cursed normality. His ears were too long, his nose too short. He was tall, but bony. And had it not been for his long-legged speed on the dirt track, he would've been branded a full-blown nerd by the time he reached junior high. But he discovered early on that a lot of chicks responded quite well to his boy-next-door persona. And because of this slight edge, he'd scored with women much earlier than many of his good-looking, studly friends.

"It's nice being legal, isn't it? " Monique asked.

"Sure is."

"I remember when I was a year or two shy of it." She frowned. "Couldn't do anything without explaining myself. Couldn't smoke or drink, or stay out late. And getting a guy in the sack without

198

worrying about that stupid statutory rape thing sure was a bummer."

He squirmed in his seat. This chick was incredible. *Talk dirty to me, baby...* For a moment he thought he'd died and gone straight to Heaven.

Reluctantly he decided to change the subject – if only to ease the uncomfortable throbbing between his legs. "What do you do, Monique? For a living. That car of yours. It's a real honey. But aren't they a tad pricey?"

She smiled. "It was a gift. My husband was a rich man."

"Was?"

"Al died last year. Heart attack."

"I'm sorry." It was difficult to hold back. Not that a heart attack was anything to snicker at. The image of this gorgeous fox hammering the old boy to death, then paying the mortician extra to wipe the smile off the corpse's face, was something out of Mad Magazine.

Monique shrugged. "Al wasn't quite sixty. He'd started his own business when he was young and kept it up till he dropped. I told him a hundred times to let the others run it, to enjoy himself while he still had time." She sighed. "But Al was a stubborn man."

Incredible. How could anyone spend all his time running a business with something as fine as this number waiting for him at home?

"What's wrong?" she asked.

"Wrong?"

"You keep shaking your head."

He reddened. "Sorry. I was just thinking."

199

"What were you – *damn*!" Her gold bracelet suddenly dropped onto the table, then slid to the floor. "That stupid thing's always coming off." She made a move to retrieve it.

Kevin bent down and scooped it up. It was difficult to ignore those gorgeous, tanned gems resting beneath the table. So instead of ignoring them, he helped himself to a healthy eyeful and then took his time coming back up from his pleasant trip.

"Thank you." She opened her bag and dropped it inside. "You'd think something costing close to two grand would come with a decent clasp." She picked up her drink. "Now. What were we talking about?" When he didn't reply, she laughed. "Oh, yes. About what you were thinking."

His cheeks flushed. "Nothing, really..."

She smiled and moved closer. Their faces were only a foot apart. Her lilac perfume and the shampoo scent in her hair enveloped him. "I'll bet I know," she whispered. "I'll bet it's the same thing I'm thinking."

His face grew even hotter. He squirmed, cursing himself for wearing such tight trousers. "Wh-What were you thinking?" He felt hot and sloppy. Was it the drink? Or the effect this babe had on him?

She moved her mouth even closer. "I'll bet you were thinking of getting me between the sheets, weren't you, big boy?"

His heart fluttered. The temperature of the room increased.

"Well?" Her tongue darted out and flicked lightly against his bottom lip. Her hot touch turned into an electric jolt rushing down his limbs.

He began nodding and soon wondered if he'd ever stop. He'd suddenly turned into one of those stupid toy bobber dogs he'd seen in the rear windows of cars.

"You have a girlfriend, Kevin?"

He couldn't remember if he did or not. Then it came to him. Katie Warden. The girl he'd been trying to catch for how many months now? Six? Seven? He couldn't remember that, either. Right now, he couldn't even remember his own name. "No," he whispered, and his heart skipped a beat.

"No one?"

He shook his head. The room grew even hotter. *Did they just turn off the air-conditioning? This was Florida, dammit.*

"I find that hard to believe. A nice-looking guy like you?"

He shrugged. A thread of guilt drifted slowly past, making him flinch. "I've been ... seeing someone..."

"I knew it. Is it serious?"

"No. Not serious."

"How long have you been seeing her?"

"A couple of ... weeks."

"And it's not serious?"

"No..."

"I guess she's stupid, huh? Not knowing what she's missing."

He nodded. "Stupid. Yep. She's stupid, all right."

201

What the hell are we talking about, anyway? It was hard getting past this woman's scent, those luscious lips. Those tits...

"A lot of girls are stupid," she said. "Not knowing the kind of men they have. What to do with them. How to treat them. I find that amazing. Don't you?"

He nodded. He couldn't concentrate on anything but those full red lips. So close. So wet.

Suddenly they touched him, tantalizing his sensitive flesh. Her strawberry lipstick, even more intoxicating than his drink, made him tremble. The warm tension in his lap turned hot. He squirmed. Something embarrassing would happen if she didn't ease up. But he just didn't care.

Her hot breath singed his cheek. "Let's find a room."

The tension in his lap had turned into a hot coal. He took a breath. "I ... need to wait ... just for a minute–"

"I understand." Her eyes lowered. "Tell you what. I'll wait for you outside. Then, when you can ... when you're able to walk, join me." She touched his cheek and slid out of the booth.

He couldn't take his eyes off her perfect ass as it gyrated toward the front of the big room.

He waited until his heart settled down. It took forever for his erection to ease up. Then he got up and hurried outside.

***

Monique closed the motel room door and dropped her bag on the round table in front of the

202

window. "Take off your clothes, Kevin. Stay a while."

He could hardly breathe. Hot in here. Very hot. He couldn't take his eyes off her.

"What's wrong? Shy?" Smiling at him, she reached up and pushed her hair over her shoulders, showing off her tits.

"I-I don't know..." *I must be dreaming ... but I don't remember falling asleep. This is the most vivid wet dream I'll ever have in my life. Everything's moving so slow ... so hazy...*

"Are you ... a *virgin*?" Still smiling, she moved toward him. "Is that why you're so ... hesitant? Never made it with a girl before?"

"It's ... not that..." His tongue ... so hot ... so swollen in his mouth. Useless.

She reached out. Her hands circled the back of his neck. An electric charge shot down his spine. His feet seemed bolted to the floor, and he couldn't dispel the feeling or command himself to move. All he could do was watch her face coming closer. He *wanted* to be powerless, to be dominated. Wasn't that every man's dream? To become a sex goddess's plaything? He owned a couple of those B&D mags, mixed in with his Playboys and nudie rags in his closet. Big color shots of a gorgeous brunette covered in leather, administering pain and torment to her helpless, trussed-up male slave.

"Oh my..." She looked down at him. Her eyes grew. Her left hand pulled away from his neck, sliding down his chest, stopping over his throbbing erection.

Trembling, he closed his eyes.

Her sudden hot, open-mouthed kiss did him in. The hot eruption permeated through him. He sagged as his legs gave way. Everything went dark.

***

When he opened his eyes, he was lying on the bed. Everything was dark.

A door opened. A woman wearing a black bra and black laced panties leaned against the open doorway.

Katie? Katie Warden? His vision was too blurred ... he couldn't be sure ... but he thought it was Katie. It had to be. The light-brown hair was definitely hers.

"K-Katie?" His tongue filled his mouth. He tried sitting up, but something was holding him down. A giant weight kept him lying on his back. Even his arms felt like lead. "Wh-What are you doing here?"

"I should be asking you the same thing. What are you doing here with a hooker?"

None of this made sense. How'd Katie get here? And where was the other chick? The gorgeous brunette? What was her name? Monica? Mona? Monique? Everything kept spinning around...

"Well? Why are you here?"

He opened his mouth. Nothing came out.

Katie took four long steps toward him and stopped just a foot short of the bed. "Why are you doing this to me, Kevin? I thought we had a good thing going."

"We ... d-do..."

"Then why'd you come here?"

"I d-don't ... I–"

"Where is she, Kevin?"

"I ... don't know..."

She moved away, then disappeared into the darkness of the room. A moment later, she reappeared. She approached the bed and sat on the edge of the mattress. Kevin squinted. Katie had somehow turned into Monique. He blinked a few times, and Monique turned right back into Katie. Good. He wanted Katie, not Monique. Monique was fine ... and hot ... and sexy ... but Katie was the one with the money.

"Poor baby ... I think your friend deserted you."

He said nothing. He couldn't get over how great Katie looked. She'd always seemed too skinny. She'd let him cop a feel once or twice before, but there wasn't much to her knockers. Now? Those babies were fabulous. They wanted to pop right out of that black lacy bra. *Bring 'em here, baby ... I've got just the thing for 'em.* She'd been hiding them from him. That was it. She was keeping the best things to herself. Waiting for the right moment to let him have it all.

Katie shrugged one beautiful bare shoulder and winked. "Well, now that we're alone, why don't we do what we were gonna do anyway? I mean, if you're gonna go to a hooker, you might as well get it from someone who really likes you, huh?"

He tried to speak, but his tongue grew thick and heavy again. He settled for a furious nod.

"Why don't we play a little game first?"

That sounded just fine. "A g-game ... uh-huh ... a game ... we'll play a game..." *A game. Hide the banana, maybe? Jerk the monkey? Smoke the cigar? Yes. A game.*

She stood, spread her legs, and placed both hands behind her back. It took her two tries. Or maybe he'd only seen it that way. His eyes seemed to be playing tricks on him. She'd gotten up, but only part of her stood – maybe just half of her. The rest of her – her aura? – remained on the mattress. Then it realized how stupid it looked still sitting there, so it evaporated and became Katie once again.

Far out, man...

"What kind of game would you like to play, Kevin?"

I've died. I'm in heaven now...

He lay there, the ponderous weight holding him down, his breath escaping him in short sighs.

"How about if we play a new kind of game?"

"F-Fine ... *new* game..."

"This will be a kind of mind-game. Is that all right with you?"

"Mind ... fine ... far out ..."

"Close your eyes first. Then I'll tell you to pick up something and listen to it. But you can't cheat, or I'll just have to leave you here all by yourself."

"No cheat ... close eyes ... listen..."

"There's an object on the bed beside you, near your right hand. Pick it up, put it to your ear, and listen to it. It'll give you a recorded message that'll say what exactly I'm supposed to do to you. Understand? For instance, it could say I'm supposed to make love to you with my mouth ... or tongue ... and that's exactly what I'll have to do–"

206

"All right, *all right* ..." This was too fucking much. He didn't know how much longer he could take this. "Pick up ... listen..."

He groped for it. A round mass. Heavy. Metal. Heavy metal? He wanted to giggle. *I'm picking up heavy metal and I ain't even a radio! I'm so funny...*

It was a jagged metal rock with a crescent-shaped handle attached to it. *Heavy, man. And far out as well.* He couldn't help the giggle trickling out his nostrils.

"That's it. Grab it there, easy now. No peeking. Bring it up to your ear, tilt it a little ... that's it ... a little more ... now listen."

He listened. He heard nothing coming from the tube. This damned heavy metal mass wasn't telling him shit. What the hell kind of stupid game was this, anyway? "I c-can't hear *any* fucking thing..."

"There's a button right in front of your index finger to increase the volume. Go ahead and press it now. Do it carefully, and don't shake it, or you won't be able to hear the message. That's it. I think you've got it now."

The room started jumping again. The bed was vibrating. *What the fuck is going on? No peeking, my ass. I need to know why the fuck this room—*

He opened his eyes. *A gun? Why the fuck am I pointing a gun at my—*

The deafening explosion brought ecstasy – and oblivion – to a final level.

***

The woman slid behind the wheel of the rented CL600.

As she drove off, she removed the brown wig and fluffed out her own short, sandy-brown hair. She dropped the wig on the seat beside her and relaxed. A smile of satisfaction took over her face as she settled back in the comfortable leather bucket seat.

This phase of the plan was complete. The next would begin without her assistance.

PART II

Balancing the Scales

CHAPTER 16

Sunday Evening, the Second Week

Lounging in the comfortable La-Z-Boy in his den, Richard Warden struggled to focus on the televised local golf match.

He was much too obsessed with the crowd and groped for the zoom feature on the remote whenever a redheaded woman became visible.

His hangover had finally subsided. When it did, he realized his stomach was empty and his nerves were shot. But he hadn't wanted to leave his sanctuary and rejoin the family. He wanted to stay here, where he felt safe. In this room, he could do whatever he wanted. He could lock the door, turn off the phone, put on a movie or golf match, fix a drink, and settle in. He owned condos in the Keys and at Disney Village, cabins in the Appalachians, Lake Placid, and Aspen, but preferred to stay in this cool, comfortable room.

His phone buzzed. He checked the display. Bob Dalgren. With a deep sigh, he switched it on.

"Richard ... we need to talk." The attorney's voice was choked, strained.

"What's wrong?"

"There's trouble."

Great. That was one word he didn't need to hear right now. "What the hell has happened now?"

"It's Kevin Cassidy. The boy's dead. Stuck a thirty-eight in his mouth and pulled the trigger."

"*What*?"

"That's ... not all."

"There's *more*?"

"There was a note. Suicide note."

Suicide? Cassidy? This was totally ridiculous.

"Richard? You there?"

"Go on."

"The note ... it's addressed to Adrienne."

"Adrienne? Why the hell would he–"

"Cassidy named you the reason for his suicide."

***

Jumpy and pale, Bob Dalgren waited in the lobby of Police Headquarters in downtown Orlando.

As soon as Richard pushed through the heavy glass door, Dalgren whisked him down the hall, to a small ten-by-ten room marked *Interviews*.

They weren't alone. Two men in dark suits stood near the door. A woman wearing glasses sat in a chair, a notepad perched on her thigh. A small tape recorder had been placed in the middle of the table.

The taller of the two men closed the door behind them. He introduced himself as Detective Albert Skinner of Homicide, who was handling Kevin Cassidy's case. The other man was also a detective. His name was Bronson. The woman, who remained anonymous, kept her ballpoint pen balanced directly above her notepad.

Bob Dalgren took over. His voice was official, emotionless. "Richard, we've asked you here to clear up this nasty business before the press has a chance to turn it into a circus. I've informed these men it would be better if you came in rather than Adrienne. I also told them you'd cooperate fully, that it would be in your best interests to clear up this matter as quickly as possible, and that you wouldn't attempt to impede the progress of this case by hiding behind any of the Articles of the Constitution. You're not under arrest, and you've come here of your own volition."

Skinner pulled out a chair and gestured for him to sit. Richard dropped into it and tried to ignore the heavy thumping in his head. "I'd like to know what's happened first," he said in a shaky voice.

Skinner nodded. "First of all, Mr. Warden, we appreciate your coming in. Especially considering the other vital problems presently facing you and your family."

"*Other* vital problems?"

"We understand family grief. That nasty business with your son and Thomas Cravell."

Richard said nothing. He was ashamed to admit that his son's senseless murder had somehow vanished from the picture. When your life takes a sudden, inexplicable downward plunge, remembering only one catastrophe at a time becomes a clumsy way of keeping your sanity.

"We understand how difficult this is, happening so close to your other family tragedy. We don't like what happened here, and we're all very eager to get this cleared up as soon as possible."

Richard squirmed on the hard wooden seat. He desperately wanted a strong drink. "Just tell me what the hell is going on and why I'm implicated in this suicide."

"We don't think it was a suicide." Skinner pulled his hands out of his pockets and sat on the edge of the table. "We questioned two people working at the motel where Cassidy was found. Apparently a woman paid for the room. We think she might have been a hooker."

"Cassidy was with a *hooker* when he was seeing my little girl?" He could feel his blood pressure rising steadily.

"Richard..." Dalgren put a hand on Richard's arm. Richard pulled away.

"He got the hooker and the room for the afternoon," Skinner said. "Then he took a thirty-eight hollow-point slug less than an hour later."

"That makes no sense," Richard said, trying to keep his anger on low boil.

"Suicides don't work this way. They get the room, have a few, then wallow in their own self-pity for a while. Gives them the courage to bite the big one. This boy went there with the hooker, got his rocks off without removing his pants, then bit the big one."

"*Without* removing his pants?"

"Exactly."

"Doesn't work, does it?"

"Not at all."

"Are you sure the woman was a hooker?"

212

"The description sounded like one. A high-class, expensive one. Lots of hair, tight-fitting outfit, heavy perfume."

"Why would he get the hooker if he was just going to wet his pants?"

Bronson shrugged. "At first we thought maybe he wanted to have a little fun before he cashed in his chips but got too excited when the woman took him into the room."

"And now?"

Bronson said nothing.

"What makes you tie this in with Adrienne and me?"

"Suicide note." Bronson pulled out a piece of white paper from a folder and handed it to Richard. "This is a copy. Original's at the lab, being tested."

"For handwriting?"

"Prints. Note was typed."

Richard began reading. Its contents made the hair stand up at the base of his neck.

Mrs. Warden,

I can't go on with this charade anymore. I don't want to stay away any longer. I don't think I'll ever be able to be with another woman ever again. Kate's a terrific girl. When we're together, I think of how wonderful it would be to share my future with her.

You're the best friend Kate could ever have. And even though you talked to your husband and tried to convince him that I have only Kate's best interests at heart, I realize how impossible this situation is.

213

I know I must go on, but I can't. Life is too complicated. I realize I'm not from the same circle as the rest of you, but I still think I could have made Kate truly happy. And although I love her very much, I can't have this much love in my heart without being able to share—

Richard slammed the paper onto the tabletop. The secretary flinched. Bob Dalgren turned pale. The detectives looked grimly at one another.

"This is bullshit. I don't believe a fucking word of it."

Skinner leaned forward. "You're saying your wife never tried talking to you about the situation with Cassidy?"

"My wife didn't even *like* the asshole. I even remember her telling me she was gonna talk to Katie about him, hopefully get the girl to come to her senses."

"Why's that?" asked Bronson.

Richard ran a hand briskly through his hair. "Cassidy had ulterior motives."

"Like what?" Skinner asked.

"We think he was after our money."

The detectives exchanged a long, solemn look.

"Now what's *that* for?" Richard asked.

Skinner sat back down on the edge of the table and crossed his arms over his chest. His angular face had wrinkled up. "You've just substantiated something for us."

"Substantiated what?"

"The fact that Kevin Cassidy was after your money."

214

Richard silently cursed himself for having a big mouth.

Dalgren said, "Richard, I think you and I need to talk this over."

"What the hell for? I'm guiltless here, dammit."

Skinner pushed the piece of paper toward him. "You didn't finish reading the note, did you?"

"I read enough." He didn't want to give them the satisfaction. It was bad enough they were accusing him of something disgusting. Why should he add to their amusement?

"I suggest you finish reading, sir." Skinner nodded. "You are mentioned very strongly in the next-to-the-last paragraph."

His head spinning, Richard picked up the note.

...I can't have this much love in my heart without being able to share it with such a terrific lady like your daughter. But I know this can never be, since your husband has already threatened me with death if I don't stay away.

I can't go on, and I hope you, and especially Kate, don't hate me for what I'm about to do. But living a life without Kate is like death anyway. What's the difference between being dead and living a dead, useless life? I only hope you and Kate will find it in your heart one day to forgive me.

Kevin

He let the paper drop gently to the table. His tongue filled his mouth. Cold sweat beaded his broad forehead. *What the fuck is happening here?*

He'd talked a number of times to Adrienne about Cassidy. He didn't like how the boy always avoided his eyes in their presence. He'd told Kevin how much his daughter meant to him, that Katie was the one thing he was most proud of, and that he was going to make sure whoever married her did it for the right reasons. He'd told Cassidy that he was on the alert for gold-diggers, and that Katie, being the sweet, naïve thing she was, would always be vulnerable.

Now he was racking his brain to remember if he'd ever threatened the boy. If anything he'd ever said could be misinterpreted. If the boy had misunderstood his message and, in a demented state, turned it completely around.

"No!" He slammed his fist down. Once again the secretary jerked in her seat. "I *never* threatened that boy – *ever!*"

The vertical line between Skinner's brows disappeared. "Who else would know about this?"

"I have no idea." He loosened his tie. None of this made any sense. He felt trapped in some crazy dream.

Bob Dalgren rested a gentle hand on Richard's shoulder. "Are you telling us the truth, Richard?"

Richard couldn't believe Dalgren would even ask him such a thing. He shot the attorney a dark, scorching look. "Of *course* it's the truth, dammit. Why the hell would I lie about any of this? The whole thing is so damned incredible!"

Skinner sighed. His eyes were no longer kind when he spoke. "We believe you're lying, Mr. Warden. We're now reasonably certain you're the one with the strongest motive here. The woman who checked in at the motel room. The hooker. We have a false name, but we have a very good description. Black hair, hazel eyes, very good figure. Between twenty-five and thirty years old. Very attractive. She put down a license number on the room registration form that puzzled us until we fed it into our databanks."

Skinner's eyes had become black coals. "The license matches the plate number on one of your own cars, Mr. Warden. And the suspect vehicle, a red Mercedes CL600, is one of three cars parked in one of your private spaces in the garage across the street from WarCo offices in downtown Orlando."

CHAPTER 17

Monday, the Third Week

"Tell me the truth, Richard."

The tone of Bob Dalgren's deceptively soft voice was harsh. "Otherwise, you're gonna fry for this, and there won't be a damned thing I can do to help you."

They sat in Richard's WarCo office overlooking the city of Orlando. At nine in the morning, the Florida sun was already bright and powerful. But the beautiful, sunshine-filled morning could not lift the dark, suffocating hood covering him.

He couldn't get the police description of Cassidy's hooker out of his head. Black hair. Hazel eyes. Twenty-five to thirty years old. Attractive. Good figure. Someone Cassidy had picked up at some bar on the way over to the motel room? Or had she picked him up?

Why in heaven's name would Cassidy want a hooker in the first place? And why on a *Sunday*, of all days? He was dating Katie – why would he want to jeopardize their relationship? And why take the hooker to a motel room, then eat a .38 slug? What exactly was the woman's part in this? Why would she pay for the room?

Last of all, why would Cassidy implicate him in a suicide note?

At the wet bar, Richard coaxed two inches of strong Napoleon brandy into a glass. Despite Dalgren's frown, Richard raised the glass and let a portion of the warm, potent stuff ignite a pleasant little fire in his aching gut. He lowered the glass and looked his friend in the eye. "If I knew anything else about all this, I'd certainly tell you."

"The only reason your ass isn't in jail is because of all the strings I had to pull to keep you out of it."

Jail. That awful word again. It had been three years since he'd heard it. Strange, how quickly those three years had passed...

"Did you kill the boy?" The attorney's face had become as impassive as a stone wall.

Richard's head throbbed. "Of course not."

"Did you have it done?"

"Why would I do *that*?"

"Because you didn't want him around Katie."

Richard flung up an arm and nearly spilled the brandy. "But why should I kill the boy? Don't you think I could've bought him off? Like I said back at Police Headquarters, Cassidy wanted money. I could see it in his eyes. Why would I kill him when maybe five or ten grand would keep him away?"

"Is that *all* it would've taken? Five grand? Ten? Or was the boy thinking more like six or even seven figures?"

Richard sighed. "Cassidy was small-time. Ten grand would've done the job."

"But that never came up. Or *did* it?"

"I talked to the boy once. Hell, Katie was even present. Ask her if you don't believe me. And that one time actually turned out rather pleasant. Adrienne was in the next room. Ask *her*."

Dalgren's expression remained impassive.

Richard couldn't believe his own friend was pulling away from him. This was incredible. He'd known Dalgren nearly twenty-five years. How could the attorney think for a moment that Richard would dig into his pockets to have a stupid kid removed permanently from the face of the earth?

"The cops didn't think Cassidy typed the note in the first place," he told Dalgren. "The prints on the paper were his but looked like they'd been forced onto the paper."

"Which brings us to the next question."

Richard waited.

"Who *did* type the note?"

"Damn if I know."

"You know absolutely nothing about this mess."

"I've already said that."

Bob Dalgren rubbed the back of his neck. "Who was the hooker, Richard?"

Richard slumped in his chair. Skinner's description had been bugging him ever since he'd come home. *Black hair. Hazel eyes. Good figure. Attractive. Twenty-five to thirty years old.*

Thousands of them were parading around. Hell, they were everywhere. Females with good bodies, lots of hair, perfect tits, and great smiles. Go to the beaches, public pools, motels, tourist traps. Turn on the TV. Surf the channels. Watch any commercial. They were everywhere ... young babes with beautiful tits and hair and thick, pouty lips. Over the last couple of decades, they'd become the norm. Gorgeous chicks abounded all over the continent – not only on TV and movies, but in pawn shops, movie theaters, drugstores, restaurants, doctors' offices, veterinary offices, specialty shops and supermarkets. Hot babes could be seen at local shoe stores, stocking shelves, or working behind the counter.

However, something about all this was very, very wrong...

The big question remained. Why had every single aspect of his life gone down the crapper since he'd met Brittany Weber?

He finished his drink. "Bob, something's bugging me about all this, but if I tell you what it is, you'll think I've lost my nut."

"Try me anyway."

"I strongly suspect the woman behind all this is Brittany Weber."

Dalgren sat up. "The same woman you told me about the other day? The redhead with the abusive husband?"

"The one and only."

"Have any idea how she ties in? You are saying you think she might be the one who took Cassidy to the motel?"

"I'm not sure."

"Then what *are* you saying?"

Richard tried piecing together something that would in some way sound coherent. But even though certain things were nagging at him, they just didn't click. "I wish I knew."

221

"Tell me about her again. Everything. Start at the beginning."

Richard told him the whole story. Everything he could recall.

"I remember why you hired Cravell to follow her," Dalgren said later. "I also remember how weird it seemed, Cravell and your son killing one another only days later, behind the Stonehenge. Didn't it seem strange to you?"

Richard nodded.

"My God." Dalgren's face turned pale. "Now Cassidy turns up dead. Don't you know how this looks?"

"It's starting to smell really foul."

Dalgren got up and began pacing. "First of all, you meet a beautiful woman and want to have an affair with her."

"It never got off the ground."

"Because of her vanishing acts?"

"It certainly had nothing to do with me. I met her whenever she wanted, wherever she wanted. I was more than ready for action. I never felt more helpless in my life. It was like I'd gone back to high school, for God's sake."

"Keep going. We might get lucky with this."

Richard glared. "You're sounding like you might be enjoying this, Bob."

"I'm just trying to open it up so we can actually see what it is."

Richard put down his glass and sighed. Dalgren was right. This had to be done. The only way was to put it beneath the magnifying glass and explore

222

every detail, no matter how miniscule or insignificant it seemed.

"I tried having an affair with this woman. I couldn't help it. She's gorgeous. I lusted after her, but she disappeared because of that damned ex-husband no one else ever saw. She called me one night and set up a date at the Stonehenge. I met her there and we had one drink."

"Just one?"

"She got upset when we started talking about her ex. She spilled her drink on her dress, jumped up, and ran to the ladies' room to clean up. She later told me her ex was in the lobby and followed her into the john, then threatened her." The heat had already begun climbing up his back. "I sat in the bar with my thumb up my ass, waiting for her to come back. When she didn't, I got drunk." The heat made him shake. He managed to control it, but the darkness quickly returned, as well as the smothering blanket.

"Richard?"

Stay with this. It has to be done. He took a deep breath. The blanket fell away, and the darkness gradually cleared. You're almost there. "A little later, some people came in talking about a double shooting across the street. I was still drinking, of course. I was drinking because that's what I do, and no one can possibly do it better than me–"

"Richard, stay with me."

Focus. "Anyway, I was drinking because I was pissed off. And hurt. And humiliated. Brittany hadn't come back. She wouldn't because that's

223

what she does, and she does it really well. She's an expert at it–"

"Richard..."

"I kept lifting my elbow. I was pissed ... and horny ... and hurt. I was about to be stood up again. I knew it, but that was all I cared about, even though my son was less than a hundred yards away ... lying dead in the wet grass ... his face ... blown off ... and all I ... all I cared about ... all I fucking cared about was getting laid!"

For the first time in three years, Richard Warden burst into tears.

***

Later, after Bob Dalgren had brought him a washcloth and a box of tissues from the bathroom behind the wet bar, Richard sat in front of the tinted window, feeling just as lost and pointless as the insignificant slivers of clouds floating around in the deep blue skyline.

Dalgren sat facing him. "What was your son doing out there?"

"You already know. He was with a woman."

"Anyone else see her?"

"Police have all that."

"They questioned a dozen employees at the Kingston, who all said the same thing – a knockout blonde with nice clothes."

Something tugged at Richard. He turned away from the window. "Kind of hard to ignore someone who looks like that, huh?"

"Exactly."

"No matter where she goes, people will notice her."

224

Dalgren shrugged. "Then what was she doing while Nick and Cravell were outside, gunning one another down?"

Richard stared at his friend. The significance of all this hadn't registered before now. "Apparently she disappeared."

"No one saw her after the shootings?"

"That's how it looks."

"So ... she met Nick at the Kingston or went there with him. Then, for some strange reason, Nick left her, walked outside, crossed the street, and engaged in a shooting contest with a private eye working for you."

The phone rang. Dalgren answered it. He listened for about ten seconds before he gawked at Richard. Then he spoke softly into the phone. "Who the hell let them in the house?"

Richard noticed the blood draining from his friend's face. "What is it?"

Dalgren raised his voice. "Get the security guard to lock the damned gate until we get there."

"Bob?" Richard's pulse hammered. "Tell me what's happening."

Dalgren pocked his phone and jumped up. "We've got to get back to the house. News of Cassidy's death leaked to the press, and they rushed to your place before anyone could stop them."

"Shit." Richard turned beet-red. "Adrienne and Katie ... they *know*?"

"I'm afraid so."

***

Two patrol cars blocked the front entrance of the Warden estate.

The uniforms waved Bob Dalgren and Richard through, resuming their posts when Richard's black Cadillac and Dalgren's Ferrari roared up the paved drive.

The house was like a tomb. The shades were pulled, the blinds closed. No lights shone. Renata was busily dusting the living room furniture when Richard and Dalgren rushed into the house. She didn't look up when Richard approached her.

"Where's everyone, Renata?"

She used her feather duster to point toward the hall staircase.

"Both Katie and Mrs. Warden?"

"*Si*. They cry."

Richard's heart skipped a beat. *This is great. Just great*. He swallowed the lump in his throat and turned to Dalgren. "I'd better ... check on Katie first." Katie would most likely give him the benefit of the doubt. He'd need such reassurance before he saw Adrienne.

He plodded up the stairs in the manner of a man approaching the gallows. His daughter's quiet sobbing could be heard as he approached the door. His heart thrashed. *Oh, for a drink...* His arm weighed a ton. *It's just fear – nothing else. Rise above it. Think high-class*.

He tapped lightly and eased open the door. "Can I come in, baby?"

Gazing out the rear window, Katie sobbed quietly from her armchair. She sat with her legs pulled up, her slender arms wrapped tightly around herself. Keeping in what little composure she had left, no doubt.

226

He closed the door, crossed the room, and sat on the edge of the bed. A hot revulsion formed in his gut. He'd done this. He'd inadvertently reached inside this sweet little girl's delicate bosom and pulled out her tender, loving heart.

"Katie."

She turned slowly. Her big brown eyes glistened with tears. Her cheeks were streaked. The little makeup she wore had mixed with the tears, streaking both cheeks with jagged brown trails. "Daddy?" Her voice had become the broken whimper of a small child. "How *could* you?"

My God. She believes them...

"How could you ... have done ... what they say?"

"Listen, honey." He reached out for her. She pulled away. It was like a slap in the face. His daughter had never rejected him before. He wanted to scream. "Katie, I want you to tell me what you heard. What the reporters said."

She took a deep breath. "They said ... they said Kevin ... killed himself. He left a note. It said you and Mom–"

"Listen, baby. I don't know how or where they got their information, but someone at the police department obviously has a big mouth and messed up their facts. Or maybe the reporters did this – I don't know. All I know is, someone's trying to make a mess of our lives and–"

"*Why*, Daddy? Why would someone *do* such a thing?"

"I've told you what a man in my position goes through. How people envy power and success. My

227

competitors – even my allies – will stop at nothing to take as much from me as they can. They start up rumors, spread vicious lies, manipulate people. They'll do everything they can to make me stumble or fall."

"But Daddy..." Confusion covered her face. "Kevin's dead. I know you and Mom didn't really like him. I could tell. But you didn't – you couldn't–"

"Baby, I would never have done anything to hurt your boyfriend. You know that." He'd once considered hiring Cassidy just so he could send him to the California offices and get him away from Katie. He'd even wanted to bribe one of the Singapore reps to take on Cassidy at War-Met. At the time, he thought he was doing the right thing. Now? Even though he was convinced someone had set him up, he still wanted to purge his guts.

"Did Kevin ... did he *really* kill himself, Daddy?"

Now was not the time to tell his daughter what the police had determined.

"We don't know, baby. Not yet."

Katie sniffed. "I honestly don't think he did. Kevin didn't let things bother him. He was always laughing, joking around."

"The case is still open. The police will eventually find out what happened."

"What those reporters said ... it's true, isn't it? I mean, about Kevin's note saying you and Mom didn't like him?"

228

He placed a hand on her bare arm. It was very warm. "Yes. I'm afraid some of what they said was true."

"Then ... what *wasn't* true, Daddy? Tell me what they screwed up."

He thought it over carefully. The difficult part had come. He knew to tread lightly. He didn't want to hurt his daughter any more than she already was. "I think ... someone else did this and wants me to be blamed for it." He shrugged. "It's the only thing that explains all this."

Her eyes grew. "Who ... would *do* such a terrible thing?"

Although he wasn't absolutely sure, it seemed highly possible that one of his enemies had paid some resourceful, highly intelligent female to orchestrate this elaborate scheme. But he couldn't reveal this to his daughter. It wouldn't help to tell Katie her father was being manipulated sexually by a woman hired by a competitor or enemy. "Someone with a grudge against me."

"But going by what you just told me, it could be one of many people."

"That's right."

"Then ... how will you know who it is?"

"I won't. Not until I make a list and narrow it down."

"Won't that take ... quite a while?"

He nearly smiled. Katie couldn't possibly realize how cruel her question sounded. "What other options do I have?"

She thought it over. She appeared so young and innocent. He suddenly saw her as she'd been when

229

he'd held in his arms on their way from the hospital, just twenty short years ago. "Daddy? Why didn't you and Mom like Kevin?"

It was time for a little finesse, to come up with something that wouldn't hurt her feelings. "Baby, your mother and I are particular about the boys who come around. This has nothing to do with Kevin. If you remember, we've given all your boyfriends a rough time."

Katie smiled. "I remember."

"We're just being protective. All parents react the same way."

Katie abruptly turned back to the bedroom window. "I ... said some things to Mom when the reporters left. Awful things."

"Why, baby?"

She shrugged. "Maybe it's because I've always been jealous of her. I mean, she's prettier than me, and everyone knows it. I guess I was so upset with the reporters, I just lashed out at her."

"Katie, you're a very pretty girl."

"Remember that Cuban gardener we used a while back? I don't know if she told you, but he was always watching her. Especially when she went outside for a swim. I spent a lot of time out there, too, but he was only interested in Mom."

"Good thing he didn't bother you. Otherwise, I would've decked him. What happened?"

"You know Mom. She keeps everything to herself. But when I asked her why the gardener liked her instead of me, she just gave me one of her dark looks and left the room. She fired Miguel the next day."

Adrienne had told him the man was incompetent. It was so like Adrienne, quietly firing a domestic for interfering with the natural order of things. "Your mother's a good woman, baby. Never forget that."

"What are you gonna tell her, Daddy?"

He sat forward and rubbed his temples. Once again, everything had turned dark and cold. "I wish I knew."

***

Dressed in her red silk bathrobe, Adrienne slouched on the edge of the bed.

Her hair was damp and matted. She'd obviously taken a shower but hadn't bothered to dry her hair. She seemed to be gazing at the rear window, but Richard suspected she wasn't looking at anything in particular. The half-empty glass in her lap told him she'd been hit hard. Adrienne seldom drank.

"Ade?" He edged slowly toward her. "This is all a huge, horrible mistake."

She raised the glass and finished her drink. She didn't reply or acknowledge his presence.

"Someone's doing a number on us."

Still no reply. This wasn't going well at all.

"I'm pretty sure one of my competitors—"

"I'm getting a divorce." It was said flatly, without any trace of emotion.

"Ade, please. Let's talk this out first."

She slammed the glass down onto the marble surface of the night table and stood. She trembled slightly, but he could tell she was keeping it under control. "I've had it, Richard."

231

"It isn't my fault."

She shot by, heading for the bathroom.

"How could you even think I'd actually kill a boy just because I didn't like him?"

She spun around and stood defiantly, fists on hips. Her eyes smoldered. "You think it's because of *that*?"

"What *is* it, then?"

"It's your loathsome habit of going after anything in a skirt. Your wheeling and dealing. That disgusting power thing. Your lying to your friends, your associates, the kids, me – everybody. I'm tired of standing in the shadows, supporting you. Watching what I say. Being diplomatic until I want to scream." Her eyes continued to smolder. "But most of all, it's Nicky, God rest his soul. Nicky, my one and only son." Her eyes glistened. "Why is he dead, Richard? Why haven't we talked about this? Since the funeral, you've barricaded yourself in your den. We haven't spoken since ... since that day..."

"I thought it best to give you and Katie your space."

"Our *space*!" Her laugh sounded like a grunt. "We're a *family*, Richard. Hasn't that highly developed corporate brain been able to recognize something as basic as a *family*? Even after three decades? A family shares its grief. When a member dies, the brood gathers together. It doesn't shuffle off by itself to drown itself in drink."

"I ... wouldn't have been ... very good company," he said softly.

"He was our son, Richard. Our *son*!"

He couldn't speak.

"Why was our son murdered by ... by your friend?"

Damnation. Adrienne was blaming him for Nick's death. She'd seen Cravell only once. He'd been to the house briefly. But how could she think her own husband would be instrumental in their boy's murder?

"Adrienne." His throat had suddenly become constricted. "You don't think that ... that ... you honestly don't think I had Cravell *kill* Nick?"

Her silence, coupled with the quiet trembling, told him the worst.

He took a cautious step in her direction. "Nick was my son, too. My blood. I loved the boy. Why would you think–"

"You and your fucking corporantics." It came out flatly. For Adrienne, it was the only statement necessary. She'd used the made-up word before, referring to his wheeling and dealing, his manipulations, the methods by which employees were steered and guided, and enemies punished.

He'd never enjoyed operating this way, but it was the only game in town, and he'd learned to excel at it. It was true that, in his long corporate career, he'd been just as ruthless as anyone. But unlike many of his competitors, he'd never actually done anything really despicable. Nothing horrible enough to keep him awake nights. Except for that one unexpected nightmare.

He tried eliminating it from his mind, but it refused to stay buried. During the past two weeks, it had become more and more unburied. He couldn't help thinking how someone had been deliberately stirring the pot, bringing every sick, disgusting detail of it to the surface of his consciousness.

"Nothing to say, Richard?"

"I swear to you I had nothing to do with–"

Her laugh, cold and bitter, chilled him. "You can actually swear to me at this stage of the game?" She shook her head. "Don't screw around on me all these years and then try the Boy Scout approach. It doesn't suit you."

Using sheer willpower, he forced his anger back into the darkness. Sure, she was dead-on about a lot of things, but when it came to this, she couldn't be more wrong. "Nick's death was not of my design. I didn't even know he was out there in the first place. And I sure as hell have no idea what he was doing–"

"He was with a *woman*. Being his father's *son*. *That's* what he was doing."

"But how can you blame *me*?"

Her eyes blazed. "As much as I loved our son, I also hated him. I blame you for the hatred, just as I blame you for everything else. He was, after all, formed in his father's image. He favored you, learned the things you wanted him to learn, then did the things you wanted him to. He was bright and hungry. You gave him his own company and started him so close to the top, he had just as many enemies as you do the day he started at Directron. And there he was – a carbon copy of Richard Warden. The divine clone. In five more years, he would've owned Directron, and there would've been two of

234

you out there, wheeling and dealing and screwing and drinking."

Adrienne forced out another laugh. "Isn't that so wonderfully, predictably American? Another Joseph Kennedy family saga."

He couldn't speak. The words had hurt deeply. He'd obviously had no idea of the actual depth of her hatred for him.

"Nick ... wanted success," he said softly.

"He wanted it because of you."

"And because of that, you blame me for his death?"

"That and other things. The fact that he was murdered by one of your associates. He'd still be alive and well if he hadn't been at that hotel with that hooker." She moved sluggishly to the night table and poured another drink from the bottle beside the glass. She suddenly looked exhausted. "I'm only glad – if that's the proper word – that my beautiful son died before he could become even more like you. I'm glad he couldn't pull what you managed three years ago." She raised the glass.

"That's not fair." A jab of heat singed the back of his neck.

"What's fair, Richard? Losing your son in a gunfight? Or to a drunk driver?"

"That's enough!"

Adrienne regarded him curiously. A hint of triumph glistened in her eyes.

"I don't have to stand here and listen to this," he said softly.

"Then get out of my bedroom." She made another move for the bathroom. Then she stopped,

235

turned, and shot him another chilling look. "Like I said, I want a divorce. But I'll be kind – I won't use Bob. I've decided to use my father's attorney, Benny Hollander." She forced out a smile. "That way, Bob won't have to worry about split loyalties while you're getting soaked."

She didn't know what she was saying. She couldn't. It was the grief. The sorrow. She had to come to her senses. "Adrienne, we need to talk about this."

"Nothing to talk about. I've had it. I can't go through this again."

"I told you I had nothing to do with Cassidy's death. Or Nick's. I'm being set up!"

"Richard, I married you because I loved you. You married me because you needed someone to fuck whenever it was convenient. We had Nick, then Katie. Then, between your infernal bed-hopping and your daily corporantics, you never had time for me again. I put up with it for the children. After a while, it didn't hurt anymore."

"I just think we should–"

"I had a talk with Benny earlier today. He told me I could get hold of much of your projected wealth if I could prove infidelity. I told him that would be no problem at all. Just four years ago, I hired a professional to follow you around for two weeks."

He couldn't speak. He was stunned.

She laughed bitterly. "That's all it took. Two weeks, and I have dozens of photos of you entertaining three different women at restaurants and motels. Isn't that simply hilarious?"

236

The chills oozed slowly down his spine.

"I was ready to leave right then, of course, but just a few months later, you upset everything by going to that Tampa convention and pulling your stupid, nasty stunt–"

"Enough!" He sat down heavily on the cedar chest and massaged his aching temples.

"For me too, Richard."

"Adrienne..." The words stuck in his throat. "I ... need you to ... to stick by me. Please..."

"I've stuck by you for thirty years. That mess in Tampa nearly killed me. Like I said, I was on my way out the door when that happened. Bob managed to sweet-talk me into coming back and sticking by you. He wanted me with you. It looked good for the stockholders. The competitors. The press."

"I ... didn't know..."

She sighed. "As much as I love Bob, he is a replica of you. Not once did he ask how *I* felt about that horrible mess."

"I'm ... really sorry..." Why hadn't Dalgren told him? It made him wonder what else the attorney had kept from him.

"Nicky's death nearly killed me, too." Adrienne wiped away a tear. "I cry for no reason. I don't sleep. I don't eat. I'm on three different medications. I'm a mess, and quite frankly, I no longer care if I live or die."

He wanted to say something but knew how pointless mere words would be. Nothing would fix any of this.

"Tonight, I'm going to get good and drunk. Tomorrow I'm going to deal with the hangover. I'm moving out Wednesday. I'll be at the folks' place for a while. But I promise I'll be back here shortly, watching you pack. I intend to take this place from you."

"Adrienne..."

She disappeared in the john. The door slammed shut.

"Adrienne!"

The sound of her weeping drifted softly from the room.

***

Later that day, Bob Dalgren came back from OPD Headquarters to share the latest on the investigation.

"Apparently, the lab found alcohol and traces of ketamine in Cassidy's bloodstream," Dalgren said, coming into the study and heading straight for the coffeemaker on the credenza near the French doors.

"Ketamine?" Richard sipped his bloody Mary. He wasn't familiar with the drug.

"Ketamine hcl. It's a horse tranquilizer. It was the most commonly used anesthetic in the Vietnam War."

"What else is it called?"

"It has several street names – Special K, Super C, Super Acid, Baby Food, Jet, Honey Oil, and many others. The chemical was common with the RAVE party crowd a few years ago, but it still seems to be circulating."

"Why?"

"It's easy to buy and goes hand in hand with the date rape drug GHB, and Ecstasy. Since Cassidy

238

was a college student and had apparently been to one or two RAVE parties within the last six months, police think he might have taken the drug himself."

"Anything more on the suicide note?"

"It was covered with Cassidy's prints, but judging from the pattern, it looked like someone had made the boy handle the paper after he was dead."

"How about the gun?"

"Saturday night special, most probably. The serial numbers were filed off. You can buy those all day at most pawnshops. The only prints on the gun and on the bullet casings belonged to Cassidy."

Judging by what Skinner had said, the mysterious brunette wouldn't even be mentioned in the event of a trial. Skinner, Bronson, and two other detectives conducted an extensive investigation, but came up empty. Dalgren said that unless they came up with something tangible, any mention of a 'mysterious woman' would be thrown out.

However, Dalgren's hunch about the CL600 paid off. Just a few phone calls convinced Skinner and Bronson that Richard's car hadn't left its parking space during the specified time. The fact that the plate could've been removed from the car, attached to a different car of the same make and year, then returned after Cassidy's murder, proved a definite possibility.

An attendant working the eight-to-eight shift told police the switching could easily be done. Attendants were always present during the day-shift hours, but their rounds were staggered. The cameras in the garage were stationary, covering the elevator areas, breezeways, and exits. Richard's black

Cadillac was parked behind a concrete pillar. Parking across the aisle near the elevators, ducking around the pillar, then switching the plate, would not be difficult.

"Someone's definitely trying their best to bring me down," Richard said. "I can't do a damned thing because I have no idea who's doing it."

"Then we'll just have to find out who is behind it, won't we?"

"Just like that?"

"We've got to take this one down to the wire." Dalgren drank more coffee. "We need to go back five, maybe even seven years, putting together everything we know about your enemies. The way it looks, someone in your past has gone to a lot of trouble to put a kink in the works. Someone with a serious grudge."

Richard picked up his bloody Mary and downed it. "Do you have any idea how many people I've had to squash during the last seven years?"

"Knowing what I do about you and your business dealings, that number must be staggering."

"Why settle on seven? Why not ten? Or fifteen?"

"Someone who's been given the shaft isn't going to wait very long to return the gesture. I don't think anyone is patient enough to wait longer than just a few years to get their revenge. If you'd screwed someone really bad, they'd have blown your head off by now."

He didn't like his friend's matter-of-fact tone. "Thanks very much for the vote of confidence."

Dalgren shrugged. "People are crazy nowadays. Their priorities are out of whack. This materialistic society of ours has been going down the tubes the last few decades. Folks will spend twenty-five, thirty thousand dollars or more for a car they'll keep for a year or two, then run it into the ground. Nearly a mill for a house, a grand for a TV, a hundred for a good meal for two. Even if gasoline reaches a hundred bucks a gallon, you'll never catch your average American observing the speed limit."

"You're right. Money means nothing anymore."

"Actually, people don't seem to care about anything. Watch the eleven o'clock news. You'll see drive-bys, muggings, car-jackings, kidnappings, incest, mutilations. Women are murdering their husbands for as little as five thousand dollars in insurance money. Newborns are being tossed into dumpsters and public toilets because their mothers simply don't want them. Pets are being starved, burned alive, or tossed out of moving vehicles. Times have changed, Richard. You know that."

Richard stared at his empty glass. His friend was right. People were going stark raving mad over nothing, and here he was, someone who'd humiliated and destroyed people most of his adult life, wondering who would do such terrible things to him. "You're absolutely right. There's a psycho out there."

"And we've got to find him before Cassidy's investigation poses a threat. There's also the issue of Nick and Cravell to think about. The cops have already started calling me on that one. I won't be

241

able to keep them away from you or Adrienne much longer."

"How close are they in the Cassidy investigation?"

"Other than what I've told you, they don't have much – which is bad. We'd better give them something tangible real soon. Otherwise, I'm going to have to find some other legal way of keeping you out of jail."

"What do you mean by 'real soon'?"

"I think we'd better have something by Friday, at the latest."

He couldn't be serious. "This is Monday. Isn't that rushing things just a bit?"

Dalgren sighed, then nodded.

Richard didn't like his friend's somber expression. "Do you honestly think we can find something out by Friday?"

"Doesn't matter. We don't have much of a choice."

CHAPTER 18

Tuesday, the Third Week

Richard Warden arranged to talk with Lou Berchfeld early that morning.

Richard decided to confide in his old friend for several reasons. He wanted Berchfeld to know what was happening to him and his family. He also wanted to find out if Lou had any idea who might be angry enough to go on a revenge campaign. Berchfeld was a trusted executive. WarCo employees opened up to him.

Berchfeld came in and sat right down. His normally genial expression was tense. Something was obviously troubling him. "We don't need this," he said right off. "It's taken the corporation much effort to get the stock back up during the last three years."

The old fart could be such a pain. Richard had lured him away from IBM fifteen years ago with a delicious seven-digit offer, with more than a quarter of a million shares of stock. Berchfeld didn't like complications – especially when they threatened the status quo.

"I know all about that, thank you." Richard didn't need yet another reminder of that mess. "I've paid for it, believe me."

"Agreed." Berchfeld fidgeted, making crunching sounds on the seat as his broad butt mashed down on the leather. "It's just that, well,

243

with our labor problems abroad – that mess with the robotic arms, not to mention the instability of the Dow–"

"We've had problems before. We'll weather this out."

Berchfeld continued as if he hadn't heard the interruption. "We don't need another major setback. The market has been so temperamental. The Koreans and Chinese are upsetting everyone with their progressive nuclear programs. Then there's OPEC, Iraq, and this damned terrorism scare–"

"I'm also aware of current events, thank you."

"Three years ago, WarCo practically went belly-up. It's taken all this time to get back on track. Now we're looking at your son's murder, which – I'm sure you're aware – has already affected Directron and Hubnetrics–"

"Don't forget for an instant who's been in the center of all this," Richard said edgily.

Berchfeld sighed. "Point taken."

Richard fixed a drink. He offered Berchfeld one, who declined with a scowl. Richard circled his desk and sat. "Like I said a minute ago, we've all been through hell before. You remember your IBM days, don't you? That wasn't exactly a cakewalk either, was it?"

Berchfeld stroked his chins. "With IBM, it was corporate espionage. But back then, that kind of thing was the trend. AT&T had it. So did MCI. So did the others. When that madness happened, you brought the guilty parties in, sat them down, gave them mandatory buyout packages, and made them

sign waivers in front of your corporate lawyers."
Berchfeld sighed. "But with WarCo, it's different."

"How?"

"It's ... well, it's you, Richard."

Richard blinked. *Now* what was this man
getting at?

"When the CEO of a major corporation
becomes more high-profile than the most
controversial news figure, something has gone
terribly wrong."

Richard said nothing.

Berchfeld trudged on. "I came to this company
because of your generous offer and because the
IBM nonsense was getting to me. Don't
misunderstand me – I appreciate what you've done
for me and for my career. I'm fifty-eight, have a net
worth of nearly ten million, two houses, and a
condo in Miami – all because of WarCo. What I'm
trying to say is this – I'm ready to go. That Tampa
mess almost ruined us. But my wife convinced me
to tough it out. As luck had it, the corporation
survived. I took a loss, but we all did, and since we
didn't panic, we didn't lose much but some time
and a little self-esteem."

A dark look took over the man's heavily-jowled
face. "But what's been happening lately scares me.
You've seen what's already happened with
Directron stock, haven't you?"

He'd gone into his website half an hour ago and
watched it drop from 40 to 36.7. Before Nick's
death, the stock had been 42.5 and steadily
climbing. It had been in the low forties for more
than a month and was holding steady between 42

245

and 42.8 the last two weeks. Initially Richard had wanted to attribute the sudden drop to the current instability of the world's markets. But now, after the fifth drop in just a few days, the message was clear. The stockholders were pulling out.

"Have you seen what Hubnetrics did yesterday?" Berchfeld asked.

The sister company of Directron, headed on the West Coast by a nervous fag named Donald Meeson, had quietly announced a merger. "I don't know what that asshole's doing, but I definitely need to talk to him."

"He's jumping ship." Berchfeld's voice rose in pitch. "Meeson's trying to get in with Cisco for some stability. He figures Cisco's close relationship with Rockwell International will benefit Hubnetrics." Berchfeld shrugged. "Hell, he could be right. Especially when you consider how much business Rockwell does with Cisco as far as lab work, research, and experimentation."

"He's young. He's nervous."

"He's also very bright. He knows what coming down."

"And what do you think is coming down, Lou?"

Berchfeld shrugged. "Corporate disaster. When the son of a major CEO is murdered, that makes news. But when, just days later, the boyfriend of the CEO's daughter commits suicide and implicates–"

"Don't tell me *that's* already out." This was getting worse and worse.

"In the *Sentinel* this morning."

Richard groaned.

246

"How's Adrienne taking all this?"

Richard shrugged. "You know women."

"They're human beings – just like we are. I wouldn't be surprised if Adrienne isn't considering jumping ship as well–"

"There's no call for that kind of talk." Richard wanted to wring Berchfeld's thick neck.

"Sorry. Just thinking out loud."

"Do that kind of thinking in private."

"The point I'm trying to make is this. You're gonna have your hands full. The papers, the police – not to mention your stockholders. Everyone's gonna be after you, and I don't envy your position."

"That's why you're leaving?"

"I'm a coward. I admit it. I just don't want to be anywhere close when the bullets start flying again."

"I understand."

"I'll have Peggy draft up my resignation by Friday afternoon. Effective for any time you deem fit. Suitable?"

"A little sudden. But suitable."

"One question – if I'm not out of line."

"What's that?"

"Why were you implicated in Cassidy's death?"

"I didn't approve of him."

"Why not?"

"I thought he was after the family money."

Berchfeld sat back in his seat and began chewing his lower lip. He was obviously about to make another stupid judgmental statement.

"You have daughters, Lou."

"Two. Both grown and married."

247

"Did you approve of their boyfriends?"

A snort. "Of course not."

"Did you kill *any* of them?"

Berchfeld gave him the strangest look.

***

After lunch, Richard drove to Bob Dalgren's Altamonte office.

It had taken Richard two hours to assemble his list of potential enemies. The world of a CEO was a large one, bringing him into contact with hundreds of people over the years. Discarding names of those who had died recently as well as those who had profited from their mistakes or left the country was a tedious task.

Dalgren scanned the list, which consisted of more than two dozen names. "First thing we must do is attach dates to the names. We need a time frame. Something to give us some sort of window. Then we'll need locations, of course. And it would help if everything was up to date."

"I'll need someone to research this discreetly, Bob. Someone we can trust. I can't be bothered going into old personnel files. It would take too damned long."

"We'll hire someone for this. It'll take work, but if everything goes right, we should have this list narrowed down by Friday."

Richard sank heavily in the padded chair. Friday. It was steadily turning into a major pain in the ass. The police needed something tangible by Friday. Berchfeld would have his resignation on Richard's desk by Friday. Dalgren would have the hate list narrowed down by Friday.

248

Dalgren stared at the list. "You want Al Rossenberg heading this list?"

That was a no-brainer. "That bastard was selling illegal computer time from his desk, no less. He'd bilked us out of half a million before we caught him. When I fired him, he threatened me."

"Half a million's a good motive for revenge. Especially when he could've easily made another couple of million if you hadn't caught him."

"He got off easy."

Dalgren returned to the list. "Why is Oscar Worthington near the bottom?"

Richard didn't want to get into this with Dalgren. The nasty business was over with, for one thing. It made him feel guilty, for another. "Oscar isn't the type to set out to ruin anyone."

"How can you be so sure?"

"The man's over seventy. He's an inventor. Stick him in a lab, give him the right equipment and he's happy. He doesn't even need a woman when he's got a stocked lab."

"Speaking of women... How's his wife?"

"How the hell should *I* know?"

"I hoped you could at least remember what that woman went through. It hasn't been *that* long ago."

"People have accidents all the time. You mend, you forget, you move on."

"Kind of callous."

"Life generally is."

Dalgren went back to the list. "You could be right about Oscar, but we'll still go ahead and have everyone researched. I don't want to eliminate anyone just because we *think* he's not the vengeful type. Oscar could be coming after you with the help of someone else who might be just as angry. I think it would be in our best interests to assume everyone here is capable of payback, directly or indirectly."

"You're running the show."

The attorney put the list down. "Why isn't the McDermitt woman's name here?"

"Who?"

"You've forgotten already?"

Richard sighed. *Tampa again.* "I was only thinking of former employees and competitors. She's the farthest thing from my mind."

"That's really cold, Richard."

The guilt that had tortured him earlier came back automatically. "Like I said, you move on. I have. I'm sure she has, as well."

"That's open-minded of you – as well as impractical. And to repeat my question, why isn't her name here?"

"I don't consider her much of a threat."

"Don't you think this woman would have a major axe to grind?"

"That's ancient history, Bob. I fucked up. It's that simple. I know it and so did everyone else when it happened. I was also punished for it."

Dalgren sat back and stared at him.

"Something's bugging you. Go ahead. Spit it out."

"Richard, you weren't *really* punished for that bit of work."

"How's that?"

"You were slapped on the wrist."

250

"I don't consider what I went through a mere slap."

"If anyone else had done the same thing–"

"I'm not anyone else."

"Of course you're not. Which is precisely what I'm getting at. You're a corporate CEO. A very high-profile, rich, important man–"

"I don't like your tone, Robert."

Dalgren hadn't heard him. "...who drove to a convention, picked up a hooker–"

"Bob." This was getting really old. "I paid off the woman. I paid off the courts. I paid for an expensive rehab program–"

"Which you never finished."

Richard glared at his friend. When he spoke again, his voice was barely above a whisper. "I've been walking on eggshells ever since."

"You should be walking on eggshells the rest of your life."

"What the hell are you driving at?"

Dalgren's expression was solemn. "Just this. I honestly don't think you fully appreciate the result of your actions."

"The hell I don't."

"Then if I repeat them–"

"There's no need to do that."

"Richard, your actions were what got you in the mess in the first place. Your drinking. The fact that you got behind the wheel of an automobile drunk–"

"I know all that, Bob. I was the one who did it – remember?"

"Yes, I remember. We all do, unfortunately."

251

He'd been blind drunk. Somehow, that crucial detail helped him accept the fact that he'd actually done the ghastly deed. The booze had done it. The hooker made him drink more. *She'd* done it. How could Richard Warden, father of two, have done such a horrible thing? But he had. He'd killed a little boy.

But as much as he hated himself for doing it, as much as he wanted to do away with himself for committing such an unforgivable act, he realized he had to move on. It was human nature. Life went on. In spite of its horrors.

"Yes. I did everything you just said. I'd give my entire fortune to be able to go back in time and undo it, to bring that poor little kid back from the grave ... but I can't. I've grown to accept it. I just wish other people – yourself included – would accept it as well."

"I've accepted it, Richard. Believe me."

"Then why this godawful rehash? Must you put me through this again?"

Dalgren sighed and sat back in his chair. "The McDermitt woman should be on this list. At the very top of it."

"Bob ... I paid her off..."

"Yes. You gave her five million dollars for her son's life, and for this you think the two of you should be square."

Richard bristled. Said like that, it made him feel like some sort of lowlife. But he was a lowlife, wasn't he? Anyone who runs over a helpless little kid is a lowlife. "What's really on your mind, Bob?"

"I just think we'd better find out where she is."

Richard shook his head. "I don't think she's got it in her."

Dalgren watched him closely as he took a slug of coffee. "I think Marie McDermitt is just as capable of pulling your legs out from under you as anyone else you've burned in the past. I fully understand how fragile the state of affairs can be. How one miniscule imbalance can shift everything. How one drop of water can crumble a rock. How the slightest vibration can destroy the works."

"You're talking about a skinny twenty-year-old girl of meager background, with no college degree. I don't even think she finished high school—"

"What's *that* have to do with anything?"

"Nothing, really. Just the fact that she isn't even well-educated."

Dalgren laughed. "Coming from you, that sure is rich. You more than anyone should know how powerful women are. A female with a double-digit IQ, a third-grade education, and a decent set of knockers, can have the President of the United States crawling around on his hands and knees, whimpering like a whipped puppy."

Dalgren was right. Women had the upper hand. Perhaps this was why he'd never placed them in key positions. Why he'd always harbored a deep-seated resentment for them. Why he'd never actually let them get into his mind. Why he'd always disapproved of Adrienne, no matter what she did. Why he'd gone to great lengths to dominate as many women as he could.

Women were smaller, weaker, and softer, yet they could easily drain a man of all his power. They made a man feel guilty ... and despicable. They were all whores. And they couldn't be trusted.

Brittany Weber topped them all. She'd entered his life, gave him a sample of her sweetness, a promise of her passion, then discarded him – just as he'd been doing with women all these years. And during this time, Nick was murdered, Katie's boyfriend was murdered, Katie had become a whimpering, pathetic mess, Adrienne was suing him for divorce, Directron and WarCo and Hubnetrics were sinking, Berchfeld had jumped ship–

My God. He suddenly felt weak and woozy, as if he'd just gotten off a rollercoaster. "Bob ... did you ever meet Marie McDermitt?"

"I was handling everything for you. Don't you remember?"

Richard had stayed out of sight during the proceedings. He hadn't set foot inside the courtroom—only in chambers, and only with the judge and the attorneys present. The case made the *Tribune*, *Sentinel*, and *Herald*, but Richard stayed away from the papers and refrained from seeing or reading anything about the story. He'd convinced himself it was the only way he could survive this. He'd also convinced himself that if he didn't actually see the victims, they didn't exist.

He forced himself to concentrate on more rational matters. "Describe her, Bob."

Dalgren shrugged. "Nothing special. Five-four, maybe a hundred pounds, flat-chested. Pretty face, but plain. Light brown hair, light brown eyes. Very fragile, but I'm sure that was because of what she was going through. Her mother stuck close to her during all that, but there didn't seem to be anyone else."

"No husband?"

"Wasn't married."

"The girl was living with her mother?"

"In one of the lower-income neighborhoods just a few blocks from the Convention Center."

Richard sighed. The scene with Adrienne suddenly came back in a hot fury. Her wet smoldering eyes. The hatred oozing from every pore. But most of all, the words that hadn't penetrated his thick skull until this instant. *"What's fair, Richard? Losing your son in a gunfight? Or to a drunk driver?"*

"You okay?" Dalgren asked.

"No. But I think I might be. One day."

"Maybe when this is all over, you can take some time off."

"Do me a big favor," Richard said.

"If I can."

"Check out the McDermitt girl, okay? I paid her five million for her son. At the time, I was dumb enough to think that much money would be enough."

Bob Dalgren rested his forearms on his desk blotter. The lines of irritation on the attorney's forehead had disappeared. "And now?"

Five million dollars. Would that figure help him to forget his son? Would it even begin to make things right? Would it change anything with Adrienne? With Katie? With Kevin Cassidy's family? Somehow, any amount would be a slap in the face.

255

"Pocket change," he said sourly.

***

Adam Brooks placed the brown paper bags carefully on his desktop.

He removed his windbreaker and hung it on the coat rack behind the door. The morning had started off cool but had quickly climbed nearly twenty degrees. It would probably reach the mid-eighties again – typical for this time of year. Quite comfortable, actually.

He sat, propped up his feet, and stared at the desk. One of the bags contained a pint of Wild Turkey. The other, a small bottle of V. S. Hennessy. He wanted to sample the Hennessy but decided to wait. Too many things on his mind right now. He needed a clear head.

First Warden's kid, then his daughter's boyfriend. This was getting ridiculous. It reeked of some sort of vendetta. Hard to prove, of course, but what were the odds? You're having a drink with a redhead you're about to escort into the closest hotel room while your son is behind the hotel, shooting it out with a private eye you'd just hired.

Why did you hire the private eye? To murder your son? That was a stretch, even for a ruthless businessman like Warden. The man's son was his pride and joy. His bid for immortality. The continuation of the Warden estate. The future of WarCo – of Richard Warden's name. There was no way the man would want his son dead.

And what was the deal with the daughter's boyfriend? Too much pressure from dating the daughter of a wealthy man? That was something that could be understood. He knew nothing of Cassidy but could imagine the kid showing up to pick up the daughter for a date and coming face-to-face with Richard Warden. As the kid nervously waited for the girl to make her appearance, Warden might put an arm across the boy's shoulders and whisper something like this: *You've come to collect my daughter, huh, kid? I need to give you a list of the ground rules you'll be expected to follow. First of all, you will not hurt her. You will not make her cry. You won't anger or embarrass her. You'll be the perfect gentleman and will take a bullet for her, if necessary. If you do not adhere to any of these rules, I'll make one phone call, and we won't have to worry about you bothering anyone ever again...*

Threats or not, the kid probably felt totally out of his element. He knew he'd better act proper – at least while in the presence of the girl's father. What the girl did outside the mansion was an entirely different matter. She might be a reckless slut, for all they knew. But as long as Cassidy remained in the father's sights, he knew he'd better behave himself. Like most fathers, Warden regarded his daughter as his princess. He would not permit her to be exposed to the negative aspects of society.

The phone rang. Bob Dalgren's name showed on the display. Adam was reluctant to take this. He was still coming to grips with what happened behind the Stonehenge Hotel. After much agonizing thought and logic, he felt less guilty about it, but it still bothered him, and he knew it probably always would. He finally decided to pick up. "How goes it, Robert?"

"You really don't want an answer to that," Dalgren said flatly.

"Of course not. I know better. What's up?"

"You've heard about Kevin Cassidy, no doubt?"

"The story was on the tube as well as the Sentinel. What the hell's going on with Warden?"

"How about if I just tell you what's happening to his corporation as a result?"

"Well, since stockholders have never been among the most stable people in the universe, I'd try a wild guess and say they've already started bailing."

"Right about that. However, that's the least of the man's worries."

"You're kidding."

"I wish I was. WarCo's crumbling, Directron's dropping like a rock, the cops want to nail Warden for his daughter's boyfriend's death, and his wife is about to split. And if she does, it will definitely collapse what's left of the corporation."

"How does his daughter's boyfriend's death figure into this?"

"The boy committed suicide under suspicious circumstances. And the fact that it happened at a very vulnerable time doesn't help."

"Hmm ... I guess it's safe to say the man's career just encountered a snag or two."

"You always were good at delivering the clever understatement."

"And it's also safe to say WarCo stock will soon be affordable?"

"Another understatement."

"What do you need from me?"

"You remember the drunk-driving case Warden was involved in?"

The homicide made front-page news a few years earlier. Adam had no idea what had transpired, but since the item had been killed so quickly, he assumed Warden had used his connections to pull a few heavy strings. "I remember hearing it on the news."

"The girl whose son was run over by Warden. Know anything about her?"

"Nothing."

"Name's Marie McDermitt. She'd be in her late twenties now. Think you can find her for me?"

"Tampa, wasn't it?"

"She lived with her mother. Mother's name, as I recall, is Harriet. Daughter wasn't married, but that was three years ago. Find out where she is and what she's doing."

"How long do I have?"

"Three days."

Adam gave a low whistle. "Isn't that cutting it a little close?"

"We didn't know what was happening until recently. And we're quickly running out of time. The Orlando Police are chomping at the bit. It won't be long before they bring Warden in for the collar. That Cassidy kid."

"What does McDermitt have to do with all this?"

"We're developing a list of vengeful enemies. Her name popped up."

"A hate list? For a CEO? You're kidding, right? Why not look for guys who want to nail a Hollywood bimbo? You'd have a shorter list."

"I know, I know. But I need you to look her up. All right? I'd like to get her done first. If she doesn't pan out, I'm gonna need you to look up some others."

"How many are on this list?"

"Twenty so far, but I did a scan on my own and found another dozen or so."

"And you need all this done in three days?"

"Incredible as it seems, yes."

"You surely don't expect me to–"

"I'm contracting a larger firm to handle the others. This place usually does the heavy digging for my colleagues during big cases. I'm calling them as soon as I've finished talking with you."

"Why do you want me on top of this particular girl?"

"Um, care to rephrase that?"

Adam snorted. "Sorry. I forgot I was talking to a scum puppy."

"Have some respect. I'm an attorney."

"Same thing. But why pick *me* for this?"

"You work faster than most of the other investigators I've hired. I need speed here, as well as a good nose."

"But why this girl? I would think Warden would want his business rivals scoped first. They'll obviously have more money and resources to burn up. The girl probably left the state as soon as Warden bought her off."

"I'm calling the shots on this one. I just think she would be more pissed at him than anyone else. He murdered her little boy and walked away. I don't think she'd hightail it – not with that much hatred and grief eating away inside her."

"All right. I'll get right on it."

"For this, I'm paying five K, plus expenses."

Adam nearly fell out of his chair. Five grand in three days. More than five times his usual rate. Warden obviously faced some seriously heavy fire.

"I'll keep in touch."

***

Adam immediately went online, selecting Hillsborough County first, then Manatee, and did a scan on names. When neither revealed anything useful, he moved on to Pasco, then Polk, and stopped with Lake. He found plenty of McDermitts, but none with the correct first names or initials.

The next step was to phone Bill Kloss, his friend and contact on the staff of the *Tribune*. Adam left a voicemail message, picked up the bottle of Wild Turkey, and broke the seal. A clean glass sat on the credenza behind him. Since he was working and needed to stay sharp, he poured just one inch and put the bottle in his desk drawer. He lifted the glass, coaxed the warm whiskey into his mouth, and let it slide softly down his throat.

He sat back and relaxed. Funny how a little whiskey made you feel better than all the therapy in the world.

Whiskey had helped him through the rough, dark days toward the end of his five-year marriage, during Judy's tireless campaign to convince him to

261

choose a more profitable and less dangerous career. She wanted him to become an investment broker. Her father had amassed quite a chunk of change in that field.

When her daily nagging yielded no positive results, she accused him of not wanting to provide properly for his wife. When that didn't work, she tricked him into talking to a marriage counselor. That trip turned out to be the kiss of death for their marriage. He saw no point in listening to some self-righteous bitch tell him what he should do to make his marriage work. He hadn't wanted his marriage to work in the first place. He was perfectly content to live with Judy. But after being beaten down from months of her persistent urging to make their relationship legal, he'd finally agreed to the wedding.

It made him wonder, time and time again, why he'd let her con him into doing something he really didn't want to do. That was a no-brainer. Judy was a skinny blonde with large jugs. And she was good in bed. Case closed.

As always, when thinking about his ex-wife, he wanted another drink. He decided against it. Kloss would call soon, possibly with something Adam could use to get this investigation going.

Too much booze was all right when you were home, the workday was over, and you didn't have to go back out or get behind the wheel of a car. If the day had been rough, you deserved a good mellow. If you were going through hell, a few drinks definitely helped. Otherwise, you stayed away from the bottle entirely.

Richard Warden was a prime example of not staying away from the bottle. How could a man in his position get behind the wheel of a car so totally shitfaced that he could run over a kid without even realizing it? It shouldn't have happened in the first place. Warden shouldn't have been operating the car drunk. The kid shouldn't have been crossing the street.

He wondered what kind of mother Marie McDermitt had been. The papers hadn't said much about her. Warden, with his money and connections, had put a lid on everything. But it really didn't matter what kind of mother Marie was ... or that her son didn't have much savvy about crossing the street. An important, high-profiled dickhead had unwittingly killed someone, then bought his way out of it.

The phone rang.

It was Bill Kloss. "What the hell have you got yourself into this time?"

"Lighten up. Found myself respectable employment, for a change."

Kloss chuckled. "How'd you get it? Craig's List?"

"Would you believe I used my charm?"

Kloss laughed loudly.

"My bubbling personality?"

"All right. If you're not gonna tell me the real reason ... whatta ya need?"

"The Richard Warden manslaughter case. Remember it?"

"Hell, I happened to be one of the dozen or so reporters foaming at the mouth when we were ordered off the story. We could've been on Sixty Minutes and made a million getting our autobiographies out. But the order was to kill it and forget about it."

"By whom?"

"All I know is, the big shot who owns the *Tribune* gave our boss an ultimatum. Then the shit trickled down and splattered the rest of us."

"Damned shame. It might've done a lot for more effective drunk-driving legislation."

"They've been cracking down in the past ten years or so, but it just won't work as well as they'd like. People are gonna drink and drive. And they're much too lazy and too arrogant to bring a designated driver with them when they drive to their favorite bar. It'll never actually stop unless they close down every single bar in this country. By the way, why are you asking?"

"Know what WarCo's up to these days?"

"Enlighten me."

"Richard Warden's son, high up in Directron Digitals, gets murdered. Just days later, Warden's daughter's boyfriend eats a bullet and implicates the old man."

"Wait. Now that you mention it, I do recall reading something online from the Sentinel. Something about WarCo stock taking a swan dive." Kloss clicked his keyboard. "Look at that. Ten full points since yesterday. Ouch."

"Looks like Warden's fair game."

"Love it when a big shit falls. Makes news, shows some order to the world. It also gives us job security. Where do you fall in this?"

"Warden's attorney asked me to look in on McDermitt."

"Warden think she's after him?"

"They're building a hate profile for Warden."

Kloss boomed laughter. "A hate profile? For a multi-millionaire who thinks nothing of chucking thousands of jobs with a single phone call? You're killing me."

"Dalgren wants me to check it out."

"Tell me what you need."

"Marie McDermitt. Anything you can find."

"Gimme a few minutes."

***

Bill Kloss called back ten minutes later.

"No known address. I checked with DMV, then three other sources. I went into our databanks and did a search and a scan. Nothing, until the obituaries came up."

"Keep going."

"Marie was living with her mother until early last year."

"The girl moved out?"

"All we know is that Mrs. McDermitt is now of the deceased genre, passing on the thirteenth day of June, last year."

"Shit. Do you have an address?"

"She spent her last days in Clearwater. Wanna know the particulars?"

"Definitely."

***

The Hospice of God's Children sat quietly on a sandy strip of scrub oaks and pines just a few miles outside the city of Clearwater.

Fronting Belleair Beach, it faced the Gulf and provided an excellent view of the jagged, finger-like islands extending beyond Clearwater Pass.

The huge, three-story refurbished beach house sat in a cul-de-sac peppered with scrub oaks. A barbecue grill, swings, shuffleboard court, gazebo, exercise path, and walkway littered the sloped property.

Adam was met by a large middle-aged black woman with a fabulous smile and a warm, friendly manner, who introduced herself as Jade. She took his hand in both of hers. He instantly felt as if he'd known her for years.

"Fay's in her office, Mr. Brooks–"

"Adam."

"She asked me to come and fetch you, Adam."

He followed her up the winding brick walk.

A heavyset woman dressed in white pushed an old man in a wheelchair down the brick path, toward the dock. The man coughed wetly, turned, and spat into the bushes. A skeletal woman with a shock of white wispy hair sat smoking a cigarette in the gazebo, while watching the waves splashing.

The house boasted large, spacious rooms, stucco walls, and tall ceilings. A heavy mixed scent of antiseptic, cigarette smoke, and coffee drifted through the rooms. Jade led him down the hall, past several closed doors, to a large, comfortable room facing the Gulf.

Fay Hawkins was a small delicate woman about sixty-five years old, with a permanent smile fixed to her face. The dimples in her sunken cheeks remained even when she'd stopped smiling.

266

Jade brought them pink lemonade and quietly whisked out of the room.

Adam and Fay sat side-by-side in front of the open French doors, as the late afternoon whitecaps pushed sluggishly toward shore.

"What did you want to know about Harriet? "Fay sipped her lemonade but didn't look at him. She seemed hypnotized by the approaching sunset.

"Whatever you can tell me will be great."

She turned to him. "Why are you interested? Tampa's a pretty good jaunt from Orlando. Takes about two hours, doesn't it? This must be important."

"I'm looking for Harriet's daughter Marie. You probably know her."

"I knew nothing about Marie. I saw her when she dropped off her momma. Then she vanished."

"And you never saw her again?"

"Not once. Poor Harriet. I don't think she would've died when she did if that daughter of hers had given her the time of day. Woman was barely fifty, for pity's sake. That's young. But you should've seen the poor soul. Looked well over seventy."

"What did she die from?"

"She was a heavy smoker. It started in her stomach with ulcers, then moved to her lungs. It had spread to her bones by the time she finally had it looked after. But by then it was too late. Her daughter admitted her to a cancer ward, but some things just take their natural course and—"

"Where'd Marie get the money?"

"Why, from that court case." Fay gave him a suspicious look. "You knew that."

Adam nodded. "I knew that."

"That girl went through hell, her little boy dying like that, and my heart goes out to her. But when she dumped her own momma right there at a cancer ward and gave them half a million dollars before turning tail – well, that just put her in the same class as that asshole that ran down her son. In my eyes, anyway."

"Any idea where she went?"

"Nope."

"I need to find her."

Fay blinked. "You workin' for that character that ran down her kid?"

"Someone seems to be after him."

Fay smiled.

"I take it you're not wild about the man."

Fay shrugged. "I never could hide my feelings well."

"His attorney thinks Marie might be the one putting the screws to Warden, and we need to find out if it's true."

"How much are you bein' paid for this?"

"Five thousand."

"That's a nice chunk of change."

"It'll pay my rent and electric bill. It might even put some extra food in the fridge."

From the wooden balcony, the reflection of the sunset in the sleek surface of the water exploded in a shimmering pyramid of flickering gold. A cool breeze trickled in with the tide.

Fay sat back and stared at him. "Like I said, I can't help much. I saw the girl once, and that was that. When the cancer people couldn't do anything, the girl picked up her momma, brought her here, then left. She did have a look at the room, but once she walked down that hall, we never saw her again."

That sounded unusually cold. If the girl didn't care much about her mother, would she have anything inside her that would translate as love for her little boy? Or was she just one of many people who didn't get along with her mother? Women often had strange relationships with their mothers. Adam had known several women who hated their mothers. His sister Renee even went through a three-year phase where she wouldn't talk to their mother or acknowledge her presence.

"Did Harriet talk about her?"

"She didn't say much, but you couldn't blame her, the cancer settling in and all."

"Even though you only saw Marie that one time, can you describe her?"

"Didn't make much of an impression. She wasn't much to look at – not that I'd ever say something like that to Harriet. Harriet thought she was a beauty queen. Mothers, you know."

"Yeah. I know."

Fay crossed her slender arms beneath her tiny bosom. "What do you plan to do for your attorney friend?"

"I have to find out if Marie's actually the one doing all this damage to Warden. I have no idea what I'm looking for. But finding her would be a

269

good place to start, and I'll be in a better position to go from there."

"Then what?"

"I wish I knew."

"What do *you* think of that Richard Warden character?"

He saw no reason to lie to this woman. "I can't stand wealthy, powerful men. They step on people, humiliate and destroy them, their lives, their dreams. They think nothing of wiping out a man's career, retirement, or pension, just to acquire more stock or another piece of property. Life's a game for them. They seem to have lost their grip on reality."

"We think alike, Adam."

He wanted to tell her about his sister Renee. Fay was obviously the type of person who'd understand. But he had to get back to Orlando. Bob Dalgren was counting on him, and they didn't have any time to waste. "The only reason I'm doing this is because I need the money. I realize that what I do for a living requires a certain code of ethics, and that I have to view certain things from several different perspectives. But in my opinion, Warden deserves everything he's getting."

Fay watched him as she drank more lemonade.

"Answer your question?"

Her dimples deepened when she lowered her glass. "And then some."

CHAPTER 19

Wednesday, the Third Week

Richard Warden crawled out of bed, forced his exhausted body into a pair of designer jeans and a sweatshirt, and stumbled down the stairs. After a light breakfast of dry toast, coffee, and four maximum-strength aspirins, he plodded down the hall to his den.

The phone was already ringing itself silly. *Hell with it.* He didn't want to talk to anyone this early. And he didn't care who it was. Berchfeld could go to hell. So could Jack Koslo, Ken Olson, and the rest of them. He didn't even want to talk to Bob Dalgren right now. If that was Dalgren calling, it could only be bad news. Good thing he was alone in the house. He could let the goddamned phone ring all day if he wanted to.

Adrienne had packed her clothes, jewelry, stocks and bonds, marched out the front door, and took the Porsche. There were no good-byes, no farewells. She'd already made it clear she'd return only after she'd legally reclaimed the estate.

Katie had also packed her things and moved in with some of her girlfriends in an apartment complex not far from Rollins. She'd said very little to him since his visit to her bedroom the other night. The shock of losing her brother, then her boyfriend, had been too much. She obviously felt the need to get away from her father, who was a grim reminder of what happened.

But that wasn't all of it. Stockholders had been demanding an emergency meeting for two days. They wanted to discuss the unwanted publicity of the murders. They were afraid this kind of media hype would eventually bring about a collapse of WarCo stock. The heads were anxious to hear the story from the horse's mouth so they could get with their international contacts and quell rumors that would certainly cause a breakdown in contracts, both abroad and nationally.

Nosy reporters had already run wild with the Cassidy story. Since they weren't given permission to use what was leaked from the police report, they injected their own venom to come up with enough dramatic material to keep the story hot.

Bob Dalgren, thank God, had skillfully handled the mess with Cassidy's parents. The Cassidy's started calling shortly after their arrival in Orlando and hadn't stopped until Dalgren threatened them with a restraining order. They'd then driven to the estate but left when Richard's security guard informed them they were trespassing, and that the family did not want to speak with anyone.

Don Meeson had also become a nuisance. He'd left more than twenty voicemail messages, demanding to know what was being done with Directron stock. He threatened to go ahead with the Cisco merger, hinting that Hubnetrics could legally break loose from WarCo altogether and be taken over by Rockwell if Richard didn't soon get back with him to clear up several key items.

Hilda Dern, vice president of WarCo, and the others – Margo Caltron, Dennis Ruiz, and Sam Hopkins – equally high on the board, demanded appointments. Stockholders suggested an official inquiry and threatened to pull their resources if not given the information they demanded.

War-Met's overseas strike threatened to escalate, making further robotics arms manufacturing impossible and postponing all current contracts. Ken Olson was unsuccessful in getting their Washington contact to serve as buffer for the test program handling the toxic waste issue. Olson was even more unsuccessful in reaching Richard to inform him of this latest blunder. As a result, the Singapore workers had abandoned the plant in protest.

Richard fixed a bloody Mary. Nothing wrong with fixing a drink this early, was it? He'd already had breakfast and was thirsty. This was his house, and he was going to do as he pleased.

He sat facing the locked door to his den. It was a massive door, one that reflected his presence and attitude. Made of polished oak, the door was painstakingly crafted. It had cost him nearly five grand. It was his favorite door. When it was locked, he knew damned well that no one else would ever gain entry.

He sipped the strong drink.

The answering machine clicked. The recorder's volume was turned down. Whoever wanted to talk could leave a message, or they could go fuck themselves. Every last one of them could go fuck themselves, and he would be more than happy to watch them while they did it.

As he sat listening to the clicking of the infernal machine, the heat increased within him. He suddenly felt the need to vent his anger. He began to shake. The past events had taken their toll. It was becoming difficult to breathe. The pressure brought on by everything during the last two weeks had rapidly become unbearable.

Nick's senseless murder headed the list. The hot fury billowed through him – rage for his son being killed, and frustration for not being able to strangle Cravell for killing the boy. Anger and confusion for Kevin Cassidy, whose senseless murder had implicated Richard. Resentment and hatred for Adrienne, who wanted to take so much away from him, even though none of this was his own doing. Hurt for Katie, who'd abandoned her father in his moment of need. And the police. And the reporters.

He slammed down the glass. The drink landed on its side on the table and splashed the back of his hand. He might as well answer the damned phone. It was their fault for all this, so they should hear about it. Their fault for his wet hand, his spilled drink, his entire life going down the shitter.

He snatched up the receiver and put it to his ear. He was about to yell into the mouthpiece when he suddenly stopped. It was her voice on the line. Brittany. He sat back, forcing himself to listen, while his pulse thrashed wildly through him. "...really sorry about what's been happening, and

274

would very much like to get together so we might..."

The bitch. The conniving, coldhearted bitch. Everything in his life had gone down the shitter since she had waved him over to her table at Gino's just two short weeks ago. Had it only been two weeks? Could a quarter of a century of building an empire be destroyed in just two short weeks?

He held the receiver to his face. The coolness of the vodka and tomato juice trickled down his wrist, dampening his sleeve. "Hello, Brittany," he said finally. A flood of heat oozed down his back. At first he thought it was residual anger, but when he heard her sigh on the line, he wasn't so sure. And why wasn't he sure? His life was practically destroyed. How could all this anger and hurt dissolve so quickly?

"Oh, Richard! I'm so glad I finally got hold of you..." She sounded upset. "I've been trying to find you for *days*!"

Yes, the anger had dissolved. Worse, it took him considerable effort to remember why he'd been angry in the first place. The answer finally reappeared in his thoughts, and with it, the anger. He forced the other images aside. They were clear, pleasant images, yet they had no place in his head right now. He forced away the sight of her in a short, tight skirt, walking toward him. He forced away the memory of her coy smile somehow beguiling with practiced innocence. He forced away the glimpse of her artfully exposed cleavage, lightly tanned and rounded, waiting for his hands and mouth to fully explore...

275

"Richard...?"

He tossed everything aside and forced his mind back on the issues at hand. And there were many – too many to actually think about at the moment. A lot was at stake right now. He should not be acting like a stupid kid anymore. It was vital at this moment to stick to the facts – such as why this woman was calling, for starters. Because no matter how he felt, how much he wanted to rip her clothes off and fuck her half to death, he had to face facts.

He had to start thinking like the old Richard Warden. He had to somehow dig in and find a fix on the shambles of his life. He had to do what he did three years ago – squirm out of the wreckage and dig his way back out. Last but not least, he had to find out what this woman wanted from him.

"Brittany … why are you calling?"

"I feel really bad about how I treated you Saturday. That was so uncalled for. It was terrible of me, and I truly apologize. Can you ever forgive me for treating you like that?"

The hairs on the back of his neck bristled. She'd reduced him to a worthless bum with the arch of a brow. Transforming him into common refuse. Now she wanted his forgiveness. Why? Did it stand to reason that she actually did feel badly about her behavior that afternoon? Even if she did, should he forgive her? And what if he did? Would they go on as before? A phone call here, a dinner date there? Would their relationship actually progress? Would they finally end up sleeping together?

Or would something else happen? This woman was the kiss of death. Who would die next? Lou Berchfeld? Bob Dalgren?

"Can you *please* find it in your heart to forgive me, Richard?" she asked in a soft voice.

"I ... had it coming." He could not believe the words stumbling out of his mouth.

"I had no cause to talk to you like that, and I want to kill myself every time I think of what I said."

"You ... had every reason to be angry with me." *What the hell's happening to me?*

"Because you hired a private detective to follow me? Because you were worried about me and wanted to make sure nothing happened to me?"

"That ... wasn't the only reason I hired Cravell." He heard himself saying it but was powerless to stop. In this woman's presence, he found himself powerless to do much of anything.

The resulting silence told him he'd stumbled into a bottomless abyss. *I've done it again. My big mouth. But I have no choice. I never have a choice with this woman...*

"What's the other reason, Richard?"

"I ... wanted to ... to find out more about you."

Another silence.

You idiot. His pulse raced. Would she put him in his place again? Curse him again? Tell him she never wanted to see or hear from him again?

She sighed. "Richard, I'd like very much to see you."

He couldn't believe what she just said. Not only was he out of control, now he was hearing things.

277

"Richard? Did you hear me?"

"I'm ... not sure."

"Don't you ... want to see me?"

"What about your ex?" That had always been the issue before.

"He's dead."

"What?"

"Eric was killed two days ago. I'm free now."

***

Tired from the previous day's driving, Adam Brooks entered his office shortly before ten that morning.

From what Fay Hawkins had told him, finding Marie McDermitt wasn't going to be easy. When he'd asked her what she thought Marie did with the money she got from Warden, Fay had said, "I'll tell you this. We might not know exactly where she is or what she's doing, but with all the dough she got for her boy, she can afford to do exactly what she's always wanted to. Five million bucks would put a new spin on things for anybody, especially somebody from her background. And while I don't know that much about her, I can make a pretty good guess what she's doing with the money. I know what *I'd* do."

Adam didn't have to wait long for her to explain. "If she's like any other woman who lost a child, she wouldn't accept the boy's death very well. Her little boy would be everything to her. With her baby lying in the ground, and the man responsible walking around free, she'd probably go nuts."

278

Adam remembered saying, "One woman going up against a wealthy, powerful man with nearly unlimited resources? That would be insane."

"Damned right," Fay had agreed. "Think about it. What would you do if some rich drunk took away the one thing you truly loved? Would you just lie down and accept it? Or would you take the money he threw in your face and use it against him to fight back?"

Adam sat in his office chair, sipping coffee. What Fay said certainly put a new twist on things.

His cell phone rang shortly before noon.

It was Bob Dalgren. "Any luck?"

"I found Harriet McDermitt's hospice in the Clearwater area. She's been dead nearly a year."

"Damn."

"She wouldn't have been much help anyway. She and her daughter weren't close. Apparently Marie's a cold fish. Definitely not the type to show her emotions to anyone."

"That's not the impression I got when I saw her. The girl was genuinely broken up over her son's death. She was hysterical and had to be sedated. She was very lethargic during the inquest, most likely due to the medication. They told me she'd collapsed when she viewed the boy's body—"

"They let her *see* the kid?"

"The mother tried to intervene, but the old woman wasn't well herself, and couldn't keep Marie from going in there. From what they told me, Marie collapsed even before they pulled down the sheet. Which was most fortunate. Most of the boy's face was gone. Being dragged half a block on rough road surface would tend to do that."

Adam grimaced. "So, the girl literally came apart. Not the sort of behavior you'd expect from someone who's supposed to be a cold fish." Adam started to question Fay's brief analysis of the girl, then realized someone who showed that much emotion after losing the one thing in her life that she loved would probably shut down inside. And become a cold fish.

"I've seen plenty of women who were real ball-busters," Dalgren said. "Except when it came to their kids. Marie was an unwed mother probably used and left by some uncaring young bastard. All she had was her mother and her kid. She probably considered the boy her one true friend."

"Um-hmm. And what happens when that special someone is taken away? I imagine it would be like someone reaching into your chest and ripping out your heart. And then the asshole who's done this to you doesn't even have the balls to face you. He simply pays someone else to say he's sorry, then tosses money at you to forget about it."

"Yes," Dalgren said softly. He sighed. "That person Warden paid to deliver his monetary apology was me."

Adam figured Dalgren had to be feeling like a heel right about now – assuming that Dalgren did actually suffer human feelings. "How difficult was it?"

"I still lie awake some nights, thinking about it. But let's get back on a less painful subject. Tell me about your talk with the hospice people."

"Woman who runs the place doesn't much care for Marie. Apparently the girl dumped her mother at one of the cancer hospitals in the Tampa Bay area, wrote them a check for half a mill, then split. 'Here's Momma, she's dying anyway, take this money for your troubles, sayonara.' That's the end of that."

"Didn't she ever go back to see her?"

"When they found out the cancer was terminal, the girl picked up her mother, took her to the hospice, and dumped her again. Didn't even attend the funeral. This makes me wonder where she went and why she was in so much of a damned hurry. I'm gonna start poking around. Got a picture of the girl?"

"I've got a friend at Orange County Courthouse. I'll ask her to find some fiche on the case. If I recall, there was only one picture taken of Marie McDermitt, and that was when the press surprised her coming from the morgue."

"Wow, that *was* low."

"I'll have my friend scan it and fax it over. May take a little while."

***

Like most private eyes, over the years Adam had developed a cadre of resources, many of them not exactly members of Club Respectable.

South Orange Blossom Trail was the prime spot in the Orlando area for tittie bars and strip joints. Despite countless attempts by the city to clean up that section, peep shows, strip clubs, adult video stores and porno palaces continued to flourish. Old

281

buildings painted outrageous colors peppered the streets, making the area a gaudy eyesore.

Many of these businesses employed young women to dress in skimpy bikinis and sit in lounge chairs at the curb to attract potential customers. It wasn't unusual at all for these girls to work both sides of the street, interfering with the hooker trade. All's fair in the world of advertising.

Adam parked in the small sandy lot behind the lavender one-story block building with its neon sign flashing *Girls Galore*, and walked up to the street entrance, where a girl about twenty years old in a flesh-colored two-piece sat in a lounge chair. She was wearing a large pair of sunglasses while reading a paperback romance novel.

Adam grinned. This sight always amused him. Stick a skinny, half-naked girl in front of a porno shop, and it'll guarantee instant business. It didn't matter one bit how many traffic accidents it caused or how many cops showed up with fines. It only showed how greedy these people were.

"Delores in?" he asked.

The early evening air was cool. Gooseflesh covered the girl's arms and legs. She barely looked up from her book. "In the office." Someone honked their horn as they roared by.

"Would you like a sweater?"

She continued staring at the paperback. "I'd love a blanket. Support me when Del fires my ass for not showin' enough?"

"And deprive you of the elegant style of living you're used to?"

"I'm a regular princess."

"Can't afford a princess. I'm just your average paycheck-to-paycheck kind of guy."

"Just my luck."

He went inside the dark, stale-smelling room, where lowlifes of all shapes and sizes scurried up and down the long narrow hall like cockroaches, sniffing for peepholes and other sizzling items of interest. A short bald man about sixty years old hobbled around in a loose CPO jacket, covering his crotch with his hands.

A middle-aged woman sporting heavy, mouse-colored hair sat behind a desk in a small, cluttered office at the end of the hall. Her dark-rimmed glasses were perched vicariously on the tip of her long nose. Her face had once been pretty, but too much hard life had desecrated the picture years earlier. She didn't look up when he came in, but she raised her dark eyes in his direction. "So what brings you here?" As she sat back, her chair squeaked in protest.

"I need a little help." Adam sat down facing her desk. Hard to believe she was his age. She appeared ten years older. She and Adam had attended the same high school. Back then, she was slim and animated, with a good face and nice figure. Now, twenty years and three husbands later, she looked haggard and drawn, her face a history of the rough life she'd led – first as a biker chick, then the wife of a con man who'd done time for embezzlement, drugs and spouse abuse. Over the years, she'd learned to manage money and stayed in business by keeping her places clean and servicing the right public officials. And getting to know every bit of dirt there was about everyone in Orlando.

"You didn't come in for a quickie, I take it."

He smirked. "Heard of Richard Warden?"

She scowled. "Owns WarCo and probably half a dozen other smaller companies, and probably a bunch of others no one even knows about. I lost some serious cash on RKW, so I'm kinda down on the bastard."

"What do you know about Warden himself?"

"Fucks anything in a skirt. Flashes money around, which lets him do what he pleases." She sat forward and propped her elbows on the desk blotter. "He's been here a coupla times, but I never saw him. Likes Tina to massage him, slap his ass with a ping-pong paddle, then give him head. He tips, but not as much as he should." She shook her head. "He's just a bully with money. No one here likes him."

"Heard about what's happening with WarCo?"

"Stock's down. You got a stake in it?"

"I'm working for his attorney. Someone's been putting the screws to the man."

"About damn time. Things tend to catch up, no matter who you are."

"Know anything about that Tampa homicide case he was involved in about three years ago?"

"Hell, it was all over the news. His fat ass should've been tossed in Stark, but I guess some people can buy their way out of anything. Damn press was havin' a field day until Warden opened up his wallet and shut it all down tight."

"Remember what the boy's mother looked like? I'll be getting a picture of her, but I wanted to check with you first, on the chance that maybe she came here for a job. She'd be in her mid- to late twenties. Five-four, brown hair, brown eyes, plain-looking, thin, flat-chested."

Delores smiled. "That could easily fit half the young gals in Central Florida. But now they're all buyin' bigger tits and lips before they reach the ripe old age of eighteen. Once they get a tit and lip job, you can't recognize 'em anymore. Any scars? Marks? Tatts?"

"None that I know of. At least on the outside."

Delores frowned. "You're not makin' this easy."

"I've only got a day or so to find her."

"Lemme poke around some."

"I'd appreciate it."

"How much? Cash is a great way to show your gratitude."

"And I thought my charm was irresistible."

"You forget how long I've known you."

"How about fifty for any kind of useful info?"

She frowned. "I spend more than that on mascara."

"Want some advice?"

She blinked. "You tell me I need to spend more, you can just take that cute little ass of yours and—"

"I was gonna say you really know how to put it on."

285

She laughed. "So do you. And it ain't gonna work this time. I don't get out of bed for less than a hundred."

"Two hundred, then. More if I'm really pleased."

"My business *is* to please."

Adam thought about making another tasteless remark, but decided he'd better quit while he was behind. "Give me a call when you get something. Thanks, Del."

***

Giovanni's, a popular Winter Park eatery, boasted romantic elegance.

Vines and plants clung to the cedar beams. Wine bottles hung from posts. A large stone fireplace filled a corner of the main room. Ornamental tile covered the floor. The small, square tables were decorated with beautiful floral centerpieces highlighted by flickering candles.

Richard could hardly contain his excitement as he slid into the corner booth where Brittany sat waiting for him. She wore a sleeveless black blouse and white skirt. Three gold necklaces accentuated the smooth area above her cleavage. She also wore golden earrings and a gold watch. He took in every delicious detail and tried to convince himself once again that this beautiful creature had absolutely nothing to do with the sudden, inexplicable unraveling of his life.

She smiled. "It's good to see you. It's been much too long. As I said earlier, I shouldn't have gotten so angry the other day. I'm so sorry."

"I really did have it coming. Anyway, we're together again, so why don't we just enjoy ourselves?"

After the waitress took their orders, Brittany said, "I read something about your president resigning. This can't be because of all your other troubles, can it?"

"Lou Berchfeld's deserting me after fifteen years. He says he wants to retire, but I know him better than that. A lot has happened the last few days, and—"

"You mean he's leaving because of what happened with your son?"

"Among other things."

"But how can he just abandon you after so long?"

"Please, Brittany. Let's not ruin our evening."

"You're right. I'm sorry, Richard."

The waitress brought their brandy on a tray with a bottle of Remy Martin. They clinked glasses. Richard sipped the excellent liqueur and wondered how he should proceed. He wanted to ask her so many things, but it didn't seem the appropriate time. He was experiencing a genuine mellow. He wanted to relax and forget about everything else.

But even so, he kept wondering what was going on in this woman's mind. Despite her beauty, her warmth, he couldn't ignore his suspicions. His longing for her had suddenly taken a back seat. The cold-minded businessman in him had returned, turning his attentions to more important issues. He couldn't shake the strong suspicion that something about this woman just wasn't right.

287

"If you don't mind my asking, what happened to Eric?"

"He died in a barroom fight. He started going crazy right after that last episode at the Stonehenge. I knew it was only a matter of time. He acted tough, but he wasn't. Do you know what I'm talking about? If you're gonna be an ass-kicker, you should be able to kick ass. Does that make sense?"

"Of course. But no matter how tough you might be, you're always going to come across someone who thinks he's tougher."

"Eric never listened to anyone. The fool walked into a bar half-drunk, then started some mindless argument with one of the bikers there. Stupid, huh?"

"Very."

"The biker was small, but bikers carry knives and guns, so you really don't want to mess with them, right?"

"Right."

"Eric was half-looped and feeling sorry for himself. Some things never change. The biker was also drunk. He wanted to cause trouble too, so there they were, busting up the place, until the barman chased them outside with a shotgun."

Richard could only wonder what this woman saw in the jerk in the first place. Bad boys. Women were drawn to them like flies to garbage. It was so disheartening.

"Outside, the biker knocked Eric down and slammed his head into the pavement a couple of dozen times, and pretty soon my ex was no longer bothering anyone again."

"I'm sorry, Brittany."

She shrugged. "Why?"

"A man you once loved is dead."

"That love died years ago."

"But it still hurts when someone you once cared for destroys himself, doesn't it?"

Brittany sighed. "I guess so."

"At least there weren't children. Or *were* there?"

Brittany was silent for a moment. She contemplated the snifter in front of her face. Richard couldn't help seeing the dark, faraway look in her eyes.

"No kids."

He couldn't help noticing how different her voice sounded. How the faraway look stayed in her eyes. She'd somehow slipped away, yet he had no idea why she had or where she'd gone.

She was still gazing at the snifter when she whispered, "Why are men so stupid when they're drunk?"

His temples pounded. It was time to change the subject. Despite his initial urge to relax, he knew there were more urgent matters to discuss. "Brittany, I don't know if you've heard, but my wife left me."

She snapped out of her dark moment.

"A lot has been happening to me, to my family, to the corporation. Nick's murder started it. Then things just began to snowball – first at home, then–"

"Your wife can't possibly blame you for all that, can she?"

"It's a long story, and I don't really want to go into it right now."

"I understand."

"Do you?"

"I think I do."

Of course she did. Her ex. The stalking. The changing of vehicles and residences. She knew just as much about pain and torment as he did. "I told you about my wife for a specific reason."

"Is this ... about us?"

"Brittany, I think what we have already is enough for a terrific relationship."

"You've wanted to have sex with me ever since we first met, Richard. Is that what you're basing this on?"

He sat back. Her statement hadn't sounded malicious but had the same impact. Why had she said it? How could she take what was planned as a romantic moment and turn it into something so sordid?

He suddenly remembered other instances. Things she'd said, suggested. His drinking. His wealth. The unpleasant scene outside the restaurant. Not to mention her haunting question not five minutes ago. Why are men so stupid when they're drunk?

Once the confusion within him had diminished, he found the courage to stammer, "Why ... did you say that?"

"It's true, isn't it?"

"But you make it sound so ... so dirty."

"You think having sex with me is dirty?"

"That's not what I meant." He was about to fall flat on his face. *Keep your wits about you, or you'll soon face a repeat of the other day.* "Brittany, it's true, I was really very attracted to you when we first met."

"And now?"

"Even more so."

"Then what's the problem?"

"When you say it like that … it sounds like ... like you're a hooker or something."

"What makes you think I'm not?"

The discussion with Skinner, Bronson, and Dalgren came back to him in a warm rush. Kevin Cassidy and a hooker getting a room. A very good-looking hooker. Brunette. Attractive. Good figure. Twenty-five to thirty years old. He swallowed a thick, gooey lump. His face grew warm.

"Don't worry, Richard. I'm not."

He reached for his drink. He heard himself say, "I didn't think so." He took a long, refreshing pull of the fiery liquid.

"I could be, you know. You can't tell a hooker by how she looks or dresses. The expensive ones, that is."

"You're right about that." He had more of the drink. *Take it easy...*

She picked up the bottle and splashed more in his glass, then replenished her own drink and raised the glass for a toast. "Our future relationship," she said.

His face flushed. "Are you serious?"

"Of course."

***

After coffee and dessert, Brittany said, "Would you like to go somewhere private?"

Richard's heart fluttered. "Of course I would. Very much."

She reached out and brushed his cheek with her fingertips. Her touch, an electric jolt, caused his blood to race. She fiddled with her purse. A moment later she removed something and handed it to him. It was a key card to one of the rooms behind the restaurant.

He tentatively held it in his opened palm, his eyes jumping from the key to Brittany, back and forth. He remembered the other times he'd wanted to take her to a room and make wild, passionate love to her. The times she'd walked out on him and didn't return until some other terrible thing had happened in his life. His eyes drifted from the card in his palm before returning to her. His lips had become rough sandpaper.

"You're not embarrassed, are you?"

"I-I just didn't ... expect this."

"I'm not what you'd call predictable, am I?"

The key card remained in his opened palm. He didn't want to wrap his fingers around it, for fear of crushing it, or making it disappear. "Are you ... I mean, are you certain you want to–"

She snapped her bag shut. "You go on ahead. I need to freshen up first."

His heart sank. "But you can freshen up in ... in the bathroom there."

She reached out and touched his lips, sending another electric surge blazing through him. "Sometimes we women need our privacy to keep the mystery alive. And don't forget about that grand

292

entrance we're all so fond of. What's wrong? Don't trust me?"

"It's just that ... I really don't think this is happening."

She slid out of the booth, bent over the table, and kissed him lightly on the cheek, causing his heart to sputter and his member to throb. "It's happening." Her hot breath warmed his entire body, and he trembled.

Then she straightened, picked up her purse, and headed for the restroom.

***

Tense, hot, and fully aroused, he reached the motel room and tried opening the door with fingers that had turned to putty.

Fortunately, he'd placed the brown bag with the fresh bottle and glasses at his feet on the concrete walk. Otherwise, he would've dropped it.

After several clumsy tries, he finally got the door open. His eyes shot to the beds. Which one would they pick? Didn't matter. Maybe they could alternate. First one, then the next. He and Brittany. Both naked. Making love. And it would be wonderful.

He bent, picked up the bag and glasses, and stumbled into the room without incident. *So far, so good. I'm fine. Just fine.*

Stripping out of his clothing quickly proved harrowing. Three times he lost his footing and fell onto the bed.

Finally, he was lying naked beneath the single sheet, only the bathroom light on. His mind reeled with vivid images of them coupling, but he forced himself to focus on other things. He had to somehow maintain a clear head while waiting for her. He couldn't humiliate or embarrass himself. He was a mature, successful man. The days of his losing control were long over.

But putting his thoughts somewhere else quickly proved fruitless. The most beautiful woman he'd ever known was meeting him here in just a few minutes. He was clearly unable to concentrate on anything else.

The bottle of Remy Martin sat on the table between the double beds. He could have a quick belt before she came. But he declined, preferring instead to open the bottle after they'd made love for the first time.

He forced himself to relax. *Don't go crazy. It won't be long before she comes to the door.*

He waited. Half an hour, then an hour. Two hours. It was nearly one in the morning when he realized he'd been stiffed once again.

He spent the rest of the night diligently trying to drain the bottle of Remy Martin.

CHAPTER 20

Thursday, the Third Week

The scanned photograph of Marie McDermitt slipped through Adam Brooks' fax line promptly at nine-fifteen in the morning.

Adam pulled the scan from the machine and found his magnifying glass from the desk drawer. For the next ten minutes, he carefully studied the picture. The result, taken from at least twenty feet away, was grainy and didn't make its trip too well through the fax line. But it was enough to give him an idea what the girl looked like.

Marie was dressed in faded jeans, tee-shirt, and tennis shoes. She looked much younger than twenty-five as stated by the news reports and court records. Her narrow shoulders, tiny waist, and slender arms and legs made her look like someone's little girl. She was flanked by a tall, well-dressed man – lawyer? – and a short, broad, middle-aged woman – Harriet? – and needed help staying on her feet as they moved down a dark corridor.

The picture was taken just days after Danny McDermitt was killed. The girl's sandy-brown hair was dirty and matted, her face haggard and streaked, her complexion pale. The woman at her side was crying and holding Marie tightly by the arm.

Adam laid down the magnifying glass, got up, and poured a cup of strong chicory coffee from the brew station on the table. He drank it black, with no sugar. Just what he needed right now. This was difficult to look at objectively. His hackles had risen sharply.

The poor kid never had a break. Made pregnant at seventeen by some jerk with a short-term memory, she was forced to raise the kid by herself. It was just the three of them – the kid, Marie, and her mother – but since Momma worked, Marie had to fend for herself. Odd jobs, panhandling – anything she could find. It was rough, but she managed. A small handful of years later, just as things were beginning to settle, a drunken big shot came along and took her little boy from her.

The story was nothing new. Adam's sister had been given the shaft in much the same way. Renee had fallen for an arrogant jerk with money. After getting her pregnant, he vanished from the face of the earth. Luckily for Renee, Adam and their mother were there to pick up the pieces. His sister, once very attractive and personable, turned into something barely recognizable. Formerly conscientious about her hair and makeup, she went for days, even weeks, without washing her hair or putting on clean clothes.

With the help of family friends, Renee eventually began caring for herself, if only to bring a normal, healthy baby into the world. She rebelled at first, choosing instead to wallow in her own self-pity, but gradually convinced herself that her family and friends were right. Reverting back to her former self could be the smart way to go. Torturing herself was the worst thing she could do for herself and her baby. Becoming beautiful, sweet Renee once again would be her one true victory. But seven months later, the baby died minutes before it was born.

Although Renee had managed to recover most of her former self-esteem, the death of her unborn child was just too much. With it came the loss of the true meaning of life, along with her will to go on. The bottle helped, but after a while it failed to do the job. Pills replaced the booze. They seemed to be much more effective. After a while, she thought she might have the horrendous pain licked. But the pills, as with the booze, eventually stopped working. Once again Renee was forced to take a further step into the boundless maze of self-destruction. She began mixing the pills with the booze, and lost the battle just one year later, when she mixed too many of the wrong pills with too much whiskey. Renee was twenty-four years old.

Adam drank more chicory and hoped the throbbing sore in his gut would ease up. He'd wanted a belt, but it was too damned early. He had work to do. This was nasty business. He was dealing with the living. Renee was dead. Her worries were over. If there was a God – and Adam was certain there was – Renee was now happily reunited with her son.

The phone rang.

"Get the scan?" asked Bob Dalgren.

"Studying it now."

"Think it'll help?"

"It might if I circulate it around. Maybe someone saw her."

"Maybe."

"What's the big man been doing lately?"

"Haven't seen him. He's due to call. There's so much we need to hash out, Berchfeld leaving and all."

"You involved in that?"

"I'm involved in all his matters."

"Lucky you."

"It pays the bills."

"I'm sure it does."

A pause. "Got something on your mind?"

Adam hesitated. Now wasn't exactly the right time for this. *The living. I'm dealing with the living. Renee wouldn't like it one damned bit if I fucked up because—*

"Adam?"

"I guess I just don't understand how a conscientious guy like you can stomach such avoidable injustices. I mean, you're an attorney, for God's sakes."

"What are you getting at?"

Adam sighed. *Careful. You don't want to piss off someone paying you five K for three days' work...*

"Warden ran over a kid. Ran over him and dragged him. Destroyed a family. How'd you manage to get that taste out of your mouth?"

Dalgren sighed heavily. "I don't condone any form of murder, intentional or otherwise. I just forced myself to get the man the best legal counsel available, then stood back far enough away so I didn't dirty my hands."

"Good game plan."

"The only one in town." He was silent for a moment. "Otherwise, I would've spat in his face. Something else on your mind?"

"Just thinking out loud."

"Some attorneys have consciences, Adam. I'm one of them. But there are times we have to force that aside to put bread on the table."

"I understand."

"Call me when you've got something."

***

Someone was pounding on the door.

Richard sat up. His temples pulsated loudly. Stupidly he surveyed his surroundings. At first he didn't know where he was. Then it dawned on him. *The motel room. Remy Martin. Brittany. Bitch.*

The door clicked, opened an inch. "Anyone here?" A woman's voice. "Gotta clean room."

"Give me ten minutes."

The door pulled shut.

His head a searing blister, Richard forced himself out of bed. On the table separating the beds, the near-empty bottle and glasses served as a seething reminder of last night's shambles. He wanted to toss them through the window. As he stared at the bottle, the pounding in his head increased dramatically. For God's sake. He'd drunk nearly a full bottle of Remy Martin in one night. *Goddamned cock-teasing slut.*

It took him several minutes before he could stand. He took one step. The room shifted, making him nauseous. He sunk back down on the mattress and gently massaged his temples. The pounding subsided. He stood up again. The room swayed. He managed a slow, careful step toward the bathroom. Great. Three, maybe four more, and he'd clear the doorway. Then he could grab the doorframe, push his way in, and hold on to the counter.

He took two more steps. He eventually reached the sink, wisely avoiding his reflection in the mirror. Not now. He felt like shit. He didn't need to actually see it in his face. He opened the tap with a thick gush of cold water, gathered some in his hands, and doused his face. When the initial glacial shock died down, he repeated the procedure, then groped for a towel. As he dabbed his face, Brittany's image drifted across his vision.

That was quickly followed by a name flooding into his brain like a miniature explosion. *Calvin Yates. Someone to stay away from at all costs. A man to deal with only as a last resort.*

Yates was a former Green Beret. A cold, calculating killing machine trained in virtually every known form of fighting. He was also very knowledgeable and experienced with poisons and weapons. Yates had been working for the Government for years and was assigned to a special section of the FBI. He also made extra money handling odd jobs for the highest bidder.

Richard had first heard of Yates ten years ago. One of the district managers running Lockland AeroSystems had been filtering large sums of money into a dummy account. When the account was discovered and questioned, the district manager promptly fired the accountant responsible for locating the inconsistency. The district manager quickly dusted the account, opened another dummy, then proceeded to sell computer time to the competition, transferring the new funds into the new phantom account. By the time someone higher up discovered his system, more than five million dollars had been transferred. The division manager was brought in and shown the evidence, which had been closely monitored. When enough documentation was prepared for an official inquiry, the accused district manager was officially questioned.

The district manager, a man obviously not easily frightened, informed the division and the board of inquiry that he would accept a buyout package of ten million dollars and would leave quietly only if the buyout was a done deal. Otherwise, he would simply offer his acquired knowledge and talents to the highest bidder.

The division informed him that a package would be developed in one week's time. While this was being done, the district manager's normal duties would continue until the official signing of the buyout.

A visiting dignitary arrived the following afternoon. The district manager was required to meet the dignitary at Lockland's suite of leased rooms at one of the posh resort hotels in Lee Vista Center. The dignitary was to receive carte blanche for all requests. Lockland was considering a billion-dollar contract for a giant laser project overseas, in the visitor's native country of Kuwait.

The district manager had the company chauffeur drive him to the airport, where he promptly received a phone call saying there had been some sort of mix-up, and that their guest was already waiting at the hotel. The district manager hurried to the hotel, found the room, went inside to inspect it before the dignitary could be given the key, and suffered a fatal heart attack five seconds later. It was rumored Calvin Yates was responsible.

As Richard Warden staggered unsteadily from the motel room, he knew exactly what his first order of business would be.

***

At noon, Adam Brooks, carrying the folder containing copies of the fax he'd received from Bob Dalgren, returned to the Girls Galore on South Orange Blossom.

The girl in the lounge chair, a blonde, was about the same age and body type as the one he'd seen the day before. She wore a visor to protect her face from the potent Florida sun. She sat with her eyes closed, the flimsy black scrap of bikini barely protecting her red skin.

"Hot enough?" he asked.

"What do *you* think?" She didn't open her eyes.

"Wondering if that visor's working for you."

She turned in his direction. "You're actually staring at my *visor*?"

"Actually, I came to see your boss."

"She's inside."

Delores was having lunch at her desk. The room oozed with the smell of fresh onions, garlic, and green peppers. She gently put down her Subway sandwich on its wrapper on top of her desk and took the folder he held out to her. She wiped her hands and mouth with a napkin and slid her glasses onto her nose.

"Poor kid." She shook her head. "I remember seein' her on TV when it happened, but I don't recollect her lookin' like this. I think maybe they showed her later on, when she had a chance to fix herself up. Here, she looks pretty much like a Holocaust survivor."

"You never saw her here, then?"

"Nope."

"You sure?"

"I got a damned good memory for faces, sweetie. 'Specially when they're in my establishment."

He tapped the folder. "Distribute these, okay? We need to find her."

"Where's that sweetener?"

He reached into his pocket, pulled out a small wad, and counted out ten twenties. He dropped them on the photocopies and put the rest back into his pocket.

"That's gone even if we don't find her, understand? These days, folks can't even remember their own name unless you shove money up their ass to prime them."

"Do what you can, okay? I need to find this girl."

"We'll give her helluva try."

***

At two-thirty, Adam called Bob Dalgren at his office.

"Making any progress?" Dalgren asked.

303

"I've got others trying to find Marie. How are the other suspects looking?"

"So far, dead ends. Al Rossenberg's in Australia, doing contract work for a Chicago software conglomerate. He couldn't care less about Richard Warden or his problems."

"You sure about that?"

"I got with the firm employing Rossenberg. One of their attorneys is an old friend. I asked George some things on the sly, and he told me Rossenberg was over the War-Met business. Judging by Rossenberg's present salary, I can't say as I blame him."

Adam grimaced. "I need to switch careers."

"How do you mean?"

"In my line of work, you get caught embezzling, you go directly to jail, do not pass go, do not collect two hundred bucks. In software, you get caught embezzling, they buy out your contract, give you a million bucks, maybe even get you to pose nude for one of those skin rags, then a year or so down the road, you get snapped up by another company and are given the keys to the kingdom."

"Software isn't the only profession that does that. Look at politicians."

"Another sore subject. Biggest crooks on the face of the earth."

"If you want an argument, you're gonna have to look elsewhere."

"How about lawyers?"

Dalgren chuckled. "Let's get back to Rossenberg. The man's doing fine. I don't think

304

he'd be stupid enough to hire someone to go after Warden."

"Anyone else?"

"Not yet. But they've only got a line on three names, and it's still early. A lot of things might turn up."

"Heard from Warden lately?"

"Won't answer his phone. I'm going to have to go over there if he doesn't answer soon. God knows what he's up to."

"You don't think he'd try something drastic, do you?"

"Richard's a rock. He expects others to be just like he is. Or maybe he doesn't care how others are, I don't know. The man is too damned proud to do something drastic. The drinking – as well as sex and those expensive hand-rolled cigars – are his only self-destructive vises. He thrives on stress. I've seen him get off a plane after spending three grueling days overseas, put in a full day at the office, show up for a banquet that evening, hit the bars until two in the morning, and be at the office the next day by nine, fresh as a daisy."

"That's more than I could take."

"I know a man's limitations – a normal man, that is. That's why I had to get on his case last year to make him submit to a complete physical. He'd had one during the McDermitt case. It was a condition of the rehab program. Except for his blood pressure being slightly high, Richard's in terrific shape for a man his age."

"But what he's going through now has to be excruciating. He's lost his son, his wife, and one of his corporate presidents. He's directly involved in three murders. His corporation is on the verge of collapse. I'm sure his wife will take as much as she possibly can."

"Adrienne's been showing signs of nervous collapse ever since the McDermitt case. Richard's womanizing has always been a thorn in her side. Her son's death, no doubt, was probably all she needed to re-evaluate things. Kevin Cassidy's death was certainly the final straw. From what I've learned, she's with her relatives in the Tampa area. I don't think Richard will ever be able to get her back."

"You think he'll want to?"

"They haven't been close for some time. Their marriage, as Richard once told me, was more like a corporate merger. Adrienne had some money of her own and helped him finance WarCo in its early stages. He repaid her later on by making her an equal partner in much of his dealings. I've made some adjustments to their holdings since then, but the way things stand, Adrienne owns nearly fifty percent of WarCo."

"In dollar amount, what's that come to?"

"Not including the mansion, condos, classic cars, antiques, or jewelry, a conservative estimate of WarCo and its subs would probably come to in excess of two hundred million."

"Ouch."

"Especially since Adrienne owns almost all of Directron and nearly half of War-Met."

"And you don't think he'd self-destruct over something that big?"

306

"Actually, I think he'd be more likely to cause Adrienne's self-destruction."

***

Bob Dalgren's red Ferrari pulled up the winding drive leading to the estate.

Richard Warden gazed out the front bay window and scowled, then finished his drink and set it down. *Dammit*. He had more important matters to deal with right now. But if he didn't answer the door, the attorney would think something was wrong. Dalgren would use the key Richard had given him for emergencies. It would be wise to let the man in. Besides, Dalgren could've learned something about the hate list.

He met Dalgren outside when the attorney was halfway up the walk. "You're a long way from your office."

Dalgren stopped abruptly. "Where have you been, Richard? And what have you been doing? I haven't seen or heard from you in days."

"I've been busy."

"Busy?"

Richard shrugged. "Things to do. Life can be quite demanding."

"Tell me about it."

Richard led the way down the dark hall, to the study. He'd wanted to check his messages but didn't want anyone to know what he was up to. Doing business with Calvin Yates was something a sane man didn't broadcast.

The attorney closed the door behind him. Richard picked up a bottle of Napoleon brandy from the wet bar and a clean glass from the bottom shelf.

Dalgren waved him off. "I've got to get back to the office. Some of us have to work."

"Meaning?"

"Some of us don't have the luxury of disappearing for days at a time."

Richard refilled his own glass, sank heavily into his chair, and sipped the potent liquid. "Just what are you implying?"

"My phone hasn't stopped ringing. People are demanding to know where you are and why you aren't answering your phone. Stockholders are accusing me of keeping things from them. Don Meeson's been calling me every hour on the hour, demanding to know what you're doing about that robotics arm problem. He says he's been trying to get with Ken Olson, who's still overseas, developing a deal with Singapore to get your ass off the hook."

Richard couldn't believe the little guy's optimism. He had more of his drink. "My ass won't ever be off the hook again."

Dalgren frowned. "You're not the self-pity type, Richard. We need to start working on some sort of recovery strategy here."

"I'm only giving you the facts, Bob. War-Met's gonna go the whole nine yards. Nothing will stop it. If Singapore shits in our faces, we'll take our money elsewhere. China looks good. So does Czechoslovakia. Both could use the contracts."

"You know damned well we can't go with Czechoslovakia. Their workmanship and business practices have driven our suppliers crazy. As for China—"

"Fuck China." Richard drank more brandy. "We'll mend and move on. That's the way it's always been. You lick your wounds and start all over."

"What about Adrienne?"

"What about the bitch?"

"You know damned well how much hold she's got on you. You also know she's not gonna give anything up."

"We'll buy her out."

"On what basis?"

"Offer her a lump sum."

"When can she walk off with more than two hundred mill with the portfolio she's already carrying? I don't think so."

"Give her Directron."

"She already owns most of it. As well as—"

"Toss her the whole thing and tell her to kiss my ass."

Dalgren dropped into the armchair. "What's happening with you, Richard? You can tell me. I'm your friend, dammit."

"Yes. You're my friend." Richard studied his drink. "And a damned good one at that."

"Then tell me what's going on."

Richard stared uneasily at Dalgren. Yes, Bob was possibly his best friend. And the way it looked right now, his only friend. Dalgren deserved to know what happened. He needed to know just how stupid the great Richard Warden was.

"I spent last night in a motel room, waiting for the bitch who's been destroying my life, to come in and fuck me."

309

Dalgren sighed deeply. "Richard, your world is crumbling, and all you can think of is some strange woman who has some sort of hypnotic hold over you."

"Very well said."

"For a bright, well-educated man, you're about as dumb as a box of rocks."

Richard chuckled. "Do you realize you're probably the only person in the world who can talk to me like that?"

"It's true."

"I know it is."

"And what do you intend to do about it?"

Richard grinned. Yates was a great problem-solver. In just a few days, things would be back to normal, because the woman calling herself Brittany Weber would be dead and buried. And eventually forgotten. "You know me, Bob. I'm a survivor. Always was, always will be."

"I don't like that look on your face."

"Can't help that."

"You've got to tell me what you're planning."

"Right now, I'm taking it easy, trying to develop a strategy with this mess. One thing I've always been able to do is remain totally objective. I see a problem, analyze it, then work on a strategy. You'll agree that I'm good at solving problems."

"Yes. You're very good at that."

"This is no different. It's a problem that must be fixed."

"What are you gonna do, Richard? You must have something in mind."

"Like I just said—"

310

"You're a survivor."

"Yes."

"Tell me what's on your mind."

Richard suddenly wanted to be alone. He couldn't have anyone around when he checked his messages. Yates always replied quickly. And once the deal was in the works, the target was as good as dead.

"Richard..."

"Get out of here, Bob."

"What?"

"I mean it. Leave my house. Please."

Dalgren stood up. "We've been through a lot, Richard. A lot of good and a lot of bad through the years. You've never thrown me out of your house before."

"Believe me, this isn't making me feel very good about myself."

"I'm glad. I'd hate to know that you can no longer tell right from wrong at this stage of the game."

Richard finished his drink and waited for the other man to leave.

"Richard?"

Richard gazed out the window. This was tough, but it had it be done. Dalgren couldn't know anything about this.

Moments later, after the red Ferrari eased down the drive, Richard went over to the answering machine. A large grin took over his broad features when he heard the familiar computer-generated voice.

***

311

Frustrated, Adam Brooks put the phone down.

No luck from Delores Hillman yet. Not one person she'd shown the photocopy recognized the girl.

Time was running out. If things went as they usually did, the cops would be swooping down on Warden, and they wouldn't care who'd been squeezing the big man's nuts. But Warden wasn't Adam's concern. The corporate bigwig was merely a means to a paycheck. Adam was doing this for Bob Dalgren. Each time he tried analyzing his motives, he found himself wondering if Renee would approve. What would she think if she saw her big brother running all over town, looking for a young woman who might be going after the rich jerk who'd run down her kid?

Depended on what he did once he found her. *If* he found her.

The phone rang.

It was Bob Dalgren. "Adam, we need to talk. The sooner, the better."

Adam could tell something was wrong. The despair in the attorney's voice oozed thickly, like cream butter. "What's up?"

"It's Warden. I think he's about to go off the deep end."

"You expect him to do something suicidal after all?"

"I wish it was as simple as that."

"What do you mean?"

"I'd feel better if you came by my office. We need to talk face to face."

"Sounds serious."

"It is. Very."

"Give me twenty minutes."

***

"Pour yourself a drink."

Bob Dalgren sat behind his desk, a bottle of Johnny Walker Red on the table. Two glasses stood on the green blotter in front of him – one half-filled, the other empty. "You're gonna need one."

Adam splashed some in the glass and sat. He couldn't remember ever seeing Dalgren so uptight. "What's this about?"

"I think the big man's about to do something drastic."

"In what way?"

Dalgren drank from the glass. "I have a sneaking suspicion he's about to hire Calvin Yates to clean up."

"Who?"

"Yates is an ex Green Beret who once worked as a wet boy for the Government. Now he does odd jobs for anyone who can afford his price. He's known in Washington and is in big demand to the highest bidder. He's a licensed pilot and has his own plane. In other words, he can be wherever you need him in just a few hours."

"What sort of odd jobs?"

"He arranges accidents, makes people disappear – all sorts of neat tricks like that."

"An enforcer."

"Much worse. An enforcer will break your arm, maybe a leg – because he's paid to do it. Yates goes a couple of steps beyond that."

"You said Green Beret?"

313

"Yes."

"When did he serve?"

"Served in Saudi. Mostly suicide missions. High explosives."

Adam finished his drink. "What makes you think Warden will go to him?"

"Richard's used him before."

"You're not serious."

"It happened years ago, when WarCo was just a baby. Richard wanted to merge with War-Met, which at the time was known as Digital Dynamics. He wanted to get into robotics back then because data centers were big and expensive and counterproductive and needed to become obsolete. Robotics seemed the perfect remedy."

"And...?"

"To make a long story short, a company by the name of SDC designed a robotics unit that had very little margin for error. As a result, lost CPU time decreased to less than five percent. The company filed bankruptcy soon afterwards but was bailed out by a European hardware company and renamed SDK.

"At the same time, Digital Dynamics was working on a similar robotics program that would lower the error margin even further by making the robot with less moving parts."

"Who was heading Digital Dynamics?"

"Oscar Worthington. He'd been working with robotics since 1981. He was a consultant for SDC, but when Digital gave him an offer of half a million a year for four years, with stock options and a fat benefits package, he snapped it up. He became

314

Digital's driving force for the next three years, until Richard entered the picture.

"Richard wanted to buy Digital, change its name, and send most of its robotics work overseas, where labor was cheaper. Worthington put up a stink. He'd almost finished perfecting his prototypical robotics arm. But when Richard bulled his way into the scene, Worthington nearly destroyed the prototype rather than let Richard bastardize it."

"Where did Yates come in?"

"Richard was very shrewd. He didn't contact Yates personally. Instead, he got Berchfeld's friend and golf buddy, Jason Nash, to do it. Nash found Yates and offered him a huge chunk of cash to dissuade Worthington from fighting Richard and to give up all rights to the robotics work Worthington had patented. Within the week, Worthington handed over the patent, resigned as chairman, packed up stakes, and moved out of the country. Last I heard, he was living in London, working in a small lab."

"What the hell happened?"

"No one knows for sure, but apparently Worthington's wife of twenty-seven years was involved in a serious car accident during that period. While she was recovering in the hospital, she received an anonymous phone call and was told to persuade her husband to get into a new line of work."

"And you think Warden's getting in touch with Yates again?"

"I'd bet on it."

"How can you be so sure?"

315

"I just talked to him at the estate. Rather, tried. The crazy bastard told me to leave. He obviously wanted me out of the house. I caught him glancing at his phone while I was there. He wouldn't want anyone to know what he's doing."

"But Warden doesn't even know for sure who's messing with him."

"Knowing him as I do, I'd say he's desperate enough to pay Yates to get rid of whoever he thinks has been messing with him."

"But Yates might end up killing an innocent person."

"I told you Richard was desperate, didn't I?"

CHAPTER 21

Friday, the Third Week

The nondescript man sat in the rented van, watching the Warden estate.

He'd just finished talking with his Swiss bank twenty minutes earlier. A deposit in the amount of two hundred thousand American dollars had been transferred anonymously from the holder's savings account in the Cayman Islands. Since the job was now official, all that was left was to watch his employer and wait until the female made contact again.

It was only a matter of time. He had known many women who specialized in ruining rich men. Their biggest flaw was that they never stayed very far away. They had to remain close to see their handiwork.

Calvin Yates lowered the binoculars and pulled a cigarette from his shirt pocket. It was hand-made, bought from a contact living in Istanbul. He put the sweet-smelling cigarette between his lips. He never lit it, just kept it there, like Baretta in the old 70's cop show. Calvin had smoked heavily in the old days, often exceeding sixty a day. But cigarettes were messy, smelly, and deteriorated the body. People could track you down when you left a trail of butts.

Though he did enjoy a glass of port with dinner, and a shot of vodka after a job, he didn't succumb to the cravings of mortal men. It took a superior being to handle the jobs he was offered. In the old days, he hadn't been as disciplined as he was now. Some nasty shit was passed around in Saudi, but aside from a South American joint every blue moon, Calvin Yates could go to bed clean and sober.

It was necessary to be clean and sober. Too many assholes needed to be wasted. You had to be in total control to do your job properly. Yep, way too many assholes. Like this female putting the screws to Warden. Two hundred thousand skins just to lay her sweet ass to rest. His biggest job ever. And all he had to do was make her disappear. No sweat.

He picked up the binoculars. Nothing in the living room or kitchen window. The house appeared deserted. The security guard sat at his station near the front gate, reading the paper. The garage doors were closed. The black Cadillac was parked out front. No way could Warden have slipped out. Especially when the man was drinking so much these days.

Calvin Yates frowned. You *never* drink that much when you want to stay in control. Control was the key. He had learned much about control as a Green Beret. In the old days, it was just him and his hunting knife lying in the cold sand in the middle of the night, waiting patiently to sneak up to the enemy, slit his throat, and slice off an ear to add to his collection. You needed to be in control to stay in the cold sand for twenty-four hours at a stretch. To

318

lie there, corpselike, while vipers and other critters crawled all over you.

Control came with training, with experience. The Government was good at kill-training. They taught you everything you needed to know. Calvin picked up things quickly and retained everything. After all, killing was his calling. No one did it better. A politician, pesky reporter, unfaithful wife, abusive husband. When the price was right, Calvin Yates was the Man of the Hour.

He'd told Warden three days, but he knew it wouldn't take nearly that long. Shadowing Warden would be the direct route to follow. Calvin would lay low, hidden but ready. When the moment was right, he'd set up a trap, snare the target, take her away, then quietly dispose of her body.

It had been a couple of years since he'd added the ear of a good-looking white female to his collection. Dozens of spics, blacks, and Arabs, but only eight American females so far.

He sat back and waited. As usual, his instincts did not betray him. Richard Warden appeared at precisely 12:15, whistling as he plodded down the paved drive to get into the Cadillac.

***

Stiff and sore, Bob Dalgren got up from his desk.

The morning had been hectic, to say the least. In addition to Detective Skinner calling him every half-hour, Bob was not having much luck with the other hate-list suspects. No matter what name popped up, there was always a legitimate alibi canceling it out.

319

He was just about to make a quick jaunt to the bathroom when the phone rang. It was Richard Warden. "I need you to be on standby this afternoon, Bobbie boy." The man sounded unusually chipper. "I plan on doing some serious head-chopping, and I'd like you to be the first to know about it before the shit starts splattering."

This didn't sound right. Not at all. "What's up?" he asked.

"It's Samuelson – who else? His fat ass needs to be reamed to shreds. I just went through my emails and learned that the bastard is planning to head the corporation. If he thinks he's gonna take Berchfeld's place–"

"Listen, Richard. We'd better talk about this before you call for a board meeting and–"

"Already did, my man. I caught Ellen before she left the house and told her to make the necessary calls for an emergency meeting. Berchfeld better be there, too – if he values his skin. His resignation isn't due until the end of the day, and I want him to look me in the eye and give me one good reason why he thinks Samuelson should take over."

"Lou won't cooperate. He wants out too badly."

"That's the best reason why he *should* cooperate."

Bob sighed. This was too sudden, too drastic. These emergency meetings never accomplished anything. They almost always turned into a giant shouting match. And this taking place in the middle of Richard's other problems didn't make sense. "I don't know about this..."

"I just might tell him to stick his resignation up his ass if he doesn't go along."

"But Samuelson's been an asset to War-Met for years. He's a top consultant for Ken Olson – and doing a damned good job of it, I might add–"

"War-Met's turning the Singapore contract into a shambles, and I'm blaming Samuelson for it."

"You can't, Richard. Singapore's responsible – not Samuelson. It's all because of that toxic dump, and you know damned well who's responsible for that."

"I can still blame the bastard. One of Olson's emails said Samuelson was dragging his feet on the EPA issue. They couldn't get their Washington contact out there because Samuelson kept putting Olson off for whatever reason. As a result, too much time went by. I also seem to recall Samuelson was a Vietnam protestor, and got in trouble in the early seventies when–"

"What does that have to do with anything?"

"It tells me something about the man's character. I can't have a former protestor heading one of my companies."

"This is personal, and you know it. And as I've learned from you over the years, business and personal should never mix."

"Sure, it's personal. Samuelson has made no bones about bad-mouthing me to the damned press. You remember what he said when I picked the Singapore contract over what the Japanese tried pawning off on us?"

Bob vaguely recalled Samuelson favoring the Japanese for the robotics deal. He couldn't remember much of the details, only the rumor that Samuelson had connections with Japan and could swing the contract much easier and a lot cheaper than by going with Singapore, which – as Samuelson strongly maintained – had inferior, less qualified, laborers. "Don't remember," he said.

"Bastard said I was hoisting Singapore Slings so much, I sent the work there out of sheer gratitude."

"He didn't say *that*, did he?"

"That he did. And if he thinks he's gonna plant his sorry ass in Berchfeld's chair–"

"It's up to the board. The board and the stockholders. They'll certainly disagree with you. From what I've already observed, I don't think Samuelson will have much of a struggle getting in."

"We'll see about that. When that jerk gets here–"

"He's coming here?"

"On the nine o'clock flight out of Los Angeles. He'll be at the meeting."

"Oh, God..."

Richard bellowed laughter. "We'll probably need ear plugs and room fresheners for this one. Those sphincters will be puckering so loud, they'll be able to hear them all the way to Jacksonville."

***

Inconspicuous in his Gators cap and sunglasses, Adam Brooks sat in his van in the parking garage in downtown Orlando, waiting for Warden's Cadillac to arrive.

Bob Dalgren had called half an hour ago, telling him about the emergency board meeting and

322

Richard's strange mood. "He's up to something, Adam. He's always unusually high during a hunt."

"Hunt?"

"When Richard goes after someone, he acts almost euphoric – just like he sounded on the phone."

"As if he just got laid?"

"Exactly. He's flying in Bill Samuelson from LA 'to ream his sorry ass,' as he so delicately put it. He doesn't want Bill taking Lou Berchfeld's position, and he's ready for a fight. I think my Yates theory could be right on the mark."

"That makes this easier, then."

"How so?"

"Now we know what he's up to."

"What's your next move?"

"I think I might as well scoot on over to the WarCo offices and see if a woman fitting Brittany Weber's description shows up."

"Then what?"

"That's only as far as I got in my thinking. But something tells me if I know where Warden is, I might also be close to whoever is putting the screws to him."

"You'll also be close to Yates, so be careful."

"What's Yates look like?"

"From what I've learned, the only people who've actually seen him are dead."

"Know something, Bob? You're not doing my confidence much good."

***

Richard Warden closed the office door and dropped his briefcase on his desk.

He sat and glanced at the clock on the wall. A drink, perhaps? A short one? Not a good move in this case. He wanted to be sober and sharp when he started his head-chopping program. If anyone smelled booze on him, they'd think he was drunk and wouldn't take him seriously. He'd pass this time. He didn't want to be relaxed in any way when he zeroed in on Samuelson.

His personal line buzzed. *Samuelson, perhaps?* He put it directly on speaker. "Richard?" It was Brittany.

His pulse jumping, he scooped up the receiver. His triumphant mood abruptly changed to the same frantic confusion he always experienced when talking to this woman. "Y-Yes?"

"We need to talk."

"I ... don't think so." He'd somehow assumed control once again. The business with Samuelson – not to mention that last episode with her – had brought him back to his senses. Looking at things coldly and objectively, a habit he'd neglected for too long, had come back with a vengeance.

"Richard..."

"I ... haven't forgotten the other night." Saying it aloud caused the dark memory to flash brilliantly in front of him. "I waited for you." His gut had already heated up. "At the motel. I waited all night."

"I know you did. I was in the parking lot, sitting in my car."

Frustration clouded his mind, making things blurry and out of reach. She made no sense. Why was she sitting in her car while he was waiting for her in the room?

324

"I was ... thinking things over. It was so ... unreal. So confusing. I was falling in love with you and ... it scared me. It still does." She sighed. Then, in a broken voice, she continued, "Richard, I'm in love with you, and I don't know how to handle this."

His head swam. He gawked at the door, wondering if she was out in the hall. Or downstairs in the lobby. Or sitting in the courtyard of the building next door. Or–

Stop this. You've got a busy day ahead of you, and this woman is on her way out. You're paying a professional a ton of cash to go after her, and you don't want to be anywhere close when the nasty stuff starts...

"Richard ... please ... tell me what to do."

The silence consumed him. Things were much easier when he wasn't talking to her. He remained the corporate giant – strong and impenetrable, devoid of weakness. But when he heard her voice, the barriers fell, enabling her claws to reach deep inside him and pull his heart out. But no more.

Because of this woman, Nick was dead. No matter what was said or implied, he just couldn't shake the conviction that his son would still be alive if Brittany Weber hadn't entered his life.

"Richard, I love you, and for the first time in my life, I'm totally clueless."

Fight this. The woman's poison. "Listen, Brittany–"

"I want you. I want you in my bed. Taking me. I want you inside me, filling me up. I want–"

325

"*Stop* it." Despite his efforts, he'd become fully aroused.

A pause. "Don't you ... want me?"

He swallowed a big lump in his throat. It was warm and sour. He nearly gagged.

"Well? Don't you?"

"I can never forget what's happened between us. What you did at the motel. What happened with my son, my wife, my daughter..."

"How can you blame me for that?"

"The evidence points to it. Everything in my life began crumbling when I first met you."

"I didn't lure your son to that bar. I was with you – remember?"

"I've given this a great deal of thought. One thing I've always done, always had to do, is find a common denominator. When something causes a chain of events, especially a bad chain of events, you have to find its cause so you can stop it. I have to do things this way. It's the only way I can keep my sanity. And my corporation."

"That's it, then. The corporation."

"It's all I have, all I'll ever have. I started it, got it going, and watched it grow. A lot of things have happened to me, both good and bad. The corporation is the only thing in my life that has stayed with me."

"The papers say your wife–"

"Soon-to-be *ex*-wife."

"They say she's trying to get hold of as much of WarCo as she can."

"I've got more attorneys than she'll ever be able to scrape together. Bob Dalgren alone will give her and her legal force a run for their money."

"And if you win–"

"*When* I win."

"Then you and your beloved corporation can ride off into the sunset."

"It's the only thing that's never let me down." Despite his bravado, his explanation, he suddenly felt very small and alone, consumed in darkness.

"You've let yourself down, Richard."

"Possibly."

"And you won't let yourself open up."

"For what? More tragedy? More heartbreak? When my son died, a big part of me died right along with him. True, we weren't close – my wife always said it was because we were so much alike. Two rams butting heads. But I loved the boy, gave him everything. When he died, that's when my wife decided there was nothing else left to keep us together. Then my daughter's boyfriend died. Katie blamed me because I never liked Cassidy, because I thought he was after the family money. Adrienne blamed me because it brought everything back – every damned screw-up that's happened to me since ... since that trouble I had three years ago."

"Trouble?" she asked softly.

His pulse hammered. He reached up and massaged his right temple. Only then did he realize he was sweating. He pulled a Kleenex from the box on his blotter and dabbed at his forehead. "Something I ... something I've been trying to forget."

"Tell me about it."

"This ... isn't the right time."

"Could this be about that ... that little boy?"

He couldn't speak right off. His throat had gone numb. He cleared it and took a breath. "Y-Yes." The lump he'd swallowed earlier had struggled back. "And that's all I want to say about it."

He closed his eyes and took a deep breath. The room had grown warmer. He loosened the knot of his tie. He wondered if he should have a talk with Maintenance, have them check the air-conditioning in the building.

He sat back, wiped his face, and took deep breaths. Much better. He was doing fine – better than he would've done yesterday, or the day before. Maybe he needed that last episode in the motel room. It opened his eyes, brought him back to reality. "The point is, I have no one now, and you want me to leave myself open again. For what?"

"For me. For us. I want to love you. Why won't you let things take their natural course?"

"I don't trust you. Our relationship – if that's what you want to call it – didn't start on the right track. It was a simple pickup in a bar. You were carrying too much baggage. I couldn't go home with you or take you out. I couldn't do anything I wanted to do. You said you had an abusive spouse after you."

"I really did."

"I don't know if I believe you, if I believe any of what you've told me."

"It's true. All of it was." She sighed. "But it doesn't matter anymore."

328

"But even after all that, things didn't change. We had dinner together, drinks. Then you abandoned me, and I don't think I'll ever forget that."

"I told you why I did that."

"Yes. You did."

"And it makes no difference?"

"Yes. It does."

"Then why can't we—"

"It's happening at the wrong time. I have a very important board meeting I must attend. The future of WarCo is at stake. When things started happening to me, they started happening to WarCo, too. One thing is directly related to the other. When my personal life began going down the tubes, my employees and partners started getting the shakes. Now the company wants to have someone I don't respect take over and—"

"Richard, I want to have sex with you." She sounded angry. "I don't care what's happening with your company. I'm sorry if you don't believe anything I say. It really hurts me to hear you say I'm somehow responsible for everything. All I need to know is where you want to meet me and when."

"No, Brittany."

"Richard..." Her voice had become a hoarse whisper. "Please?"

He didn't reply. *Don't even consider it. Calvin Yates is out there. Soon your life will return to normal.* He sighed and closed his eyes. *What a waste. What a terrible, terrible waste...*

"Richard, I'll take you any way I can get you..."

"Brittany." His voice was a croak. He no longer knew what was right. Just minutes ago he was hoping Yates could find her and punch her clock. Now he wondered how he could call off the hit so this beauty could finally be his. But just before this abominable weakness could take hold, reality once again made a welcomed appearance. *Yates will not cancel a two-hundred-thousand-dollar deal for the sake of a piece of ass.*

"Name the time and place." Brittany's voice was firm.

He didn't reply.

"How about if *I* do it?"

His heart thrashed. Sweat formed a glistening sheen on his forehead. *Fight this. Don't let her win...*

"The Marriott on Sand Lake Road, near International Drive. I'll leave word at the desk which room I'm in."

"Brittany..."

"Nine o'clock. Tonight. I'll be waiting."

Then she hung up.

CHAPTER 22

Friday Evening, the Third Week

The Cadillac pulled into the paved drive and stopped.

Calvin Yates watched intently through the binoculars. Warden got out and approached his mailbox. He opened the metal lid, pulled out a thick pile of envelopes, and tossed the heap in the car. Then he removed a white envelope from his jacket pocket and slid it carefully inside the box, closed the lid, left the flag down, then got back in his car. The Cadillac disappeared behind the trimmed shrubbery lining the drive.

Calvin put down the binoculars, slipped on his plain brown baseball cap, and pushed the brim down just above his eyes. He opened the glove box, found a pair of thick black wraparound sunglasses, and slid them on. A quick inspection in the mirror said that with the tank top and shorts, he looked like a native. And the mild tan from tennis and swimming helped maintain his anonymity. He wanted as much anonymity as possible. Tank top, shorts, baseball cap, light tan, and sunglasses fit the bill perfectly.

He began briskly walking the half-mile to the Warden estate. Being a ritzy neighborhood, the area saw little traffic. Its own private security force no doubt made periodic rounds, discouraging curiosity-seekers. If someone saw him and wanted to be inquisitive, he'd spot them in plenty of time and disappear in the bushes.

It took him about five minutes to reach the mailbox. He checked both directions and listened. He saw and heard nothing. The security guard's building stood behind the brick entrance, hiding him completely.

He stood there another minute, listening, his eyes constantly moving behind the wraparounds. When he was one hundred percent certain nothing was amiss, he pulled open the lid, snatched the envelope, shut the box and turned away. After another quick glance at his surroundings, he scanned the front of the envelope. One letter was scribbled rather sloppily in blue ink on its face: *Y*.

He slipped the envelope down his shorts and walked unhurriedly back to the van. The message, written in the same blue ink on plain white memo paper, was quite clear:

Marriott, Sand Lake/I-Drive, 9 p. m. room (?)

He put the envelope back in his pocket and started up the van.

***

The light-colored van pulled out of its spot behind the palmetto bush.

Moments ago, a man in jogging apparel had approached Warden's mailbox, removed an envelope, and hiked back in the direction he'd come. Adam figured it was Yates. He also suspected Yates had just been given his instructions.

Adam pulled out slowly. His beat-up white pickup was parked a mile down the road, in the side lot of the Lutheran Church at the four-way intersection. He'd bought the truck last year because it looked like it belonged to a professional painter or carpenter. Since there were so many others just like it on the roads, people rarely noticed it – which made it a good investment.

The church lot was located directly off the straight stretch leading to the Warden estate, with several pines at the corner of the property to provide enough cover. Yates would spot a tail in a second.

When Adam determined the direction Yates was headed, he pulled up to the intersection and turned left, then dialed Bob Dalgren's number. "I'm following Yates as we speak."

"Where?"

"Don't know yet. He just took something from Warden's mailbox. Then he drove off."

"I wish I knew for sure what was going on."

"I suspect Warden made some sort of rendezvous with the girl. This is the only way I know of to set her up."

"Knowing the man as I do, I'd say that would be a good guess."

Yates' van suddenly slowed down and pulled sharply into a 7-Eleven.

"Gotta go. I think I might have been spotted."

"How?"

"Don't know. But if Yates is as good as you say, he'd be extremely paranoid. Especially when so much money's involved."

Adam passed the 7-Eleven and made a right at the intersection. He pulled into a Popeye's farther down and parked in front. He wanted to use the binoculars but knew that would be stupid. Watching

Yates through binoculars when Yates no doubt had binoculars of his own would be like signing your own death warrant. Adam's windows were darkly tinted, but he still couldn't take the chance. His best bet was to disappear inside Popeye's. The dark tint of the restaurant windows might hide him. If he didn't want to lose Yates, this was a chance he'd have to take.

Adam got out and ambled nonchalantly toward the restaurant entrance.

***

Through his binoculars Calvin Yates watched the man getting out of the white pickup. His gut had told him someone was following him. He'd learned long ago to trust his instincts.

But a tail made no sense. Richard Warden was the only one who knew about this. The big man needed him. Why would he do anything to fuck up this job – unless someone Warden didn't know about was keeping tabs on him?

Richard Warden was filthy rich. Any one of his competitors could be spying on him. Corporate business was a nasty, cutthroat world. People bought and sold secrets, data, and other people. Warden hadn't built his empire by being Pollyanna. Like everyone else, Warden did what was necessary to turn a profit. No reason he shouldn't be as vulnerable as any other man in his position.

Of course, the female ruining Warden could have allies. Since she was obviously being paid to hit him hard, she wouldn't want to take chances. And from what Calvin had recently learned, whoever was after Warden would have to be backed by serious money. Bringing in a high-priced call girl to seduce and ultimately ruin the big man would be brilliant. Warden, a known womanizer, could not possibly come out ahead in that case.

Another possibility, of course, was that Calvin was being overly cautious. And he should be. Two hundred K was entirely too much money to risk. Being paranoid in this case made much more sense.

He decided to move in the other direction. If he spotted the tail again, he knew what would have to be done. If not, he could quit worrying and concentrate on the job. But right now, he had to make sure he was alone.

***

Yates's van pulled out of the front lot of the 7-Eleven and headed north.

Hunkering in the bushes behind the dumpsters, Adam cursed under his breath. *He spotted me, all right. Now he's setting a trap*. But there wasn't much else to do. He had to keep Yates in sight at all costs.

He hurried back to the pickup. Traffic was heavy and would prevent Yates from making much distance. Adam might have a little time. Luckily, he always carried certain the necessary tools to alter his appearance as well as the appearance of his vehicle. The fake mustache and goatee in the glove box would provide ample disguise. And his frayed Budweiser cap would substitute admirably for the Gators cap. So would the magnetic *NRA* and *SUPPORT OUR TROOPS* stickers that easily stuck to the doors of the pickup.

It took him just seconds to slap on the stickers. He hastily applied the facial disguise, switching caps as he pulled out and headed north.

***

Calvin coaxed the van off the main drag, into the K-Mart parking lot.

The place was packed. The usual Friday crowd with remnants of rush-hour traffic complicating things. He picked a spot in the middle of the lot, on the other side of a red three-quarter-ton Dodge Ram pickup.

He'd wait half an hour. If nothing developed, he'd go through with his plan. If something came up, he'd play it by ear.

Traffic filled the lot – impatient shoppers scanning the area for the closest place possible. It was amazing how many beat-up trucks eased by. Two or three were like the one he'd seen before, but the drivers looked different.

He waited patiently, expecting the familiar buzzing near the back of his close-shaved scalp that flared up when his sixth sense kicked in. Nothing out of the ordinary. He decided he was being overly cautious.

After giving the area one last careful inspection, he eased out of his spot, pulled back onto the main drag, and headed south, for International Drive.

***

Half an hour later, Yates's van turned off the main highway, into the front entrance of the Marriott.

336

Adam had carefully maintained several lengths behind Yates the entire trip, slipping through half a dozen yellow and red lights to make sure he didn't lose sight of the van. He wasn't worried about being stopped. The constant heavy traffic made it impossible to obey the lights.

Driving in Central Florida on Friday evenings frequently turned into a traumatic endeavor. Tourists shared the same highways with locals doing their weekend shopping or dining out. The roads stayed clogged until the wee hours of the morning. Luckily, that made it more difficult for Yates to spot a tail.

Adam passed the hotel entrance, pulling into the service station at the intersection of Sand Lake and International Drive. He swerved to the rear of the lot, turned around in front of the restrooms, and parked near the pay phones facing the main drag.

He picked up his binoculars. Though his view was mostly obscured, the narrow gap between the phones and some shrubbery revealed Yates's van in the crowded front lot of the hotel. Yates was walking in a brisk manner to the main lobby.

Adam glanced at his watch, which read 7:32. He sat back in his seat, picked up his phone, and punched in Bob Dalgren's number. The attorney answered immediately. "Where are you now?"

"Across the street from the Marriott, on Sand Lake and International."

"What about Yates?"

"He's in the hotel lobby. I'm getting a bad feeling about this."

"That girl might be in one of the rooms, waiting for Warden to show."

"Possibly. And if you're certain Warden actually hired Yates–"

"That, my friend, I'd stake my reputation on."

"Then I guess we can assume that whoever Yates is–"

Adam suddenly stopped talking. Yates had abruptly left the front entrance of the hotel.

"Adam?"

Yates hurried back to the van. He jumped in, then pulled right out. The vehicle edged slowly toward the rear of the complex, disappearing.

"I think he located the room."

"Adam," Dalgren said after a short pause, "Yates is a cold-blooded killer. I'm not paying you enough to risk your life."

"We can't just sit around while he knocks somebody off. And if it's a woman, I'll be messed up for a while."

"But–"

"I've always had a problem with murderers, professional or otherwise. I have an even worse problem with psychos who kill women."

"You have a gun, don't you?"

"And a carry permit."

"Ever used it?"

"I don't want to get the barrel dirty."

"This is no time to be funny."

"I always crack jokes when I'm nervous. It keeps me from pissing my pants. I think I'll sniff around, see what I can come up with."

"I'd rather you just leave. I won't tell anyone you're too scared to go up against an ex-Green Beret career hitman."

"How will I live with myself? I'd be branded a spineless coward and be forced to go into politics–"

"All kidding aside, I'd feel much better if you just turned right around and–"

"I'll be in touch."

***

Calvin waited tensely in the van, just fifty feet from Room 16.

Finding the bungalow had taken him a hundred bucks and just two minutes of his time.

"Redhead's in one of the bungalows in the back." The young, pimply-faced desk clerk had been very cooperative after a bribe of two crisp twenty-dollar bills. "A knockout, too. Said she'd be expecting someone later on." The clerk winked. "They're making hookers better and better these days."

"You got an extra key for that room? " Calvin had asked.

When the clerk's small, blinking eyes suddenly went blank, Calvin reached into his pocket again and extracted three more twenties. The clerk couldn't find the key fast enough.

It was now 8:17. The girl was expecting Warden at nine. If he was late, she might doze off. All Calvin had to do was slip in at the appropriate moment.   He had the chloroform ready. The syringe with the permanent stuff lay in the console in the van. All he had to do was chloroform her, bundle her up, take her out of the room, put her in the van, give her the injection, then find a good place to dump the body.

Piece of cake. Nothing was difficult when you were being paid two hundred large for one day's work.

***

The tall, skinny desk clerk took his time booking rooms for the yawning, sloppy-dressed young couple slouched over the counter in front of him.

Ten minutes later, after they shuffled outside, the clerk slipped into the back room.

Groaning, Adam tapped the ringer and waited. Nothing happened. He tapped it again. Still nothing. He was about to hit it a third time when the door pulled open abruptly. The desk clerk appeared in the doorway, an angry expression on his flushed face. "I was comin' out, man. Sometimes I need to take a leak – ya know?"

Adam suddenly felt foolish. It was pretty stupid to have a screaming match with someone who had information you needed. "I'm in a hurry."

The clerk took his time returning to his station behind the counter. "You want a room?"

"Just some information."

The clerk blinked. "Oh, yeah?"

"I'm looking for a woman who checked in recently. Perfect figure? Beautiful? Red hair?"

The clerk shrugged. "Lots of people here, man. This *is* a hotel, ya know."

"She's waiting for a man named Warden. Richard Warden. She–"

"Richard who?"

340

This was going nowhere. Adam reached into his pocket and dropped a ten onto the counter. "Richard Warden."

The clerk laughed. "Gotta do better."

Adam took out a twenty. It suddenly dawned on him that Yates had probably gone through this same drill. "Any better?"

The clerk pocketed the money. "There's a redhead here. Quite a babe."

Adam waited for more information, but the clerk had shut up. Adam reached inside his jacket and wrapped his fingers around the plastic grip of the stainless snub-nosed Colt .380. He kept the automatic out of sight but was switched off the safety. That sound alone usually scared most people.

The clerk's cheeks paled.

"Listen to me, you idiot." Adam leaned against the counter. "Someone is liable to be killed here tonight. If I find out this went down while you were trying to drain me of more money, I'm gonna come after you and shove this gun right up your asshole. Then we'll see just how many rounds make it up to that soft mass of mush you call your brain–"

"B-Bungalow D, room sixteen, m-mister." The clerk shook so badly, the keys on his chain jingled. "Out in b-back. Just before ... you reach the p-pool."

"Anything else I need to know?"

"Some other guy asked."

"Now there's a surprise. When was this?"

"About fifteen, twenty minutes ago."

"Anything else?"

"He has a k-key ... to the room."

341

Adam wanted to pull out the gun and rap the kid on the side of the head. "Why the hell did you give him a key?"

The clerk shrugged. "G-Gave me a hundred bucks."

People were such assholes...

Sighing, Adam dropped another ten on the counter and rushed outside.

***

Calvin stood outside Room 16 for ten minutes, his ear against the door, before moving the key toward the lock.

Not many people in sight. Just a few cars parked outside the rooms. Many darkened windows. This section butted up to the wooded area in the rear of the property, providing seclusion and quiet. Warden's babe had obviously chosen this area specifically.

The room could be empty. Since he didn't know which car she'd used, he didn't attempt a cursory search.

He silently inserted the key, turned the knob and gingerly nudged the door open a crack.

A long vertical beam coming from the partially open bathroom door provided the only light visible. He opened the door two inches, then three. He pocketed the key, then removed the chloroform packet from his side pocket. He waited tensely behind the three-inch gap, his breath shallow, his eyes glued to the bed.

When his eyes acclimated to the darkness, he used his off-center vision to determine shapes. This method was best for distinguishing breaks and

342

patterns in the darkness. It had never failed him in his desert training. It didn't take long to identify the long, thick tresses spilling out among the pillows.

The familiar rush of adrenaline spread warmly over his body. He carefully closed the door behind him and crept silently toward the figure in the bed.

***

Adam eased the pickup down the winding path leading to Bungalow D.

Cars were parked along the curb and in front of the other bungalows. Very few people wandered about.

Yates' van was parked behind a Ford pickup down the walk from the bungalow. The cab was dark. The tinted windows told him Yates could be sitting behind the wheel, waiting.

Adam parked on the other side of the path and flicked off his lights and ignition. He watched the van as well as the door marked 16. The motel room window showed no light.

Adam knew something about pros. They were like movie stars – they liked making the most money for the least amount of work. This would probably be swift and silent. One, maybe two minutes, and Yates would be thinking about spending all his money.

Yates had to be in the room. If Adam got out and was suckered and killed by Yates, so be it. He couldn't just sit here and wait for the woman to be murdered. It didn't matter who she was, what she'd done, or what her intentions were. He wouldn't let her be murdered.

343

He removed the Colt from his holster and got out of the pickup. Holding his breath, he tiptoed past Yates' van. *So far, so good. Yates was probably inside the bungalow. Time to hurry...*

Adam took cautious three steps toward the bungalow. The crunching of gravel close behind him made his heart leap up his throat.

***

The figure in the bed did not move.

The thick curls were strewn more or less evenly in a fan-shaped pattern on the pillow. It looked nice. And so neat. Too neat. Calvin Yates's scalp tingled all the way down his neck. This was wrong. All wrong. It stunk. The hair on the pillow ... it had obviously been arranged like that.

Had the girl prepared herself specifically for Warden, then fallen asleep waiting for him?

No. Something stunk...

His pulse thumping, he took two silent steps toward the bed. He reached out to yank down the bed sheets from the covered face. And stopped.

Irritated shouting echoed outside.

***

"*Freeze!*"

Adam heard the loud clicking of automatics behind him – and froze.

"Police! Raise your hands! Now!"

He did as he was told.

"Down on your knees! Keep your hands up! *Kneel!*"

His heart thumping, Adam obeyed. A dark figure moved to his left.

"Eyes straight ahead!"

344

The hard pavement pounded his kneecaps. He stared blankly at room 16. If only he could let these cops know what was happening in there. But maybe he didn't have to. Maybe the cop with the big mouth had just foiled what was going on inside the room. What would Yates do if he was interrupted?

It didn't matter. Yates had become very unimportant at the moment. More urgent matters faced him. The cops. How the hell did they know to come here and—

The desk clerk. The asshole was miffed over Adam's threat and decided to get even.

Frantic footsteps crunched the gravel directly behind him. His Colt was wrenched from his right hand. Someone patted him down. Handcuffs clinked loudly near his ears.

"My name is Adam Brooks," he said, finding his voice.

A strong, firm hand grabbed his left wrist and yanked it in a vicious semicircle behind his back. He winced at the sharp pain.

"I'm ... a licensed private detective."

He tried to ignore the bright heat racing up his shoulder. He winced again when his right wrist was pulled down to join the other.

"I'm licensed to carry a firearm. I'm bonded by the state of—"

"You're not licensed to threaten private citizens with your firearm," barked the cop directly to his left. Adam caught a strong whiff of onions. Onion rings – possibly from one of the fast-food places on International Drive. Too late in the day for doughnuts.

345

"Stand up!"

Before he could comply, he was jerked painfully to his feet.

A big, bulky cop appeared before him. The man's nametag said *Geller*. He went a good six-three and probably tipped the scales at two-fifty, some of it hard muscle as well as the soft roll obscuring his belt buckle.

Adam's pulse raced when Geller's nightstick suddenly appeared.

***

Sounded like cops outside.

Some idiot preying on tourists, no doubt. Calvin figured it was common here.

When he was finished with the girl, he'd have to wait before carrying her outside. This could pose a problem, but he wasn't too concerned. He had all the time in the world. Even if he–

Something caught his attention – movement to his left, behind the chair.

The darkness of the room had hindered his eyesight. Even after his eyes had adjusted, he could barely make out the dark form moving toward him.

Despite his confusion, his lightning-fast reflexes instantly righted themselves. In a flash he'd snatched the switchblade from its sheath in the secret compartment sewn into his belt. But it was too late.

Just as he made out the slender figure standing behind the dark blanket sliding to the floor, the soft *phut*! of a silenced automatic pistol sent a giant jolt of hot pain crashing through his chest. An instant later, a second *phut*! penetrated his forehead.

346

Calvin Yates slumped noiselessly to the bed.

During his fall, his outstretched hand, closed in a tight fist, pulled the pillow with him, sending the wig with the carefully arranged curtain of red hair sliding quietly to the carpeted floor.

***

The big cop pointed the nightstick directly at Adam's face. "If you're a licensed detective, why were you threatening the desk clerk?"

Adam found it extremely difficult to remain calm. Three cops stood to his rear, hands on hips. The one on his right rested his palm on the Pachmayr grip of his holstered automatic. "If you'll just bear with me for a moment–"

"Go ahead." The cop rested the nightstick on his right shoulder. "But make it good."

"I was questioning the desk clerk because I believe a felony crime is being committed on this property. The clerk was giving me a rough time–"

"I'd give you a rough time, too." The cop stuck his broad face closer. "Especially if you threatened me with a gun."

Adam wanted to ask the man if he'd ever heard of a new invention called the 'breath mint.' *Keep your cool...* "I believe someone is about to be murdered tonight. Someone in that room over there."

Geller lowered his nightstick and studied it. It was obvious the big boy wanted to use it.

"If you'll just give me–"

The door to Room 16 slowly opened. A slender woman with short brown hair appeared. She was dressed smartly in a business suit and high heels and

347

carried a large leather bag looped over her left shoulder. She glanced nonchalantly at them before turning briskly down the walk.

Adam Brooks instantly realized he'd just seen Marie McDermitt.

"*Which* room? "Geller seemed vaguely interested.

The girl disappeared around the corner. Adam continued staring after her.

"Brooks!"

He turned back to Geller. Suddenly things were perfectly clear. Relief washed through him. Yes. It was Marie. And unless he was greatly mistaken, the killer Calvin Yates was dead. "You know, now that I've had a chance to give this a tad more thought, I really can't remember if the murder is going to happen here, in Orlando, or on a TV show I just caught on Cable."

The nightstick whacked him smartly on his upper arm.

***

The cell door unlocked with a loud clang.

"You look like shit." Dressed in his usual tailored suit, Bob Dalgren came in and sat down beside Adam on the thin, lumpy cot.

Pale and exhausted, Adam smiled thinly.

"What happened with Yates?"

Adam chuckled. "Bob, my good man, I don't think we have to worry about our pal Cal any longer. Unless my guess is way off, our notorious wet-boy is dead."

"But how? What the hell happened?"

348

Adam pressed his back against the pillow propped up against the block wall. "It's really very simple. The man met up with someone better."

"Who?"

"Marie McDermitt."

Dalgren gasped. "Are you sure?"

"She's the one who's been calling the shots all along. Yates snuck in there and Marie came out two, maybe three minutes later. I didn't hear anything – that is, I couldn't hear much over that loud-mouthed cop. I don't know how she did it – knife, baseball bat, blackjack. But Yates is dead. Calvin Yates, your ex-Green Beret psycho killer, is now an unpleasant memory. If he was still kicking, Marie wouldn't have been able to leave that motel room alive."

"What do we do now?"

Adam scowled. "Get me out of here."

"Not that simple."

"What's the problem?"

"The desk clerk, for one thing. Why'd you assault him? He's filing charges."

"He's just pissed because I didn't let him take me for more money. Yates got to him first and gave him money for a key to the room. When I showed up and gave him more, the jerk decided this might be a gold mine and tried to bleed me. But when I threatened him, he wet himself and called the cops on me as payback."

"But why'd you threaten him?"

"At the time I thought the girl's life was in danger."

Dalgren thought it over. "I'll talk to him. Maybe I can get him to drop the charges."

"Just mention the forty bucks he ripped off me and see what he says."

"I doubt he'll acknowledge that. It would tend to make him look guilty."

"Mention the dead body in Room Sixteen. *That* ought to shake him up a tad. Giving a hit-man a key to a private motel room resulting in a murder should be a felony."

"You actually think Yates is lying dead in that room?"

"I'd say so."

Dalgren's cell quickly appeared in his hand. "I'd better call someone about this."

"Or we could all wait until the cleaning lady finds him tomorrow afternoon."

"That would be horrible."

"Yeah, you're right. Cleaning ladies have enough to worry about. They work their butts off cleaning up after people, don't get paid nearly enough, and have to worry about being pressured to get a green card and learn English. I wouldn't want their job."

Dalgren started pressing buttons, then stopped. "By the way, you mentioned one of the arresting cops knocking you around."

Adam rubbed his upper arm. "Big jerk named Geller slapped me with his damned nightstick."

"Are you marked? Bruised?"

"The big wuss didn't hit me hard enough."

"Unless you've got some cracked ribs, forget it."

"Just get me out of here. Marie's probably on her way to meet Warden."

"Why wouldn't she just leave well enough alone? I mean, the big man's really hurting."

"She'll probably want him to know exactly what's been going on. His destruction might not be enough."

"This is *cold*."

"He murdered her baby. As long as Warden thinks Yates is still out there, his guard will be down. She's emptied his entire household. There won't be any witnesses to worry about."

***

It was nearly midnight before Richard Warden decided to call it a night. He'd spent the last two hours in his study, downing bloody Mary's.

The board meeting earlier that afternoon didn't even enter his thoughts. Brittany's phone call had reduced the fire brewing within him to cold ashes. Instead of bulling his way into the conference room and sending Samuelson, Berchfeld, and the rest of them scattering, he'd gone in and made a short, concise announcement that the Board was quite capable of picking their next president. Then he'd politely excused himself, saying he had more urgent matters to tend to.

More urgent matters? This was WarCo, for God's sake. What in heaven's name could be more urgent?

Why, Calvin Yates, of course.

Despite his confidence in the man, Richard couldn't shake the nagging suspicion that something had gone wrong. Yates was quick and thorough –

why hadn't he called by now? Another glance at his watch told him it was 11:56, nearly three hours since Yates was to target Brittany at the Marriott Inn.

But what if Yates *hadn't* gotten there at nine o'clock?

Brittany was supposed to be there waiting for him. It wouldn't make much sense for Yates to get there right at nine. If Yates snuck in at nine-thirty, ten, or even later, Brittany might be asleep. She'd be most vulnerable and would provide a much easier target.

Richard finished his drink. He got up to mix another, but the room began to spin. He sat back down. *Easy does it. Best not celebrate just yet. Wait until you hear from Yates.*

He tried standing again. This time he succeeded. He moved unsteadily to the drink tray, mixed another, then slumped into his chair. He began getting angry all over again. *What a waste. What a damned stupid waste. Brittany, you bitch. Why did you do this to me? We could've made wonderful music together.*

She would've been the perfect companion for a man of his stature. She had the looks, the poise, the intelligence. It had been a very long time indeed since a woman had ignited such a fire inside him.

He pushed himself into a standing position and staggered out into the hall. *Too damned dark.* He might trip and kill himself. He flicked on the hall light. *There. Much better.* Now he could see the stairs.

352

He ascended them slowly, one at a time, one hand firmly cradling his glass, the other grasping the wooden rail.

He made it to the top of the stairs without incident. *Just a few more steps. Go on in there, finish your drink, then crash. When you wake up, Yates's message will be on the answering machine, giving you the good news.*

He shuffled clumsily into the dark master bedroom and flicked on the light. Movement caught his attention. Someone stood in the bathroom doorway.

CHAPTER 23

Saturday, the Third Week

Dressed in a light-blue lacy bra and matching panties, Brittany Weber slipped quietly into the room.

Richard Warden gazed numbly, his blinking eyes unable to comprehend what he was seeing. *This is a dream. Some sort of crazy, mixed-up dream.*

Or maybe it was the booze.

"Hi, Richard." Her soft voice sounded like it was coming from some far-away place.

He couldn't reply. His throat required more booze. Another healthy swallow would give him the courage he needed to face this strangeness. But his shaking hands were powerless to raise the glass.

"Why didn't you meet me to the motel?"

He still couldn't speak. It was impossible to make sense of this.

She took two slow, deliberate steps toward him. "Why did you send that other guy?"

Richard's mouth opened, but no words escaped it. The lump in his throat prevented any such function.

"What's wrong, Richard? Nothing to say?" She moved closer.

A hallucination, probably from too much booze. The stress. The frustrations. Everything was taking its toll. There was no way she could be in this room with him. *This woman is dead. She was dealt with by Calvin Yates, a professional killer. You're hallucinating because you're drunk, you feel guilty, and you're scared. Just click your fingers, and reality will coming stumbling back. And put the damned glass down...*

She took three more steps in his direction. "Since you didn't come to the motel to meet me, I guess we'll have to do this right here."

His arms began shaking. He glanced down at himself. His shoes were glistening red. Blood? The front of his trousers was also red. But his legs were cold. Not blood. Tomato juice. His drink. He'd dropped his drink on the carpet. But he couldn't remember doing it.

Now ... all you've got to do is click your fingers...

Two more steps. Her hands came up and buried themselves in his hair. Her pelvis pressed firmly against him. Her lilac scent devoured him.

She nudged him, making him back up to the bed. The heat inside him caused his whole body to shudder. "No," he managed, his tongue swollen. "Don't."

His brain tried intervening again, commanding him to fight this. *Concentrate on what's real. Don't believe any of what you see. Yates is a pro. Always gets the job done. He's an ex-Green Beret, for God's sake. The man can kill in his sleep. There was nothing to this job at all. This woman is dead.*

A dream, Richard... This woman cannot be here with you... She no longer exists... Click your fingers. Right now. This instant. Click them, for God's sake!

355

His thumb and middle finger came together ... and despite their trembling, made a faint clicking sound. He waited impatiently for the dream to end. For reality to come back.

He was in a strange motel room. This woman was some hooker he'd found for the night. He'd gone looking for someone to help him forget about this ugly mess. He wasn't even home.

A hooker, Richard. Not Brittany. A hooker. You're feeling remorse for paying Yates to get rid of her. It's messing with your head.

She began unbuttoning his shirt.

The reality of it rocked through him. Yates's plan had gone haywire. The ex-Green Beret *hadn't* succeeded after all. This woman had somehow done in Yates, then came here to finish the job.

He made one last feeble effort to get her to stop. "Pl-*Please*..."

She opened his shirt, reached down, and fiddled with his belt. He wanted to look down and watch, but he couldn't pull away from the sparkling green eyes blinking brightly less than a foot away.

"Now we can do what we should've been doing." She let his trousers drop. "Before you sent that other guy for me."

He wanted to pull his pants back up. Strange. For weeks, all he'd thought about was making love to this woman. But things had changed horribly. This was bad. And wrong. And evil. He wanted to push her away, pull up his pants and get away from her.

His arms had become slabs of beef. They hung helplessly at his sides. She'd drained every ounce of strength from him as easily as pulling a plug. It was all he could do to keep from collapsing.

Her face had become hard. Fierce. Nothing happy or fun showed in it. He saw only evil. The glittering green pools displayed hatred and anger.

Sensing the fear taking over, he began to whimper. *No dream. A nightmare... This bitch killed Yates. And now she's gonna kill me.*

Just as he began experiencing a heavy throbbing dizziness in his head, Brittany pushed him down on the mattress. Gasping weakly, Richard surrendered to the blackness.

***

Bob Dalgren and Adam Brooks reached Warden's exclusive neighborhood at 12:38.

Adam patted Dalgren's arm just as the Ferrari swung off the main road and coasted down the paved thoroughfare. "Stop here, Bob. I don't want anyone in the house knowing they're about to have visitors."

"We can go in through the side entrance." Dalgren parked just off the road, about two hundred feet east of the front gate. He doused his lights and killed the engine.

Adam peered outside. "What about the security guard?"

"He leaves at midnight. He's gone by now."

"No other security?"

"An electronic system that's hooked up to the front gate, the doors and windows of the estate, and the doors and windows of the guest house."

"I hope you have a key. I'd hate to have another run-in with that asshole Geller and his nightstick."

357

"I've got a dupe somewhere on this chain." The attorney removed the chain from the ignition. "The fence is wrought-iron in front, chain-link on both sides and in back. But there's a gap near the corner where a post couldn't be sunk because of roots. Richard likes trees for privacy. He had the fence guys work around it. We can just squeeze through that clump of scrubs–"

"Bob, I have to go in alone."

Dalgren stopped fumbling for his key. "You're not gonna do a number on me, are you?"

"It'll make things simpler if I don't have to worry about you getting in my way. Marie's probably armed. She would've had to be, to nail Yates."

"What do I do in the meantime? Play with myself?"

"You have Kleenex?"

"Be serious, now. What if ... she shoots you?"

"You should be able to hear the gunshot from here. That is, unless she's got a silencer."

"I'm deadly serious, Adam."

"I have a feeling she's not a cold-blooded murderer. Just someone who's been pushed too far."

Dalgren scowled. "What about the cops? If they find out what we're–"

"They won't unless you call them. But I don't think you will. Am I right?"

The attorney dropped the key in Adam's open palm. "Go do your thing. And be careful, dammit."

***

Richard Warden opened his eyes.

Where am I now? What the hell is happening?

358

He tried to sit up, couldn't. *My arms...*

He tried opening his mouth in protest, but his lips were stuck together. *What the hell?*

He lay on his back on the bed, his shirt completely unbuttoned and pulled open. His wrists and ankles were fastened to the bedposts with scarves. A thick strip of silver duct tape stretched across his mouth.

The woman standing beside the bed gazed down at him, then reached up and removed the luxurious red wig.

Richard gulped audibly as Brittany Weber suddenly became a brunette. The woman's burning eyes never left his. She dropped the wig on the carpet, bent at the waist, and began doing something with her eyes.

She straightened. Her liquid brown eyes held his. The green-tinted contacts glinted in her opened palm.

A wash of nausea jolted through him. *No. No. This is not ... this can't be ... happening...*

She bent and picked up the wig, then turned, approached the rocker in the corner of the room and put the contacts and the wig in her shoulder bag. The glazed smile, combined with the seething hatred in her eyes, sent chills up his spine.

Then he noticed the switchblade. She'd apparently removed it so skillfully from her bag that he hadn't even seen her do it.

A warmth emanated between his spread thighs. His bladder voided.

She tapped her palm with the flat edge of the switchblade. Her eyes were blazing coals.

He watched in terror. Each tap was like a blow to the gut. Her gaze moved downwards, from his eyes to his chest, settling finally on his damp groin. All the while, she continued tapping her palm with the knife.

He tried convincing himself once again that this was some horrible dream. This ghastly nightmare was the result of his horrendous guilt for paying someone to murder another human being. Brittany was its star because he'd been so preoccupied with her for the last three weeks. And because she was the victim.

Reality took over, interrupting his dark fantasy. *Not a dream, Richard.*

He began to whimper.

Her sudden laughter jolted him back to reality.

"Richard Warden." The name escaping her lips sounded like a curse. Her voice was soft yet mocking. "Corporate icon. Major big shot. One extremely important man."

She continued caressing the switchblade. "Look at you. Trussed up like a Thanksgiving turkey, your gut quivering like Jell-O. And you've wet yourself like a baby."

Her harsh words caused a knot of heat to swell deeply in his core. Their argument outside the restaurant thundered back. She was mocking him again. Laughing at him. He pulled at the scarves.

"What's the matter, Mr. Warden? Uncomfortable?"

Richard grunted loudly, thrashing on the mattress.

She took a corner of the tape and wrenched it off. He squealed. She pressed the sticky side of the tape on the pillow near his head and straightened.

"Earlier today, you complained you didn't know me," she said softly.

Though his mouth was free, he found that he could not reply.

"Are you smart enough to know who I am now?"

"McDermitt." The name came out thickly. His throat felt coated with warm molasses. The effects of the bloody Mary's had all but disappeared.

"*Miss* McDermitt, to you. I'm sure you know by now that there *is* no Brittany Weber. That was all a sham."

"For ... revenge."

"Retribution." She sighed. "You ... killed my boy." It came out as a groan. "And you didn't even *suffer* for it."

His mouth trembled as he found the words. "I did suffer."

"A few months in rehab? Behaving yourself for six weeks?"

"Among other things."

"Let me guess. You had to stay away from bars for a few weeks."

"It was ... a little more serious than that."

"Tell me what's serious. Tell me something more serious than burying your child. You ought to know what I'm talking about *now*, right?"

He pushed the dark images away. The funeral. The cemetery. Wendy collapsing on Nicky's casket. The crying, the mourning. There was no room for

361

any of that right now. All he could think about was himself. "What did you *want* from me? I gave you–"

"*Money*." The word was spat out. "You gave me *money* for my boy. You traded my little boy's life for *money*!" Her eyes smoldered. "Sorry, lady, I think I might've run over your child. Couldn't help it – I was drunk. No biggie, right? Let me write you a check for your troubles."

"Five million dollars is a lot of money..."

"Not nearly enough!"

Richard could not speak. Nicky's image broke violently through the chaos of his thoughts. Adrienne's words cut through him like shards of broken glass. *What's fair? Losing your son in a gunfight? Or to a drunk driver?*

"Danny was the only thing that was ever truly mine. You took him away from me and didn't even have the balls to come to me and apologize!"

"What would that have done? I had my attorney–"

"You can *fuck* your attorney! *All* you corporate pricks can fuck yourselves!"

"I-I – I'm sorry about your–"

Without warning, she slapped him viciously on the cheek.

The force of it, from so small and delicate a hand, was astonishing. The heavy wall of numbing pain slammed into his head.

"You're three years too late."

"But if you'll just let me–"

362

The razor-sharp point of the switchblade poked the soft flesh of his neck dangerously near the carotid artery. Richard gulped audibly and lay still.

She held it there for what seemed forever, then withdrew it and straightened. The madness had passed. She seemed to be in control again.

"Five million dollars." She began pacing. "I'm sure you know what that much money can buy. But let me tell you what I used it for. Just in case you haven't been shopping in my end of town."

Richard pulled helplessly against the scarves. They held fast.

"First of all, I needed tits. A dog like you goes after tits, right? As a matter of fact, a mongrel of your lowly breed won't even bother with a girl who isn't hauling around a healthy set of knockers. Isn't that about the size of it – so to speak?"

He couldn't reply.

"A really good wardrobe was next. I needed clothes that would attract a scumbag like you. I needed a sexy combination of styles. Half-slut, half-model – isn't that what turns you on?"

He still didn't speak. He was too busy wondering how he could escape this nightmare. He closed his eyes and willed himself to turn this into a dream, but when he opened them again, she was approaching the bed.

"I decided on plastic surgery for my face. Since I never liked my cheeks and jaw anyway, I had them redone. That's nothing anymore. Watch anything on TV and you'll see that they can make a fox out of a hag. I was no hag, but I needed some major work done to be perfect. Everyone knows a big shit like you will only go after someone who's perfect. You've got to be perfect. That's how things are now. Land of the rich, home of the successful. You've got to be young and beautiful or you're nothing."

He couldn't accept the fact that Brittany Weber had not been real. Nor could he accept the fact that she'd been this little bitch all along. It was so bizarre.

"I had surgery done to add swell to my cheekbones, plus a little shaving done to lose some jaw line. Collagen for the lips, implants for the tits. Whoever said money can't buy everything is full of shit."

She circled the bed. "Then, of course, I had to act the part of a slut. Not one of those cheap numbers on the Trail, but a genuine thousand-a-night job you rich jerks go for at those convention orgies."

She reached up and flipped some brown hair away from her eyes. In spite of the tense situation, the gesture was extremely sensual. Richard turned away. He couldn't think of this girl as anything but evil.

"My teacher was Miss Tonya. She runs the Chastity Club out on the Gulf. I'm sure you've heard of it."

He knew the place only too well. The hooker he'd bought the night he'd run down Danny McDermitt was one of Miss Tonya's thousand-dollar-a-night girls. The hooker's name, ironically, was Lucky. She'd told him how one night in her care would change his life forever.

364

The heat gathered in his neck. *The slut feeds me half a dozen expensive drinks, gives me a ridiculously expensive blowjob, tells me how fortunate I was to have selected her, then disappears from the motel room and lets me run over a seven-year-old kid.* The irony of all this made him want to scream.

"Miss Tonya taught me everything I needed to know," the girl went on. "She taught me how to look, how to dress, how to walk, how to talk. How to get that famous dick of yours to take over – which wasn't that difficult at all."

"Was there ... ever an ex?" he asked in a weak voice.

"What do *you* think?"

"You're insane." He just couldn't accept the idea of this girl toppling his world in just a couple of weeks.

Their argument outside the restaurant once again drifted past, this time with a different message. She'd been able to manipulate and degrade him so easily, only because he hadn't been far from the bottom in the first place. In spite of his tremendously successful status, he was, in reality, not much higher on the food chain than those loathsome creatures hiding beneath a rock at the bottom of a creek.

For the very first time in three years, Richard Warden actually felt loathsome.

"Now we get to the surveillance part of my campaign." She removed a thick coil of black wire from her bag, held it out, then returned it to the bag.

"I got the bugs fixed at your office by going in when your secretary went to lunch. Attaching them to your phone lines was a piece of cake. I did your study here in the mid-afternoons when your housekeeper was off. I bought a repairman's uniform at one of the novelty stores in town, rented a van, and did what was necessary. That's another thing your money bought me. An electronics course."

"Where'd you get ... the keys to the house?"

"Your housekeeper. I just showed up one day when your wife was out shopping and told Renata I was doing work on the guest house. I needed the keys for the main house so I could match them. She gave me her set. When I'd finished duplicating them at Scotty's, I came back and returned her set to her."

"How'd you know about the guest house?"

Marie smiled. "Everyone in the state knows about it. *Orlando Home Builders* did an article on the renovations you were making in your back yard. Wasn't that nice of them to let us all know about it? But that's what being a big shot is all about, isn't it? Having your face and life story splashed all over the place?"

Richard closed his eyes tightly and groaned.

"Renata was very helpful. I don't think she fully understood why I wanted the keys. Maybe she didn't care. What do you think?"

"That little bitch has been with us *ten years*!"

"It doesn't matter. Here's a news flash: She really doesn't care for you. In fact, she looked disgusted every time I mentioned your name."

366

His anger sent a wave of shuddering warmth through his tense limbs. His hands closed into tight red fists. "I'm gonna find that little slut and–"

"You're not gonna do *anything* to *anyone*." The blaze returned to her eyes. "You're not gonna do anything ever again."

***

The girl's voice trickled down the hall.

Adam stopped at the bottom of the stairs. The girl sounded calm. Warden, on the other hand, sounded agitated. He was probably being held at gunpoint.

Adam closed his eyes and suddenly realized how much the girl's voice sounded like Renee. The same soft, gentle, little-girl quality. Renee had died young, missing the happy moments of meeting someone special, falling in love, having a child, and sharing a warm, fun-filled life. She'd missed seeing that child grow and mature to become a person she'd be proud of. She'd missed growing older, wiser. She'd missed everything because a selfish, egotistical bastard had torn her down completely. A man like Richard Warden.

But that chapter of Adam's life was closed. A new chapter, one starring a young woman very much like Renee, remained open. This woman, scarred, damaged and heartbroken, still walked the earth. And she was lucky. She'd tracked down the man who'd ruined her life.

What now? Go up there? Talk her out of her revenge scheme? Try taking the gun away from her? Try convincing her Warden wasn't worth all this trouble? Life can be filled with great fun, huge

367

belly laughs, and quality entertainment if you'd just learn to take things in your stride.

He almost smiled. No one would believe a crock like that. What could he tell the girl that she didn't already know?

What he thought went against every principle, every belief, he'd ever stood for. He'd always possessed an abundance of scruples, of principles, and clung to the lifelong belief that a natural order should prevail in the world. Without it, civilization would be no higher, nor more evolved, than mob rule.

But along with this line of reasoning came another philosophy, this one shifting things into a semblance of reason. It told him that, no matter how senseless things seemed, there had to be some buoyancy. A justification for many of the bad things happening in life.

He was a private detective. He was supposed to be going after bad guys, stopping crimes from being committed. It didn't matter what the bastard did to this woman – Adam couldn't let her commit murder to justify the scales.

Murder is wrong. You know it as well as anyone. And if you don't know who the bad guy is in this instance, you might as well just turn in your badge right now.

His body turned numb as he ascended the stairs.

***

Using the sharp point of the switchblade, Marie McDermitt traced a faint white line on Richard's glistening neck.

368

"I could've called it quits when Nick and your investigator friend murdered one another. But since you didn't seem at all that broken up by the death of your son, I knew I still had work to do."

The realization slapped Richard sharply in the face. He'd been right about the Stonehenge fiasco. Brittany spilling her drink, then leaving. The mysterious blonde. Nick. Cravell. "*You* were the one with ... with my *son*? With *Nick*?"

"That boy sure did love his blondes, didn't he?"

"*You* were responsible for–"

"All I did was bring your son and one of your paid goons together." She shrugged. "Didn't exactly work out the way you wanted, did it?"

Nick was dead because of this cold, heartless bitch. And she'd managed to accomplish it without becoming directly involved. The hot tears singed his cheeks.

"And you were right. I was at Nick's funeral."

"But ... why?"

She grinned. "Playing with your mind. Getting those overactive balls of yours in even more of an uproar."

Issues that had come up earlier nipped at him. Clues she'd given him that he'd shrugged aside. Her comments about his drinking, his ordering people around. The one in the very beginning about Bogart's earlobe-tugging. The question, 'Why are men so stupid when drunk?' *I should've known. I should've at least caught something about all this.*

She started pacing again. "I figured you were closer to your daughter than your wife. But that was kind of obvious, judging by how you've cheated on

369

your wife all these years. Since you were closer to your daughter, her leaving would hurt even worse than your wife leaving and collapsing your corporation. Dealing with your daughter was really easy. All I did was target her boyfriend."

"*You* killed Cassidy." This realization, although considered before, hit him with the force of a sledgehammer. The blood drained from his face.

"Actually, the boy killed himself. He had a little trouble with the trigger guard. He was all thumbs, I guess you could say."

"You ... *instigated* it."

"Like your son, Cassidy went after anything in a skirt. You really ought to thank me. He would've ruined Katie, then made off with a lot of your cash. I saved you a great deal of money and embarrassment."

The heat of anger and frustration singed his flesh. "And by doing so, you've implicated me ... in his death."

She shrugged.

The rage made him grind his teeth. He tugged helplessly at the scarves again.

"I hope you've figured out by now that you're really not much of a human being. You're just one lucky son of a bitch who's been squeaking by, avoiding the rules. My son got in your way. You ran him over, no differently than you trample everyone else. Then you simply bought your way out of it."

Her eyes filled. "It was so difficult being nice to you. Talking to you. Smiling at you. Acting like someone who didn't loath your guts. Each time I

370

touched you I wanted to rush to the john and wash my hands. And scream. And throw up. And–"

"I'm sorry I'm so repulsive," he muttered between clenched teeth. "How'd you manage to get through it without slitting your own throat?"

A deep sigh. "I thought of Danny, actually. I guess I'd subconsciously programmed myself to focus past everything, to push myself until I'd gone as far as I'd planned. Danny helped me through it. Each time he entered my thoughts, you disappeared. Whenever I touched you or promised you something, I felt nauseous. The image of Danny's face, his beautiful smile, his bright brown eyes, healed me instantly."

He couldn't reply. There was nothing he could say to fix any of this.

"Yes, even though my beautiful little boy is dead, he's still with me. You may have destroyed his physical body, but you'll never be able to destroy what he was. He was an angel, and he'll be with me forever. That precious child was the best part of my life. And when you took him away, you–"

"I *said*, I'm *sorry*!" He lay back, his heart thrashing from the exertion.

Marie acted as if she hadn't heard him. "He was innocent. A little boy. But you know what? He has me to speak for him now. It was your worst mistake to take him from me. His innocence turned fatal to you–"

"I *said*, I didn't *mean* it! I was *drunk*! I had no idea what I was *doing*! And I *did* pay for it, I really and truly–"

"How'd you pay for it, Warden? By making a deal to go to rehab? Sure did work, didn't it? You still drink like a pig. A filthy, disgusting pig."

Richard tried one last time to pull loose. He went limp, his heart racing.

"The jerk who knocked me up was no better than you. When he'd finished with me, he walked out of my life. I tried getting in touch with him. All I wanted was some money to help me buy groceries during my pregnancy. But he couldn't care less. He got what he wanted and moved on."

He wanted to cover his ears. Her story was too frighteningly familiar. How many women had he used? How many had he discarded? Dozens. And he hadn't given it a second thought.

But he quickly reminded himself those women wanted his money. They cared nothing about principle or self-respect. They had no shame, no guilt. Only anger when the payoff wasn't as much as they'd expected. And this girl was no different from any of them. She spread her legs for someone she'd met casually, then panicked when things turned serious. Groceries, hell... She wanted the slob to pay for the kid. She'd gotten pregnant because she was too stupid to use protection, then turned nasty when she realized she'd be facing her dilemma alone.

This was not his fault. None of it was his doing. The only thing he'd confess was his colossal drunkenness. He hadn't meant to run over her kid. At the time, he hadn't even realized what had happened. It was Lucky's fault. She'd seduced him, fed him booze, got him off, took his money, then left him for the wolves. Everything bad happening to him was the result of a slut.

He wanted to scream, but he was too weak and too scared, and knew no one would hear him. His closest neighbor was nearly a quarter mile down the road. The situation was hopeless. He was a dead man.

She sat down beside him, pulled the strip of tape from the pillow, and slapped it back over his mouth. He groaned and tried to twist away, but she poked his flesh with the knife, and he grew still.

"Now I have to put you out of my misery." She leaned on an elbow just inches away. Once again, the switchblade moved frighteningly close to his exposed flesh.

His cold, calculating mind had disappeared forever, jumping ship with Adrienne, Katie, Berchfeld and the others. Leaving him completely alone. He whimpered weakly. *I'm going to die.*

The knife moved downwards, tracing circles around his exposed chest. It moved in a straight line down to his swollen belly, stopping at the navel and tracing a large circle moving clockwise, growing larger and larger, until the tip suddenly stopped just short of his groin.

"I think we'll start here."

Richard sobbed loudly, brokenly. *Our Father, Who art in heaven...*

"Maybe I'll just slice them off and wait to see how long it takes for you to bleed out."

Richard's moans grew in volume. A sheen of sweat covered his ashen face.

"Or maybe I'll perform a Lorena Bobbitt, then call nine-one-one and have them save your sorry ass at the last minute."

The room grew thick with the warm, pungent smell of Richard's bladder voiding a second time. Marie opened his trousers to expose the damp undershorts. The knife moved dangerously close to his sensitive, unprotected flesh.

Richard sobbed loudly. He could no longer see through the warm tears. *My dear, sweet Jesus...*

She shifted on the mattress, raising one leg, and bringing it back down, until she straddled his left thigh. She knelt before the target area, the switchblade in both hands. A sleek smile covered her face.

Please, God, please ... please don't let her do this to me!

Marie pressed the sharp blade of the knife firmly against Richard's testicles and gradually increased the pressure.

Richard Warden groaned one last time. His entire body went slack. *Please! God in Heav–*

His head grew hot. His heart thrashed like a fish on a line. Every muscle in his body stood out in knots. His skin turned ice-cold. Something big and slimy filled his throat. Through his tears, he saw the image of a distorted form standing over him, holding a heavy black blanket before him. Something hot and huge exploded deep within his chest. The heavy blanket dropped over his glazed, tense form.

Everything turned black and still.

***

Adam stood in the doorway of Richard Warden's bedroom.

Pulling on a pair of jeans in front of the balcony window, Marie McDermitt regarded him cautiously. A luxurious red wig sat on the rocker beside her.

Richard Warden lay motionless on the bed, held fast by scarves. His mouth was covered with duct tape, his body drenched in sweat. His glossy eyes were wide-open, staring unseeingly at the ceiling. The ammonia stench of urine lingered in the room.

"Is he dead?" Adam asked.

Marie continued dressing, buckling her belt. She reached for a red tank top from the rocker. "Heart attack. I think his high blood pressure finally did him in."

Adam approached the bed and felt for a pulse. There was none.

She shrugged into a lightweight jacket. "You're the guy I saw at the motel. It looked to me like you were being arrested."

"I managed to slip away."

"What were you doing there?"

"I was hired by Warden's attorney to find you."

"Why?"

"We sort of thought you might be the one responsible for ruining the man."

A hard look covered her face. "And now that you know?"

He pulled the tape from Warden's face, then began loosening the scarves. "The scarves are to prevent cuts and marks on his wrists and ankles, as well as marking up the bedposts, right?"

"Very good."

"The cops'll have a time with this one, anyway. They only work with the obvious."

She said nothing.

"I imagine the red stuff on his pants is spilled tomato juice."

"He was a sloppy drunk."

"They'll check his blood-alcohol level and try to determine if it did in his heart."

In the dim lighting, he was astonished to discover how much this girl resembled Renee. He knew it was merely an illusion, the drama catching up with him, but he couldn't help feeling that way. "My sister went through something much like what you went through." He positioned Warden's arms at his sides, then picked up the scarves and the tape, and dropped them beside her bag. "But she wasn't as gutsy – or as angry – as you are. Renee killed herself."

Marie McDermitt's eyes blazed for an instant. "And the bastard who knocked her up?"

"Disappeared."

Adam sighed. It was surprisingly easy and comforting, telling this woman about his sister. It had always been so much easier to keep it locked away and tell no one. But confessing the truth to her suddenly seemed the best thing to do. He instantly felt the lightness of release.

Marie pulled open her bag. The gun lay on top, in full view. He wondered if it was the gun she'd used on Yates. He said nothing as she dropped the scarves and balled-up tape inside. "I don't have to

376

worry about you, do I?" she asked, zipping up the bag.

"It ends here. If you want it to."

"What about his attorney?"

"He'll be satisfied with what I give him. Bob Dalgren isn't fond of Richard Warden, either."

She shook her head. "These men. How can they ... how can they do such horrible things? And get away with them?"

"People worship power. They forgive all that goes with it. When someone does as he pleases and gets away with it, he is envied and feared. And allowed to roam free."

"Even after running down an innocent little boy?"

"But, as we both know, Warden really didn't get away with it."

She turned toward the bed. "No, he really didn't."

Adam approached the doorway, stopped, and glanced at her. Now she didn't resemble Renee. She didn't look like anyone he'd ever seen before. Now, she seemed extremely young and vulnerable. Just as she probably was before her son was killed.

"I'm going downstairs to call Bob. He'll be coming in through the side entrance. This should give you about fifteen minutes before he calls nine-one-one. Can you get out some other way?"

"The back way, down the other staircase. There's a small gate on the other side of the garage. I duped the key to the lock. That's how I got in."

"You have wheels?"

"The church at the end of the block. I'm parked in front."

He approached the doorway:

"What's your name?" she asked.

"Adam Brooks."

The makings of a smile softened her tense features. Framing it were light traces of dimples. He wondered how this girl – this woman – looked when she was genuinely happy. He guessed it had been more than three years since she was.

"Thanks ... Adam." Then she brought up a hand to wipe her right eye.

He left the room, turned on the hall light, and hurried down the stairs. He didn't want to watch her cry. Marie McDermitt needed privacy. He realized that she'd finally reached the end of the worst chapter of her life.

EPILOGUE

The Following Friday

Adam watched Marie McDermitt from a distance.

She knelt before the grave and laid the lilacs neatly on the grassy dirt. Then she bowed her head in prayer, but that only lasted a few seconds. The sobbing quickly took over. She pulled a tissue from the pocket of her lightweight jacket and wiped her eyes. Her coppery-brown hair glistened in the morning sun. From where he stood, she looked like a little girl.

After depositing the dead lilacs in a garbage bag, she got to her feet. For another minute or so, she stared at the grave. Then she turned and trudged down the paved walk, where her car, an older model Honda, was parked just off the winding cobblestone road.

When she saw Adam, she stopped moving. She didn't resemble the cold, calculating woman who'd stalked a corporate giant and sent him to his early demise, but an innocent little girl suddenly faced with something she couldn't quite grasp. This innocence was probably not exactly new to her. He suspected she'd looked this way most of her young life. It was an innocence that attracted men, that made the worst of them want to violate it. Her innocence wouldn't have changed much if her child had not been killed. It only vanished when her

379

maternal instincts kicked in, turning it into something deadly and fatal. But once her campaign to avenge the death of her son had been completed, that aura had returned and would probably remain with her until the natural process of age touched it, turning it into a soft, quiet beauty.

He told himself once again that he'd done the right thing in helping her. Had he brought her in, the headlines splashing the tabloids would've been devastating. He could only imagine what she would be called by the press – especially the *paparazzi* – during what would inevitably become another trial of the century. The 'sophisticated' crowd would dub her 'The WarCo Killer.' Generation X would lovingly call her 'Psycho Babe.' The drinking crowd would refer to her as 'that piece of trash who'd brought down a software magnate.'

She'd be tormented by a misguided society that glorified and worshipped all the wrong things. A culture that made heroes out of murderers, cult figures out of sociopaths. The same civilization that rewarded youth, beauty, and physical prowess – and punished wisdom, morality, and knowledge.

TV specials and movies would be made about her. Big-name publishers and greedy agents would clamor for a multi-million-dollar book deal. Sleazy talk show hosts would communicate with her directly from her cell, encouraging the audience to ask her mindless, improper questions.

As the years passed, she'd join the ranks of the country's most notorious killers and murderers. To boost tired ratings, the press would return after a decade or two. An anniversary special would be hastily put together. *Biography* would air her tragedy again and again.

Richard Warden would be given the same sort of questionable fame. His widow and daughter would be interviewed, as well as his friends and associates. Fortune would provide a special issue dedicated to him. The feature would include interviews by all those who'd respected and feared the great man's genius.

But with all that false glitter and malignant publicity, not one word would be wasted on Danny McDermitt, the little seven-year-old boy who happened to be crossing the street at the wrong time. In the greater scheme of things, the life of a little boy proved nothing more than a blemish on the smug, engorged face of the most powerful and morally bankrupt society on earth.

"Adam?"

He moved closer. The wind shifted, pushing the sweet scent of lilacs in her hair, and the clean fragrance of her bath soap his way. "I'm surprised you remembered."

The breeze caused some hair to fall over her right eye. It was too short to pin behind her ear, so she just let it alone. "I always remember people who are good to me."

"I really didn't do much. You deserved a break."

She turned back to the grave. When she spoke again, her voice was distant. "There was an open field across the street from our apartment house, where lilacs grew wild. An older man owned the property. He didn't mind people picking them,

381

because he lived a few miles away and couldn't take care of the place as much as he wanted to. I'd stop and pick a few on my way home from work."

She sighed and cleared her throat. "Danny was almost six when he found out how much I liked them. He began going over there from time to time in the early spring to bring me a handful. Since there was never much traffic, the area was reasonably safe. And he was never gone very long. I'd put them in water and display them on the windowsill. When Danny saw them starting to die, he'd go back to get me more."

She sniffed. "My son was crossing the street to bring me fresh lilacs the afternoon Warden..." Her shoulders slumped. Adam wanted to help her, but she collected herself and took a deep breath. "How did you ... find me?"

"I went through the transcripts of the trial and found Danny's birthday. I figured you'd be here."

"I promised Danny his killer would be dead by his tenth birthday." She blinked. "I just made it."

"With a few days to spare."

"Did you find this place ... in the transcripts, too?"

"I went to the hospice where your mother died. They told me a few things about you and your son."

"Poor Momma." More tears filled her eyes. "I really wanted to care for her properly. But I needed to start working on my plan so I could keep my promise to Danny. You probably think I'm horrible, my mother dying alone, and all."

"Originally, but I grew to understand what you were going through. When Bob Dalgren told me you'd collapsed in the morgue–"

"Danny ... was my life..." Her eyes glistened in the sunlight. "I hadn't been a very good daughter, getting pregnant and all..." She pulled some tissues from her pocket and blew her nose. "But when Danny was born, and I held him in my arms in the hospital, something happened, and I was never the same. He was so small and delicate and helpless. When I brought him home, Momma noticed the change in me right away. 'Angel's little angel,' she called him, and from the day he was born, we were inseparable. From then on, Danny was the reason for my existence."

"Maybe one day you'll have another child."

She sighed. "I had so much trouble giving birth to him, they told me I'd never conceive again. That's something else that made all this hurt so much."

He followed her to her car. "Maybe we could meet for coffee one of these days?" He hadn't wanted it to sound like a pickup. In fact, he hadn't planned to say anything like it at all. Maybe it was because of Renee. Something about this young woman made him feel genuinely good inside. She'd gone where no one should ever have to go. The important thing was that she'd come back.

Perhaps this is what made him feel so differently about things. Her doing what she'd set out to do had restored his faith in the human condition. This was something he'd missed since he'd lost Renee.

"Are you sure … you'd like … being in the company of … of someone like me?" she asked.

"I think you'll be just fine. Especially when you finally decide to start living again."

Her beautiful smile lit up her face. "I've already decided that. Only moments ago, I could feel Danny telling me … telling me to let go. 'Be happy, Mommy,' I heard him say. His voice was a clear as yours." She blinked. "Does this make me sound … like a fruitcake?"

"I'm not exactly the right guy to ask."

"How come?"

"Most people think *I'm* a fruitcake."

She smiled. Then she looked down, and her smile dimmed as if someone had switched off the light inside her spirit. "I'm *so* messed up..."

"I've got news for you, kid. We're *all* messed up."

"Your sister. Were you close?"

He nodded.

"You'll have to tell me about her some time."

"How about over coffee and maybe a big slice of fresh apple pie?"

She laughed. "Persistent, aren't you?"

"About *some* things..."

"There's a little coffeehouse just down the road, overlooking the Gulf. It's quiet, and they don't come over to your table every two minutes to bug you."

"Sounds good."

She frowned. "I don't know if they have pie, though..."

"I'll settle for a doughnut. I *am* sort of a cop, right?"

She laughed again. "Let's go have some coffee."

He followed her down the winding path that would take them out of the darkness that had been Marie McDermitt's life the last three agonizing years. That path was now bright with sunlight. He felt certain it would lead them both to a brighter, better future.

OTHER WORKS BY DAVID BERARDELLI

THE APPRENTICE
THE WAGON DRIVER
STEPPING OUT OF MY GRAVE
ESCAPE CLAUSE
THE FUNNY DETECTIVE
JUST A SIMPLE ERRAND
WORKING FOR A MOB BOSS
AND DARKNESS FELL
AFTER DARKNESS FELL
IN ANOTHER REALM
BEYOND RECOGNITION
LOOKING FOR A DEAD GUY
THE NIGHTMARE COLLECTOR
HIDDEN
BEYOND GUILT
A RIPPLE IN TIME
HUNTING THE TALL BLONDE
AWAKENED
THE PLANNING COMMITTEE
WINTER SCENE

Titles available through:
Fiction4All
Gravestone Press

www.ingramcontent.com/pod-product-compliance
Lightning Source LLC
Chambersburg PA
CBHW010821250626
47172CB00004B/957

9781786957696